The Visionary Shakespeare

Alexander C. H. Tung

The Visionary Shakespeare

Alexander C. H. Tung

Copyright © Showwe Information Co., Ltd.

ISBN 978-986-221-807-5

Published by Showwe Information Co., Ltd.

1F, No.65, Lane76, Rueiguang Rd., Nei-Hu Dist., Taipei, Taiwan 114

· Contents ·

Preface
1

Chapter 1
The Most "Lamentable Comedy"
of Romeo and Juliet: Shakespeare's Ironic Vision
5

Chapter 2
Kingship and Counterfeit:
Shakespeare's Deconstructionist Vision in *Henry IV*
39

Chapter 3
Signification and Equivocation:
Shakespeare's Semiotic Vision in *Macbeth*
83

Chapter 4
The "Strange Eruption" in *Hamlet*:
Shakespeare's Psychoanalytic Vision
119

Chapter 5
The Jew and the Moor: Shakespeare's Racial Vision
153

i

Chapter 6
The Two Lears: Shakespeare's Humanist Vision of Nature
195

Chapter 7
The Nietzschean and Foucauldean Prospero:
Shakespeare's Vision of Power
231

• Preface •

In his influential book titled *The Visionary Company*, Harold Bloom groups together such Romantics as Blake, Wordsworth, Coleridge, Byron, Shelley, Keats, Beddoes, Clare, and Darley. In his view, all such Romantics are visionaries: they each possess "a vision, a way of seeing, and of living, a more human life" which, according to Blake, is a power of the imagination to bring forth "a representation of what eternally exists, really and unchangeably."

Here let me emphasize: Shakespeare, before the Romantics, is an even greater visionary in the Blakean sense, and all great literary creators — those before and after the Romantics as well as the Romantics themselves—are among the visionary company that are imaginative enough to bring forth representations of what eternally exists, really and unchangeably.

With his vision, Shakespeare has written a great number of plays and poems that enjoy a popularity and universality no other writer has ever achieved. Various reasons can be given for Shakespeare's popularity and universality. An important one is that his works often represent "what eternally exists, really and unchangeably." That is, his works often manifest visions that can impress us with their insights into the eternal aspects of life.

This book contains a collection of seven papers that I have written and published over the past twenty years as my interest in Shakespeare grew stronger and stronger. In those seven papers, luckily I have enough vision to see that there are a variety of visions directing Shakespeare's dramatic representations of life. In six of the papers I have variously called those visions ironic, deconstructionist, semiotic, psychoanalytic, racial, and humanist visions. In two of the papers I have particularly referred to the visions as belonging to the "vision of nature" and the "vision of power." For me, in fact, all the Shakespearean visions do "see into the life of things," to use Wordsworth's phrase, and do find the eternal nature or recurrent history of life.

Theoretically speaking, a vision is not a whim or a short-lived dream. It is a view developed through a long time of experience in the writer's heart and head. Therefore, every vision is prone to appear not in a single work but in more than one work of the same author if the author has produced a succession of works. Thus, as each Shakespearean vision is supposedly a vision accompanying Shakespeare throughout a long time, not to say all, of his life, the vision should appear in more than one work of Shakespeare's. Indeed, if we check Shakespeare's oeuvre carefully, we can find that his visions do appear over and over. However, in discussing each Shakespearean vision, I think it necessary to focus on one work or just a few works, where the vision is most manifest.

Hence, I hope it is understood that Shakespeare's ironic vision of life is to be found not just in *Romeo and Juliet*, though the vision is seen in the spotlight of that one work. Likewise, Shakespeare's deconstructionist vision is to be found not just in *Henry IV*, his semiotic vision not just in *Macbeth*, his psychoanalytic vision not just in *Hamlet*, his racial vision not just in *The Merchant of Venice* and *Othello*, his vision of nature not just in *King Lear*, and his vision of power not just in *The Tempest*. When I chose to focus on a certain vision in the spotlight of one single play or a few plays, I was aware that the vision could be seen elsewhere in Shakespeare. It was only for the sake of facilitating discussion that I seemed to connect a certain vision restrictively to a single work or a few works.

In discussing Shakespeare's various visions, I know I need to provide sufficient evidence for each point I want to make. In the effort to support my points with evidence, I find, to my great joy, that I can often, additionally, bring forth some original and interesting findings, and some of my textual interpretations are indeed highly plausible. For instance, I find that *Romeo and Juliet* can be considered as a "play-without-the-play" (as *Pyramus and Thisbe* is performed as a "play-within-the-play") of *A Midsummer Night's Dream,* and that the play is a "comitragedy" rather than a pure tragedy, in which the name "Romeo" is an instance of bawdy wordplay, suggesting "Roe me O!". In *Henry IV*, I find, the prince is to train himself in accordance with the teaching of Machiavelli's *The Prince*, and Falstaff is both a "false staff member" and a "true staff" to support Prince Hal in his training. In *Macbeth,* I find, there are six types of ambiguities connected to its central theme, signification and equivocation, and both Macbeth (the son of "Beth") and Lady Macbeth have "the second's complex," which makes them too ambitious to be content with their being second in position. In *Hamlet*, I find, Hamlet (the "little ham") feels both consciously and unconsciously that he has "most weak hams" in facing and trying to counteract the strength of the two great hams, that is, his spiritual, true father (his Super-ego) and his corporeal, false father (his Id); thus, his "strange eruption" is but a tragic symptom of his Oedipus complex, sexually involving his mother Gertrude (Ophelia being her displacement) as the real poisonous "spear" to stab him to death. In *The Merchant of Venice* and in *Othello*, I find, the Jew and the Moor are two typical figures representing two basic types of racism: intrinsic racism and extrinsic racism, which stem from racial pride and racial prejudice. I find that in Shakespeare's vision, we can always find a Shylock locked up shyly in his racial ideology since he cannot shy away (from) his racial "bond," and the Shylock is always accompanied by an Othello crying "Ot, hell, O!" for villainous misuse of racial consciousness since he himself cannot discard the racial "handkerchief" that binds his head. In *King Lear*, I find two Lears: the unnatural Lear and the natural Lear. I find Lear learns, too late, two lears (lessons): the difference of human nature, and the disparity between appearance and reality in nature. Also, I find he learns, at last, the lear that nature is above art; but he does not learn the lear that natural justice is not equivalent to human justice. Finally in *The Tempest*, I find, Prospero is a Nietzschean hero striving with his Will to Power to become a Superman, and yet he is after all only a Foucauldean Everyman exercising his power for the mundane aim of Prosperity.

Even only from the titles of the papers, readers may know that I have adopted "new" critical approaches for these Shakespearean studies. Indeed, I have adopted such approaches as called New Criticism, psychoanalysis, deconstruction, and semiotics; I have approached Shakespeare through humanist ideas and through Nietzsche's and Foucault's ideas; and I have joined in one of the fashionable cultural studies: the study of racial consciousness. Yet, what I have done with these Shakespearean studies is actually not for the sake of newness in approach. The newness in approach is, rather, just a testimony of Shakespeare's universality: he can be profitably studied with any approach, old or new.

Aside from the seven visions discussed in this book, Shakespeare has other visions, of course, that are worthy of our exploration. Besides his racial vision, for instance, Shakespeare certainly has his vision regarding class and gender. Regarding history, Shakespeare, I believe, may have a vision close to that held by scholars of New Historicism. In effect, scholars have already touched upon quite a number of Shakespearean "ideologies" which are not called visions but are no other than visions. It is to be hoped that in the future, others may bring forth more studies of Shakespeare's other visions, so as to prove Dryden's remark that the poet-playwright has "a most comprehensive soul," indeed.

• Chapter 1 •

The Most "Lamentable Comedy" of Romeo and Juliet: Shakespeare's Ironic Vision

I. An Impure Dramatist

Playwrights can be called "pure" or "impure" dramatists, depending on whether or not they write purely one single sub-genre of drama. Some famous classical dramatists were thus "pure" because they chose to write either purely tragedies or purely comedies. When we say there were three great tragedians (Aeschylus, Sophocles, and Euripides) and one great comedian (Aristophanes) in the Greek Period while there were two remarkable comedians (Plautus and Terence) and one remarkable tragedian (Seneca) in the Roman Period, we are suggesting this sense of purity. The classical dramatists' pure devotion to either Thalia (the Muse of comedy) or Melpomene (the Muse of tragedy) is an obvious fact although we cannot fully understand why they should stick to such "purity." Some later playwrights followed their purist tendency, but others simply ignored it. In the neoclassical France, for instance, Moliere wrote comedies only while Corneille wrote both comedies and tragedies. Yet, pure dramatists have definitely become very rare since the classical times. Many distinguished comedians (e.g. Ben Jonson) and tragedians (e.g. Racine) of later times actually attempted both genres. In the case of Shakespeare, we do not even know whether we ought to call him a comedian or a tragedian as he excels in both types of plays.

Shakespeare's impurity involves another complicated matter. He is impure not only in the sense that he is not devoted purely to a single sub-genre of drama but also in the sense that a play by him is often not purely a comedy or a tragedy no matter what sub-genre the play's title may indicate. We commonly tell people that Shakespeare wrote three types of drama (history, comedy, and tragedy) or four types (the three plus romance), and scholars have been classifying or discussing his entire oeuvre on the basis of this understanding. However, we know at the same time that Shakespeare seldom observed the classical or neoclassical rule of the so-called "purity of the genres." That is why people like Dryden and Johnson had to defend his mixing tragic and comic scenes, and today we can still debate on the use of "comic relief" in his tragedies.

Different reasons can be given, of course, for Shakespeare's impurity. We may attribute it, for instance, to what Neander/Dryden calls his "largest and most comprehensive soul" (Dryden 149), thinking that purity is narrowness; Shakespeare's soul is too great to allow anything to contain only one single element. Or we may follow Johnson to assert that Shakespeare is "the poet of nature"; his drama is "the mirror of life"; his scenes, therefore, contain both the comic and the tragic in life (Johnson 208-9). But here I am not to build my argument on any previous authority. In this essay I will contend that Shakespeare's impurity is a result of his ironic vision—a vision which enables him to see the necessary co-existence of opposites, and a vision which finds its most vivid expression in the play about Romeo and Juliet.

II. A Play "Without" the Play

We all know that the-play-within-the-play is a conventional dramatic device often employed by Elizabethan and Jacobean playwrights to further the central action and sometimes to help develop the central theme of the play. The best-known Shakespeare's play within the play is, of course, the one Hamlet uses to "catch the conscience of the king" (2.2.601).[1] But no less noticeable is the Peter Quince play in *A Midsummer Night's Dream*. This play, as Peter Quince tells us, is titled "The most lamentable comedy, and most cruel death of Pyramus and Thisbe" (1.2.11-12). It is presented in the *Dream*, as we see, to serve as an entertaining interlude to the celebration of the three wedded couples. If we probe deeper, we will find this play-within-the-play not only provides an amusing finale to an evening of delight but also echoes the pronounced themes of the *Dream*. For, despite the rustics' bungling enactment, the story of Pyramus and Thisbe surely demonstrates that "the course of true love never did run smooth" (1.1.34) and, worse still, death "did lay siege to" true love, making it "momentany as a sound,/Swift as a shadow, short as any dream,/Brief as the lightning in the collied night" (1.1.142-5).

If "The most lamentable comedy, and most cruel death of Pyramus and Thisbe" is a theme-echoing play within the *Dream*, then *The Most Excellent and Lamentable Tragedie, of Romeo and Juliet* (as the good quarto edition of 1599 titles the play) is a play without ("outside of") the *Dream* to echo the same themes. For, like Pyramus and Thisbe, Romeo and Juliet are crossed in love through familial hindrance and they meet their tragic fate through rash misinterpretation.

In fact, the play of *Romeo and Juliet* corresponds to the play of *Pyramus and Thisbe* not only in theme but also in tone. In his lecture on *Romeo and Juliet*, Northrop Frye says that the play has more wit and sparkle than any other tragedy he knows, that "we may instinctively think of it as a kind of perverted comedy," and that it might be described "as a kind of comedy turned inside out" (33). Then he asks, "If we tried to turn the play we have inside out, back into comedy, what would it be like?" His own answer is:

> *We'd have a world dominated by dream fairies, including a queen, and the moon instead of the sun; a world where the tragedy of Pyramus and Thisbe has turned into farce; a world where feuding and brawling noblemen run around in the dark, unable to see each other. In short, we'd have a play very like A Midsummer Night's Dream, ...(33)*

Indeed, *Romeo and Juliet* can be treated as a mock-serious play because it has too much comic wit and sparkle in it. Just as the tragedy of Pyramus and Thisbe can be turned into farce by the rustics' perverted performance, so the tragedy of Romeo and Juliet can be performed in the manner of a farcical comedy, too. In this connection, we can conclude that *A Midsummer Night's Dream* has a play-within-the-play (the Peter Quince play of Pyramus and Thisbe) and a play-without-the-play (the Shakespeare play of Romeo and Juliet), both of which can be performed comically as they are similar in theme and tone.

III. A Successful, Bad Play?

Talking of performance, we know Shakespeare's *Romeo and Juliet* has been very popular on the stage and on the screen. But the success of presentation does not engender high esteem among professional critics of the play. Frequently, in fact, the play has been thought of as still immature or even bad, although as Shakespeare's tenth play and third tragedy (to follow the scholarship of Sir Edmund Chambers) it can be counted as one of the three masterpieces (the other two being *Richard II* and *A Midsummer Night's Dream*) to establish "the first high crest" of Shakespeare's poetic career (Coghill 11).

Two drawbacks have often been pointed out to account for the failure of the play. One is the lack of that rhetorical control which marks Shakespeare's great period, and the other is the improper use of mere chance to determine the destiny of the hero and the heroine (Kermode 1055). Indeed, abundant rhetoric—especially the stilted language of Petrarchan conceits along with the wordplay—has flooded the play. Granting that Shakespeare's audiences in the early 1590s really "expected characters on the stage to talk in high-sounding phrases and to make long speeches on every occasion, full of rhetorical devices, stuffed with mythology and bookish similes" (Harrison, *Introducing*, 166), in many cases the rhetoric has really been purchased at the cost of such elements as logic, reason, propriety and truth which normally go with tragedy. As will be discussed below, we can enjoy such rhetorical language only if we can regard it not as a serious tragedy but as a frolicsome play.

As to the matter of chance, we feel A. C. Bradley is right in saying that in most of his tragedies Shakespeare "allows to 'chance' or 'accident' an appreciable influence at some point in the action" (9). But, Bradley also tells us, "any *large* admission of chance into the tragic sequence would certainly weaken, and might destroy, the sense of the causal connection of character, deed, and catastrophe" (10). So, in his opinion, Shakespeare really uses chance "very sparingly" (10).

In actuality, the phrase "very sparingly" does not apply to *Romeo and Juliet*. In this play many things can be imputed to chance. According to Nevill Coghill, Romeo and Juliet are battered by successive blows of fortune :

> *It chances that her only love is sprung from her only hate, it chances that Mercutio is killed by Tybalt when Romeo, with the best intentions, comes between them, and Mercutio is hurt under his arm, it chances that the Friar's letters to Romeo are not delivered, it chances that Romeo reaches the tomb a moment before Juliet awakens from her drug, and takes his own life thinking her dead, it chances that Juliet is left alone with her lover, his lips still warm, and there is no one to stay her from stabbing herself. (16)*

To these we may add: it chances that the servant who is sent to invite the Capulet clan to the family feast meets Romeo on the way and unwittingly asks Romeo to read the list for him, thus giving Romeo a chance to know that Rosaline is among the invited, and thus making Romeo determined to attend the feast; and it also chances that Juliet's profession of love at the window is overheard by Romeo, thus speeding their mutual love and speeding up their tragic end.

If too much chance is bad for tragedy, it is not necessarily so for comedy. In a footnote Bradley adds that "the tricks played by chance often form a principle part of the comic action" (10). We can agree to this idea. That is why one critic can claim that the final scenes of *Romeo and Juliet*, although tragic in outcome, are comic by nature inasmuch as everything hinges on accidents of timing" (Rozett 154). And that is also why another critic can remind us that "many critics of the play have found its structure flawed in the way in which, in its first half, it seems to develop like a comedy, and then, in the second half, hustles towards tragedy by the stringing together of improbable accidents and coincidences" (Brennan 52). From critical opinion like this we can plainly see that we must look at the play's plot structure in the light of comedy if we want to appreciate it well and judge it right. If we insist on looking at it from the perspective of tragedy, our conclusion will always be close to this:

> *...the deficiency of the tragic patterns that are clearly inherent in Romeo and Juliet is sometimes ignored in the process of overpraising the play. Indeed, the vast popularity of the play with audiences in Shakespeare's time (four quarto editions before the First Folio), down to this very day, as well as some delightful poetry and tightly woven dramatic suspense, are not to be ignored. It has many moments of fine melodrama, which would not have been bad had Shakespeare meant his play to be a melodrama. But the play seems to have aspired for more ("fatal loins," "star-cross'd lovers," "death-mark'd love"). These expectations, however, fail to materialize. With the unfolding of the action it becomes clear that the very foundations of tragedy, fate and human insight, are here replaced by fortuitousness and ignorance. (Oz 136-7)*

Aside from the two above-mentioned drawbacks (too much rhetoric in language and too much chance in plot), as a tragedy *Romeo and Juliet* also suffers criticism for lack of logic or reason in action. One critic, for instance, thinks it strange that

> *the rival houses have mutual friends. Mercutio, Montague Romeo's close acquaintance, is an invited guest at the Capulets' ball. Stranger still, so is Romeo's cruel lady, Rosaline, who in the invitation is addressed as Capulet's cousin. It is odd that Romeo's love for her, since she was a Capulet, had given him no qualms on the score of the feud. When Romeo is persuaded to go gate-crashing to the ball because Rosaline will be there, there is no talk at all of its being a hazardous undertaking. Safety will require, if ever so much, no more than a mask. On the way to the ball, as talk is running gaily, there is still no mention of danger involved.*

> *Indeed, the feud is almost a dead letter so far. The son of the Montague does not know what the Capulet daughter looks like, nor she what he is like. The traditional hatred survives only in one or two high-spirited, hot-blooded scions on either side, and in the kitchen-folk. (Charlton 56)*

Another critic reminds us that no original cause is assigned to the ridiculous street brawl and he questions: "How do Sampson and Gregory come to be wearing swords and bucklers since they seem to be neither gentlemen retainers nor hired bravoes of the house, but lower domestics and clowns absolute?" (Harbage 140). For a third critic, it is inconceivable that with Tybalt hardly buried, and Juliet weeping for him, they should urge Paris' suit for Juliet, and Capulet "has shaken off the mourning uncle and turned jovial, roguish father-in-law in a trice" (Granville-Barker 32). For me, it is simply absurd that Capulet should send a servant unable to read the list to invite the guests listed, that the apothecary should sell Romeo the poison, not fearing death penalty, just after the exchange of a few words, and that the Capulets should leave their vault so unguarded that Romeo, Paris, Friar Laurence and others apparently can come and go freely.

The lack of logic or reason in action, as some critics have noticed, is often the result of Shakespeare's trying to speed up the action by compressing the time over which the story stretches. In all earlier versions of the story, it is observed,

> *Romeo's wooing is prolonged over weeks before the secret wedding; then, after the wedding, there is an interval of three or four months before the slaying of Tybalt; and Romeo's exile lasts from Easter until a short time before mid-September when the marriage with Paris was at first planned to take place. (Charlton 54)*

But in this Shakespearean play all this is "pressed into three or four days" (Charlton 54). No wonder that we feel "Romeo has hardly dropped from the balcony before Lady Capulet is in her daughter's room" (Granville-Barker 33), and the travel between Verona and Mantua seems as easy as the travel between the Capulet house and Friar Laurence's cell, or as short as the travel from the public street to Capulet's orchard.

If we wish to dwell on Shakespeare's illogical or unreasonable arrangement of time and action in *Romeo and Juliet*, we can surely think out many other examples. And if we wish to evaluate the play as a serious tragedy, this lack of logic or reason is certainly another shortcoming. However, if we can judge this play as a comedy, we will be able to overlook this fault. For, after all, comedy is associated with "mirth, " "levity," "the sunny malice of a faun," not with "profundity," "gravity," "density of involvement," "earnestness" (Merchant 3).

IV. Mock-Tragedy or Comitragedy?

So far I have been emphasizing the comic aspects of *Romeo and Juliet*. But since the word "tragedie" is used in the title of the play, can't we just consider the play as a tragedy? We can, of course. But we shall then need to define the word "tragedy" very broadly. If we take the word as a synonym for calamity (this is in everyday and newspaper practice) or accept Byron's simple distinction in *Don Juan* that "All tragedies are finished by a death, /All comedies are ended by a marriage" (Canto III, 65-66), then the play is no doubt a tragedy since it ends with the calamity of more than one death. Perhaps we have reason to believe that Shakespeare must have had this broad sense in mind when the work was being given its title.

It is sometimes suggested that Shakespeare wrote *Romeo and Juliet* under the influence of Chaucer. His concept of tragedy, therefore, "can be roughly fitted into the theory of tragedy outlined and illustrated by Chaucer's Monk, a theory taken from Boethius whom Chaucer had translated: Tragedye is to seyn a dite of a prosperite for a tyme, that endeth in wrecchidnesse" (Coghill 13). This Medieval theory emphasizes the role of Fortune:

> *She turns her wheel and we rise upon it to a fickle joy; she turns it still and we fall into some awaiting Hell-mouth. Our fall has nothing to do with our deserts, for though Fortune may laugh to see pride humbled she is no less delighted to turn her wheel against the innocent. (Coghill 14)*

For people of the Middle Ages, therefore, tragedy was "simply a story which ended unhappily, offering a warning that, if one were not careful, a final unhappiness would be one's own lot too" (Leech, *Tragedy*, 15). If Shakespeare really took his notion of tragedy from the Medieval concept, the notion is still a simple one. On the basis of that notion, *Romeo and Juliet* can still be easily understood and favorably evaluated as a "tragedy."

But the trouble is: later critics, especially those who are well versed in academic definitions of tragedy, would try to judge the play on the criteria provided by Aristotle, Nietzsche, Hegel, Bradley, or any other authority. In consequence, they will find the play unsatisfactory as a tragedy or think that it is at best "a naïve version" of tragedy in comparison with his later mature tragedies like *Hamlet, Othello, King Lear, Macbeth, Anthony and Cleopatra,* and *Coriolanus* (Oz 138).

Here I must point out that Shakespeare himself was not well versed in any academic definitions of tragedy. Actually, he never meant to follow any strict classical rules of play-writing. In the case of *Romeo and Juliet*, we find what he wanted was just what any common playwright would want: a play actable on the stage and profitable for its presentation. This means that he had to consider the conditions of the theater and the audience. Now, we are not very clear about how he considered these matters. But it so happened that he chose to mix tragic and comic elements in the play.

To mix the tragic with the comic is to make neither a pure tragedy nor a pure comedy. What is the proper way, then, to call such a hybrid play? Is it a tragicomedy? The term "tragicomedy" does imply the mingling of tragic and comic elements.[2] Yet, it usually also implies a happy ending. If so, I do not think an ordinary reader will regard the ending of *Romeo and Juliet* as a happy one and therefore describe it as a tragicomedy.

If not a tragicomedy, what then? Regrettably, it seems that we have no set term for it and so we have to invent a new one. Shall we call it a mock-tragedy, considering that it is not a true tragedy but something in imitation of a tragedy? This epithet, we feel, is still improper. For, we may expect a mock-tragedy to be, just like a mock-epic, a work employing the lofty manner and the high and serious tone to treat of a trivial subject and theme in such a way as to make both subject and theme ridiculous. But we find we can in no way say that *Romeo and Juliet* has a low or trivial subject or theme presented in a lofty or serious manner or tone. Is love and marriage a low subject? Is feud and fate a trivial theme? Are the dialogues in the play all serious in tone? Do the characters all act in a lofty manner? Besides, the word "mock" has the double senses of "ridicule" and "mimic." A mock-epic not only parodies an epic but also makes fun of the epic as a genre. Furthermore, a mock-epic is always a satire: it satirizes a person, idea, institution, etc., for some folly or vice. By analogy, can we think of *Romeo and Juliet* as a mock-tragedy in the sense that it parodies a certain tragedy, makes fun of tragedy as a genre, and satirizes something?

No Shakespearean scholarship has as yet proved that *Romeo and Juliet* ever attempted to parody any existing tragedy. Nor can we find any trace in the play to prove that it pokes fun at tragedy as a genre.

For me, this parodic element is to be found in the Peter Quince play of Pyramus and Thisbe instead. In *A Midsummer Night's Dream*, as we know, Peter Quince and other artisans have really poked fun at the genre of tragedy as they perform the tragic story in a most farcical manner. In truth, as the *Dream* supposedly comes after *Romeo and Juliet*, the performance of *Pyramus and Thisbe* in it can be said to be a parody of *Romeo and Juliet* since the two plays, as mentioned above, have similar themes and tones.

However, *Romeo and Juliet* is not comical or farcical throughout. I cannot agree to the idea that the first half of the play "seems to develop like a comedy" while the second half "hustles towards tragedy" (Brennan 52). The structure of this drama is not so neatly divided. I can agree, however, that all characters in the play, including the hero, the heroine and their parents, behave comically at times. Nevertheless, the scenes where Death impends or descends are not without their pathos. Underneath the characters' comic behavior, to be sure, may lie the strain of satire directed against, for instance, parental authority, unreasonable feud, artificial or ritual love, etc., in general, and Tybalt's provocative temper, Mercutio's jesting humor, the Nurse's garrulous manner, etc., in particular. But to place the play in the category of satirical comedy is also beside the mark. For, no matter what folly or vice it may aim to attack, the play with its unhappy ending does not give us the effect of "poetic justice"; it, rather, renders that of pity. I agree that "the dangerous fault of the two lovers is their extreme rashness" (Stauffer 30). But their rashness is their "tragic flaw," not their comic defect. It is to be pitied rather than scoffed at. It follows, therefore, that if we have to invent a genre name for the play, we should prefer "comitragedy" to "mock-tragedy," seeing that the play does not really take "mock" for its end. By the way, this term is better than "tragicomedy" in that it suggests not just the mingling of comic and tragic elements but also the line of plot development from comic potential to tragic reality as seen in the play.

V. The Sonnet and the Oxymoron

We have mentioned above that Shakespeare has sped up the action of *Romeo and Juliet* by compressing the time over which the story stretches. The speeding up of the action naturally helps dramatize the story—that is, to keep the characters acting and moving. However, within the dramatic scenes, we find, the sped-up action is often blended with lyrical outpourings of the characters' interior monologues or confessional dialogues. The language in such lyrical outpourings is often like the language spoken in a love poem, especially a Petrarchan sonnet, because it is characterized by the extensive use of artificial imagery and elaborate figures of speech. Perhaps Shakespeare, indeed, intended to use that language to cater to his audience's taste. But it is also likely that his intention was led by his favorite style of writing at that time.

It is generally recognized that Shakespeare composed *Romeo and Juliet* in his most lyrical period, that is, the period around 1595 when *Richard II* and *A Midsummer Night's Dream* were also produced. In fact, the play was written in the heyday of the sonnet, too. It is noted that in England the popularity of the sonnet form "was directly due to the publication of Sir Philip Sidney's *Astrophel and Stella* in the spring of 1591" and "the most important collections of sonnets—Daniel's *Delia*, Lodge's *Phyllis*, Constable's *Diana*, Drayton's *Idea*, Spenser's *Amoretti*—all appeared within the next five years" (Harrison, *Complete Works*, 1593). Some scholars have also noted that Shakespeare was obviously influenced by Sidney's sonneteering when he wrote *Romeo and Juliet*. Brian Gibbons, for instance, has a detailed discussion of how the play is close in feeling to Sidney's *Astrophel and Stella*.[3] Anyway, some dialogues in the play (most notably the first words exchanged between Romeo and Juliet at the ball in Act I, Scene V,

17

92-105), as well as the two prologues preceding Act I and Act II , take the form of a sonnet. This fact is enough evidence for us to believe that Shakespeare's zeal for following the vogue of sonneteering has affected his composition of this "comitragedy."

But how deeply has the sonnet vogue influenced the play? In content, the play certainly deals with the conventional theme of a sonnet, i.e., love. Romeo's unrequited love for the unattainable Rosaline at first and his fated love for the unmarriageable Juliet later are both suitable themes for sonneteering, indeed. Significantly, Romeo does try to sonnetize in the play. So in Act II, Scene IV, Mercutio, referring to Romeo, tells Benvolio: "Now is he for the numbers that Petrarch flowed in" (39-40). But what avails for a sonneteer like Romeo? Physically he cannot get the rose (Rosaline) at first and he has to lose the jewel (Juliet) at last, for all his verbal efforts.

The sonnet, as we know, is full of non-referential language, with its obvious hyperbole, celestial compliments, paradox, and other elaborate figures of speech. Such language is usually hollow in sense and feeling. In *Romeo and Juliet*, it is often observed, a good many lines typify such language no matter whether they form a complete sonnet or not. For example, the fourteen lines (81-94) spoken by Lady Capulet in Act I, Scene IV, to urge Juliet to fall in love with Count Paris are notoriously too insensible and tedious as they play with the far-fetched conceit that Paris is a book. Other lines of similar nature include these spoken by Juliet when she knows Romeo's hand has shed Tybalt's blood:

> *O serpent heart; hid with a flowering face.*
> *Did ever dragon keep so fair a cave?*
> *Beautiful tyrant, fiend angelical,*
> *Dove-feather'd raven, wolvish-ravening lamb!*
> *Despised substance of divinest show!*
> *Just opposite to what thou justly seem'st!*
> *A damned saint, an honorable villain!*

O nature what hadst thou to do in hell
When thou didst bower the spirit of a fiend
In mortal paradise of such sweet flesh?
Was ever book containing such vile matter
So fairly bound? O, that deceit should dwell
In such a gorgeous palace. (3.2.73-84)

Unlike her mother, Juliet is here not laboring with a single conceit, but with a long string of conceits as she metaphorically compares Romeo to a serpent, flower, dragon, cave, beauty, tyrant, fiend, angel, dove, raven, wolf, lamb, saint, villain, book, palace, etc. If she could stop at a metaphor only, her feeling might ring true and she might have better sense. But this unnaturally long string of conceits just robs her of any sincerity she could boast of.

While the above-quoted passage betrays Juliet's lack of true feeling, it nonetheless expresses in a way her true understanding of life. Throughout that passage lies her understanding that in real life two conceptually opposite elements often can exist together: a serpent heart with a flowering face, a fierce dragon with a fair cave, a tyrant with beauty, a fiend with angelic quality, a raven with a dove's feather, a lamb with a wolf's ravening quality, a despised substance with divine appearance, a saint who is damned, a villain who is honored, a fairly bound book with vile matter, a gorgeous palace with deceit in it, etc. This understanding points to the irony of life. A person with this understanding can be said to have an ironic vision.

Juliet is indeed the person that most manifestly shows this vision. On knowing that Romeo is a Montague, she says:

My only love sprung from my only hate.
Too early seen unknown, and known too late.
Prodigious birth of love it is to me
That I must love a loathed enemy. (1.5.137-40)

19

But she is not the only person in the play that has an ironic vision of life. Friar Laurence also shows his ironic vision when his musing alone comes to the conclusion that "The earth that's nature's mother is her tomb: / What is her burying grave, that is her womb" (2.3.5-6). And Romeo is likewise aware of the ironic situation of life when to Benvolio he utters:

> *Here's much to do with hate, but more with love.*
> *Why then, O brawling love, O loving hate,*
> *O anything of nothing first create!*
> *O heavy lightness, serious vanity,*
> *Misshapen chaos of well-seeming forms!*
> *Feather of lead, bright smoke, cold fire, sick health,*
> *Still-waking sleep that is not what it is!*
> *This love feel I that feel no love in this. (1.1.173-80)*

Evidently Romeo's ironic vision as shown here is but a very common vision. It is frequently seen to crystallize in the paradoxical statements of a love sonnet such as found in Sir Thomas Wyatt's "Description of the Contrarious Passions." It is only that Romeo's description is made by the figure of oxymoron—a figure most economic in expressing the ironic or paradoxical aspects of love.

We as well as Mercutio may laugh at Romeo's oxymoronic phrases. But we should not forget that Shakespeare himself is finally responsible for the use of so many oxymora in his plays. If Romeo's oxymora are devoid of "depth" as many people suppose they are, can we therefore think that Shakespeare is also devoid of "depth" in letting him utter so many oxymoronic phrases?

The answer is in the negative. As far as *Romeo and Juliet* is concerned, we find the sonnet language employed by all the characters —call it paradox or oxymoron—is a language highly suggestive of the necessary co-existence of mutually opposing things. As Gayle Whittier

20

has put it, antithesis is "the core of Petrarchan dilemma" and oxymoron is "an extreme verbal condensation of antithesis" (31). As the two lovers move between word (the sonnet) and world (the reality), the oxymoron also moves between the decorative and the thematic. And thereby we shall find Shakespeare "bends the courtly relic of antithesis so that its opposing terms reciprocate" (31).

VI. The Playwright's Ironic Vision

I have tried to suggest above that a character like Romeo or Juliet or Friar Laurence is showing his or her ironic vision when he or she breathes out an oxymoronic phrase, although the phrase may at times sound hollow or insincere as it is found in a voguish love sonnet. Now, I want to suggest further that after all, the characters' ironic vision can be the playwright's vision, too, since it is the playwright that determines to have the characters speak that language.

To be sure, oxymoronic phrases are spoken not only in *Romeo and Juliet*. In *A Midsummer Night's Dream*, for instance, Hippolyta is speaking a very meaningful oxymoron when, referring to the sounds of hounds, she remarks: "I never heard / So musical a discord, such sweet thunder" (4.1.116-7). This oxymoron is meaningful because it suggests the ironic vision that love can have its "musical discord" or "sweet thunder" too—a vision vividly exemplified by the three wrangling couples in the play, namely, Lysander and Hermia, Demetrius and Helena, and Oberon and Titania.

Another even more meaningful oxymoron in the *Dream* is Peter Quince's calling his play a "most lamentable comedy" (1.2.11), which is later described as "A tedious brief scene of young Pyramus /And his love Thisbe, very tragical mirth" (5.1.56-7), which induces Theseus to remark also in oxymoronic terms:

21

> *Merry and tragical? Tedious and brief?*
> *That is hot ice, and wondrous strange snow!*
> *How shall we find the concord of this discord? (5.1.58-60)*

This string of oxymora is particularly meaningful in that it suggests the ironic vision that not love alone, but life as well, can always be felt and looked at from two opposing viewpoints, and the viewpoints are to be decided by the characters (i.e., the "real" persons in the story), the cast (the actors for the play), the playwright, and the audience. Pyramus and Thisbe might feel their life to be a tragedy. But Peter Quince, the playwright, and his followers (Bottom, etc.), the cast, have decided to look at it from a farcical point of view. And finally the audience (Theseus, etc.) are content to take it as a "tedious and brief" scene of "most lamentable comedy" filled with "very tragical mirth."

Now, what can we say of Shakespeare as the playwright of *Romeo and Juliet* in regard to the ironic vision of life? We believe Shakespeare may really believe that "All the world's a stage, /And all the men and women merely players" (*As You Like It*, 2.7.139-40). Hence, any supposed real story of life, be it that of Romeo and Juliet or that of Pyramus and Thisbe, is but a story to be played on the stage of the world according to the playwright's interpretation. In other words, Shakespeare is to *Romeo and Juliet* what Peter Quince is to *Pyramus and Thisbe*. He has as much freedom as Peter Quince to look at a tragic story from a comic point of view. And like Theseus and other spectators of Peter Quince's play, we may simply accept *Romeo and Juliet* as a "most lamentable comedy," thus construing Shakespeare's ironic vision of life.

To accept *Romeo and Juliet* as a lamentable comedy is not just a matter of willingness for us. The playwright, Shakespeare, has already directed that play that way. Many scholars have touched on the play's comic aspects and the comic devices used in it. One critic, for instance, has pointed out the use of comic character types—"the young lovers, the obdurate father, the loquacious and devoted Nurse, and the wise and manipulating Friar"—and comic strategies—"practical joking, bawdy wordplay, flights of poetic fancy, teasing, and comic testing" (Rozett 155). Here I will single out the device of wordplay, especially the pun, for a penetrating discussion of the ironic vision.

VII. The Pun as Wordplay

Jokes are not always mere jokes. Occasionally some serious intent may hide behind a joke. Likewise, wordplay, the most common way of joking, is not always playful. Some truth of great import may lurk behind a playful word. As the most common device of wordplay, the pun, in particular, can carry weight with its lightness, since by definition a pun contains two meanings in the same sound or word. Shakespeare is notoriously fond of wordplay. *Romeo and Juliet* is said to be one of Shakespeare's most punning plays: "even a really conservative count yields a hundred and twenty-five quibbles" (Mahood 391). But are such quibbles really just the golden apples for which Shakespeare has turned aside from his career and stooped from his elevation (Johnson 213)? M. M. Mahood does not think so. For him, Shakespeare's wordplay is functional in *Romeo and Juliet*. According to his examination, wordplay holds together the play's imagery in a rich pattern and gives an outlet to the tumultuous feelings of the central characters. By its proleptic second and third meanings it serves to sharpen the play's dramatic irony. Above all, it clarifies the conflict of incompatible truths and helps to establish their final equipoise. (391) Mahood is quite right. But my own finding is: the wordplay has also helped to clarify the play's themes and the playwright's ironic vision.

As we know, the play opens with Sampson and Gregory, two Capulet servants, joking with puns. On the surface they are talking about how brave they should be when engaged in the quarrel between the two houses. However, they are also cracking bawdy jokes since phrases like "thrust his maids to the wall," "cut off the heads of the maids or their maidenheads," "Me they shall feel while I am able to stand," and "I am a pretty piece of flesh," (1.1.16-28) are used. The bawdy intention is so obvious that we can easily recognize sexual implications, too, in such phrases as "Draw thy tool" (1.1.30) and "My naked weapon" (1.1.33). Yet, the wordplay here is not mere wordplay. Actually, it is a fine way of exposition for the play. It tells us that the play is to be about hate and love, feud and sex, or Mars and Venus. And it suggests the ironic vision that love and hate are close together; making love and making war are alike; lovers can really be "star-crossed" with Venus and Mars.

Other similar instances of wordplay capable of suggesting the same themes or ironic vision can easily be found in the play. Mercutio's reply to Romeo that "If love be rough with you, be rough with love; / Prick love for pricking and you beat love down" (1.4.27-8) when Romeo says, "Is love a tender thing? It is too rough / Too rude, too boisterous, and it pricks like thorn" (1.4.25-6). Peter's taunting of the Nurse: "I saw no man use you at his pleasure; if I had, my weapon should quickly have been out. I warrant you, I dare draw as soon as another man, if I see occasion in a good quarrel, and the law on my side" (2.4.154-7), and the Nurse's complaint: "Now afore God I am so vexed that every part about me quivers" (2.4.158-9). And Juliet's soliloquy: "Come, civil night, / Thou sober-suited matron, all in black, /And learn me how to lose a winning match / Play'd for a pair of stainless maidenhoods" (3.2.10-13). In this last instance, to be sure, the battle image is replaced by the game imagery. But all the same. A "match" is like a battle. And even better, the word "match" suggests also the sense of "matching two lovers."

VIII. Death and Love

A battle often, and a match sometimes, brings death. Can love bring death, too? Yes, of course. To Antony and Cleopatra, Pyramus and Thisbe, and our Romeo and Juliet. Yet, death is a pun. In its bawdy sense, to die or, even more clearly, to die in a woman's lap is to "experience a sexual orgasm" (Partridge 93). This pun often appears in Shakespeare's works, comic or tragic. In *Much Ado about Nothing*, for instance, Denedick says to Beatrice: "I will live in thy heart, die in thy lap, and be buried in thy eyes" (5.2.102-3). And in *King Lear*, the mad Lear says, "I will die bravely,/ Like a smug bridegroom" (4.6.195-6). But it is in the "comitragedy" of *Romeo and Juliet* that this pun occurs most frequently and most significantly.

In Act III, Scene III, when Friar Laurence tells the Nurse that Romeo is lying "There on the ground, with his own tears made drunk," we have this bawdy talk:

> **Nurse.** *O, he is even in my mistress' case,*
> *Just in her case. O woeful sympathy,*
> *Piteous predicament. Even so lies she,*
> *Blubbering and weeping, weeping and blubbering.*
> *Stand up, stand up. Stand, and you be a man.*
> *For Juliet's sake, for her sake, rise and stand.*
> *Why should you fall into so deep an O?*
> **Romeo.** *Nurse.*
> **Nurse.** *Ah sir, ah sir, death's the end of all.*
> **Romeo.** *Spak'st thou of Juliet? How is it with her? (83-92)*

Here the remark that "death is the end of all" obviously contains the bawdy sense that sexual intercourse ends with orgasm. The same sense

25

is secretly implied when, pretending to avenge Tybalt's death, Juliet assures her mother thus:

> *Indeed I never shall be satisfied*
> *With Romeo, till I behold him—dead—*
> *Is my poor heart so for a kinsman vex'd.*
> *Madam, if you could find out but a man*
> *To bear a poison, I would temper it—*
> *That Romeo should upon receipt thereof*
> *Soon sleep in quiet. O, how my heart abhors*
> *To hear him nam'd, and cannot come to him*
> *To wreak the love I bore my cousin*
> *Upon his body that hath slaughter'd him. (3.5.93-102)*

Here "dead" again suggests orgasm while "a poison" may refer to the saliva-like excretion during sexual intercourse, and to "sleep in quiet" is usual after orgasm. And the same bawdy sense is suggested in Romeo's exclamation that "How oft when men are at the point of death/Have they been merry!" (5.3.88-89), and in Tybalt's warning— "Turn thee, Benvolio, look upon thy death" (1.1.64) —when he saw Benvolio "drawn" among Sampson, Gregory and Abram whom he refers to as "these heartless hinds" (1.1.63), which as a quibble has the meanings of both "cowardly menials" and "female deer without a male hart to protect them." Finally we find the pun in the context where Mercutio jestingly tries to "conjure" Romeo:

> *The ape is dead and I must conjure him.*
> *I conjure thee by Rosaline's bright eyes,*
> *By her high forehead and her scarlet lip,*
> *By her fine foot, straight leg, and quivering thigh,*
> *And the demesnes that there adjacent lie,*
> *That in thy likeness thou appear to us. (2.1.16-21)*

The word "dead" can mean "quiet sleep after orgasm" here. This is certified when a few lines later Mercutio adds: "I conjure only but to *raise up* him" (2.1.29, my italics).

In Act V, Scene III, Romeo asks himself, "Shall I believe / That unsubstantial Death is amorous, / And that the lean abhorred monster keeps / Thee [Juliet] here in dark to be his paramour?" (102-5). Our answer for him is "Yes," because in this play death or Death can also be such a personified lover besides suggesting orgasm. That is why Juliet can say, "Come, cords, come, Nurse, I'll to my wedding bed, / And death, not Romeo take my maidenhead" (3.2.136-7); Romeo can say, "Come death, and welcome. Juliet wills it so" (3.5.24); and finally Capulet can tell Paris: "O son, the night before thy wedding day / Hath Death lain with thy wife. There she lies, / Flower as she was, deflowered by him" (4.5.35-7).

Meaning "orgasm" or representing "a lover," death is naturally to be expected and received with pleasure. Julia Kristeva observes: "Juliet's jouissance is often stated through the anticipation—the desire? —of Romeo's death" (306). But Juliet herself also expects death. That is why she can cry out, "Give me my Romeo; and when I shall die..." (3.2.21); and finally, when she finds Romeo has poisoned himself, she stabs herself, saying: "O happy dagger, / This is thy sheath. There rust, and let me die" (5.3.168-9). It is to be noted here that the "happy dagger" is what Romeo brings with himself. Thus, Juliet's death by the dagger is perfectly symbolic of the lovers' consummation.

IX. Ro-me-O!

In *Romeo and Juliet*, instances of bawdy wordplay are really too many to be all cited for discussion here. But before we leave this topic, we must discuss the hero's name also in the light of bawdy wordplay, because it can help us clarify the playwright's comic or ironic vision as well.

Very few scholars have ever given a thought to Shakespeare's calling the play's hero Romeo. As the play's direct source was Arthur Brooke's poem, titled "The Tragical History of Romeus and Juliet," people just pass "Romeo" for a variant of "Romeus," not knowing that Shakespeare has made this variation evidently on purpose.

In Act II, Scene IV of the play, let us recall, Mercutio is making fun of Romeo's name and shape when he comments: "Without his roe, like a dried herring" (38). "Roe," as we know, refers to the milt or sperm of the male fish here. Thus, Shakespeare / Mercutio evidently has in mind the idea that the "Ro" in "Romeo" can pun on the word "roe" and stand for a male's sexual organ or sexual power. So, Romeo "without his roe" will certainly leave him lamenting with "me O!" Furthermore, "Ro" can actually pun on the word "row," too. Now, imagine Juliet calling "Ro-me-o!" What can it suggest? "Row me, your boat, O!" Or "Give me your roe O!" with "Ro(e)" as a dative verb? Anyway, will it avail anything for a doe to call a dear hart which has his ro(e) only in name?

In Act III, Scene III, let us recall again, the Nurse is reproaching Romeo for his inability to "rise and stand for Juliet's sake" when she says, "Why should you fall into so deep an O?" (89-90). The "O" here is, of course, a pun on the word "woe." But it also suggests a woman's sexual organ since the letter is shaped like a hole.[4] This reading can be justified in contrasting the "O" with the "I" which Juliet uses, notoriously, to pun on the words "Ay" and "eye" in Act III, Scene II, 45-50. If we read the context carefully, we will find that Juliet's "I" actually suggests the male sexual organ too, since it is shaped like a bar just as the number "1." With this understanding, then, imagine Juliet crying "Ro-me-o!" again. What can it further suggest? "Roe / row me, the woe!" or "Roe / row me, the woman!"? Anyway, to roe / row the doe will certainly come to woe, and that is their dole.

Finally, let us recall that the entire play ends with this concluding couplet: "For never was a story of more woe / Than this of Juliet and her Romeo" (5.3.308-9). By rhyming "woe" with the last "o" in "Romeo," the Prince is evidently associating "o" with "woe." For the Prince the final result of Juliet and her Romeo's romance may really be woe. But is this Shakespeare's conclusion, too, since he is the playwright that wrote the lines for the Prince?

Very unlikely, I think. Shakespeare's attitude towards this play is most probably like Peter Quince's attitude towards his play of Pyramus and Thisbe in *A Midsummer Night's Dream*. It is true that he does not obviously try to turn tragedy into farce as does Peter Quince. But since there is so much wordplay in this drama, we are naturally led to think that Shakespeare actually had rather a comic view when he composed the play. He as well as we readers might think: Since Juliet is "a rich jewel... / Too rich for use, and for earth too dear" (1.5.45-6), her "true knight" (3.2.142) is destined not to possess her. In reality, neither man nor hart nor fish ever tries to roe / row a jewel. To do so and then come to woe is just a destined comic tragedy to be acted by players who can still be playing with words when death has come to the hero.

X. The "Comic Relief"

"Comic relief" has been a controversial term among Shakespearean scholars. It involves chiefly two theories. One is an affective theory. It takes the audience into consideration. For a theorist of this kind (e.g. Dryden) the word "relief" means "lessening or removal of pain, anxiety, etc." So A. P. Rossiter calls it a "relaxation theory." The main idea of this theory is: the audience has to be relieved of their unpleasant feelings in watching a tragedy with the interruption of certain "healing laughter"—a comic scene, for instance. The other theory is an objective theory. It is concerned with the structure of the work. This theory takes the word "relief" to mean, in a sculptural sense, "prominence or distinctness due to contrast." So we can call this theory a contrast theory. Its central idea is: a comic element is introduced into tragedy for the purpose of setting a tragic element (a theme, tone, character, etc.) in sharp relief against the comic element introduced. Rossiter tells us that for Shakespeare the relaxation theory is quite inadequate since there seems to be too much "relief" in his tragic works and "not seldom where there has not been enough tension to need *any*" (279). Rossiter is right. If we take *Romeo and Juliet* for an example, we will find that there is indeed too much "relief" in it; the audience certainly need not be relieved so intensively with so much wordplay. In Act IV, Scene V, for instance, Peter and the musicians' teasing each other with wordplay concerning "Heart's ease" and "silver sound" is unnecessary if it is to serve as a "comic relief" for the audience. For the audience knows all too well that Juliet is not really dead at that time.

If the relaxation theory is not satisfactory, how about the contrast theory? Rossiter observes that "the true Shakespearean 'relief' trades in apparently wanton incongruity, where every risk is taken in using discord or clash; where the most heterogeneous *moods* are yoked by violence together, and no 'classical' principles can discern if it is with controlled purpose" (280). Rossiter is again right here. If we examine *Romeo and Juliet* as an example, we will find that Shakespeare has really taken the contrast and collision of opposites to extreme lengths. And we certainly find the violent yoking together of heterogeneous moods in many places. For example, at the end of the play when Romeo, Juliet and Paris are all dead, every character is supposed to be in a sad mood. But the Prince is made to address Montague with wordplay: "Come, Montague, for thou art early up / To see thy son and heir now early down" (5.3.207-8). The same incongruity is seen in

Capulet's using a conceit to talk of his daughter's death—"Death lies on her like an untimely frost / Upon the sweetest flower of all the field" (4.5.28-9)—and in Romeo's "conceited" protest against the grave: "Thou detestable maw, thou womb of death / Gorg'd with the dearest morsel of the earth... " (5.3.45-8). Indeed, "so often did the 'conceited' Shakespeare play with words when he might be working with feeling that the critics cried out in protest" (Eastman 18). The critics' protest is against the gay while Romeo's protest is against the grave.

If both the relaxation theory and the contrast theory of "comic relief" fail to justify Shakespeare's mingling comic and tragic elements in *Romeo and Juliet*, is there any other way to justify it? There is one, I think. The idea of "comic relief" can be considered in the light of the author's vision as well as the audience's psychology or the play's structure. That is, we can make an expressive, rather than affective or objective, theory for *Romeo and Juliet*. But before we do that, we need to talk about Mercutio first.

Readers or audiences of *Romeo and Juliet* are often impressed with the merry character of Mercutio, which is best expressed in the wordplay with which he tells Romeo that he has been fatally wounded: "No, 'tis not so deep as a well, nor so wide as a church door, but 'tis enough, 'twill serve. Ask for me tomorrow and you shall find me a grave man" (3.1.97-99). We really wonder why he should still be jesting when death is approaching him. We know he is being ironic. Yet, we know, too, that he surely can become a grave man only after he has entered the grave.

We cannot know for sure why Mercutio should have such a merry character. But we can be certain that he has a comic view of life. He cannot bear to see Romeo groaning for love, nor can he see himself groaning for life. He can really make light of love and life although he is not unaware of the strife and stress in them. Joseph Porter agrees with Clifford Leech that there is an angriness in Mercutio which is a link with such later Shakespearean tragic heroes as Hamlet, Othello, Lear, and Macbeth (Leech, "Moral Tragedy," 75). But our general feeling is: Mercutio is a jester, not a tragic hero. I agree that there is as much fire as air in him. But his light air has been blowing so constantly over his heavy fire that we feel he is at best a Byronic hero crying that "if I laugh at any mortal thing, 'Tis that I may not weep" (*Don Juan*, Canto IV, 25-6).

Now, Shakespeare in his thirties, I may assume, has a tinge of the Mercutio character although as a playwright he is even more akin to Peter Quince in being able to treat the tragic matter comically at some aesthetic distance. Anyway, there is no doubt that Shakespeare has a comic vision to see the romantic irony that one can laugh at one's own solemnity. And the comic vision is also an ironic vision. It helps Shakespeare see the necessary co-existence of mutually opposing things. It is this vision that makes him an impure dramatist bringing forth both comedies and tragedies and mixing comic and tragic elements in the same play. It is this vision, too, that makes him compose the comedy of *A Midsummer Night's Dream* with a tragic play-within-the-play (Peter Quince's *Pyramus and Thisbe*) performed farcically, and at the same time compose the tragedy of *Romeo and Juliet* with so many comic attributes that it seems to serve as a tone-and-theme-echoing "play-without-the-play" of the *Dream.*

If we have the same comic or ironic vision, we will be able to regard *Romeo and Juliet* not as a bad tragedy spoiled by the abuse of chance in plot and that of rhetoric in language, but as a successful "comitragedy" blending tragic reality with comic potential. Furthermore, we will be able to appreciate the sonnet language, especially the oxymoronic phrases, that we find permeating the play. Meanwhile, we will also be able to discover that Shakespeare's comic or ironic vision has actually made his habit of wordplay and his particular fondness of puns. With this discovery, we then understand that death in this play can be associated with sex or love, and that the hero's name, if torn apart into "Ro-me-o," can significantly suggest the co-existence of sex or love with woe. This understanding then leads us to the conclusion that if we want to criticize the play in terms of "comic relief," we should adopt neither an affective theory of relaxation, nor an objective theory of contrast, but an expressive theory of vision. We should suppose that Shakespeare, with his Mercutio-like personality, is equipped with a comic or ironic vision of life in producing the play. He is aware of life's irony and is always ready to typify the romantic irony of having serious matters treated playfully. Thus, the play ("sport") is really *within* the play ("drama") while the play ("drama") is also *without* ("lacking") the play ("sport").

With this conclusion, however, I know I still cannot invalidate others' conclusions. For instance, I must admit that if one is to regard the play as a "problem play," the problem therein can be about "the lack of intimacy between parents and children" (Singh 43). And if one is to regard the play as a "festive play," one may surely see the lovers "commit two serious abrogations of community ritual by their secret marriage and by the fake funeral for one not dead" (Liebler 150). In fact, I find I must hold with Shakespeare, too, that the play is an "Excellent Conceited Tragedie" as indicated in the title of the 1597 quarto edition. But, in that concession, I also must point out that the word "Conceited" is also a pun. On one hand, it means that the play is full of Petrarchan conceits. On the other hand, it means that the play is well "conceived" (i.e., imagined)—so well "conceived" indeed that we may see Shakespeare's comic or ironic vision vividly expressed in its mingling of comic and tragic elements. If we have the same comic or tragic vision, we will then be able to find some "comic relief" not only in the sanguine fact that the lovers' deaths will bring an end to the two houses' feud and bring peace to everybody (Leech, "Moral Tragedy," 73), but also in the visionary fact that the two lovers' deaths have at last devoured the "love-devouring death" (2.6.7); for them death is not only sex and love but also eternal marriage. And, thus, just as poison, for Friar Laurence, can be medicine too, so tragedy, for Romeo and Juliet, can also be comedy. This irony will finally make us perplexed to accept the aforesaid simple distinction that "All tragedies are finished by a death, / All comedies are ended by a marriage." And in that perplexity we may feel we can call this play a "most lamentable comedy"—just as Peter Quince calls his *Pyramus and Thisbe*—if we prefer not to call it a "comitragedy."

Notes

1. All parenthesized references of Shakespeare's plays in this paper are to the editions of the Arden Shakespeare.
2. It is said that the term "tragicomedy" derives from a reference by Plautus to the unconventional mixture of kings, gods and servants in his own play *Amphitruo* as "tragico-comoedia." See J. A. Cuddon, ed. *A Dictionary of Literary Terms*, p. 711.
3. See his Introduction to the Arden Edition of *Romeo and Juliet*, pp. 43-52.
4. Compare H. J. Oliver, ed., *The Merry Wives of Windsor* (London: Methuen, 1971), IV, I, 42-59, for the quibble on "O."

Works Consulted

Bradley, A. C. *Shakespearean Tragedy*, 3rd ed. London: Macmillan, 1992.

Brennan, Anthony. *Shakespeare's Dramatic Structures*. London & New York: Routledge, 1988.

Charlton, H. B. "Shakespeare's Experimental Tragedy." *Twentieth Century Interpretations of Romeo and Juliet*. Ed. Douglas Cole. Englewood Cliffs, NJ: Prentice-Hall, 1970. 49-60.

Coghill, Nevill. Introduction. *Romeo and Juliet*. By William Shakespeare. London: Pan Books, 1972. 7-19.

Cuddon, J. A., ed. *A Dictionary of Literary Terms*. Harmondsworth, England: Penguin Books, 1982.

Dryden, John. "An Essay of Dramatic Poesy." *Criticism: The Major Texts*. Ed. Walter Jackson Bate. New York: Harcourt Brace Jovanovich, 1970. 129-60.

Frye, Northrop. *Northrop Frye on Shakespeare*. New Haven & London: Yale UP, 1986.

Granville-Barker, Harley. *"Romeo and Juliet*—The Conduct of the Action." *Twentieth Century Interpretations of Romeo and Juliet*. Ed. Douglas Cole. Englewood Cliffs, NJ: Prentice-Hall, 1970. 19-39.

Harbage, Alfred. *A Reader's Guide to William Shakespeare*. New York: The Noonday Press, 1963.

Harrison, G. B. *Introducing Shakespeare*, 3rd ed. London: Penguin, 1966.

———, ed. *Shakespeare: The Complete Works*. New York: Harcourt Brace & World, 1968.

Johnson, Samuel. "Preface to Shakespeare." *Criticism: The Major Texts*. Ed. Walter Jackson Bate. New York: Harcourt Brace Jovanovich, 1970. 207-17.

Kermode, Frank. Introduction. *Romeo and Juliet*. The Riverside Shakespeare. Boston: Houghton Mifflin, 1974. 1055-7.

Kristeva, Julia. "Romeo and Juliet: Love-Hatred in the Couple." *Shakespearean Tragedy*. Ed. John Drakakis. London & New York: Longman, 1992. 296-315.

Leech, Clifford. *Tragedy*. The Critical Idiom. London: Methuen, 1969.

——. "The Moral Tragedy of *Romeo and Juliet*." *English Renaissance Drama*. Ed. Standish Henning, et. al. Carbondale: Southern Illinois UP, 1976. 59-75.

Liebler, Naomi Conn. *Shakespeare's Festive Tragedy*. London & New York: Routledge, 1995.

Mahood, M. M. "*Romeo and Juliet*." *Essays in Shakespearean Criticism*. Ed. James L. Calderwood & Harold E. Toliver. Englewood Cliffs, NJ: Prentice-Hall, 1970. 391-404.

Merchant, W. Moelwyn. *Comedy*. The Critical Idiom. London: Methuen, 1972.

Oz, Avraham. "What's in a Good Name? The Case of *Romeo and Juliet* as a Bad Tragedy." *"Bad" Shakespeare: Revaluations of the Shakespearean Canon*. Ed. Maurice Charney. London & Toronto: Associated UP, 1988. 133-42.

Partridge, Eric. *Shakespeare's Bawdy*. London: Routledge & Kegan Paul, 1968.

Porter, Joseph A. *Shakespeare's Mercutio*. Chapel Hill & London: U of North Carolina P, 1988.

Rossiter, A. P. *Angel with Horns: Fifteen Lectures on Shakespeare*. London & New York: Longman, 1989.

Rozett, Martha Tuck. "The Comic Structures of Tragic Endings: The Suicide Scenes in *Romeo and Juliet* and *Anthony and Cleopatra*." *Shakespeare Quarterly*, 36.2 (1985): 152-64.

Shakespeare, William. *As You Like It*. Ed. Agnes Latham. The Arden Shakespeare. London & New York: Methuen, 1975.

——. *Hamlet*. Ed. Harold Jenkins. The Arden Shakespeare. 1982.

——. *King Lear*. Ed. Kenneth Muir. The Arden Shakespeare. 1972.

——. *The Merry Wives of Windsor*. Ed. H. J. Oliver. The Arden Shakespeare. 1971.

——. *A Midsummer Night's Dream*. Ed. Harold F. Brooks. The Arden Shakespeare. 1979.

——.*Much Ado about Nothing*. Ed. A. R. Humphreys. The Arden Shakespeare. 1981.

——. *Romeo and Juliet*. Ed. Brian Gibbons. The Arden Shakespeare. 1980.

Singh, Sarup. *Family Relationships in Shakespeare and the Restoration Comedy of Manners*. Delhi: Oxford UP, 1983.

Stauffer, Donald A. "The School of Love: *Romeo and Juliet*." *Shakespeare: The Tragedies*. Twentieth Century Views. Ed. Alfred Harbage. Englewood Cliffs, NJ: Prentice-Hall, 1964.

Whittier, Gayle. "The Sonnet's Body and the Body Sonnetized in *Romeo and Juliet*." *Shakespeare Quarterly*, 40.1 (1989): 27-41.

* This chapter first appeared as a paper in 1998 in National Chung Hsing University's *Journal of the College of Liberal Arts*, Vol. 28, pp. 195-222.

• Chapter 2 •

Kingship and Counterfeit: Shakespeare's Deconstructionist Vision in *Henry IV*

I. From History to History Play

It is sometimes jokingly said that "history" is a portmanteau word made up of "his" and "story," and that it indicates that the world's histories have been male stories, that is, stories told by male historians mainly about male figures and male "businesses." This joke may, of course, sound pretty credible to those feminists who are constantly taking pains to find more evidence of "patriarchal" dominance and oppression in our society. But I am not one of those feminists. I do not believe in such an etymological "story." Still, however, I must admit that although a joke is seldom considered a truth, it can at times contain some partial truth if only we are willing to give it a second and serious thought. Take the present case for example. If only we think of such historians as Herodotus, Thucydides, Gibbon, etc., in the West or Ssu Ma-ts'ien, Pan Ku, Ssu Ma-kuang, etc., in our country, we cannot but agree that as most famous historians, East and West, have been male, it is likely that the world's histories have been written in male perspectives, thus focusing chiefly on affairs of male interests. This fact can be applied to writers of history plays. *Henry IV*, for instance, is written by a famous male playwright (Shakespeare) chiefly on such male concerns as war and power.

In fact, history is not only mainly a male story. It is often seemingly a particular male individual's story. This particular male individual is what we call the monarch, the single supreme ruler of a state, e.g. a king or an emperor. Just call to mind Alexander the Great, Julius Caesar, Napoleon, etc., or Ts'in Shih-huang, Han Wu-ti, T'ang T'ai-chung, etc. Aren't their "personal stories" hardly distinguishable from the stories of their states? The same is true of history plays. Take *Henry IV* again for example. It is surely Henry IV's story or, as we will discuss below, actually a story of Henry V.

We know the word "history" is an ambiguous word. It denotes both a series of events and the record of such a series of events. History in the first sense refers to the true beings and true happenings in time; history in the second sense refers to the spoken or written account or report of history in the first sense. The former is the origin or the cause of the latter. All historians are narrators of the first-sense history although their narratives (histories) are often based on others' narratives (the second-sense histories).

It is well-known that Plato regards literature (especially dramatic poetry) as twice removed from reality; for him literary works are at best nothing but imitations of appearances, copies of copies, or counterfeits of lies. Plato's disciple Aristotle thinks more favorably of literature. For him the poet is not only imitative but also creative. He even treats poetry as a more philosophical and higher thing than history because the historian writes of what has already happened; the poet writes of what could happen—one tends to express the particular while the other tends to express the universal. Today, however, most people still presume that literature is mostly fictive while history is factual. Thus, they deem it a joke to say history has nothing real except names of persons and places whereas literature is all real except, again, names of persons and places.

Seriously considered, the joke is not wholly untrue. Today, the so-called New Historicists have repeatedly emphasized that history can be available to us only in the form of "representation"; all historians' histories are textualized narratives; history is no other than literature in terms of its creative process: both are products of imagination, thus neither is purely objective and neither is absolutely "true." Take our present topic for example. Can we say Shakespeare's *Henry IV* plays are historical counterfeits or lies while their supposed "sources" are historically genuine facts?

Regarding this point,, Paola Pugliatti in his *Shakespeare the Historian* remarks interestingly, thus:

> For the Tudor historian, history-writing was not the outcome of enquiry; rather, it almost implied the obligation not to enquire further once what was taken to be the acceptable tradition was established. Almost invariably, writing about history was considered a matter of re-writing and telling a matter of re-telling. Strategies were elaborated to present uncertain facts or to offer different versions of the same event. (32)

> ...Consequently, historical truth ended up being a side-effect of certain texts, established by their declarations of orthodoxy and of ethical engagement, but above all by their practice of reproduction, and validated by frequent quotation of the chosen model. The guarantee of the text's reliability, therefore, was entrusted to openly declared intertextuality rather than to engagement in historical research. (33)

If Pugliatti has said the truth, what can we say of Shakespeare's history plays and their supposed sources?

It is often noted that the main sources of Shakespeare's *Henry IV* are Holinshed's *Chronicles of England, Scotland and Ireland*, Samuel

Daniel's *The First Four Books of the Civil Wars Between the Two Houses of Lancaster and York*, and an anonymous, popular play called *The Famous Victories of Henry V.* Now, if we examine these supposed main sources carefully, we will find at least these facts: first, Daniel disagrees with Holinshed on some important points of detail—for example, "Holinshed has Glendower fighting at Shrewsbury, whereas Daniel says that the Welsh were absent" (Smith 13). Second, "Daniel, and following him Shakespeare, made Hotspur a generation younger, and the Prince of Wales a little older, so that they could be shown as rivals of about the same age" (Morris 8). Third, from the *Famous Victories* Shakespeare took the tale of Hal's misspent youth and the name "Oldcastle" for Hal's disreputable misleader, but, owing to the strong objection from the descendents of the real Oldcastle's widow, Shakespeare "changed the name in the first printed copy to Falstaff" (Smith 13). These facts suggest: first, history books tend to give different versions of history and, therefore, a history play has to choose a version to base its material on (in the case of Glendower and in that of Hotspur, Shakespeare chose to follow Daniel rather than Holinshed). Second, external power is liable to force any writer to lie about a certain fact (in the Oldcastle case Shakespeare had to use a counterfeit name). So, history is full of contingencies. Playwrights as well as chroniclers often cannot stick to a single truth. They are often equally flexible fabricators.

In truth, both chroniclers and playwrights often envision certain guiding truths when they write histories / plays. Holinshed, for example, is said to interpret history from a Tudor standpoint. His *Chronicles*, it is said, "stresses the disastrous consequences for England of the deposition and murder of Richard II by Henry Bolingbroke" (Smith 13). In accordance with Holinshed, E. M. W. Tillyard in his *The Elizabethan World Picture* holds that the literature of the Elizabethan period has for its center the ideas of divine order, the chain of being, and the correspondences between earthly and heavenly things. Hence, for Tillyard Shakespeare's English history plays helped to build up "the Tudor myth," which saw a "universally held" and "fundamentally religious" historical "scheme" governed by divine providence in the history beginning with the "distortion of nature's course" by deposing and murdering Richard II, through "a long series of disasters and suffering and struggles," to end with the restoration of legitimacy and order under the Tudors (Tillyard 1962, 362).

But did Shakespeare really intend to uphold the Tudor myth? There have been, to be sure, quite a number of scholars adhering to the providential theory.[1] Nevertheless, opponents to Tillyard and his followers have been as numerous and strong. According to Phyllis Rackin, rebellion against the Tudor myth has taken two forms: either to refuse any ideology or political propaganda by reminding us of Shakespeare's universal qualities of human nature and experience, or to demonstrate that the myth never existed or that Shakespeare was actually debunking rather than dramatizing the myth (40-41). "Both new historicism and cultural materialism reject the Tudor myth school's assumption that there was an 'Elizabethan mind' whose thinking was everywhere conditioned by a conservative 'world picture'" (Rackin 42). Surely, in recent decades, very much of the criticism of Shakespeare's English history plays "has centered on various versions of an issue framed in Shakespeare's time as a conflict between providential and Machiavellian theories of historical causation": the former "looked backward to an older feudal world and upward to transcendent spiritual authority to oppose change and justify hereditary privilege," while the latter, "by contrast, validates change, mobility, and individual initiative" (Rackin 43). But, obviously, "the newer generation, in our time as in the sixteenth century, prefers the Machiavellian version of historical causation, explaining history in terms of force, fortune, and practical politics" (Rackin 43).

Here I must confess that I am one of "the newer generation." I agree that in his history plays generally, and in the two parts of *Henery*

IV particularly, Shakespeare shows a provable advocacy of the Machiavellian view of historical causation. Yet, in the meantime I must also acknowledge that Shakespeare was a patriot, he did share with many of his contemporaries the fear of disorder coming from civil strife due to unsuccessful succession to the throne, and he might therefore be reluctant to argue openly and clearly against the divine-right theory associated commonly with royal privilege. In effect, as I will discuss below, we will find there is a deconstructionist vision embedded in Shakespeare's political understanding, whether we choose to review his chronicles in terms of providentialism or Machiavellianism.

II. Deconstructionist Ideas

To discuss Shakespeare's deconstructionist vision we need an introduction to deconstructionist ideas first. But, deplorably, deconstructionism as a school of thought is most difficult to define, and deconstructionist ideas often involve terms, some of which being neologisms, very hard to explain satisfactorily. What follows is just a simplified summary for our present purpose.

Deconstruction as a term is usually said to originate in the writings of the French philosopher Jacques Derrida in the late 1960's. As a philosophical activity, it is said to be "a critique of concepts and hierarchies" (Fowler 54). According to Derrida, Western philosophy has been led by a partiality which he calls "logocentrism." "Logos is a Greek term that can specifically mean 'word,' but also carries implications of rationality and wisdom in general, and is sometimes reified as a cosmic intellectual principle" (Fowler 54).[2] To be logocentric is to construct a system of thinking on the basis of a term as its structural center and to venerate it much as one venerates the

Word of God, not knowing that to stick to the certainty, identity or truth of that central term is to "repress or forget other elements which thus become the un-thought, and sometimes the unthinkable, of Western philosophy" (Fowler 54). Examples of such logocentric terms include *being, essence, substance, truth, form, beginning, end, purpose, consciousness, man, God,* and so on (Selden & Widdowson 144).

Logocentrism is accompanied by the "metaphysics of presence," which is the idea of taking an extra-system entity, a point of reference or a center of authority for the ultimate fundamental or principle, or the last invariable origin or source, not knowing that nothing in the world is ever so self-sufficient, so unqualified and so unmediated as to be able to serve as absolute knowledge, original truth, or determinate signification. Such a metaphysics is a delusion, a mistaking of *being* for *presence*. In his "Structure, Sign and Play in the Discourse of the Human Sciences," Derrida says, "all the names related to fundamentals, to principles, or to the center have always designated an invariable presence—*eidos, archē, telos, energeia, ousia* (essence, existence, substance, subject) *ale-theia,* transcendentality, consciousness, God, man, and so forth" (1978, 279-80).

If no "presence" can be found in this world of signification, what is there in our thinking systems? All ways of thinking involve concepts and terms, that is, involve language as a symbolic system. In de Saussure's view, words are signs made up of two parts: a mark, either written or spoken, called a "signifier," and a concept (what the mark causes to exist in one's mind) called a "signified." The relation between signifier and signified is arbitrary. In the system of signification, all signifiers as well as all signifieds are different in that they are distinguished from one another by certain opposites or contrasts. Now, in expanding de Saussure's linguistic thinking to the thinking of all thinking systems, Derrida tells us that in thinking we are really forever using certain concepts with their supposedly equivalent terms to represent or signify some other concepts with their also supposedly equivalent terms. But now, since no "presence," that is, no ultimate, original, and permanent signified can be found to serve as the center of the logos (because in practice every concept or signified can serve as a signifier to signify some other concept or signified), the only invariable in all thinking systems is the phenomenon of *différance*. As we know, *différance* is a portmanteau term coined by Derrida to denote in its French original both difference and deferment. This neologism, therefore, aims to suggest at least two things: the use of signs based on differences in the course of signification, and the endless deferment of meaning since meaning is "always relational, never self-present or self-constituted" (Hawthorn 43). In fact, Derrida identifies three main meanings for the term in his *Positions*:

> First, **différance** *refers to the (active and passive) movement that consists in deferring by means of delay, delegation, reprieve, referral, detour, postponement, reserving... Second, the movement of* **différance**, *as that which produces different things, that which differentiates, is the common root of all oppositional concepts that mark our language, such as, to take only a few examples, sensible / intelligent, intuition / signification, nature / culture, etc. ...Third,* **différance** *is also the production, if it can still be put this way, of these differences, of the diacriticity that the linguistics generated by Saussure, and all the structural sciences modeled upon it, have recalled is the condition for any significant and any structure. ...From this point of view, the concept of* **différance** *is neither simply structuralist, nor simply geneticist, such an alternative itself being an "effect" of* **différance**. *(8-9)*

Derrida himself has used other terms to refer to, signify, represent, or explain the phenomenon of *différance* in *Positions* and elsewhere. The term *trace*, for instance, takes from Freud (in "Note on the Mystic

Writing Pad") the idea that the written message can still be left in the trace of writing (just as that imprinted on the wax of children's writing pad). But the term is "radicalized and extracted from the metaphysics of presence" (Derrida 1978, 229), only to mean "the erasure of selfhood, of one's own presence" because it is "constituted by the threat or anguish of its irremediable disappearance, of the disappearance of its disappearance" (Derrida 1978, 220). So, in thinking, all concepts are but traces of traces.

The idea of "trace" is connected with the idea of "gram." For Derrida, the gram is the most general concept of semiology, and he prefers to call this science of signs "grammatology." In his *Of Grammatology* Derrida attacks the classical type of logocentrism which he calls "phonocentrism" because it privileges speech over writing and treats writing merely as a contaminated form of speech. In fact, just as Freud conceptualizes the unconscious mind as "constituted by writing in the form of an arche-writing or ur-writing in the brain which precedes all physical writing and, even, all speech—both phylogenetically and ontogenetically," so Derrida asserts that "no perception is virginal or direct, but is given meaning by a pre-existing arche-writing" (Hawthorn 8). It follows, then, that for Derrida all thinking systems are after all grammatological systems; all concepts are "grams" displayed in *différance.*

Besides *différance*, Derrida also uses the term "supplement" to designate the unstable relationship among signs, concepts, traces, or grams. In French, "suppléer" means both "to add something to" and "to take the place of." Thus, supplementality is the phenomenon of addition plus substitution. Now, in Derrida's view all thinking systems involve the addition / substitution of one thing to / for another. For instance, one may, as does Rousseau, consider writing as merely a supplement to speech. But for Derrrida writing is also a substitute for speech, just as a sign is taken to stand for another sign, a trace for another trace, a gram for another gram.

Once we understand the possibility of making all signs "supplement" other signs, of tracing all traces to other traces, or of writing all grams about other grams, we will realize that we are in a world of semiological or grammatological "dissemination," where the seeding and potential growth of meaning is endless because in the absence of stable signifieds all signifiers can be freely adopted to serve as seeds of meaning. Indeed, we can all become "players of signs." Only that by "play" we mean not only play as in "to play a game," but also play as in "to play the piano," "to play a fish," etc. In other words, the play of signs for dissemination can be "playful" or "non-playful," depending on the nature of the "play."

Playful or not, our play with signs often betrays our propensity towards constructing "violent hierarchies." To assert, for instance, that speech precedes writing, or nature precedes civilization, or good precedes evil, is to privilege one concept / term over another while upon close examination we will find the two opposing / contrasting concepts or terms are mutually defined and thus should be placed on the same plane instead of being violently placed one above another to form a "violent hierarchy." Without hierarchical thinking we will be able to say speech is a species of writing, nature is a state of civilization, and good is a degree of evil, just as we can say writing is a species of speech, civilization is a state of nature, and evil is a degree of good.

To deconstruct a logocentrism, a thinking system, or a violent hierarchy is to find an / the "aporia" therein. An "aporia," as we know, is an apparently irresolvable logical impasse. As Alan Bass, the English translator of *Writing and Difference*, has explained, Derrida has adopted the Greek term to indicate the situation we find "once a system has been 'shaken' by following its totalizing logic to its final consequence"; it is often "an excess which cannot be construed within the rules of logic, for the excess can be conceived as *neither* this *nor* that, or both at the same time—a departure from all rules of logic" (Derrida 1978, xvi-xvii). For example, in trying to deconstruct J. L.

Austin and John Searle's speech act theory that a performative utterance must be a "serious" statement rather than a joke or something said in a play or poem, Derrida can argue that both a real courtroom oath and an oath people play in a film or book belong to a repeatable sign-sequence. Since they come from the same source of "reiterability," we can hardly say any is "parasitic" upon the other, or any is logically prior to the other. Therefore, a joke or a Hollywood court oath can be as "serious" as a "serious" pledge made anywhere.

The deconstructive method, as shown in seeking an aporia, is certainly rather sophistic in nature. In trying to find an aporia, a deconstructionist views a thinking system as essentially a matter of rhetoric: "thinking is always and inseparably bound to the rhetorical devices that support it" (Norris 61). Consequently, the maneuvering of "tropes" is all important and necessary, as such American deconstructionists as Paul de Man, Harold Bloom, Geoffrey Hartman, and J. Hillis Miller may agree. Yet, as Barbara Johnson has also observed, "*Deconstruction* is not synonymous with *destruction*." "It is in fact much closer to the original meaning of the word *analysis*, which etymologically means 'to undo'—a virtual synonym for 'to de-construct.' " "The de-construction of a text does not proceed by random doubt or arbitrary subversion, but by the careful teasing out of warring forces of signification within the text itself. If anything is destroyed in a deconstructive reading, it is not the text, but the claim to unequivocal domination of one mode of signifying over another" (5).

On the basis of the deconstructionist ideas as summarized above, we may now proceed to discuss Shakespeare's deconstructionist vision in the two parts of *Henry IV*. We will see that Shakespeare's texts not only show his critical difference from the historians who have provided sources for him, but also, either explicitly or implicitly, try to undo or deconstruct many logocentric thoughts by displaying the myth of presence, the violent hierarchies, the apparent aporias, etc., in signs, traces, etc., which are reiterably kept in a state of dissemination and *différance*, while the playwright together with the players or characters in the plays "play" the game of language or rhetoric to the extent of almost unthinkable ingenuity with revisionary insights.

III. The *Prince* and the Prince

In the first section of this essay I have suggested that Shakespeare leans towards Machiavellianism rather than providentialism in respect to the problem of historical causation. Now, in this section, I will further clarify that Shakespeare's Machiavellianism, as shown in the *Henry IV* plays, is a deconstructionist stance directed against the authoritative doctrine of providentialism. But, before I do that, I must clarify first the Machiavellian ideas, lest we should be misled by detractors of Machiavelli, who have been abundant among people, East and West, since the Renaissance Period.

It is said that no fewer than 395 references to Machiavelli were catalogued in Elizabethan literature (Lewis 65), and yet very few biographers of Shakespeare, if ever, have been bold enough to claim Machiavelli's influence on Shakespeare. That Shakespeare did know Machiavelli's name is out of question. In *Henry VI, Part 3*, he lets Richard (afterwards Duke of Gloucester) mention Machiavelli in a monologue that comes to these lines:

> *I'll drown more sailors than the Mermaid shall;*
> *I'll slay more gazers than the basilisk;*
> *I'll play the orator as well as Nestor,*
> *Deceive more slyly than Ulysses could*
> *And, like a Sinon, take another Troy.*
> *I can add colors to the chameleon,*

> *Change shapes with Proteus for advantages,*
> *And set the murderous Machiavel to school.(3.2.186-93)*

In these lines Machiavel is indeed an incarnation of the Evil One himself. This understanding, pronounced by Richard, is not necessarily Shakespeare's only understanding of Machiavelli. But, regrettably, even distinguished scholars would equate Shakespeare's with Richard's understanding. That is why although so many scholars, among them T. S. Eliot, have seen the Machiavellian influence on Shakespeare, yet they have almost univocally asserted that Shakespeare's Machiavellian figures are restricted to such wicked ones as Edmund, Iago, and Richard the Third, forgetting that a good king can be a Machiavellian as well.

In fact, in Machiavelli's mind, only a successful (hence "good") ruler can live up to his standards of the prince. A failure fit for tragedy is never a rightful Machiavellian. We must know that the Renaissance Period was teeming with various "conduct books" (including Castiglione's *The Book of the Courtier*, Thomas Elyot's *The Book Named the Governor*, and of course Machiavelli's *The Prince*), which were intended to teach different ranks of people, especially high-ranking powerful men, how to conduct themselves so as to ensure their success and the benefit of the state. So, as a conduct book, Machiavelli's *The Prince* was to teach how a prince should conduct himself. The teachings concerning political means therein might sound "horrible" to many moralists. Yet, its purpose was a moral one: to let the prince recognize the true political reality. We admit that Machiavelli's *virtù* should be distinguished from the moralist's *virtue*. But I cannot agree that "what is good in the world of politics is *entirely unrelated* to and *generally the opposite* of what makes for goodness in the moral life" (Charlton 90, italics mine). I must maintain that a politically strong king can be a good king, and Prince Hal in *Henry IV* is indeed "the Machiavel of goodness" (Danby 91).

What are most impressive and offensive in Machiavelli's *The Prince* are these most often-quoted statements:

> *...a prince must know how to make good use of the nature of the beast, he should choose from among the beasts the fox and the lion; for the lion cannot defend itself from traps and the fox cannot protect itself from wolves. It is therefore necessary to be a fox in order to recognize the traps and a lion in order to frighten the wolves. Those who play only the part of the lion do not understand matters. A wise ruler, therefore, cannot and should not keep his word when such an observance of faith would be to his disadvantage and when the reasons which made him promise are removed. ...he who has known best how to use the fox has come to a better end. But it is necessary to know how to disguise this nature well and to be a great hypocrite and a liar. (58-59)*

Here Machiavelli is telling a truth no experienced politician can deny. If we consider the "princely" figures in the *Henry IV* plays in the light of this truth, we will soon understand the role-relationship among the four principal characters: King Henry IV plays both the lion and the fox, but Prince Hal, "the lion's whelp" (Pt. 1, 3.3.146)[3], plays both roles even better than the King, while Hotspur, the "child of honor and renown" (Pt. 1, 3.2.139), poses only as the lion and Falstaff, who has been called "the king of companions" and "the prince of good fellows" (Goddard 25), poses only as the fox. This accounts for Prince Hal's success in contrast to others' failure, but this in no way lessens the Prince's honor. We respect him as much as the Elizabethans or the Prince's contemporaries.

If Shakespeare agrees understandably with Machiavelli that the prince must act as both the powerful lion and the cunning fox, he is by the way proposing that powerful kingship is necessarily connected with hypocrisy and cheating, not just with divinely—ordained right or inherited royalty. So the problem of succession—allegedly a problem very much in most Elizabethans' mind—is to be solved not by providential privilege but by "natural selection," that is, by contest (as seen in the jungle) among opponents who vie by strength and by craftiness into the bargain.

Thinking in this line, we will realize that Shakespeare has deconstructed the medieval faith in the "sacred kingship" of a God-anointed monarch. Meanwhile, he has also deconstructed the Elizabethan belief (and often our belief, too) that order is the norm; disorder is the exception. As we can witness in all Shakespeare's English history plays, power struggle among the mighty and the wily never ceased for long: "Disorder *was* the natural state of man, and civilization a matter of pure expediency," although "such a way of thinking was abhorrent to the Elizabethans (as indeed it always has been and is now to the majority)" (Tillyard 1962, 28, italics mine). *Henry IV, Part I,* let us recall, opens with King Henry IV wishing for peace and for a chance to go "as far as to the sepulcher of Christ" (1.1.19). But no sooner were the wishes uttered than the tidings of more rebellious battles everywhere came to worry the king. And from then on, even after the decisive Shrewsbury Battle, the Lancaster House had to face one trouble after another. In the end of *Henry IV, Part 2,* Prince John forebode that "ere this year expire, / We bear our civil swords and native fire / As far as France" (5.5.105-7). To make wars abroad, as we know, is but a political strategy to make temporary peace in one's own nation. Indeed, as far as Shakespeare's history plays are concerned, disorder in the form of riot or war, rather than order in peace, definitely occupies the central stage.

In the *Henry IV* plays, however, it is the Prince rather than the King that figures most importantly on the central stage. Prince Hal, the future Henry V, is actually the prince who plays the lion and the fox most successfully not only in facing the rebellious camps but also in dealing with his father, his brothers, his riotous company, and all others. It is owing to his disguised prowess that he could defeat Hotspur, to his seeming earnestness that he could win his father's final approval and his brothers' trust, to his cheating wisdom that he could associate with and get rid of Falstaff's gang, and to his gesture of uprightness that he could win the hearts of all his subjects. He is unquestionably "Shakespeare's studied picture of the kingly type: a picture to which his many previous versions of the imperfect kingly type lead up" (Tillyard 1943a, 110). Apparently, the *Henry IV* plays show Prince Hal's "progress from dissolute heir apparent to responsible monarch" (Traversi 4). In actuality, the Prince knew clearly from the beginning what he was doing: "I'll so offend, to make offence a skill, / Redeeming time when men think least I will" (Pt. 1, 1.2.211-2). What a subtle fox he already was!

IV. The Work and the Play

Once we recognize Prince Hal as a Machiavellian fox occupying the central position of the stage, we will be able to read *Henry IV, Parts 1 & 2*, as a deconstructive text aiming not only to subvert the logocentrism of the providential concept of historical causation, but also to subvert many other logocentrisms or "violent hierarchies" underlying the two works or plays which for many critics are actually but one work or one play about the same hero, Hal.[4]

To begin with, let us look at the plot. We see in both parts of *Henry IV* a serious plot twines with a comic one. The serious plot comprises the plotting scenes, the battling acts, and other serious matters connected with the King, the princes, the lords, etc., whose speeches are not jokes because they mean what they say, and whose concerns are not trivialities because they bear on the affairs of the state.

In contrast, the comic plot comprises the tavern scenes, the ludicrous acts, and other funny matters connected with Falstaff, the Eastcheap guys, and other low-class commoners whose conversations are mostly frothy jokes and whose concerns are mostly private, trivial affairs. So, it is only natural to say the serious plot is the main plot and the comic one is the subplot. For one signifies "work" while the other signifies "play."

But this serious / comic or work / play division is a "violent hierarchy. " To privilege the serious over the comic or work over play is a logocentrism because, upon further consideration, we find the division has its own aporia; the comic turns out to be no different from the serious and (the) play *is* (the) work.

Prince Hal is the very man that mingles the serious with the comic and the very man that knows (the) play is (the) work. Once in an apartment the Prince, hearing how Falstaff disregarded an old lord talking very wisely in the street, commented: "Thou didst well, for wisdom cries out in the streets and no man regards it" (Pt. 1, 1.2.86-7). This joking comment implies in fact Prince Hal's acceptance of the proverb, his understanding that wisdom can be found even in the streets, and his belief that one should not disregard wisdom because of its place of occurrence. So, it is not surprising that the Prince seeks to increase his wisdom by mixing with "the false staff" outside of the court.

What has the Prince learned, then, in the tavern? For one thing, he must have learned the truth suggested by Falstaff that "the true prince may (for recreation sake) prove / a false thief" (Pt. 1, 1.2.150-1). We know Prince Hal refused at first to join Falstaff's plot of robbery, but later he joined with Poins in robbing the robbers "for recreation sake." On the surface, this act appears to be nothing but play in the sense of sport. Yet, if we think deeply, we will realize that this play is also a practice, a principal practice as to how to rob the world—much like the lion's whelp practicing in sport how to hunt for prey. This interpretation is intensified by Gadshill's remarks:

> *I am joined with no foot-land rakers,*
> *no long-staff sixpenny strikers, none of these mad*
> *mustachio purple-hued maltworms, but with nobil-*
> *ity and tranquillity, burgomasters and great onyers,*
> *such as can hold in, such as will strike sooner than*
> *speak, and speak sooner than drink, and drink*
> *sooner than pray—and yet, 'zounds, I lie, for they*
> *pray continually to their saint the commonwealth,*
> *or rather not pray to her, but prey on her, for they*
> *ride up and down on her, and make her their boots.*
> *(Pt. 1, 2.1.72-81)*

These remarks, though made sportingly, have pinpointed the difficulty of telling statesmen from highwaymen, of claiming oneself as "a true man" rather than "a false thief" (as Gadshill did to the Chamberlain), because "*homo* is a common name to all men" (Pt. 1, 2.1.90-3)—all men, high and low, are thieves—the only difference is: some men (the great ones) can openly rob the commonwealth with impunity while others (the small ones) are often threatened with justice even if they commit but petty larceny. So, symbolically Prince Hal's playing the sport of holdup men is an imitation of the politicians' playing the tricks of stealing a state. Usurpation of a kingdom is a kind of robbery. The lords' "serious plot" is actually not "high" above the louts' "comic plot." This truth was recklessly revealed by Hotspur when, upon finishing his rebellious "noble plot" with his father and uncle, he exclaimed, "O, let the hours be short, / Till fields, and blows, and groans applaud our sport!" (Pt., 1, 1.3.273 & 295-6). The violent hierarchy of serious / comic or work / play is thus deconstructed.

The double plot of *Henry IV* is accompanied by the dubious logos called "honor." Curtis Brown Watson has pointed out that "Shakespeare's heroes, like the great lords of Elizabeth's court, feel an allegiance to Christian as well as to Greek and Roman ideals, but

Shakespeare reflects a concept of honor—of moral esteem dependent on the public recognition of virtue—whose philosophic roots lead directly back to Aristotle and Cicero" (73). That is, Shakespeare's heroes may take honor for eternal, heavenly fame as well as for public esteem, but Shakespeare seems to regard honor, as did Machiavelli, Montaigne, and Seneca before him, as primarily a matter of public esteem. Thus, honor for Shakespeare is liable for deconstruction if it is mistaken for a sort of "presence," an ultimate truth to live on.

In a sense, all the plot details of *Henry IV* are centered on the theme of honor. The King, the princes, the archbishop, the lords, and all other "worthy" people's serious acts and "noble" scenes are all intended to "buy" honor as a lasting fame in heaven and on earth, whereas the "false staff," the gadders, the loafers, the cheaters, and all other "unmerited" fellows' comic acts and "ignoble" scenes are all left with shame or dishonor. However, is honor really an attainable "presence"? We have seen Hotspur forever hotly spurred on by honor. To him, "it were an easy leap / To pluck bright honor from the pale faced moon, / Or dive into the bottom of the deep, / Where fathom-line could never touch the ground, / And pluck up drowned honor by the locks" (Pt. 1, 1.3.199-203). King Henry IV called him "the theme of honor's tongue" (Pt. 1, 1.1.80) from the beginning, imagined "every honor sitting on his helm" (Pt. 1, 3.2.142), and exclaimed: "What never-dying honor hath he got / Against renowned Dauglas!" (Pt. 1, 3.2.106-7). Yet, in one single battle at Shrewsbury, Prince Hal could boast to crop all the budding honors on Hotspur's crest to make a garland for his own head (Pt. 1, 5.4.71-2). When Hotspur was fatally wounded, he cried out:

> *O Harry, thou hast robbed me of my youth!*
> *I better brook the loss of brittle life*
> *Than those proud titles thou hast won of me;*
> *They wound my thoughts worse than thy sword my flesh:*

> *But thoughts, the slaves of life, and life, time's fool,*
> *And time, that takes survey of all the world,*
> *Must have a stop. (Pt. 1, 5.4.76-82)*

He knew only too late that honor as the name for military prowess is unreliable. But this is a truth already known to Falstaff, who reasoned about death and honor thus:

> *Well, 'tis no matter, honor pricks*
> *me on. Yea, but how if honor prick me off when I*
> *come on, how then? Can honor set to a leg? No.*
> *Or an arm? No. Or take away the grief of a wound?*
> *No. Honor hath no skill in surgery then? No.*
> *What is honor? A word. What is in that word*
> *honor? What is that honor? Air. ...*
> *Therefore I'll none of it. Honor is a mere*
> *scutcheon. (Pt. 1, 5.2.129-140)*

So he did not like "such grinning honor as Sir Walter hath" (Pt. 1, 5.4.59). He chose to live with dishonor and even dishonorably tried to steal honor by claiming that he himself had killed Hotspur.

If honor is just a word, is but air, or is a mere scutcheon, it has no real "presence," then. The highest honor is to become sovereign of the state. But the crown as the symbol of that supreme power is forever passable from one person to another. Bolingbroke got it from Richard II to become Henry IV by, "God knows, what by-paths and indirect crooked ways" (Pt. 2, 4.5.184). But while he was suspecting that Prince Hal had hastily attempted to take it from him, the Prince realized that the imperial crown signified not only power but also care, which "keep'st the ports of slumber open wide / To many a watchful night" (Pt. 2, 4.5.23-4). So he told his father king that he actually upbraided the crown by saying that "thou best of gold art worst of gold" because "thou, most fine, most honored, most renowned, / Hast eat thy bearer up" (Pt. 2, 4.5.160-4).

We do not know for sure whether or not Prince Hal was telling the truth earnestly about the crown. Anyway, the crown is indeed not a "full presence" capable of signifying in any circumstances the supreme power of a king. In some cases, it can be just a transient trace, a mocking supplement on the owner's head, just like the cushion put on Falstaff's head when he was playing Bolingbroke in the play-within-the-play.

Talking of the play-within-the-play, we find it has at least a fourfold construing of deconstructive ideas. First, Falstaff's suggestion that "This chair shall be my state, this dagger my scepter, and this cushion my crown," coupled with Prince Hal's reply that "Thy state is taken for a joint-stool, thy golden scepter for a leaden dagger, and thy precious rich crown for a pitiful bald crown" (Pt. 1, 2.4.373-7), has told us the deconstructive idea that anything can be a symbol of anything or the idea that any signified can again serve as a signifier, and thus *différance* is inevitable. Second, in this travesty Falstaff's playing Bolingbroke "in King Cambyses' vein" (Pt. 1, 2.4.382) has told us the fact that the world is full of different symbols for the same thing. Here Falstaff clearly claims to stand for the king (he is in fact regarded as the King of Eastcheap). Later, at Shrewsbury, we find "The King hath many marching in his coats" (Pt. 1, 5.3.25). We know Bolingbroke is the "true" king now. But the King used to be Richard II before. Even now, there is also Mortimer, who is said to be the proclaimed heir to Richard II. And we have Harry Percy, too, who is called "the king of honor" (Pt. 1, 4.1.10). So, the world of *Henry IV* has really witnessed the "dissemination" of "player-kings," that is, people who play the role of king in one sense / way or another. And it is Prince Hal, the ideal prince and future King Henry V, alone, that can "penetrate the surface of names and things" and culminate the search for a player-king (Allman 19). Third, if Falstaff can displace

Bolingbroke as Prince Hal's father in the play-within-the-play, it is possible to consider other symbolic displacements of father and son relations. In Richard Wheeler's psychological analysis, such displacements include Hal and Hotspur as sons to Henry IV, Northumberland and Worcester as weak and deceitful fathers to Hotspur, and the Lord Chief Justice, whom Hal makes "a father to my youth" (Pt. 2, 5.2.118), besides Henry IV and Falstaff as fathers to Hal (Wheeler 159). In fact, when the Prince became King Henry V, he also assumed the stance of father to his brothers, as he said, "I'll be your father and your brother too" (Pt. 2, 5.2.57). Symbolic displacements as such render the sense of "father" unstable and make possible the reiteration and dissemination of the father / son hierarchy. Fourth, the fact that Falstaff and Prince Hal each in turn played the other's father suggests that the father / son relationship is indeed a violent hierarchy at times. If to father is to teach, we may well agree with Wordsworth that in a sense "the child is father of the man." In the case of Prince Hal, for example, it turns out that he was the man to teach his father king the true significance of the crown, and the man to teach Falstaff, his "playful" father, the inadequacy of mere play without work. From Prince Hal we may even go further to consider Hotspur. Hotspur's death has certainly taught his father not only the vanity of fame but also the importance of military superiority.

Now, to return to our consideration of the characters, we admit that Falstaff can indeed represent Misrule while Lord Chief Justice represents Rule. But this character contrast does not necessarily imply that Shakespeare has endorsed the Rule / Misrule hierarchy, privileging the former over the latter. To be sure, Lord Chief Justice's final triumph and Falstaff's shameful ending might incur that association. And Prince Hal's understanding that "If all the year were playing holidays, / To sport would be as tedious as to work" (Pt. 1, 1.2.199-200) certainly calls for Rule rather than Misrule. But we must realize that in terms of Rule and Misrule, all rebellious personages are in a true sense embodiments of Misrule. In the *Henry IV* plays, who has not typified Misrule? Bolingbroke, who rebelled against Richard II? Hotspur, who rebelled against Bolingbroke? Hal, who acted like a profligate against honor? Even Lord Chief Justice can be viewed as an unruly man who could not check his own sense of justice. I agree that "Shakespeare dramatizes not only holiday but also the need for holiday and the need to limit holiday" (Barber 51). But "the need to limit holiday" is built on the assumption that the holiday impulse, i.e., Misrule, is always already there challenging and threatening Rule. The Machiavellian view of historical causation is actually allied with the carnivalesque spirit and the libidinous drive of Id to overthrow the conscious rationale of Rule.

V. Names and Name-Calling

Like honor and dishonor, Rule and Misrule are after all but words employed to call certain abstract qualities which prove no more stable than the personages who are supposed to possess the qualities. In fact, all names betray the same inconstancy. In the two parts of *Henry IV* Shakespeare has fully utilized names and the method of name-calling to suggest this basic deconstructive idea and bring forth his themes.

It is pointed out that in Tillyard's study "the sequence of plays from *Richard II* to *Henry V* were constituted as a central chapter in the great nationalistic 'epic' of England" (Holderness 21). The sequence of plays comprises the two parts of *Henry IV* along with *Richard II* and *Henry V*, and is, as we know, often referred to as Shakespeare's second tetralogy of English plays. What is meaningful is: Alvin Kernan has called this "epic" of England the *Henriad*. This means that the four plays actually depict how King Henry came to establish his kingdom, much as the *Aeneid* depicts how Aeneas came to establish the Roman

Empire. But the trouble is: Who is the King Henry in the *Henriad*? One may readily reply, "Henry IV, Bolingbroke, of course." But is it? Unquestionably? Can't it be Henry V, Harry of Monmouth, instead? If we judge by the two parts of *Henry IV*, we soon find that the son has actually replaced the father in importance, whether we consider the plot, the characterization, the theme, or the quantity of appearance on the stage. We have said above that the plays actually center on Prince Hal. So, the plays are actually two preceding parts of *Henry V*. To interpret this deconstructively, we can say: no matter whether Shakespeare had made it so intentionally or not, the play's title has no true "presence" because it signifies not what it is, but what comes after to replace it. In brief, the *Henriad* exemplifies indeed the phenomenon of *différance* in the titles of the plays.

Within this *Henriad*, now, we find we have four Henrys: King Henry IV, Prince Henry of Wales (later Henry V), Henry Percy (Earl of Northumberland) and his son with the same name but nicknamed Hotspur. What do the four Henrys signify? There are obvious differences, of course, among the four: two are old and two are young, two are fathers and two are sons, two are the ruling party and two are the rebellious party, two are the winners and two are the losers, etc. But all four have the same aim: to gain honor, which means kingship. Yet, in trying to achieve that aim, these four have behaved quite differently. Harold Goddard has pointed out that "on the day when Henry deposed Richard he became a double man, one thing to the world, another to his own conscience" (10). Goddard has also pointed out that besides the two elder Henrys we have two younger Henrys in the same house: the Henry who is "but man" and the Henry who is "Prince" (20). In my analysis, the four Henrys represent four different combinations of the lion and the fox: Hotspur with the most lion and the least fox, Hal with the least lion and the most fox, Bolingbroke with more lion and less fox, and Northumberland with less lion and more fox. But it turns out that the most foxy person, rather than the most lion-like one, is the most successful in politics: kingship is gained mostly by counterfeit. By this "natural" dissemination of Henrys, then, Shakespeare has deconstructed the violent hierarchy of "the lion over the fox" or "strength over craftiness."

Although all the four Henrys figure importantly in the plays, "Henry" is after all but a common name like John and Dick, rendering no particular meaning in itself. In the plays, however, many names have obvious suggestions which upon further consideration may prove conducive to the understanding of Shakespeare's deconstructionist vision. Take, first, the name "Falstaff" for example. "Falstaff" naturally suggests "false staff," and Falstaff is indeed a false staff member of Prince Hal's in the sense that he is "false" in character but acts as an assistant or advisor of the Prince. Yet, in what sense can we call Falstaff "false"? Certainly, he is deceitful to Prince Hal, Mistress Quickly, and others. He is perfidious to his religion. And he is treacherous to his country. And certainly he is not a genuine knight: he practices counterfeit chivalry and fake militarism, being a braggart soldier all immersed in cowardly lies and cheating lives. But is he really only that? If we compare his falseness with the kingly figures', can't we say he is but another fox? In the plays, indeed, there are suggestions that Falstaff is like Reynard the Fox in the medieval beast-fable, who struggles for power against the powerful wolf Isengrim, King Noble the lion, Chanticleer the cock, etc. In Pt. 1, III, iii, Falstaff calls the Hostess of Boar's Head Tavern "dame Partlet the hen" (50). That has already hinted at the beast epic. In Pt. 2, I, ii, when Lord Chief Justice warns Falstaff not to wake a sleeping wolf, he replies, "To wake a wolf is as bad as smell a fox" (152-4). This reply clearly suggests that while the Lord Chief Justice is a wolf, Falstaff is himself a fox. This comparison makes better sense when later the Hostess complains that Falstaff "stabbed" her in her own house "most beastly in good faith" and asks Master Fang to "hold him sure" and Master Snare to "let him not 'scape" (Pt. 2, 2.1.13-25). These details of comparison suggestively make the world of *Henry IV* a jungle of beasts, where only the fittest can survive, and the fittest are often the most cunning of foxes.

In this connection, when we return to Falstaff as a foxy companion to Prince Hal, we begin to be aware that instead of being a false staff member, Falstaff is actually a true teaching sample for the Prince. He is the Prince's true "support" ("staff" in the sense of being a stick or rod for aid in walking or climbing, or for use as a weapon). Or, at least, he is the Prince's real help for the time being ("staff" in the sense of being a composition of plaster and fibrous material used for a temporary finish and in ornamental work). Falstaff's principle is: to live is to lie. So, to counterfeit death is only a foxy way of lying in order to live. Likewise, to counterfeit weakness is only a way of lying for power. What he believes in is not "false stuff," but "true stuff" alive with means for survival. Therefore, the name Falstaff, along with the person's life, serves to deconstruct our complacent faith in the absolute "presence" of truthfulness in contrast with sheer falsehood, and to tear down the violent hierarchy of privileging truths over lies.

It is often suggested that Falstaff is a rich amalgam of comic types; he is the morality Vice, the traditional Parasite, the *Miles Gloriosus*, the Corrupt Soldier, and the Fool as well. The *Henry IV* plays are, of course, far from morality plays. Nevertheless, the naming of such characters as Falstaff, Shallow, Silence, Fang, Snare, Mouldy, Shadow, Wart, Feeble, Bullcalf, and Rumor does add some allegorical color to the plays. As allegorical figures, these characters do bear the traits their names suggest. However, the names coupled with the persons' behavior often bring about some deconstructive effect. In the Induction of *Henry IV, Part 1*, for example, Rumor is made to tell the truth that he is "a pipe / Blown by surmises, jealousies, conjectures, / And of so easy and so plain a stop / That the blunt monster with uncounted heads, / The still-discordant wavering multitude, / Can play upon it" (15-20), although he knows his office is to "noise abroad" untruthful tidings. This self-deconstruction of Rumor's is in effect rendered more meaningful by the pipe metaphor and the fact that he is painted full of tongues. The pipe metaphor suggests that rumors are but sounds "played" out, and the full-of-tongue painting suggests that rumors are a dissemination of utterances. Such sounds and such utterances are naturally without any "presence" of truth, thus only temporarily fulfilling the hearers' desires and deconstructively forming a *différance* of signs or traces.

As to the figures of Shallow and Silence, it is easy to see that they are made to satirize the two main demerits of justices. We know Shallow and Silence are two country justices. Shallow once told his cousin Silence that he had been "called anything" and "would have done anything indeed too, and roundly too" (Pt. 2, 3.2.16-7). But in one soliloquy Falstaff told us:

> *I do see the bottom of Justice Shallow. Lord,*
> *Lord, how subject we old men are to this vice of*
> *lying! This same starved justice hath done nothing*
> *but prate to me of the wildness of his youth, and the*
> *feats he hath done about Turnbull Street, and*
> *every third word a lie, duer paid to the hearer than*
> *the Turk's tribute. (Pt. 2, 3.2.296-301)*

So, Shallow is shallow of judicial virtues, and deep in vile practices. That is why he only helped Falstaff recruit such soldiers as Mouldy, Wart, Feeble, and Bullcalf. But a Shallow justice needs the aid of his cousin Silence. When Shallow told Falstaff that Silence was in commission with him, Falstaff said, "it well befits you should be of the peace" (Pt. 2, 3.2.90). Then we as well as Falstaff could find that Silence actually was never silent: he talked about foibles and sang merrily all the time. He was only silent about the justices' vile practices. Thus, Shallow and Silence are two allegorical figures Shakespeare employed to remind us that on one hand, the name does sometimes suggest the substance (Shallow is shallow of virtues and Silence is silent about truths). Yet, on the other hand, the name is more often than not a misleading trap (Justice Shallow and Justice Silence are never just: Shallow is deep in vices and Silence is noisy about follies).

The ironic turning of names in sense is most impressively exemplified in the case of Hotspur. In the beginning of *Henry IV, Part1*, Travers came to tell Northumberland that a gentleman had told him that "rebellion had ill luck / And that young Harry Percy's spur was cold" (1.1.41-2). This report made Northumberland respond with puzzlement, "Ha? Again! / Said he young Harry Percy's spur was cold? Of Hotspur, Coldspur?" (1.1.48-50). This puzzlement is in actuality accompanied by a sudden awareness that the name is but a name; the person can mockingly become quite other than his name.

Since the name is not necessarily the person or the thing at times, it stands to reason that naming is not so important or significant as we suppose it is, and consequently names can be changed without changing the essence of the persons or things bearing the names. However, in real life people do prefer using some names to others under certain circumstances. In the plays, for instance, Prince Henry is variously called Harry, Hal, and many other names befitting the addressers' statuses and circumstances. We know, of course, there is some difference between Falstaff's calling him "Hal," "lad," or "boy" and the King's calling him "Harry," or "son." But the difference makes no essential difference in the Prince's character. This truth is easily explained by the fact that we have two Bardolphs in the plays (just as we have four Henrys). One Bardolph is a lord against the King; the other an irregular humorist in Falstaff's company. Besides, we may be reminded that in the plays we have a place called Gad's Hill, which sounds no different from Gadshill, another madcap in Falstaff's company, though spelled differently. Facts like this may teach us that names are indeed arbitrary signs given to stand for persons or things. This truth, already pronounced by Juliet's observation that "That which we call a rose / By any other word would smell as sweet" (*Romeo and Juliet*, 2.2.43-44), is de Saussure's linguistic truth and Derrida's deconstructive truth as well.

Yet, humanity is ever so often beguiled by names. In *Henry IV*, even the Eastcheap madcaps care so much about their names. So Falstaff asked this favor of Prince Hal: "when thou art king let not us that are squires of the night's body be called thieves of the day's beauty: let us be Diana's foresters, gentlemen of the shade, minions of the moon; and let men say we be men of good government, being governed as the sea is, by our noble and chaste mistress the moon, under whose countenance we steal" (Pt. 1, 1.2.23-9). This demand for euphemism, as we know, is very common. But euphemism never changes the nature of the grain. Highway robbers are still highway robbers, whether you call them St. Nicholas' clerks or any other name as suggested by Falstaff.

Still, people think names have "presence" of something. So, in addition to trying to euphemize their own names they often attempt to detract others by calling them bad names. Name-calling is, of course, not always serious. It can be a sign of intimacy or even become a game, a sporting contest, among friends. Once Prince Hal called Falstaff "this sanguine coward, this bed-presser, this horse-back-breaker, this huge hill of flesh—," and Falstaff reacted by calling him back: "you starveling, you eel-skin, you dried neat's-tongue, you bull's-pizzle, you stock-fish—O for breath to utter what is like thee!—you tailor's-yard, you sheath, you bow-case, you vile standing tuck" (Pt. 1, 2.4.237-44). We know they were being humorous in calling each other names. But when name-calling is not meant for jokes, it can be a serious wound to the named target. We need only to remember that Hotspur's rebellion arises first with the King's calling Mortimer a traitor and refusing to "ransom home revolted Mortimer" (Pt. 1, 1.3.91). Indeed, the two parts of *Henry IV* are a show of who is best called a traitor and who best deserves the name of king.

VI. Sword Wars and Word Wars

To decide who is the traitor or who is the true man (particularly the true prince) usually needs evidence, pro and con. But, curiously enough, people East and West often decide the matter by force. In *Richard II*, let us recall, Bolingbroke and Mowbray were asked to settle their dispute by having a trial by combat at Coventry. Although, as the story goes, they were prevented at last from proving their true or false characters by such a contest, we know dueling was then, as it is still now, an acceptable way of settling a quarrel. In truth, international wars and civil wars can be regarded as large-scale duels involving many more men with many more deadly weapons for more public, rather than private, causes. In *Henry IV*, therefore, the wars between the Lancaster House and the rebellious camp can be seen as duels with swords to settle the problem of legitimacy in kingship.

But *Henry IV* is not merely a series of battles with soldiers and swords. On the stage, we see sword wars are always preceded by word wars. Besides, word wars are practiced not only in the serious plot but also in the comic one. What is most significant is: the results of the sword wars seem to depend invariably on the results of word wars. In Part 1 of *Henry IV*, for instance, how many word wars do we see before we come to the decisive Shrewsbury battle? In Act I, scene i, we see King Henry IV is grieved to hear new hostilities by the Scots and Hotspur's retention of the Scottish prisoners. For the King these things mean that a crusade to the Holy Land has to be delayed again by civil tumult. In scene ii, we then see Prince Henry matching wits with Sir John Falstaff. This match is certainly a word war (usually called a debate) about the theme of purse-taking as a "vocation." In scene iii, we see the King arguing with Hotspur about Mortimer. This argument is also a word war, and it leads not to humor but to rancor. In Act II, scene ii, we see Falstaff and his company robbing some wealthy travelers first, and then we see Prince Hal and Poins setting upon the robbers next in disguise. These highway robberies are two small-scale sword wars. Then in scene iv, we see Prince Hal defeat the boastful Falstaff in the Boar's Head Tavern by finding an aporia in the latter's tall tale. This defeat is one of language. In Act III, scene iii, Falstaff picks a quarrel with Mistress Quickly to beguile her of the money he owes her. Prince Hal joins in and proves against Falstaff. Finally Falstaff obtains Hal's pardon by his witty rhetoric. This tavern scene is obviously a series of word wars. In Act IV, scene iii, Sir Walter Blunt comes from the King to ask the Percys about their grievances. Hotspur grasps the opportunity to recount the King's faults. Later in Act V, scene i, Worcester visits the King's camp and presents the Percys' grievances again. But the King's reply is: "...never yet did insurrection want / Such water-colors to imprint his cause" (79-80). The mutual thrusts with words naturally cannot stop the impending sword war. Hence Prince Hal challenges Hotspur to "try fortune with him in a single fight" (100). But his challenge is mixed with such praise of Hotspur that the ever-haughty Hotspur will lose alertness with him on the battlefield. That is why he can vanquish him later in action. So, the sword war results, partly at least, from the word war.

In the second part of *Henry IV*, the acts and scenes are likewise intermingled with word wars and sword wars. In Act 1, scene i, Lord Bardolph and the messengers are contending for truth about the outcome of the Shrewsbury battle. That is a word war. In scene ii, Falstaff is really engaged in a word battle against Lord Chief Justice, who charges him with "living in great infamy" (135) and "misleading the youthful Prince" (143). In Act II, scene i, Mistress Quickly has entered a suit against Falstaff for a large sum of money he owes her. But Falstaff soon mollifies Quickly by his appeasing tricks. He wins this word war as before. In scene iv, there is a brawl between Doll Tearsheet and Pistol. The wrangle finally makes Falstaff so furious that he thrusts at Pistol and wounds him in the shoulder. This sword war, blending with word war, makes Doll claim that Falstaff is "as valorous as Hector of Troy... " (216). Later in the same scene, Falstaff makes an unflattering description of Hal, but when the Prince presents himself, Falstaff claims that he deliberately dispraised the Prince to prevent unworthy folk attaching them to him. This shows that Falstaff is really a tough fighter in any word war. In Act IV, scene i, Westmorland comes to Gaultree Forest to negotiate with the Archbishop of York. Although Mowbray advises against surrender without a battle, the Archbishop favors Westmorland's proposal of meeting with Prince John. In the next scene, Prince John promises that the rebels' grievances will receive attention and persuades the Archbishop to dismiss his troops. But immediately after the dismissal, Prince John orders the arrest of the Archbishop and the rebellious army soon disperses. These two scenes show the effect of good skills in two forms of word war (negotiation and promise) in aiding a sword war. In scene v, the King thinks that Hal is impatient for his death. Hal refutes this accusation with an eloquent statement of his love. Father and son are thus reconciled. (Their word war comes to armistice.) In Act V, Falstaff continues to gull Shallow and others while Hal, now King Henry V, declares his respect for the Lord Chief Justice and reassures his love for his brothers and subjects. Finally, to the surprise of Falstaff and his fellow rogues, Hal disavows his connection with them and banishes them. The Prince's word skill has outwitted Falstaff at last.

From the above explication, we can see that word skill in word war is indeed part of the warrior's vital business. Both a prince like Hal and a rogue like Falstaff need to develop various word skills for various forms of word wars, just as they need to develop various sword skills for various forms of sword wars. We may laugh at Hal and Falstaff's practicing how to answer the King's angry scold. But we must know that the rhetorical art is certainly as important as the martial art to a military man. When Hotspur confesses that he has "not well the gift of tongue / Can lift your blood up with persuasion" (Pt. 1, 5.2.77-8), he has half certified his final failure. It takes a man like Hal to know the real importance of rhetoric and to pity Francis, the next-to-dumb apprentice tapster: "That ever this fellow should have fewer words than a parrot, and yet the son of a woman! His industry is up-stairs and down-stairs, his eloquence the parcel of a reckoning" (Pt. 1, 2.4.96-9). The Prince has taken pride in his own gift of tongue: "I am so good a proficient in one quarter of an hour that I can drink with any tinker in his own language during my life" (Pt. 1, 2.4.17-9). In fact, Hal "masters not only the jargon of the drawers but his father's abstract, Latinate periods, the 'princely tongue' that lets him praise Hotspur 'like a chronicle,'" and the 'unsavory similes" and complex puns that make him Falstaff's match" (Sundelson 110). So, he is not just a "king of courtesy" as the drawers have said he is. He is a "king of language" as well.

Falstaff is Hal's only rival in language skill. Perhaps he is better considered as Hal's tutor in rhetoric or coach in persuasion. Michael McCanles observes:

> *No one quotes scripture in Shakespeare more than Falstaff, and no one is more a master of the odds and ends of manners and morals, of sermons and proverbs, and of pious exhortation. Falstaff's moral piquancy lies, therefore, not simply in his representing holiday as opposed to Henry's sobriety. On the contrary, his mastery, no less than Henry's, of the rhetoric of moral exhortation and the stances of self-righteous complacency make him an embodiment of moral ambiguity that is formidable to deal with. (98)*

Indeed, Falstaff lives on words. He escapes ill fortune through words. And we love to hear him warring with words. He may be a coward by sword, but never a coward by word. This knight's eloquence has talked himself into a braggart soldier, into a man big with bluffs and wags.

Nevertheless, he is a sophist who is able to talk us into an awareness of all the "false stuff" liable for deconstruction. His frank reflection on living and lying, for instance, has earned himself the name of "a fundamentally honest man":

> *He has two sides like a coin, but he was not a counterfeit. And Henry? He was a king, a man of "honor," of brains and ability, of good intentions, but withal a "vile politician" and respectable hypocrite. He was a counterfeit. (Goddard 35)*

In the second section of this essay, I have mentioned that deconstructionists look on all thinking systems as essentially a matter of rhetoric. Accordingly, the maneuvering of "tropes" is for them all important. If Foucault is right in asserting that discourse is always inseparable from power and that there are no absolutely "true" discourse, only more or less powerful ones (Selden & Widdowson 129, 161), then it is no wonder that in *Henry IV* the last power-winner is Prince Hal, the most eloquent speaker who speaks both prose and verse and knows when to speak what language to whom. He has two great rivals to conquer: Hotspur and Falstaff. The former he conquers in a sword war, the latter in some word wars. Sword needs strength, and word needs skill. As a foxy lion endowed with both strength and skill, the Prince undoubtedly has the advantage to vanquish all wolves and other lions or foxes. This fact helps our deconstructionists to tear down the "violent hierarchy" of placing strength above skill, or sword above word, or lion above fox.

VII. Closure and Conclusion

Deconstruction is a dynamic theory. In holding the possibility of deconstructing any construct or construction, it sees no closure in anything. In its light, history is forever a continuous process of constructing and deconstructing. Thus, history books are only tentative forms of closure. They try to close events and their meanings in certain linguistic forms. Such closures are vain. Events and their meanings are forever subject to different interpretations or closures. The history books or non-history works which serve as the sources of Shakespeare's history plays are such vain closures. But Shakespeare's history plays are themselves vain closures, too. The playwright's posterity can change his texts and the texts' supposed meanings at will. This deconstructionist reading of *Henry IV* is just an example of re-interpreting Shakespeare's interpretation of his source-providers' interpretations of the events, real or imagined, that supposedly happened to the characters, real or imagined, who supposedly existed in certain supposed period of time. In other words, this essay is nothing but another "gram," another "trace," another "supplement," or another "floating signifier" in the *différance* of Shakespeare's *Henry IV* as a system of signification in history. It surely has its aporias. Hence it boasts of no permanent closure at all.

But people are fond of closures. In a traditional essay like this, it is necessary to give a concise summary called conclusion. Below, then, is my conclusion, which, I must emphasize again, is no more than a summary of tentative closures.

Both Shakespeare's supposed sources and his *Henry IV* texts have "truths" of their own. But neither of them have "presence" of any absolute, unchangeable "truth." *Henry IV*, like any usual history, is a male story. It is written by a male author (Shakespeare) mainly about a male monarch (apparently Henry IV, but actually Henry V), and chiefly of male interests (concerning war and power). But the story does not necessarily uphold the so-called "Tudor myth." Shakespeare might wish to share Tillyard's providential view of historical causation, but he truly advocated, as a "poet of nature," the Machiavellian-Darwinian theory of "natural selection" in the "jungle

73

of politics." The entire *Henry IV*, therefore, can be looked upon as a deconstructive text aiming to unmake the Tudor myth, to undo the logocentrism of "divine right," and to tear down the violent hierarchy of privileging order over disorder, or Rule over Misrule.

It is beyond doubt that Shakespeare is deeply influenced by Machiavelli. This influence can be seen in the wicked characters Shakespeare has created: Richard III, Iago, Edmund, etc. But to be Machiavellian is not necessarily to be wicked (we need to deconstruct this myth first). A Machiavellian hero is simply a successful hero, a hero who can win power and hold it. In reality, he is not one fit for tragedy, but one fit for epic. Shakespeare's "second tetralogy" can indeed be regarded as an epic called the *Henriad*. But the national hero in it is Henry V, rather than Henry IV. And this hero is, no doubt, a Machiavellian ("a good Machiavellian," if you like).

In *The Prince*, Machiavelli asserts that a prince needs to be as strong as a lion and as cunning as a fox if he wants to gain power and keep it. Accordingly, the prince must needs be hypocritical on occasions. Now, in *Henry IV*, the Prince is Prince Henry of Wales. His father calls him Harry in the court. But his tavern friends call him Hal. This double way of calling suggests his double nature: the lion and the fox. Indeed, the two parts of *Henry IV* can be considered "as in one sense an account of Prince Hal's training for office" (Holderness 27). The training is to develop the young lion's strength and skill for power struggle. In that training, therefore, he needs not only natural growth in strength but constant practices in skill. His wild escapades with the rogues are actually his exercises for strength and skill. But "skill" covers rhetorical art (that of the fox) as well as martial art (that of the lion), of course.

Drama is primarily an art of words, not an art of deeds. (We need to deconstruct the hierarchy of deeds / words, too.) A play's acts and scenes are primarily words in dialogues or monologues, although the words can imply and incept action. Consequently, a playwright is a person well versed in the art of words. Now, Shakespeare is such a playwright. In *Henry IV*, he has so selected and arranged words for the characters that we have the impression that the characters are engaged not only in sword wars but also in word wars. In fact, the Prince therein is forever preparing for the final rhetorical as well as martial wars. In the end, as we know, he has conquered all his enemies: the foes in the rebellious camp (the Percys and others) and the friends in his own camp (his father and brothers as well as Falstaff's company). (Here Shakespeare has deconstructed the friend / foe hierarchy in terms of conquest.) And, as I have suggested above, the Prince's conquest is helped chiefly by his word skill, not sword skill, that is, by his foxy role, not by his lion-like role. (Here Shakespeare has deconstructed the sword / word or lion / fox hierarchy.) If the two parts of *Henry IV* are actually one whole play, the play is chiefly a "play" with words. No wonder we see wordplay everywhere. And Hal and Falstaff (actually Shakespeare) seem to favor it particularly.

But "play" has another meaning. It is opposed to "work." Some scholars say *Henry IV* places emphasis on the needs of "play," "misrule," "holiday spirit," "carnival feeling," etc. Yes, all work and no play makes Jack a dull boy. The old boy in *Henry IV* (Old Jack, or Sir John Falstaff) plays all the year round. So is he dull? "No!" he answers emphatically. He is right. This "playboy" is everything but dull. He is in fact a master of language, a tutor of rhetoric, a coach of persuasion, a maker of fun, an amalgam of Vice, Paradise, Fool, *Miles-Gloriosus*, Corrupt-Soldier, Clown, and what not, but surely not a dullard. Rather, he is a sophist of depth, I must emphasize. As discussed above, Shakespeare intermingles serious plots with comic ones, only to show that it is often impossible to distinguish work from play. Play may prove to be just practice for work. In the plays, the Prince's play with the Falstaff company is indeed a practice for war, an exercise for body strength and mental wisdom. When he plays the role of his father and that of Falstaff in the play-within-the-play, he is both comic and serious. Outwardly he is comic, but inwardly he is serious. Likewise, when he plays a robber of the thieves or the teaser of a tavern boy, he is also comic and serious. In any play he can always learn something to increase his strength and wisdom. For him (the) play is (the) work. By him Shakespeare has deconstructed the hierarchy of work / play.

In effect, through all the characters' (especially Hal's and Falstaff's) words and deeds, or work and play, Shakespeare has deconstructed many other logocentrisms or violent hierarchies. In the foregoing sections, I have pointed out the denial of wisdom as something learned only in the court by great noble men. The tavern is as good a place for wisdom. Statesmen are no better than highwaymen. Honor, as primarily a matter of public esteem, is but a word. The prince is but a kind of thief, and so he is as honorable as a thief. Kingship as the highest honor symbolized by the crown is passable from person to person. Besides, kingship suffers from dissemination: there are always so many claimable kings in the world. The hierarchy of sovereign over subjects is unstable. And no less unstable is the father / son hierarchy in terms of symbolic displacements. Friends can be foes. Lions can be foxes.

Shakespeare even uses names for deconstruction. *Henry IV* is actually *Henry V* in disguise. The four Henrys are but four combinations of the lion and the fox. Falstaff is a false staff member and a true support or supplement with realistic stuff. Rumor has truth. Shallow and Silence are justices deep in vice and noisy in folly. Hotspur can become Coldspur. So all names are "grams" or "traces" bearing no true substances. Yet, people are fond of good names. So the thieves want to euphemize their "vocation." And people like to call others names. But name-calling can be friendly or hostile, humorous or hurtful. Sword wars often originate from word wars, which in turn often come from name-calling. The conflict in *Henry IV* arises partly from the King's calling Mortimer a traitor. The entire play is in fact a series of word wars and sword wars between "traitors" and "patriots." But who are traitors and who are patriots? Henry IV himself is both a patriot and a traitor. And who isn't both in the jungle of politics?

Indeed, in the light of power struggle, human beings are no better than beasts. That is why Falstaff can say, "If the young dace be a bait for the old pike, I see no reason in the law of nature but I may snap at him" (Pt. 2, 3.2.325-6). But in the jungle of politics the lion certainly needs to cultivate the art of the fox in order to be an unfailing king. To put it plainly, kingship certainly needs counterfeit. In *Henry IV*, Hal conquers all by counterfeiting. He is the one who knows when to play a prince and when to play a prentice on the ground that "in everything the purpose must weigh with the folly" (Pt. 2, 2.3.178-9). It is significant that his father dies in a chamber called Jerusalem, that is, in a counterfeit Holy Land. Even at his deathbed he still recommends counterfeiting to his son: "Be it thy course to busy giddy minds / With foreign quarrel, that action hence borne out / May waste the memory of the former days" (Pt. 2, 4.5.213-5). The son, a better fox, naturally takes his advice. So, in the end of the play, he lets his brother proclaim the likelihood of a French expedition within the same year. Behind war there always hides some political purpose. Kingship is obtained and maintained, indeed, by counterfeit methods, not by genuine measures. This is perhaps the most salient point we can see in Shakespeare's deconstructionist vision of *Henry IV*, where the most foxy lion reigns in the political jungle, believing kingship is no other than counterfeit.

Notes

1. Phyllis Rackin mentions Lily B. Campbell, Irving Ribner, Andrew S. Cairncross, Robert B. Pierce, Robert Rentoul Reed, Jr., etc., in his *Stages of History,* p. 40, note 1.
2. I have often thought that the closest Chinese equivalent term for logos is "Tao" (道).
3. All parenthesized numbers hereafter refer to the Arden Shakespeare editions of *Henry IV Part 1 & Part 2,* with Harold F. Brooks, et al., as general editors.
4. In his "The Structural Problem in Shakespeare's *Henry IV*" Harold Jenkins has a good discussion of the problem of whether the two parts of *Henry IV* make two plays or just one single play. Among the one-play theorists are Dr. Johnson, Capell, Dover Wilson, Tillyard, and Jenkins himself.

Works Consulted

Allman, Eileen Jorge. *Player-King and Adversary: Two Faces of Play in Shakespeare*. Baton Rouge & London: Louisiana State UP, 1980.

Auden, W. H. "The Prince's Dog." In Hunter, 187-211.

Barber, C. L. "Rule and Misrule in *Henry IV, Part 1*." In Bloom, 51-69.

Bloom, Harold, ed. *William Shakespeare's* Henry IV, Part 1. Modern Critical Interpretations. New York: Chelsea House, 1987.

Charlton, H. B. "Shakespeare, Politics, and Politicians." In Hunter, 81-91.

Danby, John F. *Shakespeare's Doctrine of Nature*. London: Faber & Faber, 1982.

Derrida, Jacques. *Of Grammatology*. Trans. Gayatri Spivak. Baltimore: Johns Hopkins U. P., 1977.

——. *Writing and Difference*. Trans. Alan Bass. London: Routledge, 1978.

——. *Dissemination*. Trans. Barbara Johnson. London: Athlone Press, 1981.

——. *Positions*. Trans. Alan Bass. London: Athlone Press, 1981.

De Saussure, Ferdinand. *Course in General Linguistics*. Trans. W. Baskin. London: Fontana/Collins, 1974.

Dollimore, Jonathan & Allan Sinfield, eds. *Political Shakespeare: Essays in Cultural Materialism*. 2nd ed. Manchester: Manchester UP, 1994.

Dutton, Richard. *William Shakespeare: A Literary Life*. London: Macmillan, 1989.

Eliot, T. S. *Selected Essays*. London: Faber & Faber, 1980.

Fowler, Roger. *A Dictionary of Modern Critical Terms*. London & New York: Routledge & Kegan Paul, 1987.

Goddard, Harold C. "*Henry IV.*" In Bloom, 9-40.

Greenblatt, Stephen. "Invisible Bullets: Renaissance Authority and Its Subversion, *Henry IV and Henry V*." In Dollimore & Sinfield, 18-45.

Hawthorn, Jeremy. *A Concise Glossary of Contemporary Theory*. London: Edward Arnold, 1992.

Holderness, Graham. *Shakespeare Recycled: The Making of Historical Drama.* Hemel Hempstead, Hertforshire: Harvester Wheatsheaf, 1992.

Hunter, G. K., ed. *King Henry IV Parts 1 & 2: A Selection of Critical Essays.* London: Macmillan, 1982.

Iser, Wolfgang. *Staging Politics: The Lasting Impact of Shakespeare's Histories.* Trans. David Henry Wilson. New York: Columbia UP, 1993.

Jenkins, Harold. "The Structural Problem in Shakespeare's *Henry IV.*" In Hunter, 155-73.

Johnson, Barbara. *The Critical Difference: Essays in the Contemporary Rhetoric of Reading.* Baltimore: Johns Hopkins UP, 1980.

Kernan, Alvin B. "*The Henriad*: Shakespeare's Major History Plays." *Modern Shakespeare's Criticism.* Ed. Alvin B. Kernan. San Diego, CA: Harcourt Brace Jovanovich, 1970. 245-75.

Leggatt, Alexander. *Shakespeare's Political Drama: The History Plays and the Roman Plays.* London & New York: Routledge, 1988.

Lewis, Wyndham. *The Lion and the Fox: The Role of the Hero in the Plays of Shakespeare.* New York: Barnes and Noble, 1955.

McCanles, Michael. "The Dialectic of Right and Power in *Henry IV, Part 1.*" In Bloom, 97-100.

Machiavelli, Niccolo. *The Prince.* Ed. Peter Bondanella. Trans. Peter Bondanella & Mack Musa. Oxford: Oxford UP, 1984.

Morris, Helen. *Henry IV Part 1.* Macmillan Master Guides. London: Macmillan, 1986.

Norris, Cristopher. *Deconstruction: Theory and Practice.* London & New York: Methuen, 1982.

Pugliatti, Paola. *Shakespeare the Historian.* London: Macmillan, 1996.

Rackin, Phyllis. *Stages of History: Shakespeare's English Chronicles.* London: Routledge, 1990.

Ribur, Irving. *The English History Play in the Age of Shakespeare.* New York: Octagon Books, 1979.

Rowse, A. L. *William Shakespeare: A Biography.* New York: Harper & Row, 1963.

Schoenbaum, S. *William Shakespeare: A Compact Documentary Life.* Oxford: Oxford UP, 1977.

Selden, Raman & Peter Widdowson. *A Reader's Guide to Contemporary Literary Theory.* 3rd ed. New York & London: Harvest Wheatsheaf, 1993.

Shakespeare, William. *Henry IV, Part 1* The Arden Edition. Ed. A. R. Humphreys. London: Methuen, 1960.

——. *Henry IV, Part 2* The Arden Edition. Ed. A. R. Humphreys. London: Methuen, 1966.

——. *Henry VI.* The Arden Edition. Ed. Andrew S. Cairncross. London & New York: Methuen, 1969.

——. *Romeo and Juliet.* The Arden Edition. Ed. Brian Gibbons. London & New York: Methuen, 1980.

Shaw, Catherine M. "The Tragic Substructure of the 'Henry IV' Plays." *Shakespeare Survey: Shakespeare and History.* Ed. Stanley Wells. Cambridge: Cambridge UP, 1985. 61-67.

Smith, A. J. P. *Brodies's Notes on William Shakespeare's* Henry IV Part 1. London: Macmillan, 1985.

Sundelson, David. "Prince Hal's Joke." In Bloom, 109-113.

Tillyard, E. M. W. "*Henry IV* and the Tudor Epic." 1943a. In Hunter, 102-26.

——. *The Elizabethan World Picture.* London: Chatto & Windus, 1943b.

——. *Shakespeare's History Plays.* London: Penguin, 1944; New York: Collier Books, 1962.

Traversi, Derek. *Shakespeare: From* Richard II *to* Henry V. Stanford, CA: Stanford UP, 1987.

Watson, Curtis Brown. *Shakespeare and the Renaissance Concept of Honor.* Princeton, NJ: Princeton UP, 1960.

Watson, Donald G. *Shakespeare's Early History Plays: Politics at Play in the Elizabethan Stage.* Athens, GA: U of Georgia P, 1990.

Wheeler, Richard P. *Shakespeare's Development and the Problem Comedies: Turn and Counter-Turn.* Berkeley, Los Angeles, London: U of California P, 1981.

Wilson, J. Dover. *The Essential Shakespeare: A Biographical Adventure.* New York: Haskell House, 1977.

* This chapter first appeared as a paper in 2001 in National Chung Hsing University's *Journal of the College of Liberal Arts*, Vol. 31, pp. 73-113.

• Chapter 3 •

Signification and Equivocation: Shakespeare's Semiotic Vision in *Macbeth*

I. The Doubtful Theme

Shakespeare's greatness lies partly in his great interpretability. None of his works, to be sure, deserve the post-structural epithet of "open text" or "writerly text." Yet, almost every play of his induces a wide variety of interpretations concerning its theme. *Macbeth*, his shortest drama, is not an exception. There have been critics, for instance, who read the play in the light of its most obvious theme: ambition. Other critics, however, have attempted to concentrate on such other themes as fear, evil, conscience, and crime (see Campbell, Knight, Lukacher, McElroy). And still other critics may admit the plurality of its major themes. L. C. Knights, for example, says, "The equivocal nature of temptation, the commerce with phantoms consequent upon false choice, the resulting sense of unreality..., the unnaturalness of evil..., and the relation between disintegration in the individual... and disorder in the larger social organism—all these are major themes of the play" (111). I think Knights is right, and so are all other critics who choose to see only one single relevant theme. Nevertheless, I must say I am surprised to find that no critic, as far as I know, has as yet touched on the theme of signification: no one seems to have noticed that the play is as much about signs as about ambition or any other theme.

To say that the play is also about signs or signification is to bring into focus, perhaps, Macbeth's famous remark that life is "a tale / Told by an idiot, full of sound and fury, / Signifying nothing" (5.5.26-8).[1] Certainly, this cynical remark implies that life, like an idiot's tale, is a vocal sign devoid of any sense. But does this saying represent merely Macbeth's own cynical understanding of life? By letting Macbeth make such an utterance, has Shakespeare not made a comment, also, on how a person (here the protagonist of the play) interprets signs and on how signs are made to signify things?

S. S. Hussey says, "If the play is obviously about assassination it is even more about equivocation" (226). Many other critics (most notably Kenneth Muir in his Introduction to the Arden Edition of *Macbeth*) have given heed, too, to the theme of equivocation alluded to in the play (2.3.9 ff.). Yet, for them the theme is just a topical matter concerning "the trial of Father Garnet (28 March 1606) for complicity in the Gunpowder Plot" (Muir xv-xvi). They do not seem to have been aware that equivocation is a special kind of signification and the entire play can be regarded as a dramatic study of that special kind of signification.

Indeed, as I will show step by step below, *Macbeth* has embedded in it Shakespeare's most revelatory view of signs. Through the characters' appearances, speeches, gestures, and acts as well as the setting and imagery of the play, we can all detect Shakespeare's semiotic vision emerging from the process of signification and the theme of equivocation. But before we get into details, we need first to agree on some semiotic truths.

II. The Significant Truths

In his *Theories of the Symbol*, Tzvetan Todorov traces the birth of Western semiotics to St. Augustine's synthesis of classical ideas regarding symbols or signs as found in works of semantics, logic, rhetoric, and hermeneutics. Todorov quotes some important definitions or explanations of the sign from Augustine's *On Dialectics, On Christian Doctrine, On the Trinity* and other texts. Among them are these:

> *"A sign is something which is itself sensed and which indicates to the mind something beyond the sign itself. To speak is to give a sign by means of an articulate utterance."*
>
> (On Dialectics, V)

> *"A word is a sign of any sort of thing. It is spoken by a speaker and can be understood by a hearer."*
>
> (On Dialectics, V)

> *"A sign is a thing which causes us to think of something beyond the impression the thing itself makes upon the senses."*
>
> (On Christian Doctrine, II, ii, 1)

> *"Nor is there any other reason for signifying, or for giving signs, except for bringing forth and transferring to another mind the action of the mind in the person who makes the sign."*
>
> (On Christian Doctrine, II, ii, 3)

> *"For those are called words in one way, which occupy spaces of time by their syllables, whether they are pronounced or only thought; and in another way, all that is known is called a word imprinted on the mind."*
>
> (On the Trinity, IX, x, 15)

> *"The thought that is formed by the thing which we know, is the word which we speak in the heart; which word is neither Greek nor Latin, nor of any other tongue. But when it is*

needful to convey this to the knowledge of those to whom we
speak, then some sign is assumed whereby to signify it."

(On the Trinity, XV, x, 19)

From these quotations we as well as Todorov know that a sign has long been defined or understood as something indicating or representing something else, and a word is a verbal, hence sensible, sign (among other signs) used in the process of communication to transfer meaning or thought in the speaker's mind to the hearer's mind. Thus, "Words belong on the one hand to the auditory realm, on the other to the intentional realm: the intersection of these two categories yields linguistic signs" (Todorov 58).

It is often assumed that modern semiotics began with the Swiss linguist Ferdinand de Saussure. In his *Course in General Linguistics*, Saussure differentiates *langue* (the socially shared linguistic system) from *parole* (the individual utterance based on the system). He also differentiates *signifier* (the indicating or representing mark) from *signified* (the concept indicated or represented), telling us at the same time that the relation between signifier and signified is arbitrary. Thus, he has gone as far as to hint that it is possible for one to use different signifiers in one's *parole* to signify the same concept or use the same signifier to signify different concepts without deviating from the *langue* in a communicative process.

The American semiotician C. S. Peirce envisages quite a different system of signs from Saussure's binaristic or dyadic system. He is interested in semiosis, the act of signifying. For him a sign is "a First which stands in such a genuine triadic relation to a Second, called its *Object*, as to be capable of determining a Third, called its *Interpretant*, to assume the same triadic relation to its Object in which it stands itself to the same Object" (2.274).[2] Therefore, semiosis always involves "a cooperation of *three* subjects such as a sign, its object and its interpretant, this tri-relative influence not being in any way resolvable into actions between pairs" (5.484, quoted in Eco 15). For him, the interpretant is itself a sign, so the semiotic process is a recurrent one: the life of signs is one of perpetually issuing the offspring of an interpretant through the mating of a sign and its object. In fact, Saussure's signified is an interpretant in its broad sense, and Peirce's interpretant is no other than Saussure's signified perceived as another sign.

In describing the relation between a sign and its object, Peirce issues three other terms besides the term *interpretant*:

> ...*every sign is determined by its object, either first, by partaking in the character of the object, when I call the sign an Icon; secondly, by being really and in its individual existence connected with the individual object, when I call the sign an Index; thirdly, by more or less approximate certainty that it will be interpreted as denoting the object in consequence of a habit... when I call the sign a Symbol. (4.531, quoted in Fiske 47)*

Scholars often explain that Peirce's *Icon* refers to a linkage of resemblance, *Index* to an existential or causal linkage, and *Symbol* to an arbitrary linkage. This is true, but it should be noted that in proposing linkages other than the arbitrary one, Peirce has actually contradicted Saussure in *no* way, since Peirce is talking about the relation between a sign and its object while Saussure is talking about the relation between a signifier (i.e., Peirce's sign) and its signified (i.e., Peirce's interpretant).

Umberto Eco has contributed a lot in our efforts to clarify the semiotic process. He tells us that the interpretant as Peirce has postulated can assume different forms:

a) **It can be the equivalent (or apparently equivalent) sign-vehicle in another semiotic system. For example I**

can make the drawing of a dog correspond to the word
   /dog/.

b)   It can be the index which is directed to a single object,
   perhaps implying an element of universal quantification
   (<all objects like this>).

c)   It can be a scientific (or naïve) definition in terms of
   the same semiotic system, e.g. /salt/ signifies <sodium
   chloride>.

d)   It can be an emotive association which acquires the
   value of an established connotation: /dog/ signifies <
   fidelity> (and vice versa).

e)   It can simply be the translation of the term into
   another language, or its substitution by a synonym.

So the interpretant "could be equated with any coded intensional
property of the content, i.e., with the entire range of denotations and
connotations of a sign vehicle" (70). But, Eco adds, "the interpretants
are much more than this: they can be complex discourses which not
only translate but even *inferentially* develop all the logical possibilities
suggested by the sign" (70). Moreover, "the interpretant can be a
response, a behavioral habit determined by a sign, and many other
things" (70). So Eco assumes that "all the denotations of a sign-vehicle
are undoubtedly its interpretants, that a connotation is the interpretant
of an underlying denotation, and that a further connotation is the
interpretant of the one underlying it" (70). Finally, Eco assumes that
"one should even consider as interpretants all possible semiotic
judgments that a code permits one to assert about a given semantic unit,
as well as many factual judgments" (71). This final remark leads us
back to the conclusion that Peirce's interpretant, no less than
Saussure's signified, is indeed a rather vague term, as it comprises
actually anything or any response that arises from the stimulation of a
sign-vehicle (Saussure's signifier or Peirce's sign).

The term *interpretant* unavoidably connects itself with hermeneutics, the general theory and practice of interpretation. In hermeneutics, controversy has arisen as to where lies the validity of an interpretation. With a view to solving this problem, E. D. Hirsch, Jr., sets out to distinguish "meaning" from "significance" or "relevance." For Hirsch, "meaning" is what the author meant, or the author's "awareness" in constructing a text. It is the permanent or invariable in a text, hence the proper object of interpretation. In contrast, "significance" or "relevance" is anything "meaning" bears on something else—personal taste, historical period, present concerns, standards of value, etc. It is thus the object of criticism. Hirsch's idea seems to be active in Peirce's definitions for his key terms: "A sign stands *for* something *to* the idea which it produces, or modifies. ...That for which it stands is called its *object*; that which it conveys, its *meaning*; and the idea to which it gives rise, its *interpretant*" (1.339, quoted in Riffaterre 81). Obviously, Peirce's "meaning" and "interpretant" correspond to Hirsch's "meaning" and "significance."

In applying Peirce's ideas to his semiotics of poetry, Michael Riffaterre points out that there are "dual signs" or equivocal words which are situated at the point where "two sequences of semantic or formal associations intersect" (86), "being equally pertinent to two codes or texts, the meaning-conveying one and the significance-carrying one" (81). Such signs or words, he adds, function quite like puns or syllepses. Furthermore, he says, the verbal sequence progresses simultaneously as mimesis and as semiosis. "At the mimesis level, meanings of words depend entirely upon syntax and position. At the semiotic level, contrariwise, the words repeat the same information, usually a seme, or the invariant of a thematic structure" (88). Thus, he arrives at the conclusion that the poetic sign has two faces: "textually ungrammatical, intertextually grammatical; displaced and distorted in the mimesis system, but in the semiotic grid appropriate and rightly placed" (165). And the reader's "manufacture of meaning is thus not so much a progress through the poem and a half-random accretion of verbal associations, as it is a seesaw scanning of the text, compelled by the very duality of the signs—ungrammatical as mimesis, grammatical within the significance network" (166).

III. The Equivocators

In Act II, scene iii, of *Macbeth*, Shakespeare makes the drunken Porter utter, among other things, this remark: "Faith, here's an equivocator, that could swear in both the scales against either scale; who committed treason enough for God's sake, yet could not equivocate to heaven: O! come in, equivocator" (8-12). It is suggested that the Porter is here alluding to Father Garnet, who went under the name of "Farmer" and was accused of equivocation in the trial of the Gunpowder Plot (see Muir 59, note 9), although we know the Porter is plainly addressing an imagined person coming to his imagined hell. A few lines later, the Porter jokingly tells Macduff that drink provokes three things: nose-painting, sleep, and urine. Then he goes on to say:

> *Lechery, Sir, it provokes, and unprovokes: it provokes the desire, but it takes away the performance. Therefore, much drink may be said to be an equivocator with lechery: it makes him, and it mars him; it sets him on, and it takes him off; it persuades him, and disheartens him; makes him stand to, and not stand to: in conclusion, equivocates him in a sleep, and, giving him the lie, leaves him. (28-35)*

Towards the end of the play, when a messenger comes to tell Macbeth that he has seen a moving grove, Macbeth confesses that he begins to "doubt the equivocation of the fiend, / That lies like truth" (5.5.43-44).

And when Macduff says he was untimely ripped from his mother's womb, hence not born of a woman, Macbeth yells: "...be these juggling fiends no more believed, / That palter with us in a double sense" (5.8.19-20).

From the above-quoted lines, we know the text of *Macbeth* has clearly pointed out three equivocators: namely, an imagined person in the Porter's mind, "much drink," and the fiend or the "juggling fiends" who should be identified with one or all of the Weird Sisters. But are the play's equivocators confined to these clearly referred to in the text? Are there any other characters or things in the play that "swear in both the scales against either scale"; that "provoke and unprovoke," "make and mar," and "persuade and dishearten"; that "lie like truth" and "palter with us in a double sense"? Our answer is definitely "Yes." Empson holds that all the lords in the play are meant to be ambiguous as each plays his own game during this period of confusion (143). I think Macbeth himself and Lady Macbeth, at least, are the other two main equivocators comparable to the three Weird Sisters.

At the outset Macbeth is depicted as "Bellora's bridegroom," brave, valiant, and worthy in contrast with the "most disloyal traitor, / The Thane of Cawdor" (1.2.53-5). Cawdor's treachery leads Duncan to the conclusion that "There's no art / To find the mind's construction in the face" (1.4.11-12). The irony is: this conclusion is even more fitting if Duncan can survive to comment on Macbeth's treachery. For, as the upshot shows, Macbeth is Duncan's "peerless kinsman" (1.4.58) not only in bravery, but also in traitorous behavior. His peerlessly equivocal character has ultimately made him peerless indeed, in the sense that no one else can compare with him, and in the sense that he is devoid of any degree of nobility as he becomes a tyrannous, treacherous king.

Macbeth is aware of his own double personality. When Duncan names Malcolm the Prince of Cumberland, he says in an aside: "That is a step / On which I must fall down, or else o'erleap, ...Let not light see my black and deep desires" (1.4.48-51). But it is his lady that sees most clearly his equivocal character:

> *Yet do I fear thy nature:*
> *It is too full o 'th'milk of human kindness,*
> *To catch the nearest way. Thou wouldst be great;*
> *Art not without ambition, but without*
> *The illness should attend it; what thou wouldst highly,*
> *That wouldst thou holily; wouldst not play false,*
> *And yet wouldst wrongly win. (1.5.16-22)*

In Lady Macbeth's eyes, this Bellora's bridegroom is at the same time both unjustly ambitious and holily mild. In other words, he has the manly desire for greatness, but without the manly nature of illness. To her he seems to be a mere woman full of the milk of human kindness. Or, we may say, there are two Macbeths: the ambitious, manly Macbeth and the conscientious, womanly Macbeth. And it is these two Macbeths battling against each other that make the tragedy.

It is to be noted that Lady Macbeth urges her husband to be a man, but her teachings are often the feminine means of cheating:

> *Your face, my Thane, is as a book, where men*
> *May read strange matters. To beguile the time,*
> *Look like the time; bear welcome in your eye,*
> *Your hand, your tongue: look like the innocent flower,*
> *But be the serpent under 't. (1.5.62-6)*

Under her incessant teachings, as we know, Macbeth sometimes yields to ambition and sometimes resorts to conscience. Hence his remark: "I have no spur / To prick the sides of my intent, but only / Vaulting ambition, which o'erleaps itself / And falls on th'other" (1.7.25-8). And hence his hesitation to kill Duncan, and his remorse after killing him.

After Macbeth becomes king, however, he has lost most of his conscientious self. Consequently, he schemes to murder Banquo and Fleance, and gives orders to slaughter Macduff's whole house. But even at this atrocious time Macbeth is not entirely without conscience. His strange manners at the banquet betray not only his fear at the sight of Banquo's ghost but also his awareness of his own wickedness. It is after he has "supp'd full with horrors" (5.5.13) and found life empty of meaning that he can be said to have completely lost his conscience. But this is then the time for his unfeeling attitude towards everybody's death, including his wife's.

Lady Macbeth is no less equivocal in character than her husband. At the outset, she seems to have really unsexed herself and filled herself "from the crown to the toe, top-full / Of direst cruelty" (1.5.42-3). But we must remember: she dare not kill Duncan herself because she finds him resembling his father in sleep (2.2.12-13). And she breaks down worse, if not sooner, than Macbeth. While Macbeth feels he has murdered the innocent sleep, she actually suffers from "slumbery agitation" (5.1.11): her belief that "A little water clears us of this deed" (2.2.66) has actually plunged herself into the queer act of washing her hands continually in her sleepwalking scene. If Macbeth's life is taken by Macduff when his ambitious self has overthrown his conscientious self, Lady Macbeth's life is taken by herself when her conscientious self has vanquished her ambitious self. At the end of the play, she is called Macbeth's "fiend-like Queen" (5.9.35). Surely, she is another "juggling fiend." She has been playing with equivocal words and devices like the Witches. Yet, she is equivocal not just in being both fiendish and womanly, but also in being manly and womanly or being ambitious and conscientious like her husband.

As to the things that equivocate, they are not limited to "much drink" and ambiguous words, of course. Almost anything significantly described can be an equivocator for something. We know, for example, the weather in the play is both fair and foul. The heath, "the setting for the asexual witches," is "*blasted* in a double sense—both barren and accursed" (Mahood 134). The court, in the drunken Porter's imagination at least, is both a court and a hell. The time is often both light and dark. When Duncan is murdered, Rosse says, "...by th'clock 'tis day, / And yet dark night strangles the traveling lamp" (2.4.6-7). The season when Duncan comes to visit the Macbeths is "a season of imperception" in which the delicate air attracts the martlets only to prove that it is but "St. Martin's Summer," the transitory period with unseasonably mild weather for migratory birds to depart rather than to stay (Doloff 328-9). The stealing away of Malcolm and Donalbain is interpreted both as a consequence of their parricide and as a consequence of others' regicide. Likewise, Macduff's flight to England is interpretable both as an act of wisdom and as an act of fear, according to Rosse (4.2.4-5). Besides, Rosse is puzzled to find that "cruel are the times, when we are traitors, / And do not know ourselves" (4.2.18-9), just as Macduff's son is puzzled to find that his father can be called a traitor, and that as liars and swearers, traitors are to be hanged by honest men while the former are far more than the latter in number. If we read the play carefully enough, we will even conclude that Shakespeare, after all, is himself the greatest equivocator of all. But before we come to the conclusion, we need to study the nature of equivocation.

IV. Six Types of Ambiguity

In Section I, I have said equivocation is a special kind of signification. The primary point which makes it special is: it has a double or doubtful meaning, that is, it is ambiguous in sense, in reference, or in situation. So equivocation is equivalent to ambiguity. An equivocator is someone or something that makes ambiguity in a process of signification.

William Empson, as we know, has observed seven types of ambiguities in English verse including Shakespeare's. But Empson's typology, as we must also know, is far from scientific and it is restricted to verbal ambiguities. To do full justice to Shakespeare's equivocal ambiguities in *Macbeth*, I think we need only the distinction of six types divided into three contrasting pairs as explicated below.

The first pair is lexical ambiguity vs. syntactical ambiguity. Lexical ambiguities refer to those arising from lexical items (i.e., words) which possess more than one meaning or reference. When Lady Macbeth says, "To alter favor ever is to fear" (1.5.72), for instance, the word *favor* can mean both "countenance" and "friendly regard." It is therefore a case of lexical ambiguity. When ambiguities arise not from lexical items but from syntactical factors (i.e., ways of arranging words in order), we then have syntactical ambiguities. A good example of syntactic ambiguity is seen in Act V, scene i, when in sleepwalking Lady Macbeth says, "Fie, my Lord, Fie! a soldier, and afeared? What need we fear who knows it, when none can call our power to accompt?" (34-6). The syntax here is ambiguous because the last question can be split into two questions (and thus with a different interpretation): "What need we fear? Who knows it, when none can call our power to accompt?" (see Bishop 78-9). Another example occurs in the first one and half lines of Act I, scene vii uttered in thought by Macbeth. Some critics say the lines should be: "If it were done, when 'tis done, then 'twere well. / It were done quickly" (1-2). Others say the correct reading is: "If it were done, when 'tis done, then 'twere well / It were done quickly." The two different readings make a good case of syntactical ambiguity (see Muir 36, notes 12 & 1-7).

The second pair is verbal ambiguity vs. situational ambiguity. Both lexical and syntactical ambiguities are verbal ambiguities since they derive ambiguities from word meanings or ways of arranging words. But a case of ambiguity does not necessarily stem from verbal details. It can stem from situational details, too. For example, after

95

Lady Macbeth has drugged the grooms' possets, she finds "That Death and Nature do contend about them, / Whether they live, or die" (2.2.8-9). The situation is ambiguous in that the grooms can be said to be both alive and dead.

The third pair is intentional ambiguity vs. affective ambiguity. In a communicative process, the speaker may utter ambiguous words intentionally (consciously for a certain purpose) or unintentionally (without knowing he is being ambiguous). When the third Apparition tells Macbeth that he cannot be vanquished until "Great Birnam wood to high Dunsinane hill / Shall come against him" (4.1.934), the Apparition is intentionally making an ambiguous statement to mislead Macbeth into bold action. In contrast, when Lady Macbeth tells her husband to "look up clear" and explains that "To alter favor ever is to fear" (1.5.71-2), she does not intend to make the word *favor* mean both "countenance" and "friendly regard" at the same time; the ambiguity is unintentionally made. Yet, intentional or not, an ambiguity is either felt or not felt on the part of the object. Normally, to feel an ambiguity will directly bring about a certain effect. When Macbeth sees the ambiguous presence of a dagger before him (II, i), for example, he is puzzled and discouraged. Sometimes, however, not to feel an ambiguity will also cause a great effect. What makes Macbeth boldly rush into action, for instance, is his ignorance of the third Apparition's intentional ambiguity. Anyway, if an ambiguity is intended, we call it an intentional ambiguity. If an ambiguity has effect, we call it an affective ambiguity.

If we examine *Macbeth* closely in respect of its inherent ambiguities, we will find that all the six types of ambiguity as introduced above are prevalent in the text. Many lexical ambiguities, for instance, coexist with puns. And puns, moreover, function in the play to "connect subject and object, inner force with outer form, the poetic vision with the characters in action" (Mahood 41). When Macbeth says, "The very firstlings of my heart shall be / The firstlings of my hand" (4.1.147-8), for example, the word "firstlings" can mean "firstborn young" as well as "the first results of anything, or first-fruits." This ambiguity is particularly meaningful if we consider the fact that "Macbeth has no children but acts of violence against the children of others" (Mahood 135). When Lady Macbeth says, "I'll gild the faces of the grooms withal, / For it must seem their guilt" (2.2.56-7), the word "gild" does pun with "guilt" and it not only has the local significance but also helps to intensify the play's overall theme of crime and theme of masking. Likewise, when Banquo says, "...how our partner's rapt" (1.3.143), the word "rapt" puns with "wrapped," referring therefore both to what Christopher Pye calls "politics of rapture" (the theme of inner repression) and to what Cleanth Brooks calls "cloak of manliness" (the theme of outer sham).

Many of the abundant syntactical ambiguities in *Macbeth* also echo the play's themes. The riddling line "To know my deed, 'twere best not know myself" (2.2.72), for example, has been interpreted quite variously in supposing that the subject who does the knowing is Macbeth himself, who has just murdered Duncan. Such interpretations include: "If I am to come to terms with what I have done, I shall need to avoid self-scrutiny"; "If not being lost in my thoughts means seeing clearly what I have done, I'd better remain lost in my thoughts"; "If I must look my deed in the face, it were better for me to lose consciousness altogether"; "Better be lost in thought than look my deed in the face"; and "It were better for me to remain permanently 'lost' in thought, i.e., self-alienated, than to be fully conscious of the nature of my deed" (quoted in Pye 151). According to Pye, such readings have missed the line's literal sense: "To know the deed, I must not know myself"—that is, the sense that "the crime is indistinguishable from its disavowal" (151). In reality, as a line addressed to Lady Macbeth, who has just told Macbeth not to be lost so poorly in his thoughts, it can also mean "If you want to know my deed, you had better not know myself." This reading, then, suggests that Macbeth's deed (killing Duncan, losing himself in thought, or any other deed) is often not in keeping with his character—a fact implied in the fair-is-foul theme or the theme of conscience-in-conflict-with-ambition.

Most of the situational ambiguities in *Macbeth* are absorbed in its plot. Whether the Witches' solicitings are good or evil, whether Malcolm's escape is due to his parricide or someone else's regicide, whether Fleance's fleeing is for avoiding Macbeth's murder or for having murdered his father, whether Macduff is wise or foolish to leave his household behind while he flees to England, and whether Lady Macbeth is wise or foolish to spur her husband's ambition on and on—problematic situations like these are interpreted differently by different characters in the play before the things become clear in due time. Such ambiguous situations have in effect served to intensify directly the theme of equivocation besides adding interest to the play's plot development.

As to intentional ambiguities and affective ambiguities, we can say all the equivocators' words and manners, including the Witches', the Macbeths', and Malcolm's, have time and again been brought forth intentionally to mislead victims, conceal crimes, test characters, etc. And such intentional ambiguities do often achieve their purposes, thus becoming affective ambiguities. We know, for instance, the Witches have succeeded in cheating the Macbeths, and Malcolm has succeeded in testing Macduff's loyalty by disparaging himself dubiously with verbal ironies. Macbeth's false talks and false appearances are certainly not so successful as his lady's or the Witches'. In terms of effect, however, Macbeth's intentional ambiguities do have the negative effect of betraying himself. So, on the whole, we can assert that the play is a process of turning intentional ambiguities into affective ambiguities. If the play's main setting is a battlefield, it is a setting not only of soldiers fighting with weapons but also of equivocators fighting with intentional ambiguities. In a sense, then, the play is a combination of sword wars with word wars. And this feature is proclaimed by the keynote of equivocation at the very beginning of the play.

V. A Battlefield of Ambiguous Signs

Macbeth begins with the first appearance of the Weird Sisters. It is noted that "Cuningham thought that this scene was spurious, because no dramatic object was gained by its introduction," and "Granville-Barker concurred" by stating that "Apart from such an opening being un-Shakespearean... The scene... is a poor scene and a pointless scene," whereas Coleridge remarked that the scene "is to strike the keynote... of the whole play," and so Knights declared that "every word of which... strikes one dominant chord" (Muir 3). This note explains that this first scene is indeed equivocal with regard to its significance as well as its authenticity. This equivocal possibility of interpretation, however, leaves me no doubt as to the scene's function. I agree with Coleridge and Knights that the scene "is to strike the keynote of the whole play" and it "strikes one dominant chord"—that is, the note or chord of equivocation. Let us examine the details.

The scene begins with the first Witch asking: "When shall we three meet again? / In thunder, lightning, or in rain?" (1-2). Some critics see syntactical ambiguity in these two lines. So Hanmer suggested this emendation: "When shall we three meet again /In thunder, lightning, or in rain?" Anyway, we know the Witch is asking to know *when* they will meet again in a certain situation. The question "In thunder, lightning, or in rain?" is to continue, not to answer, the when-question. But this second question implies the equivocal nature of the situation: it has rained so much with such thunder and lightning that the Witches find it hard to say they have met in thunder and lightning or in rain. So, by introducing a syntactical ambiguity together with a situational ambiguity into the first two lines, Shakespeare has struck the keynote or dominant chord of the entire play: EQUIVOCAL!

The second Witch answers, "When the hurlyburly's done, / When the battle's lost and won" (3-4). It is usually noted that the Witch refers the hurly-burly to the tumult of sedition or insurrection. But can't she refer it, too, to the tumult of the rainstorm with thunder and lightning? If there is such a possibility, we then find a case of lexical ambiguity in "the hurlyburly." The statement "When the battle's lost and won" is a paradox because we normally think, and say, a battle is lost, or it is won, seldom "lost and won." Upon second thought, however, we will agree that a battle is really lost on one side and won on the other side. Furthermore, we may also agree that no one side in a battle can claim a whole victory: each side actually win something and lose something. So it is correct to say the battle is lost and won on both sides. Maynard Mack, Jr., has pointed out that Macbeth wins the battle in Act I and, "by winning, loses—because of the temptations his victory and honors bring him" (69). With this understanding, then, we see the second line spoken by the second Witch has a situational ambiguity inherent in it.

After the three Witches agree to meet again "ere the set of sun" (5), "Upon the heath" (6), they together say, "Fair is foul, and foul is fair" (11). Their common statement is an uncommon one. It is "ungrammatical as mimesis," to use Riffaterre's term, because logically "fair is fair, and foul is foul." Yet, in real situations we do find: a fair-looking man is a foul person, a foul character does a fair deed, a fair day is foul for an evil-doer, a foul penalty is but fair dealing, etc. So, "within the significance network," to use Riffaterre's phrase again, the uncommon statement is "grammatical." If we examine the context, we can assert that the Witches use the words *fair* and *foul* superficially to refer to the weather as they hover "through the fog and filthy air" (12). Yet, in the bottom of their thought, they intentionally refer to the good and bad characters with their fair and foul deeds in the play. Thus, intentional and verbal ambiguities with hidden situational ambiguities have made the first scene conspicuously resonant with the theme of equivocation, which is in keeping with the characteristics of the Witches or Weird Sisters.

The second scene begins with Duncan asking Malcolm, "What bloody man is that?" "This is the Sergeant," answers Malcolm. Here *bloody* means "bleeding," or "covered with blood." But it can mean "cruel," or "eager to kill," as well. In truth, a sergeant is often covered with blood after his eagerness to shed blood in battle. Kolbe points out that "blood" is mentioned over 100 times in the course of the play (noted in Muir 5). As an ambiguous lexicon, this "bloody" has indeed foreboded a stage full of blood with many people killing and / or killed.

In telling the King "the knowledge of the broil," the bloody Captain says, "Doubtful it stood; / As two spent swimmers, that do cling together / And choke their art" (6-9). This is a simile referring immediately to the ambiguous state of Macbeth fighting against Macdonwald. But this simile is equally valid as a description of any two battling sides including Macbeth's later struggle with Macduff. One critic even holds that the two swimmers "anticipate the fate of the Macbeths" (Lukacher 191). The same doubtful situation is emphasized in the Captain's another simile:

> *As whence the sun 'gins his reflection,*
> *Shipwracking storms and direful thunders break,*
> *So from that spring, whence comfort seem'd to come,*
> *Discomfort swells. (1.2.25-8)*

Comfort is discomfort; discomfort is comfort. Fair is foul; foul is fair. To win is to lose; to lose is to win. The same philosophy, the same equivocation expressed through doubtful words and ambiguous situations.

In Act I, scene iii, Macbeth says to Banquo, "So foul and fair a day I have not seen" (38). One critic thinks it means "*Foul* with regard to the *weather*, and *fair* with reference to his *victory*" (see Muir 14, note 38). But most of us will agree that both *foul* and *fair* refer directly to the weather, indicating the existence of "fog and filthy air" to cloud the sky to such an extent that one can hardly say it is a fair day or a foul one. Anyway, this ambiguous statement certainly can serve as a symbolic statement to indicate the equivocal state in which the characters are placed or the equivocal fortune they are confronted with.

What confront Macbeth and Banquo immediately in the scene are the three Witches, who "look not like th'inhabitants o'th'earth, / And yet are on't" (1.3.41-2). These natural and supernatural beings are "borderers" even because they have beards like men. Their equivocal appearances are accompanied by their equivocal predictions. They successively call Macbeth "Thane of Glamis," "Thane of Cawdor," and "King hereafter" (48-50). They also say Banquo will be "lesser than Macbeth, and greater," will be "Not so happy, yet much happier," and will "get kings, though thou be none" (65-7). Since they utter prophecies as such, they can easily be identified with the Fates, the three women who spin the thread of life, assign destiny, and cut the thread at death. But as they are apparently "juggling fiends" playing with ambiguous words, we can say they are undoubtedly skillful equivocators.

The Witches' doubtful predictions set Macbeth doubting. After he verifies the second truth that he is Thane of Cawdor, Macbeth ponders:

> *Two truths are told,*
> *As happy prologues to the swelling act*
> *Of the imperial theme...*
> *...This supernatural soliciting*
> *Cannot be ill; cannot be good... (1.3.127-31)*

The equivocal nature of this "supernatural soliciting" has in fact started a war within Macbeth's psyche. He wavers between accepting it or not accepting it; hence between acting to fulfill it or simply waiting for the natural outcome. At first, he concludes that "If Chance will have me King, why, Chance / may crown me, / Without my stir" (144-5). But later, as we know, he does not just resign himself to chance. He acts somehow, instead, for "the imperial theme." And that brings about his tragedy.

Once, after he has thought of the horrible act of murdering Duncan, Macbeth says in fear, "And nothing is, but what is not" (1.3.142). This puzzling statement indicates the point that "Present fears / Are less than horrible imaginings" (137-8), or, as Knight puts it, the fact that "Reality and unreality change places" (*Wheel*, 153). Yet, we can also say this statement foreshadows Macbeth's final understanding that life is but a walking shadow or a tale told by an idiot signifying nothing. Anyway, the Witches' intentional ambiguity has become a strongly affective ambiguity leading not only to Macbeth's inner conflict but also to his philosophical and semiotic understanding that everything is unreal, is at most but a sign for another sign.

This philosophical / semiotic understanding, however, cannot prevent Macbeth's tragic action. As the story goes on, after Lady Macbeth's further urging, he commits regicide and becomes a murderous tyrant. Finally, he can only gain support and comfort from the Witches' further temptation embodied in the Apparitions' ambiguous assertions. The assertion that none of women born shall harm Macbeth produces a case of lexical ambiguity, as the word "born" is made to mean both simply "given birth" and more specifically "delivered through a woman's vagina." And the assertion that Macbeth shall never be vanquished until Great Birnam wood shall come against him to high Dunsinane hill, also produces a case of lexical ambiguity. For the word "wood" can refer both to an entire forest and to the wooden part of trees. So, Macbeth's downfall can be said to result, partly at least, from his ignorance of these lexical ambiguities.

VI. The Tragic Flaw

It is often said that Macbeth's tragic flaw (*hamartia*) lies in his ambition. To be sure, "vaulting ambition" is Macbeth's moral shortcoming, which makes him, like Faustus, "gulled by guileful agents of the supernatural" (Nosworthy 210). But one may also point to the error of his succumbing to the Witches' temptations and Lady Macbeth's urgings. And, certainly, we can admit that Macbeth's conscience is too weak to stand firm in its position. Besides, it is justifiable to attribute Macbeth's downfall, as we have just said, to his ignorance of lexical ambiguities or any other ambiguous state he is in. However, after considering all these possible factors, I think Macbeth's biggest tragic flaw lies in his rashness in interpreting signs (if not in performing his deeds).

Let us recall the scene when the Witches comes to tell Macbeth his future. After they have greeted Macbeth "with present grace, and great prediction / Of noble having, and of royal hope," Banquo finds that Macbeth seems to "fear / Things that do sound so fair," though he seems to be "rapt withal" (1.3.51-7). The rapture is a sign, of course, of Macbeth's accepting the promises. But why should he start and seem to fear? He says, "To be King / Stands not within the prospect of belief, / No more than to be Cawdor" (1.3.73-5). Incredibility may be part of the reason. But after Rosse and Angus come to tell him he has really become Thane of Cawdor, he thinks the first two told truths are "happy prologues to the swelling act / Of the imperial theme" (127-9), although Banquo warns him that "to win us to our harm, /The instruments of Darkness tell us truths" (123-4). For a short while he does reason whether this "supernatural soliciting" (130) is ill or good. In the process of reasoning, he says:

If good, why do I yield to that suggestion
Whose horrid image doth unfix my hair,
And make my seated heart knock at my ribs,
Against the use of nature? Present fears
Are less than horrible imaginings.
My thought, whose murther yet is but fantastical,
Shakes so my single state of man,
That function is smothered in surmise,
And nothing is, but what is not. (1.3.134-42)

From these lines, we can clearly see that Macbeth's fear actually comes from his imagining murder as the only way to make him king. Banquo does not know this. Hence his interpretation: "New honors come upon him, / Like our strange garments, cleave not to their mould" (145-6). Here we may stop to ask: Is murder really the only way to a throne? Our answer is "No," of course. One can succeed to a throne. One can be elected to it, too. But does Macbeth have any chance to succeed or be elected to a throne? He himself knows that it is highly improbable. As a general just returning from the battlefield where the owner of royal power is determined by the success or failure of uprising and slaughtering, Macbeth simply cannot imagine otherwise. Nevertheless, this imagining murder as the only way to the throne is a rash interpretation of the signs the Witches have just given him. There is a time when he persuades himself that if chance will have him king, chance may crown him without his stir (1.3.144-5). But later he forgets about it.

Before rashly imagining murder as the only way to a throne, Macbeth has rashly interpreted the Witches' hailings as true signs of his future. Otherwise, he will not be so rapt and he will not try to make the "imperial theme" come true. Why should he take the hailing signs as true? This is a problem of "depth psychology," perhaps. According to David Bleich, every act of interpreting an utterance is a *conferring* of meaning. Hence one's interpretation is the display of one's desire.

As a renowned thane newly victorious in battles, Macbeth must have thought of his greater future and may have stirred up the "imperial theme" in his subconscious ego at least. So the Witches' hailings are but clear sounds complying with his psychic drive. Lady Macbeth construes that he does have the ambition to be great. Accordingly, we may say, Macbeth's rash interpreting the hailings as true signs of his future is derived from his deep, ambitious desire. And that rashness has set going the entire course of his tragedy.

Since Macbeth tends to believe in the Witches, he cannot but worry in the meantime about the prediction that Banquo will get kings. But in interpreting this prediction, Macbeth shows his rashness again. "To get kings" immediately means "to beget kings" to him. And from that interpretation he rashly jumps to the conclusion that he must kill Banquo and his son Fleance if he is to keep his throne, considering that he and Lady Macbeth have no child to succeed as his heir. In point of fact, if Macbeth can interpret the prediction otherwise, making "to get kings" mean, for instance, "to be given kings," or "to win kings," or "to provide kings," etc., he will not suspect Banquo and Banquo's son so jealously and hostilely as to ruin himself.

Macbeth's habit of interpreting signs rashly on the basis of his own desire is seen again and again. When Duncan pronounces Malcolm his heir, Macbeth immediately envisages a step on which he must fall down or else overleap (1.4.48-9). When Duncan shows his intention to come and visit Macbeth's castle, Lady Macbeth immediately interprets this news as Macbeth's chance to murder Duncan and become king himself, using the raven's hoarse croaking as foretelling "the fatal entrance of Duncan" under their battlements (1.5.38-9). Macbeth obviously has the same interpretation since he agrees to "beguile the time" and put the night's "great business" into his wife's dispatch (1.5.63-8).

Just as Lady Macbeth along with her Lord interprets rashly Duncan's coming to their Inverness castle as Macbeth's good chance to murder Duncan and become king himself, so Macbeth interprets rashly Banquo and Banquo's son's coming to attend their Forres banquet as his good chance to root out the threats to his throne. Consequently he employs some murderers to kill them on their way out for riding before the banquet time. The result, as we know, is: Banquo is murdered but Fleance has escaped. And this result becomes immediately a sign that Macbeth cannot prevent his destiny. So he utters, "Then comes my fit again... I am cabined, cribbed, confined, bound in / To saucy doubts and fears" (3.4.20-4). It is in such a mood that he decides to go the next day to the Weird Sisters for more directions.

The Weird Sisters' directions are, of course, the Apparitions' misleading predictions made for the purpose that Macbeth "shall spurn fate, scorn death, and bear / His hopes 'bove wisdom, grace, and fear" (3.5.30-1). The predictions that Macbeth cannot be killed by a man born of woman and that he cannot be vanquished unless Great Birnam wood moves to Dunsinane hill do lead Macbeth to the quick interpretation that he is really unconquerable. Hence his bold act and final despair in combat with Macduff.

Before he meets Macduff in the battlefield, he hears Macduff has fled to England. The news immediately leads Macbeth to the conclusion that he has to act promptly. Hence his decision: "From this moment, / The very firstlings of my heart shall be / The firstlings of my hand" (4.2.146-8). And hence his surprise attack of Macduff's castle, his seizure upon Fife, his slaughter of Macduff's entire household, and his final downfall.

Macbeth has often been compared with Hamlet, seeing that the two heroes have similarities and dissimilarities. Harold Goddard has asserted that as "imaginative brothers," Macbeth and Hamlet are different in that "Macbeth begins more or less where Hamlet left off" (8), implying that one is active while the other is thoughtfully hesitant. Franco Moretti and Alessandro Serpieri have the same opinion when they say "Macbeth is pulled along by the logic of his first act; Hamlet continually postpones such an act" (65). In truth, Macbeth and Hamlet are both conscientious at times and therefore are both occasionally hesitant in performing certain acts. However, Macbeth's hasty habit of interpretation stands in high relief with Hamlet's tardy habit of interpretation. For all his disgust at his mother's speedy remarriage with his uncle, Hamlet does not rashly interpret the words of his father's ghost as all true, and so he seeks to verify them by pretending madness and designing a pantomime show. In contrast, Macbeth almost always interprets signs, including the Witches' words, immediately as true signs in line with his own desire. Ironically, of course, both heroes come to a tragic end, one for his hasty, another for his tardy, habit of interpretation.

Regarding Macbeth's tragic flaw, Wayne Booth has had a good analysis worth quoting in full:

> On one level it could, of course, be said that he errs simply in being overambitious and underscrupulous. But this is only partly true. What allows him to sacrifice his moral beliefs to his ambition is a mistake of another kind. ...Macbeth knows what he is doing, yet he does not know. He knows the immorality of the act, but he has no conception of the effects of the act on himself or on his surroundings. Accustomed to murder of a "moral" sort, in battle, and having valorously and successfully "carv'd out his passage" with "bloody execution" many times previously, he misunderstands completely what will be the devastating effect on his own character if he tries to carve out his passage in civil life. The murder of Duncan on one level resembles closely the kind of thing Macbeth has done professionally, and he lacks the insight to see the great difference between the two kinds of murder. (99)

So, for Booth, Macbeth's flaw lies in ignorance, rather than in ambition. After a good elaboration on this theme, Booth concludes that Macbeth's tragic error is at least threefold:

> *He does not understand the forces working upon him to make*
> *him commit the deed, neither his wife nor the weird sisters; he*
> *does not understand the differences between "bloody execution"*
> *in civilian life and in his past military life; and he does not*
> *understand his own character—he does not know what will be*
> *the effects of the evil act on his own future happiness. (100)*

I think Booth is right. But is it not right, too, that ignorance combined with ambition has bred rashness in Macbeth's character, which directly leads him to hasty interpretations and unscrupulous acts? In trying to justify his killing the grooms who are supposed to have killed Duncan, Macbeth confesses that "The expedition of my violent love / Outrun the pauser, reason" (2.3.113-4). This is an intentional confession of his rashness. Nevertheless, rashness certainly *is* his tragic flaw. This flaw, to be sure, is a typical flaw of tragic heroes from Oedipus onwards. In Macbeth's case, however, we find his rashness is primarily in his interpreting signs, not in his doing deeds.

VII. The Semiotic Vision

So far we have pointed out the following facts about *Macbeth*: First, it can be regarded as a play about signs or signification. Second, equivocation is a special kind of signification and equivocal signs are rampant in *Macbeth*. Third, the play's equivocators are not limited to the Witches, much wine, etc.—those clearly referred to in the text. Macbeth and his lady are in fact two other main equivocators. Fourth, equivocation is the act of producing dual signs, of making ambiguities. In *Macbeth*, six distinctive types of ambiguities (lexical vs. syntactical, verbal vs. situational, and intentional vs. affective ambiguities) are found working here and there effectively with the characters. Fifth, the play is filled with so many ambiguities that one can think the play is a battlefield not only of soldiers with weapons but also of equivocators with ambiguous signs. Sixth, Macbeth's greatest tragic flaw lies in his rash habit of interpreting signs in accordance with his desire.

Meanwhile, we have also pointed out some semiotic truths significant for our further study. A sign, we see, is anything standing for something else and a word is just a verbal sign among numerous other sorts of signs used in the process of communication. A sign, we also know, is divisible into signifier and signified, and the relation between them is arbitrary. Therefore, it is possible to use the same signifier in one's *parole* to signify different concepts. When a sign standing for an object comes to one's consciousness, however, one often produces an *interpretant* in one's mind, no matter whether the sign is an icon or an index or a symbol (according to Peirce's classification). The *interpretant* can assume many different forms; in fact, it can be anything associated with the perceived sign. In consequence, very often the *interpretant* is based not on the meaning but on the significance of the sign. And thus very often equivocal or dual signs can be employed purposely to render ambiguities so as to lead people into certain *interpretants* with widely different significances.

Now, if we consider *Macbeth* in the light of these semiotic truths, what can we find? A. P. Rossiter affirms that the theme of *Macbeth* "is not ambition, or sin, or guilt merely; but rather the equivocal nature of Nature" (219). Indeed, we have found that the weather, the time, the season, the heath, the court, the characters, the speeches, the acts, practically everything and everybody in the play can be felt equivocal in one way or another. This equivocal nature of Nature naturally leads one to call the *Macbeth*-world a "predominantly nocturnal" world, and the play a "dream play" (McElroy 209), since it is so dark, so unclear, and so uncertain in so many aspects. Yet, we must know that equivocation is a special kind of signification, a way of maneuvering signs for the purpose of ambiguity. Who, then, is responsible for the equivocal nature of Nature in the *Macbeth*-world? We admit that the Weird Sisters and the Macbeths are the main equivocators. But who makes them equivocators? The answer may be "Hecate" or "God" or "Heaven knows." Anyway, it seems that in Shakespeare's vision, the *Macbeth*-world (or actually any world where power struggle is involved) is a world of signs in which persons and things alike are made mutual equivocators, that is, they can be ambiguous or dual signs to one another since in the course of communication they can each produce intentional ambiguities and receive affective ambiguities on the basis of variable interpretants in accordance with significant variations in the equivocators' external situations or inner drives.

In this world of signs, we have certainly found the Witches trying all the time to "Double, double toil and trouble" (4.1.10). Their "supernatural solicitings" together with the phantoms they produce (the Apparitions with a bloody child, a crowned child, a show of eight kings, etc.) may be signs representing the devil's will or at least a certain supernatural being's will. The weather, the time, the season, the places, the strange happenings (unruly night with chimneys blown down, strange screams of death, feverous shaking earth, etc.), the paradoxical realities (a battle is lost and won, a farmer hangs himself on the expectation of plenty, to do harm is laudable and to do good is accounted dangerous folly, etc.), the hearsay omens (moving stones, speaking trees, etc.)—all abnormal things seem to be cooperative signs coming to support the supernatural will. On the other hand, we have also found the Macbeths trying to "make our faces vizards to our hearts" (4.2.34) because "False face must hide what the false heart doth know" (1.7.83), while Donalbain knows "There's daggers in men's smiles" (2.4.138), and Malcolm has to pretend to be a vicious prince. In fact, all characters have their own wills, and they have been making signs and interpreting signs in order that they may have their own ways to fulfill their own wills. When the little son of Macduff tells his mother that if his father were dead, she'd weep for him; if she would not, it were a good sign that he should quickly have a new father (4.2.60-3), the child has poignantly made an ambiguous remark on the relation between one's will and the sign one makes. The "new" father may be the old one (the returned Macduff) or someone else the mother has newly married. Anyway, the ambiguous relationship between the mother's will and her outward sign is like that between a king and his subject, or indeed that between any two people. It is only that a man or a woman's will, like the child's, often cannot be fulfilled, no matter what signs may have been employed to uphold it, since a human will seems to be superseded at times by Heaven's will which manifests itself in all natural and supernatural signs. It follows, therefore, that in Shakespeare's vision, there are human signs and there are non-human signs (i.e., natural and supernatural signs) in the world; as human wills interact with Heaven's will, human signs also interact with non-human signs, so much so that equivocation or ambiguity becomes inevitable.

Schopenhauer, as we know, maintains that "the desires and drives of men, as well as the forces of nature, are manifestations of a single will, specifically the will to live, which is the essence of the world" (Benét 906). This will to live, in effect, can be further divided into the will to power and the will to sex, as power and sex are the two primary means to guarantee survival. In *Macbeth*, superficially the will to power appears to dominate all scenes, since the main characters have been struggling for supreme power. Accordingly, the natural and supernatural signs as well as the human signs including the Macbeths' contrived words and deeds have been interpreted politically as related to the theme of ambition. In actuality, however, the will to sex is as strong as the will to power in *Macbeth*. Evidence of this can be seen in the fact that a good number of "innocent" terms in the play do bear a heavily sexual charge. Ralph Berry has given us many examples, including such phrases or lines as "black and deep desires" (1.4.51),

"And his great love, sharp as his spur, hath holp him / To his home before us" (1.6.23-4), "I am settled, and bend up / Each corporal agent to this terrible feat" (1.7.80-1), "Hold, take my sword. There's husbandry in Heaven / Their candles are all out" (II, i, 45), "Tarquin's ravishing strides" (2.1.55), "That which hath made them drunk hath made me bold; / What hath quench'd them hath given me fire" (2.2.1-2), "You do unbend your noble strength, to think /So brainsickly of things" (2.2.45-6), "retire we to our chamber: / A little water clears us of this deed" (2.2.66-7), "And when we have our naked frailties hid, / That suffer in exposure" (2.3.132-3), "Nought's had, all's spent, / Where our desire is got without content" (3.2.4-5), "Come, we'll to sleep. My strange and self-abuse / Is the initiate fear that wants hard use; / We are yet but young in deed" (3.4.142-4), and "To bed, to bed! there's knocking at the gate. / Come, come, come, come, give me your hand. / What's done cannot be undone, To bed, to bed, to bed" (5.1.62-4).[3] Indeed, the killing of Duncan is the doing away of the phallic symbol. Lady Macbeth has been wishing her lord to be a brave "man," accusing him of being "unmanned," and fearing he might lose his "manliness." Subconsciously she has confused "murder" with "mating," and politics with sex. To echo his lady's fear, Macbeth fears to hold the dagger, the phallic symbol, in reality or in imagination, to do the deed. He confesses that he has no "spur" to "prick" the horse, which is his intent to become king. In fact, he is overridden by his "unsexed" Lady Macbeth, the nightmarish mare that chides and chews him to urge him on and on. Terence Hawkes is right in stating that in this play "Murder is to politics what lechery is to love and equivocation is to language" (153). Sexual signs and political signs are hardly distinguishable in many ambiguous cases.

Since Macbeth and his lady often err in making hasty interpretations of equivocal signs, and since the signs they themselves make cannot convince others of their innocence nor actually pacify their own conscience, their will cannot but be frustrated. When they meet their tragic end, however, they cannot reflect upon their own flaw. Instead, while Lady Macbeth becomes a neurotic case betraying herself with signs of mental illness before she commits suicide, Macbeth imputes his failure to the equivocal nature of signs and indeed to the lack of sense in signs after he suffers from similar neurotic tension on some occasions. We can easily understand why he should blame the "juggling fiends" for paltering with us in a double sense. We can understand, too, why he should come to the nihilistic conclusion that life is a tale told by an idiot signifying nothing.

It is to be remembered that immediately after killing Duncan Macbeth says, "... from this instant, / There's nothing serious in mortality; /All is but toys: renown, and grace, is dead; / The wine of life is drawn, and the mere lees / Is left this vault to brag of" (2.3.90-4). These words are intentionally ambiguous, thus leading Donalbain to ask, "What is amiss?" (95). In effect, these words foreshadow Macbeth's habit of nullifying signs at a critical moment. To say "nothing serious," "but toys," "mere lees," etc., is as much as to say "no inherent value." Later, when Macbeth hears of his lady's death, all the poetic lines from "Tomorrow, and tomorrow, and tomorrow" to "Signifying nothing" are uttered in the same vein. To say "dusty death," "walking shadow," "tale told by an idiot," etc., is likewise to emphasize the lack of sense in life as a composite of signs. Accordingly, Terry Eagleton is right in saying that Macbeth "ends up chasing an identity which continually eludes him; he becomes a floating signifier in ceaseless, doomed pursuit of an anchoring signified" (3). And Malcolm Evans is also right in claiming that the "nothing" signified "is not merely an absence but a delirious plenitude of selves and meanings" (117). In Shakespeare's vision, in other words, an equivocal person like Macbeth, when facing a plenitude of signs with a plenitude of ambiguous meanings, is liable to get lost, thus ironically maintaining that no sign signifies anything at all, that "nothing is, but what is not."

Shakespeare is no semiotician. But from a semiotic study of *Macbeth* as shown above, we can certainly see the poet's semiotic vision: it is a world in which we are all signs inhabiting signs (to modify Emerson's "We are symbols, and inhabit symbols"), in which signs are weapons or tools used to fulfill people's wills or desires in terms of power or sex, in which equivocal or dual signs are common and ambiguities are prevailing, and in which, nevertheless, signs are easily seen through in frustration, and thus easily become mere floating signifiers mated with no stable signified or *interpretant*.

In Shakespeare's semiotic vision, in fact, there are always so many Macbeths in the world. Each Macbeth is a "son of Beth." As "beth" is the second letter of the Hebrew alphabet, each "son of Beth" seems to be a person with "the second's complex." He has the feeling of being regrettably just the second in position, and yet he has the ambition to become the first. When such a "son of Beth" is only second-rate in wisdom, he simply cannot deal well with his complex world of equivocal signification. Consequently, each Macbeth, mated with his barren Lady Macbeth, can only find that he himself is a ham actor strutting and fretting his hour upon the stage full of sound and fury signifying nothing.

Notes

1. Hereinafter the parenthesized numbers of the acts, scenes, and lines of the quoted text refer to the Arden Edition of *Macbeth* edited by Kenneth Muir.
2. The two parenthesized numbers of Peirce's work indicate the volume and the paragraph (not the page) numbers.
3. For a better understanding of the sexual implications in words like these, see Rubinstein's *Dictionary of Shakespeare's Sexual Puns and Their Significance*.

Works Consulted

Benét, William Rose. *The Reader's Encyclopedia.* 2nd ed. New York: Harper & Row, 1965.

Berry, Ralph. *Shakespearean Structures.* London: Macmillan, 1981.

Bishop, T. G. "Reconsidering a Folio Reading in *Macbeth 5.1.*" *Shakespeare Quarterly.* Vol. 46, No. 1, 1995 (Spring). 76-79.

Bleich, David. *Subjective Criticism.* Baltimore & London: Johns Hopkins UP, 1978.

Bloom, Harold, ed. *William Shakespeare's* Macbeth. Modern Critical Interpretations. New York: Chelsea House, 1987.

——, ed. *Macbeth.* Major Literary Characters. New York: Chelsea House, 1991.

Booth, Wayne C. "Macbeth as Tragic Hero." In Bloom, 91-101.

Brooks, Cleanth. " 'The Naked Babe" and the Cloak of Manliness." *Shakespeare: Macbeth.* Ed. John Wain. London: Macmillan, 1994. 192-210.

Campbell, Lily B. *Shakespeare's Tragic Heroes: Slaves of Passion.* Gloucester, MS: Peter Smith, 1973.

De Saussure, Ferdinand. *Course in General Linguistics.* Trans. W. Baskin. London: Fontana/Collins, 1974.

Doloff, Steven. "Macbeth's Season of Imperception." *Shakespeare Quarterly.* Vol. 40, No. 3, 1989 (Fall). 328-329.

Eagleton, Terry. *William Shakespeare.* Oxford: Basil Blackwell, 1986.

Eco, Umberto. *A Theory of Semiotics.* Bloomington: Indiana UP, 1976.

Empson, William. *Essays on Shakespeare.* Ed. David B. Pirie. Cambridge: Cambridge UP, 1986.

Evans, Malcolm. *Signifying Nothing: Truth's True Contents in Shakespeare's Text.* Brighton, Sussex: The Harvester Press, 1986.

Fiske, John. *Introduction to Communication Studies.* 2nd Ed. London & New York: Routledge, 1990.

Goddard, Harold C. "Macbeth." In Bloom, 5-37.

Hawkes, Terence. *Shakespeare's Talking Animals: Language and Drama in Society.* London: Edward Arnold, 1973.

Hussey, S. S. *The Literary Language of Shakespeare.* 2nd ed. Essex: Longman Group UK, 1992.

Knight, G. Wilson. *The Wheel of Fire: Interpretations of Shakespearean Tragedies.* London & New York: Methuen, 1949.

——. *The Imperial Theme: Further Interpretations of Shakespearean Tragedies.* London & New York: Methuen, 1951.

Knights, L. C. *Some Shakespearean Themes and an Approach to "Hamlet."* Stanford, CA: Stanford UP, 1959.

Lukacher, Ned. *Daemonic Figures: Shakespeare and the Question of Conscience.* Ithaca & London: Cornell UP, 1994.

Mack, Maynard, Jr. "The Voice in the Sword." In Bloom, 59-89.

Mahood, M. M. *Shakespeare's Wordplay.* London & New York: Routledge, 1957.

McElroy, Bernard. *Shakespeare's Mature Tragedies.* Princeton: Princeton UP, 1973.

Moretti, France & Alessandro Serpieri. "The Great Eclipse: Tragic Form as the Deconstruction of Sovereignty." *Shakespearean Tragedy.* Ed. John Drakakis. London & New York: Longman, 1992. 45-83.

Muir, Kenneth, ed. *Macbeth.* The Arden Shakespeare. London & New York: Methuen, 1962.

Nosworthy, James M. "Macbeth, Doctor Faustus, and the Juggling Fiends." *Mirror Up to Nature.* Ed. J. C. Gray. Toronto: U of Toronto P, 1984. 218-222.

Peirce, Charles Sanders. *Collected Papers of Charles Sanders Peirce.* 8 vols. Ed. Charles Hartshorne & Paul Weiss. Bristol: Thoemmes, 1998.

Pye, Christopher. *The Regal Phantasm: Shakespeare and the Politics of Spectacle.* London & New York: Routledge, 1990.

Riffaterre, Michael. *Semiotics of Poetry.* Bloomington & London: Indiana UP, 1978.

Rossiter, A. P. *Angel with Horns: Fifteen Lectures on Shakespeare.* London & New York: Longman, 1989.

Rubinstein, Frankie. *A Dictionary of Shakespeare's Sexual Puns and Their Significance.* 2nd ed. London: Macmillan, 1989.

Todorov, Tzvetan. *Theories of the Symbol.* Trans. Catherine Porter. Oxford: Basil Blackwell, 1977.

* This chapter first appeared as a paper in 1998 in National Chung Hsing University's *Journal of Humanities*, Vol. 32-1, pp. 195-222.

• Chapter 4 •

The "Strange Eruption" in *Hamlet*: Shakespeare's Psychoanalytic Vision

I. An Individual or a Species?

It is well-known that Samuel Johnson praises Shakespeare as " above all writers, at least above all modern writers, the poet of nature, the poet that holds up to his readers a faithful mirror of manners and of life" (Adams 330). In this praise, as we know, Johnson alludes to Hamlet's statement that the end of playing "was and is to hold as it were the mirror up to nature" (3.2.21-22).[1] In Hamlet's mind, and presumably in Shakespeare's as well, stage presentation must be true to life: "to show virtue her feature, scorn her own image, and the very age and body of the time his form and pressure" (3.2.22-24). In other words, faithful imitation of humanity and the world is the basic principle of art for Hamlet, Shakespeare, and Johnson.

But this mimetic theory has one particular problem when applied to the study of Hamlet's own character. It is obvious that when Hamlet in the play or Johnson in his Preface to *Shakespeare* talks of "nature," the word refers to human nature rather than to the great external nature so extolled by the Romantics later on. Furthermore, it refers mostly to such observable manners of life as able to embody the nature of one's virtue, vice, or folly. For Johnson, especially, the observable manners are not "particular manners" which "can be known to few, and therefore few only can judge how nearly they are copied" (Adams 330). Shakespeare's characters, Johnson asserts,

> *are not modified by the customs of particular places, unpracticed by the rest of the world; by the peculiarities of studies or professions, which can operate but upon small numbers; or by the accidents of transient fashions or temporary opinions: they are the genuine progeny of common humanity, such as the world will always supply and observation will always find. (Adams 330)*

Therefore, Johnson concludes, "in the writings of other poets a character is too often an individual: in those of Shakespeare it is commonly a species" (Adams 330).

Now, is Hamlet an individual or a species? Does Johnson mean to hold that Hamlet is an inactive type of person when he says that "Hamlet is, through the whole play, rather an instrument than an agent" (Hoy 147)? Or does he agree with most critics that Hamlet is an enigma, a puzzling individual whose conduct is largely without "poetical probability" (Hoy 147)?

For me it makes no significant difference to call Hamlet an individual or a species. What counts is whether or not Shakespeare has created a Hamlet whose behavior is explicable according to our knowledge of human nature, and whether or not this Hamlet's life and character can verify the particular vision that Shakespeare might have in this drama.

II. The Psychoanalytic Ideas

Hamlet has been an enigma, indeed, to the other characters in the play and to Shakespearean critics. His "antic disposition" (1.5.180) has been puzzling to people around him. His speech and his behavior often seem inscrutable. Even today, critics are still arguing about his personality. Is he simply a man with "an extreme sensibility of mind" (Mackenzie 149) or "an intellectual given to reason and reflection" (Knights 66) or a man "whose sense of moral excellence is uncommonly exquisite" (Richardson 147) or "a great moralizer ...marked by refinement of thought and sentiment" (Hazlitt 164-5)? Why has he kept delaying his vengeance on Claudius? Why should he seem so cruel to Ophelia? Puzzled by such questions, critics seem to have found no easy way out except probing into Hamlet's "deep psychology."

Talking of "deep psychology," one instantly thinks of today's psychoanalysis, and Freud's and Ernest Jones's connecting Hamlet with the Oedipus complex instantly comes to our mind. But we must admit that Shakespeare was born in an age when Freudian concepts were foreign or non-existing to him. As a Renaissance playwright, Shakespeare was most probably affected by the theory of the four humors. And, as A. C. Bradley has vigorously argued, Hamlet's case can be taken to be that of melancholy: "It would be absurdly unjust to call *Hamlet* a study of melancholy, but it contains such a study" (103).

Still, to impute Hamlet's tragedy to his melancholy character is an old-fashioned and not so "scientific" a way of analyzing his personality. Although Shakespeare certainly did not have any scholastic contact with our modern "deep psychology," we may still assume that his understanding of human nature or human psychology can possibly lead him to write a play with its characterization and action interpretable in terms of today's psychoanalysis.

Since Jones's Freudian interpretation, Hamlet seems to have been fixed up as a case of the Oedipus complex and as a personality "unconsciously identified with Claudius" (1983, 37). But is Jones's interpretation all plausible? Does it truly reflect Shakespeare's psychoanalytic vision? It is my contention that we now need a new psychoanalytic interpretation of *Hamlet* if we want to do justice to

Shakespeare. And this new interpretation will involve, at least, the technical terms mentioned below, in addition to the "Oedipus complex."

First, Freud's emphasis upon the *unconscious* aspects in contrast with the *conscious* aspects of the human psyche is still very useful.[2] Next, his idea of three psychic zones (the *Id*, the *Ego*, and the *Super-Ego*) can still be adapted for our present interpretation. We may doubt his assertion that all human behavior is motivated ultimately by sexuality. Yet, we may allow the idea that *libido*, or sexual energy, is a prime psychic force. Finally, we must recognize that the unconscious process may take place through *condensation* or *displacement*, and repressed desires are often expressed through the use of female (*yonic*) symbols and male (*phallic*) symbols.[3]

Besides these Freudian concepts, we also need some Jungian ideas. First, we can believe with him in the existence of the *collective unconscious*, not just that of the *personal conscious* and the *personal unconscious*. Next, we can also agree that the collective unconscious is not directly approachable; it is often found in *archetypes* (e.g., the hero, the scapegoat, the Devil, the Good Mother, the Unfaithful Wife, etc.). Then, we may accept the *shadow*, the *anima / animus*, and the *persona* as the three essential archetypes that compose the self. Finally, we may also use the idea of *projection* and that of *individuation*.[4]

After Freud and Jung, Lacan develops a psychoanalytic system of his own, based on linguistic or structuralist / poststructuralist theories. Available for us here are the three Orders he proposes to describe our tripartite personality: the *Imaginary Order* (the preverbal stage, centered in the mother), the *Symbolic Order* (the stage dominated by linguistic differences and ruled by the "Law of the Father"), and the *Real Order* (a stage beyond language, either preceding it or exceeding it).[5] Aside from this Lacanian proposal, the idea of *jouissance* which Lacan shares with Roland Barthes, Judith Butler, Richard Middleton, and others is also useful. It is the enjoyment or bliss that "gets you off," the "orgasmic rapture found in texts, films, works of art or sexual spheres," and it is "intrinsically self-shattering, disruptive of a 'coherent self.'"[6]

III. War and Woman

Shakespeare is a Renaissance dramatist. Renaissance is an age of humanist revival. Humanism is based on the understanding that a man is a man. It understands that occupying the middle link of the Great Chain of Being, man is no God and no Devil, though he aspires to be angelic and tends to become bestial at times. In other words, Shakespeare's Renaissance humanist spirit makes him face the Ego naturally, though his religious nurture teaches him to regard highly the Super-Ego and despise the Id at the same time. When Johnson criticizes that Shakespeare "sacrifices virtue to convenience, and is so much more careful to please than to instruct that he seems to write without any moral purpose" (Adams 333), he is telling us that the playwright is more on the side of the Hellenistic culture of humanism, letting loose our libido, than on the side of the Hebraic culture of asceticism, practicing to repress our desires.

Now, the best-known work of the Hellenistic culture is Homer's *Iliad*. *Iliad* is about the Trojan War. The War is for the sake of Helen. This shows that sexuality is indeed presumably the ultimate motivation of human warfare. We know the mythological gods and goddesses are all anthropomorphic. They represent mankind's desires, hopes, aspirations, etc. How many of us would not like to become the omnipotent Zeus? Yet, what does Zeus do? He seems to be philandering all the time: only loving to love and seeking for sex.

In the world of beasts, we see so many males keep "waging war" for females, just as the gods or human heroes do: he-goats fighting for she-goats, bucks battling for does, etc. This tells us that animals are forever struggling for procreation, and a particular female or some females often become, for a group of males, the target(s) worth combating for in order to win the right of mating. No matter whether the war is carried on for the immediate pleasure of sex or for the final end of survival through procreation, the female is in effect the anima, the symbolic force that attracts the males to it, just as Helen attracted the warring heroes.

In *Hamlet*, we are told that King Hamlet had a combat with Fortinbras of Norway, and won from him his lands after slaying him. Young Fortinbras then wished to avenge his father and recover the lands. But the King of Norway, uncle to young Fortinbras, curbed his invasion into Denmark. Later, young Fortinbras went on a campaign against the Polack through the dominions of Denmark. The campaign was said to "gain a little patch of ground / That hath in it no profit but the name" (4.4.18-19). But it turned out that when young Fortinbras returned victorious from Poland, the kingdom of Denmark, with the deaths of Claudius, Hamlet, Gertrude and others, was left to return to Fortinbras.

This background story seems to suggest that human beings are warlike and combatant animals, they constantly combat for lands or war for names, they often fight in the name of revenge, but lands or names may be gained without active vengeance. Underneath this suggestion, however, there is this truth: to have lands or names is to have the power to own the necessary resources for survival, including the dear women for men. In actuality, to combat or to war is to exercise our libido, and to revenge is but to fix a target for the exercise. In *Hamlet*, there is a war of revenge between Hamlet and Claudius. They fight for Gertrude. There is another war of revenge between Hamlet and Laertes. They fight for Ophelia. Superficially, on the level of the conscious, Gertrude is Hamlet's mother and Ophelia is Laertes' sister. Deep down there in the realm of the unconscious, however, Gertrude is no other than Ophelia: either is but a dear woman, an exciting anima to rouse one's libido.

So, I agree with those critics who do not take *Hamlet* for a revenge tragedy in the line of Thomas Kyd's *Spanish Tragedy*, which is just the story of a sensational slaughter in the name of revenge for one's own son or for any one murdered, and just a display of the revenger's art in carrying out his plan of vengeance. But I do not think that "*Hamlet* towers above other plays of its kind through the heroism and nobility of its hero" (Gardner 224). Instead, I think that it is just a typical play of its kind through its involving the "deep psychology" of war and woman. And I believe the central problem of *Hamlet* is sexuality although the play can be "on all kinds of problems: on fathers and children, on sex, on drunkenness, on suicide, on mortality and corruption, on ingratitude and loyalty, on acting, on handwriting even, on fate, on man and the universe" (Harrison 1968, 884).

IV. Appearance vs. Reality

Appearance vs. reality is verifiably a recurrent motif in Shakespeare. In his great tragedies especially, we find, the motif has become a predominant element in characterization and plot. In *King Lear*, for instance, we have the children who appear to be filial (Goneril, Regan, Edmund) vs. those who are truly filial (Cordelia, Edgar), the Fool who appears to be foolish but is wise in reality, and the King, of course, who appears to have power but actually has nothing to keep even his dignity and life. Indeed, the tragedy is a history of two fathers finding, at last, their "real" children (Lear finding Cordelia, and Gloucester finding Edgar) and a king coming to know his "true" subjects (Lear coming to know Gloucester, Albany,

Kent, the Fool, etc.). In *Othello*, we have the "honest Iago," who is honest only in name, not in truth, and who throughout the play tries to appear friendly, benevolent, loyal and kind to Othello and others while in reality he acts most like a Machiavellian schemer or the Devil's incarnation. And the play is a history of how Iago's true character, as well as Othello's, is found out. In *Macbeth*, we have the Witches who seem to bring good tidings and predict good future, but actually things just prove to be the opposite; we have the brave Macbeth who seems to be loyal at first but proves to be a traitor at last and who seems to win at first but is only to lose at last; and we have so many words and situations in the play which seem to be clear on the surface but actually ambiguous in depth.

Now, in *Hamlet* we find the appearance vs. reality motif occurs even more frequently. Claudius only appears to be good to Hamlet, Gertrude is a "most seeming-virtuous queen" (1.5.46), Rosencrantz and Guildenstern are actually spies on Hamlet rather than his friendly schoolmates, and Hamlet is "but mad north-north-west" (2.2.375), not truly mad beyond knowing a hawk from a handsaw. Hamlet himself is most aware of the discrepancy between appearance and reality. He reminds Ophelia that "God hath given you one face, and you make yourselves another" (3.1.144-5). He wants Horatio to join judgments in censure of Claudius's "seeming" (3.2.86-7). And he sighs to his schoolmates:

> *What piece of work is a man, how noble in reason, how infinite in faculties, in form and moving how express and admirable, in action how like an angel, in apprehension how like a god: the beauty of the world, the paragon of animals—and yet, to me, what is this quintessence of dust? (2.2.303-8)*

Hamlet is indeed most aware of "the evil reality under the good appearance" (Spencer 39).

Evidently, the play is full of ideas, images, episodes as well as characters that can suggest the appearance / reality contrast. In his "The World of *Hamlet*," Maynard Mack has discussed the ideas of seeming, assuming, and putting on; the images of clothing, painting, mirroring; the episode of the dumb show and the play within the play, together with the characters of Polonius, Laertes, Ophelia, Claudius, Gertrude, Rosencrantz and Guildenstern, and Hamlet. His conclusion is: "all these at one time or another, and usually more than once, are drawn into the range of implications flung round the play by 'show'" (52).

The idea of "show" brings us to the Freudian concept of the conscious and unconscious levels of mental activity. In this concept, the human mind is structured like the iceberg: what is shown above or appears to be seen is the level of consciousness, while what lies hidden beneath the surface or what counts as its great real weight is the level of unconsciousness. If we consider the appearance vs. reality motif in the light of the conscious vs. unconscious psyche, we may find that *Hamlet* is indeed a show of the conscious Hamlet in conflict with the unconscious Hamlet.

V. Ham-let and Den-mark

Hamlet is, of course, not a dual personality like that of Dr. Jekyll and Mr. Hide. But his personality is certainly split into a conscious self and an unconscious self. He tells his mother: "I have that within which passeth show" (1.2.85). But does he know what that is?

Freud tells us that the Id is entirely unconscious. That is what often passes show. And what are often shown are parts of the Ego and the Super-Ego. Now, the Id is the reservoir of libido, the primary source of all psychic energy, and it functions to fulfill the pleasure principle whereas the Ego and the Super-Ego serve to check or repress the Id by observing the reality principle and the morality principle.

Now, the Ghost that appears to bid Hamlet avenge him is only apparently a ghost. He is in effect Hamlet's Super-Ego, the ethical part that makes his conscience and directs him to act in accordance with the moral principle. In the deep bottom, then, there is Claudius, who is Hamlet's Id, who acts according to the pleasure principle, and who must be checked or repressed by Hamlet's Super-Ego and Ego. But the difficulty is: facing two fathers (i.e., sources) of his inner psyche, Hamlet's Ego simply cannot annul either easily. At any critical moment, his reality principle can only tell him to hesitate between the two forces. So, Hamlet's inactivity or delay in taking vengeance is the effect of his being pulled at the same time by his own Super-Ego as a good angel and his own Id as a bad angel, rather than due to the fact that the conscious call of duty to kill his stepfather is in conflict with "the unconscious call of his nature to kill his mother's husband, whether this is the first or the second" (Jones 1976, 90).

Critics have found that Shakespeare is notoriously fond of word play. But as far as I know, no critic has as yet noticed the meaningful reference to hams in Hamlet's reply to Polonius's question about what he is reading:

> *Slanders, sir. For the satirical rogue says here that old men have gray beards, that their faces are wrinkled, their eyes purging thick amber and plum-tree gum, and that they have a plentiful lack of wit, together with most weak hams—all which, sir, though I most powerfully and potently believe, yet I hold it not honesty to have it thus set down. For yourself, sir, shall grow old as I am—if like a crab you could go backward. (2.2.196-204)*

Here, the phrase "most weak hams" suggests impotence, of course. An old man like Polonius may already be suffering from "most weak hams" and may have become impotent at times in sexual intercourse. But does a man as young as Hamlet feel that he has "most weak hams," too?

No direct mention of Hamlet's sexual power is made in the play, and we can believe that he is not yet impotent, even with all his ambiguous attitude towards Ophelia. But the name "Hamlet" may suggest not only a "hamlet," a group of houses or a small village in the country; it may also suggest a "ham-let," a little ham which is not yet strong or powerful enough to counteract the strength of the great hams that his two fathers possess.

As we know, the original source of *Hamlet* is F. de Belleforest's story *Le Cinquiesme Tome des Histoires Tragiques*. In that French story, the hero's name is Amleth.[7] We do not know for sure whether or not Shakespeare changed "Amleth" into "Hamlet" with any particular purpose. But the change does make it more liable for Freudian interpretation. As the name may suggest "a little ham," Hamlet can certainly be thought of as a man not yet strong enough to compete for sex, very like a young lion or young hart that is still unable to compete for the target lioness or hind. This Hamlet, in other words, may indeed be still suffering from the Oedipus complex with Gertrude as the target female, although he is said to be already thirty years of age.[8] In Hamlet's unconscious mind, Gertrude is still his love, but his ghost father and his stepfather (uncle father) are still keeping the woman, threatening to "castrate" or "kill" him if he dares to challenge the fatherly sovereignty.

Facing this situation, Hamlet's Ego naturally feels that he is torn between his Super-Ego and his Id. That is why he often feels that things are going out of joint. After hearing the Ghost's revelation, as we know, Hamlet concludes the first act of the play by saying: "The time is out of joint. O cursed spite, / That ever I was born to set it right" (1.5.196-7). This conclusion can easily lead critics to believe that Hamlet has the habit of amplifying his personal dilemma and acting as "bonesetter to the time," only to be sacrificed so as to "allow us the satisfaction and exaltation of tragic catharsis" (Brockbank 103 &115). Nevertheless, the agony Hamlet feels now, as we must admit, is but a continuation of the former feeling that made him wish that "this too too sullied flesh would melt, / Thaw and resolve itself into a dew" (1.2.129-30), a feeling caused by his mother's speedy remarriage.

In his unconscious psyche, we may suggest, Hamlet may be delighted with his father's death (crying out, "Now that he is gone, I am free to possess her"—now that Laius is gone, Oedipus can have Jocasta), although his father's image (sometimes in the form of a ghost) may still come back and haunt him: "My father—methinks I see my father... In my mind's eye" (1.2.183-5). But what a hindrance that has come immediately! Another father has replaced the dead one, and that so speedily! The little Ham's desire, his libido, has to be repressed all the same! What can he do now? Except complaining about the frailty of woman (1.2.146) and imagining the world as "an unweeded garden" with only "things rank and gross in nature" (1.2.135-6), what can Ham-let do?

He can agree with Marcellus that "Something is rotten in the state of Denmark" (1.4.90). Moreover, he can imagine "the time is out of joint": Denmark has become "Den-mark," just as he himself has become "Ham-let" again, owing to his mother's remarriage with Claudius. Indeed, in his imagination, here is a great Den, in which the leading mark is "a beast that wants discourse of reason" (1.2.150).

VI. Mad with Method

In Act I, Scene 2, when Claudius addresses the Prince of Denmark (or, rather, Den-mark) as "my cousin Hamlet, and my son," (1.2.64), Hamlet (or Ham-let) says (as an aside): "A little more than kin, and less than kind" (1.2.65).[9] This rejoinder has caused a number of discussions about the differences in sense between "kin" and "kind" (see the long note in Jenkins 434-5). In my psychoanalytic view, this immediate reply (a purposeful "slip") from the little Ham's inner soul has accurately described the mutual relationship between Claudius and Hamlet. Hamlet is indeed a little more than kin to Claudius: he is not just his cousin and his son as stated here, nor is he just his "chiefest courtier, cousin, and our son" (1.2.117) proclaimed elsewhere to be "the most immediate to our throne" (1.2.109). He is, in addition, his rival in love, his competitor for Gertrude, and his father's or his own Super-Ego's avenger for the target woman. On the other hand, Hamlet is certainly a little less than kind to Claudius, not because he is unkind to him but because he feels that although they are apparently of the same kind (a man with beastly desire to possess the woman), yet he is truly less of the kind: he is just a Ham-let, a little Ham with but "most weak hams," an impotent in the face of the potentate father, who is the Phallus, the powerful kind in terms of sex.

Thus, the little Ham is plunged into melancholy. Hamlet himself and Claudius, as well as Shakespearean critics (e.g. A. C. Bradley), have diagnosed Hamlet's case as that of melancholy (see 2.2 597 & 3.1.167). In his *Anatomy of Melancholy* Robert Burton (Shakespeare's contemporary) has dealt with various morbid mental states, and for him melancholy "embraced everything from raving lunacy to philosophical and occasional pessimism."[10] When we read through the play, we may surely find Hamlet lost, at times, in "raving lunacy" and "philosophical and occasional pessimism." And we may agree with Bradley that Hamlet's excess of reflection "is to be considered rather a symptom of his [melancholy] state than a cause of it" (93).

What, then, is the cause? The superficial (conscious) cause is, of course, "His father's death and our over-hasty marriage" (2.2.57), as Gertrude tells Claudius. But the deep (unconscious) cause should be the little Ham's libido, which shapes itself into an "ambition" to kill the father and own the mother, or a "bad dream" in which his first spiritual father wants him to slay his second corporeal father. This "ambition" or "bad dream," as defined in Hamlet's exchange of words with Rosencrantz and Guildenstern, is "but a shadow" or "a shadow's shadow" (2.2.260 & 262). And, in Jung's terminology, "shadow" represents "the dark, unattractive aspects of the self" which the individual's impulse rejects and projects on someone or something else (Dobie 68). In *Hamlet,* the "shadow" is seen in the abundant "images of sickness, disease or blemish of the body" and "the idea of an ulcer or tumor, as descriptive of the unwholesome condition of Denmark morally" (Spurgeon 316). And it is seen in Claudius, of course, as "a villain" (3.3.76 & 77). It is this shadow that makes "the goodly frame the earth" seem to Hamlet to be "a sterile promontory" (2.2.298-99). And it is this shadow, too, that drives him at last to kill Claudius as the "incestuous, murderous, damned Dane" (5.2.330). So, Claudius is ambivalently both Hamlet's Id and his shadow.

Thus, Hamlet is truly mad in his own way. And madness is truly "poor Hamlet's enemy" (5.2.235). His madness, as is his melancholy, is expressed in "raving lunacy" and "philosophical and occasional pessimism." But this madness is expressed not only as Hamlet's conscious self (Super-Ego and Ego) striving against his "shadow," but also as his unconscious self (libidinous Id) striving for his "anima," the life force that stops him from committing suicide. Hamlet's "anima" is, of course, his mother Gertrude. Yet, by "displacement" Ophelia has obviously become Gertrude's substitute. So, in his madness Hamlet will treat Ophelia as if she were Gertrude.

Polonius, as we know, says that "there is method" in Hamlet's madness (2.2.205). And Hamlet tells his mother that "I essentially am not in madness, / But mad in craft" (3.4.189-90). In fact, Hamlet's madness is more "like mad" when he is abandoned to his unconscious self. And that is when he is at the sight or at the thought of his anima, i.e., Gertrude or Ophelia. On the other hand, he may seem "not so mad" or "mad with method" or "mad in craft" when he is controlled by his conscious self. And that is when he is confronted with his

Super-Ego (his father), his shadow (his uncle father), or other male figures.

Hamlet certainly shows no sign of madness when he hears Horatio, Marcellus and Bernado's story about the ghost, and subsequently when he goes to hear the ghost's revelation. In fact, he is prudent enough to refuse to tell his friends what passed between him and the ghost, and discreet enough to force them to swear that they will reveal nothing of what they have seen.

In the face of Rosencrantz and Guildenstern, Hamlet is all circumspect. He immediately suspects that they are Claudius's spies. He taunts them with worldly wisdom, and finally contrives to save himself and send them to death, just as a wary and scheming man will do to his enemies.

Hamlet has the wits to arrange a performance of *The Murder of Gonzago* with some lines of his own inserted, to instruct the players in acting techniques, to privately set Horatio to watch the King's reaction to the play, and to succeed in testing the King's conscience.

It stands to reason that Hamlet rejects the idea of killing Claudius while he is praying with remorse. The excuse that he would then send him to heaven at such a moment of repentance is certainly from a sound practical mind. When finally he runs him through with a rapier and forces him to drink the poisoned liquor, he may be said to be "mad' with anger. But he is then in a situation demanding that righteous act of vengeance. Thus, no one will consider him a lunatic just for the final scene.

In other scenes when Hamlet meets other male figures, including Polonius, Laertes, Osric, the grave-diggers, etc., Hamlet is likewise sane enough to either make witty remarks or act sensibly, although he may occasionally and purposely display certain "madness with method." And it is sanity, too, that enables him to ponder over the question of "to be or not to be" or reflect upon his own inactivity when he is alone.

VII. Daggers and Death

When Hamlet faces Gertrude, the scene is quite otherwise. In the chamber scene, the Queen directly says, "Alas, he's mad" (3.4.106). She says so because Hamlet has been speaking "words like daggers" (3.4.94) to her and because he speaks to the reappearing ghost invisible to her, which seems to her to be "holding discourse with the incorporal air" (3.2.118).

In this scene Hamlet is mad, in actuality, like a male animal (say, a ram) mad in due time to mate with a female (ewe) and yet somehow made to repress his desire, only to stand by watching a stronger one tup her. Under such circumstances, since his hams are too weak to vie with the stronger one's (his stepfather's) and he cannot for the time being ram away the strong opponent, Hamlet naturally can only rave at the tupped one, using "words like daggers" to attack her, besides reviling the stronger one and imagining that morality (personified by the ghost father) is on his side.

There are many references of the dagger in Shakespeare.[11] The dagger can be a weapon used to kill a man (e.g. Duncan in *Macbeth* or Caesar in *Julius Caesar*). It can also be a weapon used to kill a woman (e.g. Juliet in *Romeo and Juliet* or Emilia in *Othello*). When a female is stabbed by a dagger, the "killing" may have a sexual implication. For, the dagger with its sharp-pointed length is admittedly a male or phallic symbol in linguistic usage as well as in Freudian psychology (see de Vries 126). In *Romeo and Juliet*, for instance, when Juliet finds that Romeo has poisoned himself, she stabs herself with Romeo's dagger, saying, "O happy dagger, / This is thy sheath. There rust, and let me die" (5.3.168-9). This utterance, for all its pathetic tone, does inadvertently carry with it the pleasure associated with sexual intercourse.

So, with the dagger as a phallic symbol, when Hamlet "speaks daggers" to his mother, he is symbolically tupping his ewe, thrusting her with his verbal penis, and fulfilling his dream of possessing her as his libido will unconsciously have him do or his madness will fanatically lead him to do, since he is not yet weaned from his Oedipus complex.

In Act III, Scene iii, after Polonius comes to inform Hamlet that the Queen will speak with him presently, Hamlet tells himself:

> *O heart, lose not thy nature. Let not ever*
> *The soul of Nero enter this firm bosom;*
> *Let me be cruel, not unnatural.*
> *I will speak daggers to her, but use none.*
> *My tongue and soul in this be hypocrites:*
> *How in my words somever she be shent,*
> *To give them seals never my soul consent. (384-90)*

Here the allusion to Nero is significant, for Nero put his mother Agrippina to death because she poisoned her husband, the emperor Claudius. Here Hamlet says that he will act differently from Nero. He will not use real daggers to kill his own mother. He will just "speak daggers" to let her "be shent." And he thinks that the act may "be cruel" but "not unnatural." It is only that his tongue and soul will then "be hypocrites," since they never really want to kill her.

But this soliloquy reveals more than this superficial interpretation. In terms of sexual psychology, what Hamlet reveals here is not just his conscious determination to "lose not thy nature" or to avoid being "unnatural," that is, to keep his instinctive affection (or filial love) for his mother. It is also an unconscious determination to bring forth his "natural" instinct of sex, to let go his libido, that is, to thrust the woman with his verbal dagger, if not with his real dagger or male organ for copulation. In other words, to be "natural" here can mean

135

both to consciously observe the moral principle (to look up to one's Super-Ego) and to unconsciously observe the pleasure principle (to give in to one's Id).

The famous "chamber scene" is preceded by the equally famous "nunnery scene," where Ophelia takes Gertrude's place to receive the thrusts and stabs of the little Ham's verbal dagger. There, similarly, Hamlet is considered mad: "O, what a noble mind is here overthrown... that noble and most sovereign reason / Like sweet bells jangled out of tune and harsh, / That unmatched form and feature of blown youth / Blasted with ecstasy" (3.1.152-62). And Hamlet himself says, "Go to, I'll no more on't, it hath made me mad" (3.1.148).

John Dover Wilson is right in saying that "in the tirades of the nunnery scene he [Hamlet] is thinking almost as much of his mother as of Ophelia" (193). Wilson may also be right in asserting that "Hamlet must have overheard what Polonius said to the king" (196), and "Hamlet's accidental discovery of the intention to spy upon him has a bearing wider than his attitude towards Ophelia... It renders the nunnery scene playable and intelligible" (197). Yet, no matter whether Hamlet has discovered the King and Polonius's intention or not, the scene is still "playable and intelligible" in terms of "deep psychology." For, as we must know, there Hamlet is displaying not only his "savage side" in treating Ophelia "like a prostitute" (Wilson 194). He is also unconsciously experiencing the *jouissance* that goes with the verbal thrusts.

Much depends on the word "nunnery." It refers, literally, to a place where a maid like Ophelia "will preserve her chastity and be safe from love, marriage, and breeding of sinners," and yet, sarcastically at the same time, it also refers to "a house of *un*chaste women" (Jenkins 282: note 121). It is certainly perverse to insist on the sarcastic meaning at the expense of the literal meaning, as does Wilson in his *What Happens in "Hamlet."* Nevertheless, we must understand that unconsciously, on the level of Id, the little Ham would be all the happier to meet his target woman (be she Gertrude or Ophelia) at a brothel, where no Super-Ego will come to check his libido. Thus, Hamlet's unconscious mind is pleading earnestly when he says, "Get thee to a nunnery" (3.1.121), although his conscious mind may deny it as a joke and Ophelia, as well as all others, may take it as merely a frenzied utterance.

If to speak daggers to a woman has a symbolic, libidinous pleasure of sexual intercourse, to wish to die for a woman is to pursue the *jouissance* of orgasm. I have pointed out, in another essay, that death is often equal to orgasm in *Romeo and Juliet* (see Tung 212 ff.). In fact, this bawdy connection is seen repeatedly elsewhere in Shakespeare. In *Much Ado about Nothing*, for instance, we have Benedict saying to Beatrice: "I will live in thy heart, die in thy lap..." (5.2.102). And in *King Lear* we have the mad Lear saying, "I will die bravely, / Like a smug bridegroom" (4.6.195-6).

In *Hamlet*, there is no line that can directly associate death with orgasm except, perhaps, these: "O, I die, Horatio. The potent poison quite overcrows my spirit" (5.2.357-8). These are words said when Hamlet is about to die after he is wounded by the poisoned rapier and has snatched the poisoned cup from Horatio. The word "overcrows" suggests the crowing of a victorious cock, and a cock suggests the genital organ of a man while the potent poison suggests the female's fluid shed in coition. Here Hamlet seems to suggest that he is overjoyed (has reached orgasm) through the coition fluid that comes with the thrusts, but the poison (fluid) has triumphed over his "cock" as he is soon to die.

In sexual intercourse, to die is actually to "sleep in quiet" after orgasm, just as suggested by Juliet when she assures her mother: "Indeed I never shall be satisfied / With Romeo, till I behold him—dead... Madam, if you could find out but a man / To bear a poison, I would temper it— / That Romeo should upon receipt thereof / Soon sleep in quiet" (*Romeo and Juliet*, 3.5.93-99). Now, in *Hamlet* we have these lines:

> *...To die—to sleep,*
> *No more; and by a sleep to say we end*
> *The heart-ache and the thousand natural shocks*
> *That flesh is heir to: 'tis a consummation*
> *Devoutly to be wished. (3.1.60-64)*

As the word "consummation" can refer specifically to the completion of marital union by the first act of sexual intercourse after marriage, to die or to sleep can, naturally in this context, refer to the quiet state after orgasm. And consequently a sexual implication can also be found in the ensuing lines, particularly these: "For who would bear the whips and scorns of time... When he himself might his quietus make / With a bare bodkin?" Here, a "bare bodkin" is again a phallic symbol like the dagger, and to "make one's quietus with a bare bodkin" is to "sleep in quiet" after orgasm. Thus, this most famous soliloquy of Hamlet's (and Shakespeare's) is unconsciously in effect a soliloquy carried on by a Ham-let that dare not let go his libido to achieve his sexual consummation, rather than merely a conscious reflection upon the ethical question of "to be or not to be" in the rational Hamlet's mind. This interpretation, to be sure, is further supported by the fact that as soon as Hamlet concludes this soliloquy, he sees Ophelia coming, and as soon as he sees her, he says: "Soft you now, / The fair Ophelia! Nymph, in thy orisons / Be all my sins remembered" (3.1.88-90). If the fair nymph remembered all his sins in her prayers, wouldn't it be easier for him to sink in "the undiscovered country [pleasure] from whose bourn / No traveler returns" (3.1.79-80)?

   The theme of death, carried along the sexual path, will ultimately come to the grave. It takes Andrew Marvell to write, "The grave's a fine and private place, / But none, I think, do there embrace" ("To His Coy Mistress," 31-32). But the grave-diggers in *Hamlet* know more than this. As they joke at their work, they know the grave "lasts till doomsday" (5.1.59). What they do not know is: the grave can be a female or yonic symbol, and two men will soon come there to embrace. As we are told, when Ophelia is being buried, Laertes suddenly leaps into the grave, saying, "Hold off the earth awhile, / Till I have caught her once more in mine arms" (5.1.242-3). Upon seeing this, Hamlet also leaps into the grave, wishing to be "buried quick with her" as well. In consequence, the two men grapple with each other in the grave, with Hamlet proclaiming that "Forty thousand brothers / Could not with all their quantity of love / Make up my sum" (5.1.264-66).

This is indeed a moving scene. But it not only shows a brother's deep love and a lover's deep affection. It also symbolizes the great attraction that a target female can have for her enamored male. As we know, the grave, with its concave shape before earth is put to it, is obviously a female (yonic) symbol. To leap into it so as to die there is a "consummation" any unconscious Id may wish for. That is why earlier in Act II, Scene ii, when Polonius asks, "Will you walk out of the air, my lord?" Hamlet answers, "Into my grave?" (206-7). Unconsciously for Hamlet, the grave is Gertrude or Ophelia, for whom he would willingly "die."

Besides the grave, the cup is another female (yonic) symbol in the play. The poisoned cup is the emblem of the Fatal Woman or the Unfaithful Wife. At the end of the play, Gertrude drinks it unwittingly, Claudius is forced to drink it, and Hamlet drinks willingly the "liquor left" (5.2.347). All the three die from it. This means: woman certainly can be a ruinous "cup" for all.

V.III Patriarchy and Prison

Though a woman can be like a poisoned cup, a man's libido still seldom hesitates to approach and drink it. In the case of Hamlet, for instance, even though he complains of a woman's "frailty," he is still subject to her beauty or charm. Thus, as Ophelia describes to her father, there was a time when Hamlet looked as if "he had been loosed out of hell / To speak of horrors" while perusing her face (2.1.83-4). And, as we know, there are times in the plays when Hamlet seems to have loosed his libido to speak words with bawdy implications: e.g. "Let her not walk in the sun. Conception is a blessing, but as your daughter may conceive—friend, look to it" (2.2.184-5); "In the secret parts of Fortune? O most true, she is a strumpet" (2.2.235); "Lady, shall I lie in your lap? ...Do you think I meant country matters" (3.2.110 & 115).

But a man's sexual desire is too often repressed. In Shakespeare's age, it is said, "the father was the head of the family and its ruler" (Harrison 1966, 95). In the world of Hamlet, as in most parts of the ancient world, in fact, patriarchy is a system that constricts not only a child's freedom in marriage (as Capulet does Juliet's or Egeus does Hermia's), but also a child's "fancy" or natural desire for a sexual partner. In Act I, Scene iii, therefore, we have Laertes warning Ophelia, thus:

> *Fear it, Ophelia, fear it, my dear sister,*
> *And keep you in the rear of your affection*
> *Out of the shot and danger of desire.*
> *The chariest maid is prodigal enough*
> *If she unmask her beauty to the moon.*
> *Virtue itself scapes not calumnious strikes. (33-38)*

Then we have Polonius admonishing her, thus:

> *Affection? Pooh, you speak like a green girl,*
> *Unsifted in such perilous circumstance.*
> *...Tender yourself more dearly*
> *Or... you'll tender me a fool. (101-109)*

And then, as we know, Laertes is himself asked to bear in mind all his father's moral "precepts" (1.3.58ff.) and behave well. Polonius even sends Reynaldo to detect by wiles his son's conduct in Paris, to see if Laertes is addicted to gaming, drinking, fencing, swearing, quarreling, drabbing (whoring), etc. (2.1.26-26).

In truth, we also see young Fortinbras controlled by his uncle, King of Norway. And Hamlet, obviously, is controlled by his spiritual (ghost) father and his corporeal (step or uncle) father. His ghost father wants him to act as an avenger, a champion of virtue against incest or lechery, but the ghost says: "Taint not thy mind nor let thy soul contrive / Against thy mother aught. Leave her to heaven, / And to those thorns that in her bosom lodge / To prick and sting her" (1.5.85-88). Superficially, this is a father's warning against a son's matricide. But in deep psychology this is the Super-Ego's prohibition against the Id's incestuous instinct that goes with the Oedipus complex.

As to Claudius, the corporeal father or uncle, he simply represents, as we have said, both Hamlet's Id and his shadow. As his Id, he is attracted to the same anima, Gertrude. As his shadow, he must struggle against the prince's persona. He knows the Queen's attachment to her son, feels the son's jealous hatred against her speedy remarriage with him, and is therefore constantly on the alert for any surprise attack from the mad one on either himself or the Queen. As the powerful king and the hostile uncle / father, he represses Hamlet's desire most conspicuously indeed. He even summons Rosencrantz and Guildenstern to observe Hamlet and seeks to have the prince's life done away with.

In Act II, Scene ii, Hamlet tells the two old "friends" that "Denmark's a prison" (243), and that the world is "a goodly one, in which there are many confines, wards, and dungeons, Denmark being one of the worst" (245-6). When they say they do not think so, Hamlet then replies: "Why, then it's none to you; for there is nothing either good or bad but thinking makes it so. To me it is a prison" (249-50).

From this dialogue we can clearly see that Hamlet does feel strongly that he is himself imprisoned tightly in Denmark.

What, then, is the cause of this feeling? Is it ambition, as his friends suggest? Hamlet himself says: "O God, I could be bounded in a nutshell and count myself a king of infinite space—were it not that I have bad dreams" (2.3.254-6). What, then, are the bad dreams? Hamlet does not make it clear, though he mentions that "A dream itself is but a shadow" (2.2.260). Now, judging from this conversation along with the situation he is in, we may infer that Hamlet may have such bad dreams as: first, a latent ghost is constantly appearing to direct his behavior, to restrict his will, and to control his desire within the ethical confines; second, a potent shadow is forever there watching over him, guarding against his "mad" conduct, and threatening to strangle his freedom along with his life. And this latent ghost plus this potent shadow are no other than the little Ham's two fathers, who in a process of condensation together with all other fathers of all other families form the father image and become the governing authorities that make up the patriarchal system to repress the children's desires, especially the desire prone to incest (the Oedipus complex) or to lust.

IX. The Strange Eruption

But will a son obey his father unquestioningly and docilely all the time? The answer is emphatically in the negative. In the case of Hamlet, we see him "doubt some foul play" (1.3.256) from the beginning, when he is told about his father's apparition. After he himself talks with the ghost and is convinced that "It is an honest ghost" (1.5.144), he still dare not carry out the vengeance immediately. That is why he has to feign madness and use a pantomime together with the players' perturbing dialogue as "The Mousetrap" (3.2.232) to "catch the conscience of the King" (2.2.601). And even after he makes sure of the fact, he still hesitates to kill Claudius while he is praying, and thus he has to reproach himself again and again for being as irresolute or inactive as a coward (see the soliloquy in 4.4. 32-66).

On the other hand, we see Hamlet has been hostile towards Claudius, his stepfather or uncle father. He regards him as a villain and also suspects him of "foul play," though unable to avoid falling into his final scheme. In fact, it is against this corporeal father that the entire revenge tragedy is directed on the conscious level, though unconsciously the pressure for revenge comes as much from the good angel (the spiritual father) as from the bad angel (the corporeal father) since both seek to repress the prince's desires.

Anyway, as a son under the pressure of two fathers, Hamlet is indeed but a little Ham with his libido doubly repressed. Under such circumstances, his psychic state is not just like an iceberg with his conscious persona appearing on the surface to struggle with his Super-Ego against his shadow, while his unconscious Id is kept hidden beneath the surface to stir his soul occasionally in meeting with his anima. In effect, it is even more like a volcano with its visible top (his conscious self or persona) appearing on the surface and its unseen lava (his libidinous Id or true ego) hidden beneath the surface, only to erupt with pressure from his Super-Ego and his shadow.

In the beginning of the play when the ghost becomes a topic, Horatio, compelled by his "own eyes" (1.1.61) to abandon the theory of "fantasy" (1.1.26), says that the ghost's appearance "bodes some strange eruption to our state" (1.1.72). By that statement Horatio means, of course, that the apparition is a sign of some strange, violent outbreak that is to come to the state of Denmark. However, "our state" need not refer only to the state of Denmark. It can also refer to "our mental state." In that sense, "some strange eruption to our state" will then refer to some strange, violent outbreak as seen of Hamlet's emotion that is to come with the ghost's appearance to the mental state of all Danes. In other words, Horatio seems to have announced unawares in his ambiguous manner that the play is to be "some strange eruption" from Hamlet's psychic volcano. And Hamlet's strange eruption obviously consists of his "raving lunacy" and "philosophical and occasional pessimism," which are the symptoms connected to what the Renaissance people called "melancholy" or to any neurotic case that can be interpreted in terms of modern psychoanalysis.

X. The Psychoanalytic Vision

As Hamlet's psychic volcano erupts unconsciously now and then, what sort of person does he seem to be? Among other things, we have seen a Hamlet seemingly as mad as Orlando and as revengeful as Hieronimo. Yet, Shakespeare has not made the play into a love story like Ariosto's, nor a revenge tragedy like Thomas Kyd's. Instead, he has written a play the concern of which is primarily not with the sensational effect of mad love or mad revenge, but with the original cause of madness for love and for revenge. And, thus, the play has presented before us a vision that shows Shakespeare's deep understanding of our basic human nature.

We have argued that "Hamlet" can be "Ham-let" in Shakespeare's mind. In fact, Shakespeare is always very careful and artful in giving his characters' names. In *Hamlet*, his namesmanship is shown not only in changing "Amleth" to "Hamlet." In the original source of the play, as we know, Hamlet's father is called Horvendile, his mother Geruth, and his uncle Fengon. By replacing "Horvendile" with the "Old Hamlet" or "King Hamlet," that is, by using the same name "Hamlet" for both father and son, Shakespeare naturally suggests closer ties between the father and the son, thus helping us to claim that the ghost Hamlet is in reality the identical soul of the prince.

On the other hand, in changing "Fengon" into "Claudius," Shakespeare obviously alludes to the Roman emperor Claudius. The Claudius in *Hamlet*, however, is very different from the Roman emperor. He is the poisoner, not the poisoned; hence, he is revenged upon, rather than avenged. Furthermore, he is revenged upon by Hamlet, his nephew or stepson, unlike the Roman emperor, who was murdered by Agrippina, his wife. By this allusion, therefore, Shakespeare seems to suggest that people with the same name may also be very different in character and in fate, although they may similarly be involved in power struggle and in love affairs.

But Shakespeare's most significant suggestion lies in the Queen's name "Gertrude." Scholars have noticed that the Gertrude in the Folio edition of the play is different from the First Quarto's Gertred and the Second Quarto's Gertrard; she may still be a lusty widow, but now "her speeches and actions are characterized almost exclusively by meekness and silence" (Kehler 404), and there is no evidence now that Gertrude is an accomplice in murdering King Hamlet.[12] But scholars have not yet pointed out that the name "Gertrude" is significant because in etymology it is from Old High German *ger* (spear) + *trut* (dear, beloved).[13] When Shakespeare finally adopted the name "Gertrude" instead of "Geruth," what was in his mind?

It is impractical, of course, for us to conjecture now what might be in his mind. But the fact that "Gertrude" stands for "a dear, beloved spear" certainly can assist us in giving the play a psychoanalytic interpretation. In Section III of this paper, we have suggested that men always war for women, and Gertrude is the woman that causes a war of revenge between Hamlet and Claudius. As a dear spear, Gertrude undoubtedly has the inkling of war. But as an anima she causes not only the superficial war between Hamlet and Claudius. As discussed in Sections IV, V, and VI above, Gertrude also causes a deep war between the conscious Hamlet, i.e., the persona representing Hamlet's rational Ego and moral Super-Ego (the sane, normal Hamlet with "a noble mind" as described by Ophelia in 3.1.152-6) and the unconscious Hamlet, i.e., the "mad" Hamlet representing his bestial Id with his libido emerging to the surface or erupted out from beneath. Meanwhile, we also suggest that King Hamlet (the ghost, spiritual, ideal father) is the embodiment of the prince's Super-Ego whereas King Claudius (the corporeal, villainous father) is the incarnation of the prince's libidinous Id and his shadow.

Since the war is in its actual depth a conflict between the conscious Hamlet (outer ego) and the unconscious Hamlet (inner ego), the result is naturally a tragedy, a kind of suicide, a death that passes the question of "to be or not to be," or an end that the split personality can only wait for with the attitude of "The readiness is all" (5.2.218). So, in a sense, we see that Gertrude as a dear spear has caused not only a deep war but also a great woe: she represents not only the archetype of the Unfaithful Wife but also that of the Fatal Woman in our collective unconscious. This fatal woman brings a number of deaths in the play. But the death of Hamlet with his two fathers is the death of a trinity, of three Hams (a weak one plus two powerful ones), and it is the aftermath of having his Ego torn fatally, under the influence of his anima, between his Super-Ego (his soul, his spiritual father) and his Id or shadow (his body, his corporeal father). And thus one can aver with Barbara Everett: "Hamlet didn't delay in revenging his father, because he didn't revenge his father. In the end he revenged only himself" (118).

Ironically, then, a woman as mild and meek as Gertrude can become a lethal weapon, a beloved spear to cost so many dear lives, just as Helen does in *Iliad*. But how about Ophelia? Isn't she as mild and meek? Yes, she is even more so, and she is chaste and harmless. She is not the type of the Unfaithful Wife nor that of the Fatal Woman. In truth, her name means "a help or succor" in its Greek origin.[14] Her role in the play is not just to contrast her youth, chastity, innocence, etc., with Gertrude's age, lust, crime, etc. Nor is it just to increase the tragic sense by adding her own death to the tragedy or to "represent a quality in Hamlet's mind... that point of love in Hamlet which is the center of his true nobility" (Vyvyan 41). Besides providing occasions for Hamlet's or Shakespeare's or the Shakespearean scholars' philosophizing about beauty, virtue, death, fatalism, etc., Ophelia is actually to help demonstrate the psychological truth that in one's fancy displacement often occurs: a target woman (e.g., Gertrude) may easily be displaced by another (Ophelia). Thus, as discussed in Section VII above, she also receives verbal daggers from the mad Hamlet as does Gertrude. And her grave, as a female (yonic) symbol, is the place where Hamlet, no less than Laertes, wishes to "die" in, just as the poisoned cup, another female (yonic) symbol, is no other than Gertrude, the dear spear that kills Hamlet as well as his two fathers.

In Shakespeare's vision, then, men do often war for women. But only the strongest man can possess the target woman, in the big world or in a small village (a hamlet). In a family, the powerful one is always the father. The son is but a Ham-let, who is forever influenced and controlled by the strong Hams, his spiritual father and corporeal father. So, if the son is not weaned from his Oedipus complex, he cannot achieve individuation. He may stay somewhat in the Imaginary Order, although placed in the Symbolic Order and aspiring for the Real Order. In that case, as in the case of Hamlet, there is no "due balance between the real and the imaginary world" (Coleridge 163), and madness or melancholy will surely ensue. And more often than not the Ham-let will suffer from a conflict between his conscious self and unconscious self, involving his rational Ego, moral Super-Ego, bestial Id, and villainous shadow fighting altogether vainly for his anima, the figure ambiguously to be his spear and his cup, his poison and his love, his grave and his life all at once. Consequently, death becomes a *jouissance*, a symbolic orgasm experienced at last by the erotic male with his strange eruption in the face of his anima. Is this then a revenge tragedy? Yes, but not a traditional kind. It is a Shakespearean kind: a kind, to crack a joke by the way, that stems from the little Ham that dares to come and try to shake the dear spear cherished by the patriarch, the powerful father, the strong Ham, the Gigantic Phallus. As a playwright of such a kind of revenge tragedy, isn't this Shake-spear the "poet of nature," who sees clearly as a psychoanalyst the depths of human nature in relation to the theme of war and woman, in its sexual and symbolic aspects?

Notes

1. Hereinafter the parenthesized numbers of the act, the scene, and the line(s) refer to The Arden Edition of Shakespeare. *Hamlet* is edited by Harold Jenkins.

2. For his discrimination between the levels of conscious and unconscious mental activity, see his "The Anatomy of the Mental Personality, Lecture XXI," in *New Introductory Lectures on Psychoanalysis* (Norton, 1964).

3. A simplified explanation of these Freudian concepts can be found in Guerin's *A Handbook of Critical Approaches to Literature*, 87-94, and in Dobie's *Theory into Practice: An Introduction to Literary Criticism*, 49-55.

4. For a simplified explanation of these Jungian ideas, see Guerin, 134-39, or Dobie, 56-60. Jung's works include *Psyche and Symbol, Psychological Reflections, The Archetypes and the Collective Unconscious, Modern Man in Search of a Soul,* and *Two Essays on Analytical Psychology.*

5. For a simplified explanation of these Lacanian concepts, see Dobie, 61-64. Lacan has touched on the father-and-son relationship in *Hamlet* in his *The Four Fundamental Concepts of Psychoanalysis.*

6. Quoted from the entry "*Jouissance*" in *Wikipedia*, the free encyclopedia on line.

7. G. B. Harrison says that "Hamlet appears first as Amlethus in the *Historia Danica* written by Saxo Grammaticus in the twelfth century." See his *Shakespeare: The Complete Works* (1968), 880.

8. Hamlet's age is inferred from the Grave-digger's account of the combat between Old Hamlet and Old Fortinbras in act V, Scene 1, ll. 139-57. But this inference is problematic. See the longer note in Jenkins's *Hamlet*, 551-4.

9. This aside is a chance remark and as such it can be a verbal slip, which according to William Beatty Warner is a form of the unconscious, along with dreams, symptoms, personal rituals, defense mechanisms, and jokes.

10. See the entry of "Anatomy of Melancholy" in Benèt's *The Reader's Encyclopedia*, 33.

11. In Ad de Vries's *A Dictionary of Symbols and Imagery*, under the entry of "dagger," the references are said to appear in *Twelfth Night* (IV, ii), *1 Henry IV* (II, iv), *Henry V* (IV, iv), etc. In fact, the references to "poniards" such as in *Much Ado about Nothing* (II, i), and in *3 Henry VI* (II, i), have the same semantic force.

12. For detail about the murder of Old Hamlet, see the Ghost's explication in Act I, Scene v, 42ff. That Gertrude is innocent of the murder is also evidenced in her calm reaction to the players' pantomime and dialogues in Act III, Scene ii.

13. See the entry "Gertrude" in *Webster's New World Dictionary of the American Language* (1967).

14. See the entry "Ophelia" in *Webster's New World Dictionary of the American Language* (1967).

Works Consulted

Adams, Hazard, ed. *Critical Theory Since Plato*. New York: Harcourt Brace Jovanovich, 1971.

Bennèt, William Rose, ed. *The Reader's Encyclopedia*. 2nd ed. New York: Thomas Crowell, 1965.

Bevington, David, ed. *Twentieth Century Interpretations of Hamlet*. Englewood Cliffs, NJ: Prentice-Hall, 1968

Bradley, A. C. *Shakespearean Tragedy*. New York: Meridian Books, 1955.

Brockbank, J. Philip. "Hamlet the Bonesetter." *Shakespeare Survey*. Vol. 30. Ed. Kenneth Muir. Cambridge: Cambridge UP, 1977. 103-15.

Coleridge, S. T. "Notes on the Tragedies: *Hamlet*," in Hoy, 156-62.

De Vries, Ad. *A Dictionary of Symbols and Imagery*. Amsterdam & London: North Holland Publishing Co., 1974.

Dobies, Ann B. *Theory into Practice: An Introduction to Literary Criticism*. Boston: Thomson/Heinle, 2002.

Everett, Barbara. " 'Hamlet': A Time to Die." *Shakespeare Survey*. Vol. 30. Ed. Kenneth Muir. Cambridge: Cambridge UP, 1977. 117-23.

Freud, Sigmund. *The Ego and the Id*. New York: Norton, 1962.

——. *Three Essays on the Theory of Sexuality*. Basic Books Classics. New York: Baker & Tailor, 2000.

Gardner, Helen. "*Hamlet* and the Tragedy of Revenge." *Shakespeare: Modern Essays in Criticism*. Ed. Leonard E. Dean. London, Oxford, & New York: Oxford UP, 1967. 218-26.

Guerin, Wilfred L., et al. *A Handbook of Critical Approaches to Literature*. New York & London: Harper & Row, 1966.

Harbage, Alfred, ed. *Shakespeare: The Tragedies*. 20th Century Views. Englewood Cliffs, NJ: Prentice-Hall, 1964.

Harrison, G. B. "Introduction to *Hamlet*." *Shakespeare: The Complete Works*. New York: Harcourt Brace, 1968. 880-4.

——. *Introducing Shakespeare*. 3rd ed. London: Penguin Books, 1966.

Hazlitt, William. "Character of Shakespeare's Plays: Hamlet," in Hoy, 163-9.

Hoy, Cyrus, ed. *William Shakespeare: Hamlet.* Norton Critical Edition. New York: Norton, 1963.

Jenkins, Harold, ed. *Hamlet.* The Arden Shakespeare. London & New York: Methuen, 1982.

Johnson, Samuel. "Preface to *Shakespeare,*" in Adams, 329-36.

Jones, Ernest. *Hamlet and Oedipus.* New York: Norton, 1976.

———. "The Death of Hamlet's Father." *Literature and Psychoanalysis.* Ed. Edith Kurzweil & William Phillips. New York: Columbia UP, 1983. 34-38.

Jung, C. G. *The Archetypes and the Collective Unconscious. Collected Works of C. G. Jung.* Vol. 9, Part I. Ed. & trans. G. Adler & R. F. C. Hull. Princeton, NJ: Princeton UP, 1981.

Kehler, Dorothea. "The First Quarto of *Hamlet*: Reforming Widow Gertred." *Shakespeare Quarterly.* Vol. 46 (Winter 1995), No. 4, 398-413.

Knight, G. Wilson. "The Embassy of Death: An Essay on *Hamlet,*" in Hoy, 185-93.

Knights, L. C. "An Approach to *Hamlet,* " in Bevington, 64-72.

Lacan, Jacques. *The Four Fundamental Concepts of Psychoanalysis.* Ed. Jacques Alain. Trans. Alan Sheridan. New York: Norton, 1998.

Mack, Maynard. "The World of *Hamlet,*" in Harbage, 44-60.

Mackenzie, Henry. "Criticism on the Character and Tragedy of Hamlet," in Hoy, 148-52.

Richardson, William. "The Character of Hamlet," in Hoy, 147-8.

Spencer, Theordore. "Hamlet and the Nature of Reality." *Journal of English Literary History,* V (December, 1938), 253-77. Rpt. in Bevington, 31-42.

Spurgeon, Caroline F. E. *Shakespeare's Imagery and What It Tells Us.* Boston: Beacon Press, 1958.

Tung, C. H. "The Most 'Lamentable Comedy' of Romeo and Juliet: Shakespeare's Ironic Vision." *Journal of the College of Liberal Arts.* Vol. 28. Taichung: Chung Hsing University, 1998. 195-222.

Vyvyan, John. *The Shakespearean Ethic.* London: Chatto & Windus, 1959.

Warner, William Beatty. *Chance and the Text of Experience: Freud, Nietzsche, and Shakespeare's* Hamlet. Ithaca, NY: Cornell UP, 1986.

Wilson, John Dover. "Hamlet and Ophelia," in Hoy, 193-7.

* This chapter first appeared as a paper in 2007 in *Intergrams*, which is an e-journal of the Department of Foreign Languages and Literatures, National Chung Hsing University.

• Chapter 5 •

The Jew and the Moor: Shakespeare's Racial Vision

I. Comprehensive Soul

It is well known that John Dryden, in his "An Essay of Dramatic Poesy," makes Neander praise Shakespeare as "the man who of all modern, and perhaps ancient poets, had the largest and most comprehensive soul" (247). But what exactly did the term "comprehensive soul" mean to Neander or Dryden? The statement that immediately follows the praise is: "All the images of nature were still present to him, and he drew them, not laboriously, but luckily; when he describes anything, you more than see it, you feel it too" (247). This statement seems to explain that what made Shakespeare's soul comprehensive was his ability to grasp "all the images of nature" and render them "luckily" and touchingly. Except this apparent explanation Dryden or Neander provides no further explication in this famous essay.

In an editorial of 1998, Christopher Flannery says: "When Dryden speaks of Shakespeare's 'comprehensive soul,' he means that Shakespeare's genius plumbs the deepest depths and scales the loftiest heights of human nature and encompasses the broadest reaches of the human condition." Thus, he goes on to say, "Shakespeare's themes include virtually every interesting aspect of human life." However, the Shakespearean themes he mentions are such as "love, revenge, beauty, ambition, virtue, vice, justice, free will, providence, chance, fate, friendship, loyalty, betrayal; the interplay among passions, reason and will; truth and illusion, men and women, mortality and immortality; the vast variety of human characters and societies."[1] Somehow, he has failed to mention the theme of race.

Race is, of course, part of nature, and each human race has always had its distinctive "image(s)" formed and known in various "societies." Nevertheless, race was indeed not so important an issue in Shakespeare's England as to become a central theme of his drama. According to Michael D. Bristol, at the end of the 16th century "racism was not yet organized as a large-scale system of oppressive social and economic arrangements, though it certainly existed as a widely shared set of feelings and attitudes" (181). *The Merchant of Venice* may be a play most obviously touching on the tension of Jews in a Christian society, and thus one can argue as to whether the play is anti-Semitic or not. Yet, as the title suggests, the play is mainly about "the merchant of Venice," that is, Antonio, who embodies friendship or love of the highest degree, against usury or any mercenary form of profit that is often associated with merchants. Although the play is "otherwise called 'The Iewe of Venyce,'"[2] and it is certainly Shylock's tragedy and often performed as such,[3] most people still regard it as a comedy for Bassanio and Portia or as a tragic-comedy for Antonio. If the play, as C. L. Barber suggests, is to dramatize "the conflict between the mechanisms of wealth and the masterful, social use of it" (179), the emphasis is placed first and foremost on wealth as a personal, rather than racial, matter, for wealth is primarily one's personal, rather than racial, belongings.

Othello is another of Shakespeare's plays that has the greatest potential to develop into a "problem play" about race. In its source tale, as Susan Snyder points out, Cinthio does not dwell much on the theme of skin color, but Shakespeare dwells on it a great deal in the play (31). And as Stephen Greenblatt puts it, "blackness is the indelible witness to Othello's permanent status as an outsider" (45). Yet, as it is, the tragedy is primarily about jealousy,[4] and Othello's tragic fate lies more in his personality (e.g. his rashness or gullibility) than in his racial situation: there is no racism detrimental enough to hinder him directly through racial hatred in his military or matrimonial life. The racial problem raised in the play is, at most, but a problem subordinate to the problem of villainy, which makes use of others' personal traits as well as racial prejudices existing in a society.

Three of Shakespeare's other plays, namely *Titus Andronicus*, *Antony and Cleopatra*, and *The Tempest*, also have characters other than "the white race": Aaron the blackamoor, Cleopatra the Egyptian, and the Indian-like Caliban.[5] But who would think of these plays primarily in terms of racism? Aaron is but a convenient agent to bring forth Shakespeare's revenge theme, Cleopatra a type of love overpowering political and military power, and Caliban an example depicting the master / servant relationship or the nature / nurture contrast. In none of these plays, as in neither *The Merchant of Venice* nor *Othello*, does the theme of race ever really come to the fore to bedim other possible themes.

Although race was never Shakespeare's central theme, race and racism actually never escaped the playwright's notice. In fact, as will be discussed in this essay, Shakespeare's comprehensive soul has made him comprehend a lot of things related to the problem of race, his comprehensiveness has become an impartial attitude toward races, and his soul has created a racial vision bespeaking his comprehensiveness most impressively.

II. Racial Personae

We have mentioned five characters (Aaron, Shylock, Othello, Cleopatra, and Caliban) from five plays (*Titus Andronicus, The*

Merchant of Venice, Othello, Antony and Cleopatra, and *The Tempest*) as Shakespeare's dramatis personae that may have something to do with race and racism. But the five characters do not exhaust Shakespeare's racial personae. In *The Merchant of Venice,* at least, we have two other Jews (Shylock's daughter Jessica and his friend Tubal) and one or two Moors (the Prince of Morocco and the Moor mentioned in passing whom Launcelot Gobbo made big with child), who either directly or indirectly help make up Shakespeare's racial vision. If we count also Aaron's black baby by Tamora and Caliban's hag mother Sycorax (who is also not presented but mentioned in the play), then Shakespeare's racial personae may be said to be above ten.

Of the eleven racial personae, only four are female (Jessica, Cleopatra, Sycorax, and Launcelot's Moor), but they are enough to connect race with gender. Among the eleven characters, again, we find three Jews (Shylock, Jessica, and Tubal), five Moors (Aaron and his baby, the Prince of Morocco, Launcelot's woman, and Othello), one Egyptian (Cleopatra), and two Algerians (Caliban and his mother Sycorax, since she is said to be from Argier). Up to Shakespeare's time, as we know, any race that was non-Greek, non-Roman, or non-Christian was thought to be barbarous. So, all of the characters would have been considered barbarous if none of them had converted to Christianity (like Jessica and Othello) or had been born of nobility (like Cleopatra or the Prince of Morocco). Anyway, in Shakespeare's vision race is also linked to religion and class, besides gender.

In ancient times, the Moslem region west of Egypt in north Africa was called Barbary. It was the place where Moors (a Moslem people of mixed Arab and Berber descent) used to live.[6] The English word "Moors," it is said, is related to the Spanish *Moros* and the French *Maures* and derived from the Latin *maurus* and the Greek *mauros*, which means "dark," and the word originally referred to "the dark ones" inhabiting northern Africa because they were darker in complexion than the Europeans. Later, in the 15th century, when black slaves were brought back from west Africa, "black Moors" or "blackamoors" was the word used to distinguish the negroes from the "Moors" of northern Africa, though people often failed to make the distinction and kept calling all Africans "Moors" no matter whether they were black or merely swarthy, from north or west Africa.[7] In Shakespeare's drama, Aaron is identified as a blackamoor but Othello is said to be a swarthy Moor. To Shakespeare, "a Moor was not clearly distinguished from a black" (Asimov 609). I am of opinion that no matter whether Othello is brown or black, this particular Moor is enough to become a racial topic though critics including Coleridge and A. C. Bradley have strongly argued for the necessity of making Othello a swarthy Moor rather than a blackamoor.[8]

Racism is indeed often based on visible morphological characteristics such as skin color, hair type, and facial features. In Shakespeare's plays, as in any society or natural environment, skin color is the most conspicuous and hence important characteristic used to identify a Moor or a foreigner, or to tell a white man from a barbarian. In *Titus Andronicus*, the black Aaron is compared to a "swart Cimmerian" (*TA*, 2.3.72); in *The Merchant of Venice*, the Prince of Morocco asks Portia not to dislike him "for my complexion" which is like the "shadowed livery of the burnished sun" (*MV*, 2.1.1-2); in *Othello*, Othello is said to have a "sooty bosom" and is likened to "an old black ram" (*OT*, 1.2.70 & 1.1.88); and in *Antony and Cleopatra*, Philo mentions Cleopatra's "tawny front" (*A&C*, 1.1.6). To be sure, Othello is also said to have thick lips while Caliban is characterized as a deformed monster rather than a colored person, yet to Shakespeare's Elizabethans the Moors, the Egyptians, or the Algerians—all those African people were distinctly colored people.

Besides skin color, however, religion was another important characteristic for Shakespeare's Europeans to discriminate between themselves and aliens. It happened that Moors were usually Moslems. It followed, therefore, that Moslems were associated with colored people and a foreign race in Europe. But Moslemism was not the only religion to suggest religious difference to Christians. Judaism was another religion that made the Europeans differ from Jews. To be sure, no religion is ever conspicuously written on anyone's face: Moslemism or Judaism is a cultural manifestation, not a physical appearance. Yet, even though a white cannot easily tell himself apart from a Jew (who is not as colored as a Moor), he can observe a Jew's practice of Judaism and then find the needed difference to form his racialism. It is for this reason, perhaps, that in *The Merchant of Venice* the Christians as well as Shylock apparently equate the Jew's religion to his race and his nation.

So far we have established the fact that in Shakespeare the Jew and the Moor are the two prominent figures bearing on problems of race, owing to their nurture (religious practice) and / or nature (such physical appearance as skin color). But racialism or racism is not just a matter of the "racial personae." It is to even much greater a degree a matter of those who live with the "dark-skinned people" or with the "non-Christian unbelievers."

In his "Race and Racism," Tzvetan Todorov says, "Racism is a matter of *behavior*, usually a manifestation of hatred or contempt for individuals who have well-defined physical characteristics different from our own" (64). This statement does not apply very well to the case of Shylock in *The Merchant of Venice*, for Shylock is not identified in the play as a person with any particular skin color, hair type, or facial feature, but as a person with Jewish belief and Jewish behavior. So, through Shylock Shakespeare seems to suggest that racism does not necessarily arise from "well-defined physical characteristics" only: there are cases in which racism comes from different social conduct (e.g. Shylock's Jewish usury). Yet, Todorov's statement still holds true in that the Christians as well as Shylock do reveal their racism in their behavior, in their hatred or contempt for individuals who have nurture or nature different from their own.

Accordingly, when we discuss any particular case of racism, we should take into consideration both sides: the side that has the visible differences and the side that sees or makes the differences, that is, the side of "the other" and the side of "the self." And, more often than not, we may find that the former side is the minority while the latter side is the majority in the society in which they live together. In Shakespeare's plays, for instance, Venice is where the Jews and the Moors appear and live with the native Venetians or Italians, but the Jews and the Moors are the minority side of "the other" that has the visible differences, whereas the whites or the Christians are the majority side of "the self" that sees and makes the differences. That is why W. H. Auden can say: "Shylock is a Jew living in a predominantly Christian society, just as Othello is a Negro living in a predominantly white society" (232).

Since it takes both sides to consider any racism, any list of racial personae should contain not only those characters who are the minority others with visible differences but also those characters who are the majority selves seeing or making the differences. Consequently, Shakespeare's racial personae theoretically comprise not only the eleven characters we have just mentioned above; they should comprise all the dramatis personae in the five plays concerned, at least all the characters, white or colored, Christian or non-Christian, who have demonstrated more or less their racial consciousness: for example, Demetrius and Chiron as well as Aaron, Antonio and Portia as well as Shylock and Jessica, Branbantio and Iago as well as Othello, Philo and Octavius as well as Cleopatra, and Prospero and Miranda as well as Caliban.

Among the racial personae, however, two figures are undoubtedly most important: namely, Shylock and Othello. They are so important not just because they, through their racial actions and reactions, represent the two basic types of racism (racism owing to nurture and racism owing to nature), but also because their names, as will be clarified below, have special significance in the light of racialism or racism. In Shakespeare, character-naming is indeed "not an entirely random matter": Shakespeare's characters often "allude to, or play on, the names of themselves or others"[9] By giving the Jew and the Moor each "a local habitation and a name" (to quote a phrase from *The Midsummer Night's Dream*), Shakespeare, as we shall see, has not just made concrete two racial stories, but also made meaningful his imaginative understanding of racial problems.[10]

III. Pride and Prejudice

There is a tendency for scholars to differentiate racialism from racism. Todorov, for instance, refers to racialism as a belief in the existence of races, i.e., "human groupings whose members possess common physical characteristics," just like animal species (64-65). Such a belief is a scientific one, and hence neutral in attitude without any racial prejudice. However, racialism often becomes racism, a belief not just in inherent biological differences among various human races but also in the superiority of some races to others and thus the justification for hating or despising or even eliminating other races.[11] For Todorov, "the form of racism that is rooted in racialism produces particularly catastrophic results" (64), as Nazism is that form of racism.

Kwame Antony Appiah also uses "racialism" to denote the idea of recognizing the existence of races with certain common traits and tendencies, or inheritable characteristics called "race essence." But Appiah assumes that from the basic racialism two types of racism may develop in time. The first type is "extrinsic racism," which believes that "the racial essence entails certain morally relevant qualities," and thus, "members of different races differ in respects that *warrant* the different treatment, respects — such as honesty or courage or intelligence—that are uncontroversially held... to be acceptable as a basis for treating people differently" (5). It is through this racism that one believes negroes simply lack intellectual capacities and Jews are avaricious, and they should be treated accordingly. The second type of racism is "intrinsic racism." It believes that "each race has a different moral status, quite independent of the moral characteristics entailed by its racial essence" (6). Thus, intrinsic racism will nurse "race feeling" or "feeling of community," which is very like "family feeling," and preach for racial solidarity just as Pan-Africanism or Zionism has done, while extrinsic racism will only result in racial hatred or even oppression (11-12).

Shakespeare was no theorist and he had no scholarly expertise on racialism or racism. Nevertheless, Shakespeare has in his drama shown his comprehensive knowledge of racial problems. As a matter of fact, Shakespeare's plays have witnessed two basic types of racialism: one (represented by the Jew) is the type seeing differences or "otherness" in nurture (including religious belief and behavior), and the other (represented by the Moor) is the type seeing differences or "otherness" in nature (mainly such physical appearance as skin color). Based on these two types of racialism, Shakespeare's plays then enact a wide variety of racism. Shakespeare never dichotomized racism into intrinsic and extrinsic racism. But his wide variety of racism can be classified, too, into two sorts, quite like Appiah's assortment. In plain terms, the two categories may be called "racism of pride" and "racism of prejudice," corresponding to Appiah's "intrinsic racism" and "extrinsic racism" respectively.

It is only natural that one should love one's own race. But one cannot love one's own race without taking pride in one or more characteristics of one's own race, just as a giraffe cannot love its own species without taking pride in, say, its long neck. It may be remembered that, in *The Merchant of Venice*, Jessica says:

> *Alack, what heinous sin is it in me*
> *To be ashamed to be my father's child!*
> *But though I am a daughter to his blood*
> *I am not to his manners. (MV, 2.3.16-19)*

Jessica cannot take pride in her father's manners and her father's manners are considered to be those of a typical Jew. So, she decides to become "a Christian" and Lorenzo's "loving wife" (*MV*, 2.3.21), forsaking her cultural heritage, which all Jews share.

While Jessica is just about to become a Christian, Othello, as the play opens, "is not simply a Moor; he is a Christian" (Hecht 125). Is Othello born into a Christian family or is he converted to Christianity sometime later? We can find no answer to this question in the play. If, as many critics believe, Othello is a convert and that helps him secure his position and people's trust in Venice,[12] has he lost pride in his own race and his original faith? Again, we cannot find the answer directly in the play. According to Leo Africanus' description in *The History and Description of Africa* (1526), Barbary people were "decent, valiant, patient, courteous, honest, skillful warriors... and exceeding lovers and practicers of humanity."[13] Does Othello ever take pride in his people as such? To Iago he once says, "I fetch my life and being / from men of royal siege," and "My parts, my title, and my perfect soul / Shall manifest me rightly" (*OT*, 1.2.21-22 & 31-32). These lines imply that Othello has confidence in himself because of his noble birth, good ability, present position and "perfect soul." But does his "perfect soul" come from his Christian belief? After a brawl in Cyprus, Othello berates his soldiers by asking, "Are we turned Turks, and to ourselves do that / Which heaven has forbid the Ottomites?" This question shows that Othello is ashamed of such "barbarous" tribes as Turks and the Ottomites, which may be linked to his own Moorish race. Besides, he also favors Christianity, for he goes on to say, "For Christian shame, put by this barbarous brawl" (*OT*, 1.3.163).

Religion is not a problem with Aaron, Cleopatra, or Caliban, nor is religion a focal point in the three plays in which they are cast. But when Caliban says in an aside that he must obey Prospero because "his Art is of such power. / It would control my dam's god, Setebos, / And make a vassal of him" (*TT*, 1.2.374-6), his statement implies that power may even control a people's faith. And when at last Caliban promises to "be wise hereafter, / And seek for grace" (*TT*, 5.1.294-5), he is almost like a Jew or a Moor promising to discard his old faith and become a Christian.

Faith is part of one's nurture, not nature. As such, it is actually not part of one's racial heritage. Yet, to many people of our time as well as Shakespeare's, religion almost always seems to bond with race. That is why even today Jews are equated with Judaism and Moors with Moslemism. So far, we have mentioned three of Shakespeare's characters (Jessica, Othello, and Caliban) who have somehow become willing to accept the faith or grace of Christianity. Their self-pride, thus, does not cover the pride in their racial religion. To Shylock, however, the "bond" of union between his race and his religion is so strong that he simply cannot bear to break it. After he is forced in court to say he is content to become a Christian, he immediately asks for leave to "go from hence," saying "I am not well" (*MV*, 4.1.391-2).

To Shylock, in fact, his race, his religion, and his nation are one. He thinks he embodies all Jewish virtues and is proud of his Jewish value. He says he will not eat, drink, nor pray with Christians (*MV*, 1.3.32-33). He argues for the Jewish virtue of thrift (*MV*, 1.3.66-85). He regards "sufferance" as the badge of all his tribe (*MV*, 1.3.105). And when the time comes, he utters all his racial grievances through the "Hath not a Jew eyes..." protest (*MV*, 3.1.52-66). If intrinsic racism is to plead for racial solidarity, Shylock's racism is so intrinsic that it is not only tinged with ethnocentrism (preference for one's own ethnic group), but also with xenophobia (fear of racial difference). In a sense, then, his dislike of miscegenation (against his daughter's marriage with a Christian Venetian) is also derived from his intrinsic racism. And in all probability Tubal, another Jew in the play, is the only one left for his trust.

In the same play, the Prince of Morocco's pleading of "Mislike me not for my complexion" and his insistence that "I would not change this hue" (*MV*, 2.1.1 & 11) also demonstrate his intrinsic racism and his own racial pride. But the Moor that speaks most proudly and impressively for his own race in Shakespearean drama is Aaron. In Act IV of *Titus Andronicus* we have a moving scene. The Nurse brings to Aaron his black baby (the one Tamora has just been delivered of). She curses it as a devil and a toad. But Aaron retorts, "'Zounds, ye whore! is black so base a hue?" and then calls the baby "Sweet blowse" and "a beauteous blossom" (*TA*, 4.2.71-72). When Demetrius and Chiron threaten to kill the baby, Aaron not only protects it but also defends it, thus:

> *Coal-black is better than another hue*
> *In that it scorns to bear another hue,*
> *For all the water in the ocean*
> *Can never turn the swan's black legs to white,*
> *Although she lave them hourly in the flood. (TA, 4.2.99-103)*

In *Antony and Cleopatra*, we can also see racial pride. Cleopatra tries to compete with Octavia in height, tone of voice, gait, age, shape of face, and hair color, but not in complexion. She may not have confidence in her tawny color. Yet, she never loses her pride in being "serpent of old Nile" (*A&C*, 1.5.25). What is emphasized in the play is, of course, the Egyptian queen's personal charms that go with a woman instead of a race. However, deep at her heart Cleopatra is proud enough of her *Egyptian* charms because she is able to "conquer" the *Roman* Antony and that "broad-fronted Caesar" (*A&C*, 1.5.29).

Caliban's skin color is not a focus of *The Tempest*. In the play he is reduced to a monster, a beast or a fish. This "abhorred slave" or representative of a "vile race," nonetheless, is not without his own pride. He has imagined himself peopling the isle with Calibans. He is at least proud of being able to curse the usurpers of his land in the language they have taught him.

If we want to dwell on the topic of racial pride or intrinsic racism, we must understand that Shakespeare's entire oeuvre is set in a white-dominated culture and a Christian milieu. Therefore, all the non-white and non-Christian characters' racial pride is but a weak trace, compared with the overwhelming pride of the Christian whites that make up the majority of the playwright's dramatis personae. Think of all those who have expressed contempt for Moors, Jews or other aliens: Demetrius and Chiron; Antonio, Bassanio, and Portia; Brabantio, Iago, and Roderigo; Philo, Pompey, and Octavius; as well as Prospero, Miranda, etc. Do they not carry their racial pride to such an extent that their intrinsic racism for racial solidarity has practically become extrinsic racism that features prejudice, hatred, oppression, etc., besides contempt?

Shakespeare's characters are indeed all set in a white-centered Christendom. In the white Christians' minds, it is "the world of the saved and the civilized, apart from the pagans and the infidels" (Fitch15). In such a world, a person is automatically thought to be a white. So Hamlet's idea of "noble mankind" or Miranda's so-called "beauteous mankind" means only the whites. In such a world, too, "often enough a Christian is simply a synonym for a person" (Fitch 15). According to Robert E. Fitch, that is why Sir Andrew in *Twelfth Night* can say, "Methinks sometimes I have no more wit than a Christian or an ordinary man has" (15). And I think that is why racism can become a poignant theme, though not one of the primary themes, in Shakespeare's comprehensive soul.

The whites in Shakespeare do have various prejudices against the non-whites and non-Christians. A colored person, for instance, is often connected with lustfulness. So, Aaron is made to boast that he can fetter

Tamora "in amorous chains" and "wanton with this queen" to "mount aloft" with her (*TA*, 2.1.12-25). And Othello is directly addressed as "The lustful Moor" (*OT*, 2.1.290) though he is actually no peer to Aaron in that respect. Even a colored woman is likewise connected. So, Pompey says that he wants "salt Cleopatra" to join lust with witchcraft and beauty to "tie up the libertine in a field of feasts" (*A&C*, 2.1.21-23), while Philo is made to complain that Antony "is become the bellows and the fan / To cool a gipsy's lust" (*A&C*, 1.1.8-9). In fact, Cleopatra is repeatedly called a strumpet or a whore. In *The Tempest*, then, Caliban is called a "savage" and said to have attempted to violate the honor of Miranda.

A colored person is also often connected with sorcery. We have mentioned Pompey's reference to Cleopatra's witchcraft. In fact, when Antony suspects her, he also says, "The witch shall die..." (*A&C*, 4.12.47). Caliban, then, is said to be the "hag seed" of the "damned witch Sycorax" from Argier (*TT*, 1.2.367 & 263). Aaron is not directly imputed to any sorcery, but he is called a "swart Cimmerian," which suggests not only his black hue but also a mysterious darkness emblematic of witchcraft. Finally, as we know, Brabantio accuses Othello of practicing on Desdemona "with foul charms" (*OT*, 1.2.73):

> *Ay, to me:*
> *She is abused, stolen from me and corrupted,*
> *By spells and medicines, bought of mountebanks,*
> *For nature so preposterously to err,*
> *(Being not deficient, blind, or lame of sense)*
> *Sans witchcraft could not. (OT, 1.3.59-64)*

For the whites, a colored person is nothing but a barbarian and thus is often only next to a beast and may even be compared to a bird, a fish, or an insect. Since Caliban is a "freckled whelp hag-born" (*TT*, 1.2.283), he has to be "stied" in a "hard rock" (*TT*, 1.2.344-5). He is referred to as "a plain fish," too, and said to be "marketable" (*TT*, 5.1.266). To Scarus and others, Cleopatra may be called a "ribaudred nag of Egypt" (*A&C*, 3.10.10). She is also compared to a female duck for her "doting mallard," Antony (*A&C*, 3.10.20), besides being the "serpent of old Nile." Aaron is Tamora's "raven-colored love" (*TA*, 2.3.83), who can "sing so like a lark" (*TA*, 3.1.158). He is also a "hellish dog" (*TA*, 4.2.77). In Titus' imagination, he is also a fly, "a black ill-favored fly" (*TA*, 3.2.68) that deserves no more than killing. And his baby is compared to a "tadpole" (*TA*, 4.2.85). As to Othello, he is "an old black ram... tupping your white ewe" (*OT*, 1.1.88-89), or "a Barbary horse" to "cover your daughter" and make "the beast with two backs" (*OT*, 1.1.110-6).

For the whites, finally, a colored person is no other than a villain or a devil. Aaron and his baby are indeed repeatedly attached with the epithets of "villain" and "devil." He himself is even made to confess:

> *O, how this villainy*
> *Doth fat me with the very thoughts of it!*
> *Let fools do good, and fair men call for grace,*
> *Aaron will have his soul black like his face. (TA, 3.1.202-5)*

And, at last, he only regrets that he cannot do ten thousand more dreadful things, wishing meanwhile to become a devil to "live and burn in everlasting fire... to torment you with my bitter tongue" (*TA*, 5.2.141-50). We know Othello is not a devilish villain like Aaron, but a noble Moor. Yet, he is intentionally referred to as "an erring barbarian" (*OT*, 1.3.356). When he confesses that he has killed Desdemona, Emilia cries out, "O, the more angel she, / And you the blacker devil!" (*OT*, 5.2.131-2). Cleopatra, then, is presented as a scheming, though charming, woman throughout the play. Antony does once suspect that she has been "a boggler ever" (*A&C*, 3.13.110). Though she proves to be a true lover in the end, she is forever a cheating whore in many other Romans' imagination. Finally in *The Tempest*, as we know,

Caliban, the abject slave, is called "this mis-shapen knave" and "this demi-devil" (*TT*, 5.1.268&272).

Like a non-white, a non-Christian also suffers from prejudices. Shylock is said to be "a very Jew" and "a faithless Jew" (*MV*, 2.2100 & 2.4.37). Since he lends money at exorbitant rates, he is considered as nothing but a loan shark. He is called "the villain Jew," "the dog Jew," "the very devil incarnation," "this cruel devil," and "this currish Jew" (*MV*, 2.7.4, 2.8.14, 2.2.26, 4.1.213, 4.1.288). His desires are said to be "wolvish, bloody, starved, and ravenous" (*MV*, 4.1.138). So, his daughter's kindness towards Launcelot Gobbo only makes Launcelot say: "... most beautiful pagan, most sweet Jew!—if a Christian do not play the knave and get thee, I am much deceived" (*MV*, 2.3.10-12).

Racial prejudices are often used to justify all types of ill-treatment and evil doings. When Tamora's black baby is born, she as well as her nurse and her sons, in order to hide her secret love with Aaron, naturally wishes to "christen it with a dagger's point" or "broach the tadpole on a rapier's point" (*TA*, 4.2.70 & 85). But behind the motive is certainly the white people's prejudiced feeling that the black baby is a devil, "a joyless, dismal, black, and sorrowful issue... as loathsome as a toad / Among the fair-faced breeders of our clime" (*TA*, 4,2.64-68). When Marcus tells Titus that he has killed a fly, Titus at first accuses him of being a murderer, of "a deed of death done on the innocent" (*TA*, 3.2.56), and even expresses his deep sympathy with the fly:

> *How if that fly had father and mother?*
> *How would he hang his slender gilded wings,*
> *And buzz lamenting doings in the air!*
> *Poor harmless fly,*
> *That, with his pretty buzzing melody,*
> *Came here to make us merry, and thou hast killed him.(TA,*
> *3.2.60-65)*

But when Marcus tells Titus that "it was a black ill-favored fly / Like to the empress' Moor," Titus soon changes his tone: "O,O,O! / Then pardon me for reprehending thee, / For thou hast done a charitable deed" (*TA*, 3.2.68-70). Titus has reasons, of course, to hate Aaron, but what makes Aaron even more hateful is his black skin added to his black deeds.

Iago also has reasons, of course, to hate Othello: e.g. the reasons lurking in his complaint that "preferment goes by letter and affection, / Not by the old gradation" (*OT*, 1.1.36-37), and in his ungrounded suspicion that Othello "has done my office betwixt my sheets" (*OT*, 1.3.385-6).[14] But what intensifies his hate may be the fact that he is placed under the command of "the Moor," and an alien Moor is supposed to be not qualified for a general of the whites, nor even for the husband of a beautiful Venetian. That is why Iago should say, "We cannot be all masters, nor all masters / Cannot be truly followed... In following him, I follow but myself" (*OT*, 1.1.42-58). That is also why he should warn Brabantio that "an old black ram / Is tupping your white ewe... the devil will make a grandsire of you" (*OT*, 1.1.88-91). And that is the ultimate reason why he should carry out all his villainous scheme so cruelly against Othello.

Prospero uses Caliban's attempt to violate his daughter as a reason for ill-treating Caliban as "a born devil, on whose nature / Nurture can never stick" (*TT*, 4.1.188-9). In Prospero's and Miranda's minds, as in the minds of many civilized Europeans of Shakespeare's time, Caliban does represent a "vile race" which "any print of goodness will not take, / Being capable of all ill" (*TT*, 1.2.360 & 354-5). Therefore, all Calibans only deserve confinement in caves for servile labor, and they have to be controlled by power and threatened all the time with "old cramps" (*TT*, 1.2.371), very like what the early colonists did to the "barbarians" or "savages" of the colonized lands.

In *Antony and Cleopatra*, the Romans do not seem to have meant any ill-treatment for Cleopatra. But when Octavius says that "her life in Rome / Would be eternal in our triumph" (*A&C*, 5.1.65-66), he has meant to show the Queen of Egypt in the procession in Rome and let all Romans build their pride on the Egyptian's humiliation. It would be disgrace unbearable to Cleopatra indeed, and so she decides to die before it.

Disgrace is what Shylock often has to suffer from. He reminds Antonio that "You call me misbeliever, cut-throat dog, / And spet upon my Jewish gabardine... You spurned me such a day, another time / You called me dog" (*MV*, 1.3.106-123). He is said to be, and is indeed, merciless in court towards Antonio, but he is likewise mercilessly treated when the case turns. All the Christians, including the "fair" judicious lawyer (Portia), seem to feel no qualms in condemning the Jew severely, seizing all his property and forcing him to convert to Christianity.[15] They also seem to feel no qualms about Lorenzo's seducing the Jew's daughter and squandering the Jew's money, nor about Launcelot Gobbo's getting a Moor big with child. They can only laugh to hear another Jew's (Tubal's) report about this Jew's misfortunes.

IV. Venice and the Mediterranean

As we know, Shakespeare's plays are set mostly outside of England, and most often in Italy.[16] The numerous Italian settings may just go to show the tremendous influence of the Italian renaissance which led the entire Europe into a cultural revival after the medieval period. Yet, "the use of place and locale is not 'neutral,' but semantically over-determined" (Marrapodi, et al. 7). Italy was indeed an ambivalent country for the Elizabethans: on one hand it was the cradle of European civilization, of poetry and art; on the other hand it was, in Nashe's words, the "Academie" of political intrigue, poisoners and sinners (Marrapodi, et al. 7). So, a playwright like Shakespeare might exploit Italian historical context "as an important dramaturgical expedient for acting upon the audience's moral attitudes and contributing to the play's ideology" (Marrapodi, et al. 7), leading people to the Petrarchan or Machiavellian world. As Harry Levin sees it, whereas Petrarchism fostered the paradigms for Shakespeare's earlier plays like *Romeo and Juliet*, Machiavellianism preconditioned those of a later play like *Othello* (26).

In fact, as far as race and racism are concerned, we must know that Shakespeare's England was a marginal island immersed in Europe's continental culture (somewhat like today's Taiwan as a peripheral island immersed in China's continental culture). We have said above that Shakespeare's world was a white-centered world dominated by Christianity. For most Elizabethan Europeans, white Christians were the normal and civilized people living in the center of the Renaissance world, and Italy was the geographical as well as cultural core of this world. Consequently, white Christians of Shakespeare's time easily considered those races to be barbarous that lived away from Italy in the outskirts of the Mediterranean sea. It so happened, then, that the Turks, the Arabs, the Moors, etc., were peoples scattered off the Renaissance center. So, it is no mere accident that all the five Shakespearean plays that we have discussed herein as related to race and racism are all set in the Roman or Italian world extending to lands over the Mediterranean.

Indeed, up to Shakespeare's time, Western civilization had been a history of interactions and transactions among the peoples living in countries surrounding the Mediterranean sea, and Hellenism with its Greco-Roman tradition combining Hebraism with its Judaic-Christian tradition had been indelible influences Westerners were imbued with. As time went on, it so happened that Westerners began to think of all the non-Greek, non-Roman, or non-Christian peoples as barbarous tribes. And, as a result, the non-white peoples (the Moors, the

Egyptians, the Arabs, the Turks, etc.) with their non-Christian beliefs were considered "barbarous," fit only for racial discrimination, prejudice, and ill-treatment. Besides this, owing to religious discrepancies and other cultural factors, the Jews were also included in the list that had to face racism not only in imaginary works but also in real life.

The Merchant of Venice is otherwise called The Jew of Venice. The full title Shakespeare gives to Othello is The Tragedy of Othello, the Moor of Venice.[17] If we place The Jew of Venice and The Moor of Venice side by side, it becomes clear that Shakespeare has used the Jew and the Moor as two typical figures and Venice as a typical locale to explore among other things the theme of race and racism. The Jew stands mainly for non-Christian belief and practice, of course, while the Moor stands for non-white barbarism, in the minds of racist Europeans.

As to Venice, we must understand that it was in Shakespeare's imagination a place where a Jew like Shylock could do his loan business and a Moor like Othello could serve as a military leader. According to Isaac Asimov, Venice "at its peak was richer and more powerful than almost any full-sized nation of its time." "It was queen of the sea and a barrier against the formidable Turks." It was like "an Italian Athens born after its time." Although "the fifteenth century saw her pass her peak," and in the sixteenth century the entire peninsula of Italy, including Venice, "was reduced to misery," even in Shakespeare's time "she remained a romantic land, with the trappings of empire still about herself—an efficient, stable, and long-established government over wealthy merchants and skillful seamen with territory and bases here and there in the Mediterranean" (499-501). Shakespeare had never been to Italy or Venice. Venice, therefore, was only an imaginary existence in Shakespeare's mind. For him it was a locale where Venetians mingled with aliens, Christians met with heathens, and civilized people came upon barbarians; where not only

Petrarchism along with poetry and art but also Machiavellianism along with vice and folly prevailed and flourished among the different races. So, Maurice Charney can assert that Venice was "the corrupt, international, commercial city that fascinated Shakespeare and the Elizabethans," and that "Shylock's Venice anticipates the Venice of Iago in *Othello* and there are many ways in which Iago borrows from Shylock" (42).

If Venice was imaginably, for Shakespeare, an international city permeated with Machiavellianism as well as Petrarchism, was racism then a common attitude among the citizens? We have no exact evidence to prove the truth. But Janet Adelman has supposed that Othello is depicted "as the victim of the racist ideology everywhere visible in Venice, an ideology to which he is relentlessly subjected and which increasingly comes to define him as he internalizes it" (111). Anyway, Shakespeare has indeed presented "a Venice that lived in the Elizabethan mind, and it is the Venice of his dramatic needs" (Granville-Barker 69). And we can believe that Shakespeare did imagine Venice as a place where racism could occur naturally to people like Shylock and Othello and to those around the Jew and the Moor, and that Shakespeare chose to dramatize racism in Venice instead of London intentionally, perhaps, to have a better and more objective position in which he could concretize his views of racism.

V. The Cause and the View

We have discussed intrinsic and extrinsic racism in connection with racial pride and prejudice, we have examined Shakespeare's racial personae in connection with racial ill-treatment and evil doings, and we have pointed out Shakespeare's typical racial figures in connection with their typical locale. Now, it is time to see further, to probe into the problem of how racism is complicated by other matters in Shakespearean drama and finally to figure out Shakespeare's racial views that constitute his racial vision.

In *Titus Andronicus*, racism is complicated primarily by power struggle and dire vengeance. Aaron, the blackamoor, tries to "mount aloft" with his Gothic imperial mistress, Tamora. But the two are further involved in a series of mutually revengeful acts between two sides initiated by Titus' killing Tamora's son Alarbus. The revengeful acts bring about "murthers, rapes, and massacres, / Acts of black night, abominable deeds, / Complots of mischief, treason, villainies, / Ruthful to hear, yet piteously performed" (*TA*, 5.1.63-66). In the course of power struggle and dire vengeance, the Romans have reason to treat Aaron and his accomplice as "barbarous beastly villains" (*TA*, 5.1.97). But Titus and other Romans on his side are no less barbarous and beastly in their ferocity and cruelty. Thus, Shakespeare seems to suggest through the play that no race is ever really civilized: blacks and whites can be equally barbarous, beastly, villainous, and devilish, though a black man like Aaron may seem to have behaved more like an arrant knave or a black devil.

In *The Merchant of Venice*, racism is complicated by commerce and religion, and "the physical and emotional are bonded to the financial" (Peter Smith 176). Shylock and the Christians certainly belong to widely different "races."[18] Like the two sides in *Titus Andronicus*, the Jew and the Venetians are reciprocally engaged in revengeful acts. Shylock hates Antonio because "he lends out money gratis, and brings down / The rate of usance here with us in Venice" (*MV*, 1.3.39-40) and, of course, because the Christians have different customs and often scorn him and ill-treat him. But Shylock himself also scorns the Christians for their laxity with money and of morals. The Christians hate the Jew primarily for his mercenary attitude, of course. But, in fact, the Christians are as mercenary as the Jew. Bassanio woos to marry Portia so that he might "get clear of all the debts I owe" (*MV*, 1.1.134). Portia's "sunny locks" are likened to "a golden fleece" (*MV*, 1.1.169-70), and Gratiano says, "We are the Jasons, we have won the fleece" (*MV*, 3.2.240). The court scene with the "pound of flesh" theme seems on the surface to show the Jew's merciless cruelty towards the Christians. Yet, the Venetians and those from Belmont, for all their Christian teachings, are merciless and cruel in like manner, since they can bear to deprive the Jew of everything— his property, dignity, religion, etc. So, through the play Shakespeare seems to suggest that no race, Christian or non-Christian, is ever really without mercenary avarice, and no race is ever really tolerant or merciful enough: in the face of material profit each race is often burdened with its own "bond" of racial value, thus going not towards fraternity and love but towards hostility and hate.

In *Othello*, racism is complicated by love and marriage as well as by power struggle. We have said that Iago hates Othello for the general's method of preferment and for his own suspicion of illicit love. Iago elevates his personal revenge to a racial revenge. He tries to make Roderigo, Brabantio and other whites believe that the Moor is a lascivious "erring barbarian," and Brabantio does believe Othello to be a mountebank Moor. Iago even tries to make Othello believe that Venetian women are lax in sex—"In Venice they do let God see the pranks / They dare not show their husbands" (*OT*, 3.3.206-7)—and that Desdemona was deceptive regarding his skin color: "when she seemed to shake and fear your looks, /She loved them most" (*OT*, 3.3.211-2). So, there was a time when Othello did believe that his complexion might really become one of the reasons for his failure in marriage life: "Haply, for I am black, / And have not those soft parts of conversation / That chamberers have, or for I am declined / Into the vale of years" (*OT*, 3.3.267-9). Finally, we can assume that when Othello was told to leave his command in Cyprus to Cassio as his successor, and when he said he would obey the mandate and return to Venice, he must have felt the agony of a Moor seemingly forced to yield both his power and his woman to a white man. In other words, racism must have entered his mind unconsciously to add to his spite against his supposed opponent. That is why in explaining his affliction he suddenly yells to Desdemona, "Turn thy complexion there," and asks, "O thou black weed, why art so lovely fair?" (*OT*, 4.2.64 & 69). (The word "fair" obviously denotes both "beautiful" and "white in skin color" here.)

Othello's racial consciousness may have stemmed from his own natural understanding, but it is stirred up by Iago purposely for this Florentine white man's own personal and racial revenge (Iago is said to be from Florence). Iago does handle racial consciousness successfully with skill throughout the tragedy. In the end, for instance, when he is telling Roderigo that there is command from Venice to depute Cassio in Othello's place, he adds a lie replete with racial consciousness: "he [Othello] goes into Mauritania, and takes away with him the fair Desdemona" (*OT*, 4.2.223-4). This lie suggests as much as "This black Moor is taking his fair-skinned wife back to the black land of the Moors."[19] It is this lie that has prompted Roderigo to linger Othello's abode by trying to remove Cassio. So, the whole play contains a long story of how racial consciousness is manipulated for a wicked purpose, and Shakespeare seems to suggest thereby that racism is often exploited for a special purpose and thus it often comes to a tragic end.

No racism is manifestly exploited in *Antony and Cleopatra*. But racial consciousness does exist when Antony calls Cleopatra "Egypt," or "this foul Egyptian"; when Cleopatra refrains from talking about complexion in trying to compare herself with Octavia in many other respects; when Philo mentions Cleopatra's "tawny front" or "a gipsy's lust"; when Enobarbus refers to Antony's "Egyptian dish"; and when Pompey refers to "the lap of Egypt's widow" (*A&C*, 1.1.6 & 9, 2.1.37, 2.7.123, 3.3.11-33, 3.11.56, 4.12.10). And racial pride does exist when Octavius tries to get the Queen of Egypt to Rome and lead her in triumph. Here we may see, as did Shakespeare, that racism need not take any obvious act to reveal itself. Think how many times Shylock has been called "the Jew" instead of "Shylock" and how many times Othello has been called "the Moor" instead of "Othello." Racism does concur with appellation.

The appellations given to Caliban are "monster," "savage," and "slave." In these appellations are implied the ideas of "a deformed person," "an uncivilized person," and "an abject person." But such ideas are not used to describe an individual only. As Caliban is a typical native of his land and the land is usurped by the whites (typified by Prospero and Miranda), the appellations actually refer to all Calibans as a native race. And, thus, racism in *The Tempest* involves "colonialism" and power struggle between "the colonizers" and "the colonized."

As we can see from the plot of *The Tempest*, the power used for power struggle in Italy among the whites themselves is chiefly political and military power, but the power used for usurping the colored people's land on the island is mainly magic power, which Prospero calls his "Art." At this point, Shakespeare seems to suggest that to the inferior race like Caliban's, the white superior race seems to have mysterious power capable of overriding the powers of the natives. Such mysterious power suggests, in fact, colonists' cheating art plus military power, as used by the early settlers.

Although Prospero uses his "Art" (his magic power) instead of military or political power to usurp Caliban's land, he uses force none the less and he keeps using force to control and enslave Caliban as "the other race." Caliban, to be sure, acts like a person born abject. He would even lick Stephano's shoe for a taste of his liquor. But Prospero and Miranda have used Caliban's misdemeanor as a pretext to declare him reprobate by nature and then confine him to a rock, making him practically a slave. In their minds they have the right to be the masters: they believe their race is superior to the race of Calibans. So, through the play Shakespeare seems to suggest that the racist oppressors certainly regard their race as superior to the race of the oppressed, thus having the conscience to ill-treat the other race or do evil things to them.

VI. Shy lock, Ot, hell, O!

W. E. B. DuBois is said to have argued that "racialism is the belief that differences between the races exist, be they biological, social, psychological, or in the realm of the soul"; and that "racism is using this belief to promote the belief that one's particular race is superior to the others."[20] As mentioned above, Todorov has, in effect, said pretty much the same thing, and he added that racists even believe that "the subordination of inferior races or even their elimination can be justified by accumulated knowledge on the subject of race" (67). So far, we have discussed a lot based on Shakespearean drama in the light of racial consciousness, can we now decide as to whether Shakespeare is a racialist or a racist in the sense given by DuBois or Todorov?

As his plays have displayed it, Shakespeare may be called a racialist, but surely not a racist. He certainly recognized differences in races, but he did not see any sense in racial discrimination, opposition, oppression, or violation, not to say genocide. He was, in truth, an impartial humanitarian preaching racial liberty, equality, and fraternity.

We may recall that Aaron defends his black baby forcefully in order to save its life. For all his evil doings, he says this touchingly to Chiron:

> *Here's a young lad framed of another leer:*
> *Look how the black slave smiles upon the father,*
> *As who should say, "Old lad, I am thine own."*
> *He is your brother, lords, sensibly fed*
> *Of that self blood that first gave life to you;*
> *And from that womb where you imprisoned were*

> *He is enfranchised and come to light:*
> *Nay, he is your brother by the surer side,*
> *Although my seal be stamped in his face. (TA, 4.2.119-27)*

We can take these words for Shakespeare's pleading for racial fraternity if we cannot believe such words can come from the black devil's mouth.

Obviously, no racial fraternity is found between the Christians and the Jew in *The Merchant of Venice*. Shylock's likening gold and silver to ewes and rams, and hence his comparing the generation of interest to the breeding of "eanlings" (*MV*, 1.3.74), only adds to our impression that monetary management has robbed the Jew of his sense of fraternity. But on the other hand Antonio's calling Shylock a dog repeatedly suggests that the Christian has treated the Jew "as if he were from another species of animal than the human one" (Shell 110). So, what Shakespeare attacks in the play is all races' lack of love or friendship owing to financial avarice, and what he preaches in the play is the regaining of people's lost sense of inter-racial fraternity.

In reality, Shakespeare preaches racial equality even more obviously in *The Merchant of Venice*. We may recall these words spoken by the abominable Jew:

> *Hath not a Jew eyes? Hath not a Jew hands, organs,*
> *dimensions, senses, affections, passions? Fed with*
> *the same food, hurt with the same weapons, subject*
> *to the same diseases, healed by the same means,*
> *warmed and cooled by the same winter and summer*
> *as a Christian is? —if you prick us do we not bleed?*
> *If you tickle us do we not laugh? If you*
> *poison us do we not die? And if you wrong us shall*
> *we not revenge? —if we are like you in the rest, we*
> *will resemble you in that. (MV, 3.1.52-61)*

These words are not just words uttered by this ill-treated Jew. They are words used by Shakespeare to plead for equality among all races, wishing us to look more at racial similarities than at racial differences.

The abhorred slave, Caliban, is only eloquent enough to make a plain speech and curse the masters. But he says clearly to Prospero: "...This island's mine, by Sycorax my mother, which thou tak'st from me..." and that "...I am all the subjects that you have, / Which first was mine own King: and here you sty me / In this hard rock, whiles you do keep from me / The rest o' th' island" (*TT*, 1.2.333-46). Like Ariel, he longs for freedom. In the end, Prospero pardons all, breaks his staff, discards his Art, and sets everybody free, including Caliban and his companions. These final gestures of Prospero's imply in essence Shakespeare's pleading for liberty among all races. And this pleading is intensified by the last two lines of this play's Epilogue addressed by Prospero to the audience: "As you from crimes would pardoned be, / Let your indulgence set me free" (19-20). In Shakespeare's view, then, no individual of any race but loves freedom, although mankind with all its races is full of crimes. One can be pardoned from one's crime. But one has to be set free first. No race is really born slaves.

Yet, from what does one have to be set free in spirit? In terms of racism, one has to be set free first from racial pride and prejudice. Racial pride and prejudice are Sycorax's "cloven pines" to confine all Ariels, Prospero's cells to imprison all Calibans, and his Art to control all people, including Italians and Algerians. Racial pride and prejudice are also the real handkerchiefs to bind the aching heads of all Othellos, and the unseen handkerchiefs to bind the scheming heads of all Iagos. Furthermore, racial pride and prejudice are the Jews' "bonds" to inflict penalties on Christians, and the Christians' "bonds" in turn to persecute the Jews. Instead of such "bonds," we need "rings of love" to bind Lorenzos with Jessicas as well as Bassanios with Portias, Gratianos with Nerissas, and Shylocks with Leahs.

In Shakespeare's imagination, all races are really alike in various aspects. So, racist stereotyping is always wrong. Portia is wrong in thinking with her bias of her suitors of various nationality as mere types. A white man is not always "white" in character, and a black is not always amoral and anti-Christian.[21] If Aaron is a villain, Iago is another. If Cleopatra is a lecherous queen, Tamora is another as well. Shylock is indeed merciless, but so is Portia. Othello is certainly jealous, but so is Iago. Caliban wants to lord over his own land, but who doesn't? Jessica deserts his father for her Venetian, and Desdemona likewise deserts her father for her own Moor. The Prince of Morocco comes for a beauty, but so many others from so many other countries and races have done the same thing for the same purpose. If many a Shylock is too thrifty, many a Bassanio is too profligate. If many a Moor is as cunning and cruel as Aaron, many a white man is as scheming and wicked as Iago. If the black devil is terrible, the white devil is horrible, too.[22]

As Shakespeare tries to bring us to the awareness of racial similarities, however, his treatment of racial consciousness may have been influenced by his class consciousness. The servile Caliban is no king, nor duke. The devilish Aaron is but a slavish lover attending on a Gothic queen. But Othello is a general "from men of royal siege" (*OT*, 1,2.22). He as well as the Prince of Morocco is no black devil, but a noble Moor. So, it seems to Shakespeare that noble birth can be a compensation for ignoble complexion. We have reason to believe that the inter-racial union of Claribel with Tunis mentioned in *The Tempest* is approved on the side of the Neapolitans in consideration of royalty.

Meanwhile, Shakespeare's treatment of racial consciousness may also have been influenced by his gender consciousness. A white woman seduced by a black man, like the case of Desdemona and Othello, is considered in the play as an intolerable case of miscegenation, and their sexual intercourse is equated to sodomy.[23] But a black girl made big with child by a white servant, like the case of Launcelot Gobbo and his Moor, only serves to "further misogynistic humor" (Daileader 15). Although Antony and Cleopatra are as much to blame as Aaron and Tamora for their inter-racial lust, the former case (a white man with a colored woman) seems to be more pardonable (even much "greater") than the latter case (a black man with a white woman). Similarly, a Jewish girl like Jessica may run away with a Lorenzo,[24] but a white girl like Miranda is absolutely untouchable to a Caliban.

Notwithstanding that both Shakespeare's class consciousness and his gender consciousness may really have influenced his treatment of racial consciousness, we must conclude that generally speaking, Shakespeare's racial personae are indeed presented with a view to doing away with racism, rather than promoting it. In his mind there always seems to be a Shylock, who is indeed *a shy lock*—a shy person locked up in his own ideological house, segregated in his own racial consciousness, refusing and not daring to come out and mix with other people of a different race. Such a Shylock needs, in fact, to *shy away (from) his lock*, and gives his keys not just to Jessica, his daughter, but to everybody else so that all the valuables placed in his caskets, including his racial treasures, may be found, appreciated, and utilized.

Simultaneously, an Othello also seems to exist all the time in Shakespeare's mind. He is another victim of racism. He is always crying out not just "O! O! O!" (*OT*, 5.2.198), but "Ot, hell, O!"[25] He knows as well as we do, at last, that racism, along with other things, is always there ready to make one, "whose hand, / like a base Indian, threw a pearl away, / Richer than all his tribe" (*OT*, 5.2.347-9). And we know as well as he does, at last, that there is always a racist villain, an Iago, waiting there ready to use racism as a means to mar everything and ruin everybody so as to have his personal and racial revenge.

VII. The Comprehensive Vision

Literary themes can be particular themes or universal ones. A universal theme is often a comprehensive theme as well: it can include a number of related themes. In Shakespeare, for instance, love-and-marriage is a universal theme occurring in many comedies and tragedies. It is also a comprehensive theme, as it covers such themes as youthful fancy, foolish dotage, patriarchy, Oedipus complex, jealousy, villainy, and property, in addition to the racial theme of miscegenation. But, as far as race and racism are concerned, the most relevant comprehensive theme to cover the themes of racial consciousness, racial pride, racial prejudice, racial discrimination, racial oppression, etc., is the theme of appearance vs. reality.

It should be noted that the theme of appearance vs. reality has indeed recurred in all types of Shakespearean drama. It is of course to be found in a "comedy of errors," in which A is mistaken for B just because of their similarity in appearance. It is certainly to be found in a history play, in which power struggle leads people into intrigues and crimes that hide reality and appear innocent. It is surely found in *Hamlet*, in which the word "seems" becomes an important word ringing with significance, in *Macbeth*, in which fair is said to be foul and foul is said to be fair, and in *King Lear*, in which "nothing" is actually "something" and "natural" may prove "unnatural." As to a romance, we are reminded in *The Tempest* that we are but such stuff as "dreams are made on" and everything will "melt into thin air" (*TT*, 4.1.150 & 157): all is mere visionary appearance without any substantial reality.

To return to our present theme of race and racism, we must assert that in Shakespeare's vision, skin color or religious denomination is but an aspect of one's appearance by nature or by nurture: it takes time and wisdom, therefore, to probe into reality, to know one's real personality and to know the real situation one is in. It may be easy to identify Aaron as a devilish black villain, but not so easy to thrust Othello into the black side of murderous Moors. It may be easy to see Shylock as apparently a Jewish usurer, as overtly a relentless racial victimizer with a hoard of "jewels and stones and ducats" locked up in his personal caskets and in his racial ideology. It is not so easy to see him at the same time as actually a racial victim, as covertly a pitiable Jew with nothing left but a "bond" to appeal to the apparently fair, but actually unfair, Portia, who is actually no *Justina*, but only the partial *Portia* with her personal and racial portion, and so wants the Jew to be openly merciful but is hiddenly merciless herself.

Indeed, throughout Shakespearean drama, we can easily find a white-dominated Christendom, in which complexion and religion often serve obviously as a twofold basis for racial discrimination and oppression. Therefore, in Shakespeare's vision there are two typical figures, the Jew and the Moor, suffering forever from racism in their Venice. But we must say that in terms of racial responsibility Shakespeare's view of racism is an impartial one. For all his treatment of Shylock as a racist loan shark, Shakespeare has actually made the Jew pathetic as well as hateful and laughable.[26] And for all his treatment of Antonio as a generous patron friend of the Venetians, Shakespeare has actually made him an unjust racist, too, towards the Jews. Meanwhile, for all his treatment of Iago as a villain seemingly devoted to evil without any motive, he has actually probed into his racial psyche to find part of the reason for the Ancient's evil doings, just as he has probed into Othello's racial consciousness to find the Moor's own racism as part of the reason for his final murderous act. So, in Shakespeare's view, the Jews, the Moors, the Venetians, etc., are all alike: all races are susceptible to racism.

In treating impartially all people's susceptibility to racism, Shakespeare had his own purpose, of course. We cannot overlook his efforts, indeed, to court the favor of his spectators by looking at racial problems more through a white European's eye than through a colored person's. Yet, somehow, he was never too lopsided for us to see his real intention. In the Christendom as staged in all his drama with its apparent racialism or racism, we can actually see a great humanist Shakespeare, with a really humanitarian concern about races, with a true heart pleading in his true voice, wishing us to regard all races in terms of fraternity, equality, and liberty, and expecting us to let Aaron's "tadpole" live, let Shylock's "case" have a fair judgment, and let Caliban's "isle" witness his own freedom. Meanwhile, we also hear a voice spoken explicitly and implicitly to warn all races to guard against such racist tendencies in life as found related to an Aaron or a Titus, a Shylock or an Antonio, an Othello or an Iago, a Caliban or a Prospero, a Cleopatra or a Tamora, a Jessica or a Desdemona, et cetera, et cetera, lest racism should bring about unwanted comedies or tragedies, unworthy consequences of history or romance.

So, Shakespeare's racial vision is a "fair vision," an impartial and comprehensive vision, a vision in which no race is "all black" nor "all white," in which the Jew and the Moor, together with the Christians and the Venetians, are equally condemned for their vices, ridiculed for their follies, venerated for their virtues, and praised for their merits; a vision, actually, in which personage is not just skin deep, and barbarism is not just Barbary's unique racial badge; in which, finally, all races, in all classes of both genders and in all walks of life, are asked to see real differences between appearance and reality, rather than seek superficial differences among races in terms of nature or nurture.

But, alas, in this fair, impartial, and comprehensive racial vision, we as well as Shakespeare can always see a Shylock, that is, a racial shy lock, Christian or non-Christian, that locks oneself up shyly in racial consciousness made up of racial pride and prejudice, which is no other than a racial "bond" that binds one with racial ideology. How we wish such a one to shy away (from) the lock or the bond! And how we wish to let such a one have a bunch of keys that are made of fraternity, equality, and liberty! For only with such keys can mankind open the only real casket that stores the ideal Portia (not just a superficial portrait of her real self), that is, an authentic "fair" with her *portion* of beauty, truth, and goodness.

Yet, alas again, before we get the "fair"! For Othello is always going side by side with Shylock there! Unlike the fake and funny name "Shylock" for a Jew, the rare name "Othello" does suggest an authentic Italian man of "wish" or "will."[27] And the dramatic Othello does wish to live well in the white Christendom and love his Venetian wife. But, alas, his head is bound with a handkerchief that cannot rid him of his headache. The handkerchief is a racist handkerchief transferred from hand to hand. It is a magic handkerchief, too, exploited by a racist villain, who has used his racial contempt and hatred to justify his vice and folly. It has turned the white Desdemona into "the demon" that has a "black" lover and made her "black" lover mourning everlastingly, "Ot, hell, O!"—a sound reminding us all the time to beware of racism and asking us to replace racial pride with inter-racial respect, and to eliminate racial prejudices rather than races.

Notes

1. The editorial was titled "Shakespeare's Bare Bodkin." It appears in Ashbrook Center for Public Affairs at Ashland University.
   [http://www.ashbrook.org/publicat/oped/flannery/98/shakespeare.html]

2. The play, when entered in the Stationers' Register for 1598, was referred to as "a booke of the Marchaunt of Venyce, or otherwise called the Iewe of Venyce."

3. As the Jew of Venice, Shylock was at first presented as a horrific and grotesque figure rather than a pathetic hero. It is not until our contemporary age that he is often presented as a tragic victim.

4. Peter Davison says: "*Othello* is not 'about' race, or color, or even jealousy. It dramatizes the way actions are directed rather by attitudes, fears and delusions that rule the subconscious than by evident facts" (64). But for most critics and common readers, the play's primary theme is certainly jealousy.

5. Caliban is an Algerian mother's son but is like an American Indian in that he is also a colored person and his land is usurped by the whites. For detail about this Indian theme, see Alden T. Vaughan's "Shakespeare's Indian: The Americanization of Caliban."

6. According to Marvin McAllister, North Africa's Barbary Coast was originally settled by Amazighs or "Berbers" during antiquity and later conquered by Arabs in the seventh century. The intermixture of Africans and Arabs produced a hybrid population commonly known as Moors.

7. For the information about the Moors, see Asimov, 401-2.
8. Coleridge thought: "It would be something monstrous to conceive this beautiful Venetian girl falling in love with a veritable negro" (quoted in Bristol 194). Bradley thought "a coal-black Othello would overpower our imagination" (202), and Carol Needy also suggested that Othello "should be read not as a black at all but as a 'mestizo'—a hybrid" (Loombaq 150).
9. Quoted from Richard Coates' foreword to *Names in Shakespeare Online: A Bibliography of Proper Names in Shakespeare to 2005*, p. 3.
10. As we know, in their source stories (the first story of the fourth day of Ser Giovanni, *Il Pecorone*, and the narrative in Cinthio's the *Hecatommithi*, respectively), both the Jew and the Moor are unnamed. Thus, in giving them names Shakespeare, very probably, must have tried to make the names meaningful.
11. Todorov has mentioned five steps in which racialism becomes racism. See his "Race and Racism," 65-67.
12. Isaac Asimov, for instance, says: "It is inconceivable that the Venetians would trust a Mohammedan to lead their armed forces against the Mohammedan Turks; we must therefore further assume that Othello was a converted Christian" (616).
13. Quoted by Marvin McAllister in his "Program Notes—the Image of Othello." [http://www.shakespearetheatre.org/plays/articles.aspx? &id=113], p. 1.
14. Coleridge thought of Iago as a villain that did not require our "motive-hunting of a motiveless malignity." M. R. Ridley rejected this idea and pointed out a number of motives for Iago. See Ridley's introduction to his edition of *Othello*, p. lx-lxi.

15. Harold C. Goddard says that "as if in imitation of the Jew's own cruelty, they [the Christians] whet their knives of law and logic, of reason and justice, and proceed to cut out their victim's heart" (35). This confirms Shylock's conviction that "Christianity and revenge are synonyms" (35).

16. Charles Lamb once regretted: "I am sometimes jealous that Shakespeare laid so few of his scenes at home." This is quoted in Levin, 21, and Levin counts 11 Shakespearean plays with Italian settings aside from the Roman tragedics.

17. Harold Bloom says: "*The Moor of Venice* is sometimes the neglected part of the tragedy's title. To be the Moor of Venice...... is an uneasy honor, Venice being, then and now, the uneasiest of cities" (1987, 2).

18. John Palmer says that the play is to contrast "the narrow, alert and suspicious character of the Jew" with "the free, careless and confident disposition of the Christian"; the former trusting in his bond, the latter trusting to luck (120).

19. According to Asimov, "Maurtania was the name given in ancient times to the northwest shoulder of Africa, the region now called Morocco." It may be used here as a vague term, meaning "a land of the Moors, that is, north Africa generally" (628).

20. See "Definitions of Racism" in the entry of "Racism," *Wikipedia*. [en.wikipedia.org/wiki/Racism]

21. Both Martin Orkin and Virginia Mason see Othello as a reversal of the stereotyped black and white associations. For further detail, see Ian Smith, p. 178ff.

22. We may note that John Webster's revenge tragedy *The White Devil* was staged in Shakespeare's later years, but the idea that "the white devil is worse than the black" must have entered the dramatic circle as early as when Shakespeare brought forth *Titus Andronicus*.

23. For discussion about interracial marriages as sodomy, see Bruce Boehrer's *Shakespeare Among the Animals*, p. 20 ff.

24. James Shapiro says that even religious conversion "is not quite the same for Jewish women as it is for Jewish men." For further detail, see his *Shakespeare and the Jews*, p. 132 ff.

25. Daileader, in discussing "a devil" as the play's most recurring epithet, takes "Othello" to be "Ot-HELL-o" and "Desdemona" to be "Des-DEMON-a" (24).

26. This is an evident fact, but E. E, Stoll cannot agree on this point. See his "Shylock" in Bloom, p. 25. Leslie A. Fielder also believes that "the appeal of Shylock was not so much pathetic as horrific and grotesque" (64).

27. I think the initial "O-" in "Othello" is like the "O'-" in so many Irish names, meaning "of"; the ending "-o" is an Italian suffix indicating the male gender, in contrast with the female "-a" (as in "Portia"); and the second "l" is just a repetition of the last letter of "thel" in accordance with the spelling rule of the English language. Meanwhile, I agree with M. H. Abrams that "thel" probably derives from a Greek word for "wish" or "will" (see Abrams' introduction to *The Book of Thel* in his edition of *Norton Anthology of English Literature*).

Works Consulted

Adelman, Janet. "Iago's Alter Ego: Race as Projection in *Othello*," in Orgel & Keilen, 111-130.

Appiah, Kwame Anthony. "Racisms." *Anatomy of Racism*. Ed. David Theo Goldberg. Minneapolis: U of Minnesota P, 1990. 3-17.

Asimov, Isaac. *Asimov's Guide to Shakespeare*. New York: Wings Books, 1970.

Auden, W. H. "Brothers and Others," in Wilders, 224-240.

Barber, C. L. "The Merchants and the Jew of Venice," in Wilders, 176-192.

Bloom, Harold, ed. *William Shakespeare's The Merchant of Venice*. Modern Critical Interpretations. New York & Philadelphia: Chelsea House Publishers, 1986.

Bloom, Harold, ed. *William Shakespeare's Othello*. Modern Critical Interpretations. New York & Philadelphia: Chelsea House Publishers, 1987.

Boehrer, Bruce. *Shakespeare Among the Animals*. New York: Palgrave, 2002.

Bradley, A. C. *Shakespearean Tragedy*. London: Macmillan, 1904.

Bristol, Michael D. *Big-Time Shakespeare*. London & New York: Routledge, 1996.

Charney, Maurice. *All of Shakespeare*. New York: Columbia UP, 1993.

Coates, Richard. Foreword to *Names in Shakespeare Online: A Bibliography of Proper Names in Shakespeare to 2005*. [http://www.informatics.sussex.ac.uk/users/schoi/Shakespeare/about.php]

Daileader, Celia R. *Racism, Misogyny, and the Othello Myth: Inter-Racial Couples from Shakespeare to Spike Lee*. Cambridge: Cambridge UP, 2005.

Davison, Peter. *Othello*. London: Macmillan, 1988.

Dryden, John. "An Essay of Dramatic Poesy." *Critical Theory Since Plato*. Ed. Hazard Adams. New York: Harcourt Brace Jovanovich, 1971. 228-257.

Fiedler, Leslie A. "These Be the Christian Husbands," in Bloom (1986), 63-90.

Fitch, Robert E. *Shakespeare: The Perspective of Value.* Philadelphia: The Westminster Press, 1969.

Goddard, Harold C. "Portia's Failure," in Bloom (1986), 27-36.

Granville-Barker, Harley. "Shakespeare's Venice," in Wilders, 69-71.

Greenblatt, Stephen. "The Improvisation of Power," in Bloom (1987), 37-60.

Hecht, Anthony. "Othello," in Bloom (1987), 123-141.

Levin, Harry. "Shakespeare's Italians," in Marrapodi, et al., 17-29.

Loomba, Ania & Martin Orkin, eds. *Post-Colonial Shakespeares.* London & New York: Routledge, 1998.

Marrapodi, et al., eds. *Shakespeare's Italy: Functions of Italian Locations in Renaissance Drama.* Manchester & New York: Manchester UP, 1997.

McAllister, Marvin. "Program Notes—The Image of Othello." [http://www.shakespearetheatre.org/plays/articles.aspx?&id=113]

Orgel, Stephen & Sean Keilen, eds. *Political Shakespeare.* New York & London: Garland Publishing, 1999.

Palmer, John. "Shylock," in Wilders, 115-131.

Shakespeare, William. *Antony and Cleopatra.* Ed. M. R. Ridley. London: Methuen, 1978. Abbreviated to *A&C.*

——. *The Merchant of Venice.* Ed. John Russell Brown. London: Methuen, 1979. Abbreviated to *MV.*

——. *Othello.* Ed. M. R. Ridley. London & New York: Methuen, 1979. Abbreviated to *OT.*

——. *The Tempest.* Ed. Frank Kermode. London & New York: Methuen, 1979. Abbreviated to *TT.*

——. *Titus Andronicus.* Ed. J. C. Maxwell. London & New York: Methuen, 1987. Abbreviated to *TA.*

Shapiro, James. *Shakespeare and the Jews.* New York: Columbia UP, 1996.

Shell, Marc. "The Wether and the Ewe: Verbal Usury," in Bloom (1986), 107-120.

Smith, Ian. "Barbarian Errors: Performing Race in Early Modern England," in Orgel & Keilen, 168-186.

Smith, Peter J. *Social Shakespeare: Aspects of Renaissance Dramaturgy and Contemporary Society.* Basingstoke & London: Macmillan, 1995.

Snyder, Susan. "Beyond Comedy: Othello," in Bloom (1987), 23-36.

Stoll, E. E. "Shylock," in Bloom (1986), 15-26.

Todorov, Tzvetan. "Race and Racism." Trans. Catherine Porter. *Theories of Race and Racism.* Ed. Les Back & John Solomos. London & New York: Routledge, 2000. 64-70.

Vaughan, Alden T. "Shakespeare's Indian: The Americanization of Caliban," in Orgel & Keilen, 131-147.

Wilders, John, ed. *Shakespeare: The Merchant of Venice.* London: Macmillan, 1969.

* This chapter first appeared as a paper in 2008 in National Chung Hsing University's *Journal of Humanities*, Vol. 41, pp.233-270.

• Chapter 6 •

The Two Lears: Shakespeare's
Humanist Vision of Nature

I. The Poet of Nature

Shakespeare is often introduced as "the poet of nature." But what exactly does the epithet mean? When Samuel Johnson praises Shakespeare as "above all writers, at least above all modern writers, the poet of nature," the critic's mind is focused on the "naturalness" of the poet's dramatic presentation, that is, on the playwright's ability to "hold up to his readers a faithful mirror of manners and of life," thus creating typical characters who are "the genuine progeny of common humanity" and whose dialogues seem "to have been gleaned by diligent selection out of common conversation, and common occurrences" (330). As an advocate of neoclassicism, Johnson in fact praises Shakespeare's "adherence to general nature," his "making nature predominate over accident" (331). Yet, while praising Shakespeare's "naturalness" (which refers in effect to such neoclassic merits as "faithfulness," "commonness," "genuineness," "typicality," and "generality"), Johnson also disparages Shakespeare for the defect, among others, of "sacrificing virtue to convenience," of seeming to "write without any moral purpose," which shows that the dramatist "is so much more careful to please than to instruct" (333).

Now, we must admit that Johnson is right in pointing out Shakespeare's defect of prioritizing pleasure before instruction as well as his merit of dramatizing life naturally. However, we must also grant that it is only natural for a playwright to try to delight his readers or theatergoers first, and that Shakespeare as a delightful playwright is actually not without his moral purpose in writing any of his plays: if he has to sacrifice virtue to convenience at times, he has actually never forgot the importance of virtue. In truth, if Shakespeare "makes no just distribution of good or evil," or if he "carries his persons indifferently through right and wrong," it is not, as Johnson goes on to suggest, just a "fault the barbarity of his age cannot extenuate" (333). It is, rather, the natural outcome of Shakespeare's seeing so much of the basic nature in humanity and seeing so much of the comic and the tragic in life.

At this juncture, we may recall Hamlet's advice to the Players: "... you overstep not the modesty of nature: for anything so overdone is from the purpose of playing, whose end, both at the first and now, was and is, to hold as it were the mirror to nature: to show virtue her feature, scorn her own image, and the very age and body of the time his form and pressure" (3.2.19-24). These words of Hamlet's are no other than Shakespeare's. They express the idea that art is a truthful representation ("mirroring") of life and to be truthful is also to observe the principle of moderation, i.e. , to show *naturally* the feature and image of both virtue and vice ("scorn") in addition to showing the form and impression ("pressure") of the "age and body of the time." Therefore, for Hamlet or Shakespeare, those players are to be debased who have imitated humanity so abominably that they neither have "the accent of Christians nor the gait of Christian, pagan, nor man," and who have so strutted and bellowed that anyone might think "some of Nature's journeymen had made men, and not made them well" (3.2.31-35). To overdo anything in acting virtue or vice is to overstep "the modesty of nature" or violate the natural principle of moderation.

In point of fact, moderation (besides commonness or generality) is another essential merit for neoclassical writers like Johnson. Theoretically, Johnson should have been glad of Shakespeare's impartial treatment of both virtue and vice. Yet, as it is, Johnson's didacticism has led himself to complain of Shakespeare's essential amorality, or of his lack of "poetic justice." Johnson "knows well that in this world justice is not poetic" (Eastman 28). Yet, in view of justice Johnson seems to prefer art to nature, wishing Shakespeare would go to the extreme of depicting the ideal, rather than the real, for the sake of promoting virtue and demolishing vice. In the light of poetic justice, then, Shakespeare as the poet of nature seems to be too "natural" for Johnson.

In actuality, Shakespeare's "naturalness" or "over-naturalness," as will be shown in this essay, has much to do with his understanding of nature, which can be termed a "humanist vision of nature." But, before we come to the conclusion, we need to know first the meaning of the key word "nature."

II. The One Single Word

In his "Lear, Tolstoy and the Fool," George Orwell thus remarks with his critical acumen:

> *Shakespeare has a habit of thrusting uncalled-for general reflections into the mouths of his characters. This is a serious fault in a dramatist, but it does not fit in with Tolstoy's picture of Shakespeare as a vulgar hack who has no opinions of his own and merely wishes to produce the greatest effect with the least trouble. And more than this, about a dozen of his plays, written for the most part later than 1600, do unquestionably have a meaning and even a moral. They revolve round a*

> central subject which in some cases can be reduced to a single
> word. For example, Macbeth is about ambition. Othello is
> about jealousy, and Timon of Athens is about money.

After this, Orwell adds, "The subject of *Lear* is renunciation, and it is only by being willfully blind that one can fail to understand what Shakespeare is saying" (159-160).

Orwell's critical acumen is really worthy of our admiration. For me Shakespeare did write a number of "one-word plays," of which *Lear* is but one, and not an obvious one. If we want to give some other definite examples, we can refer to *Troilus and Cressida* with its subject of fidelity, *Measure for Measure* with its of justice, and *Coriolanus* with its of pride. However, in the case of *Lear*, I cannot agree with Orwell that "it is only by being willfully blind that one can fail to understand what Shakespeare is saying." I do not believe that Orwell was himself being willfully blind when he maintained that the subject of *Lear* is renunciation. Nevertheless, I must say that in his consideration of the play's theme Orwell was somewhat blindfolded by the main plot (the Lear plot) of the play. The subplot (the Gloucester plot) of the play simply has nothing to do with renunciation. If we take a whole view of the play, we must admit that we cannot say the play's double plot is unified by the theme of renunciation.

Ironically, it seems, Orwell has forgot his own word. He has forgotten that "Shakespeare has a habit of thrusting uncalled-for general reflections into the mouths of his characters." As anyone can see, in *King Lear* Shakespeare is so preoccupied with his general reflections on the Great Nature and our human nature that the word "nature" is noticeably repeated again and again through the mouths of the characters. John Danby has observed that *King Lear* is a drama of ideas and it "can be regarded as a play dramatizing the meanings of the single word 'Nature'" (15). I really wonder why Orwell has failed to observe the significance and effect Shakespeare has intended to produce through this single word.

To be sure, some other critics have already noticed the frequent occurrence of the word "nature" in *Lear*. G. B. Harrison, for instance, observes in his Introduction to the play that apart from the use of animal images which constantly recur, Shakespeare "effected a grim irony by the use of two words which sound throughout the play like the tolling of a knell: 'nature' and 'nothing.'" And he proceeds to interpret the meaning of "nature" in this play, thus:

> *Lear, Gloucester, and Edmund each in turn call on Nature. To the old fathers Nature is the goddess of natural affection by whose law children are naturally loyal to their parents. To Edmund—the "natural" son—Nature is the goddess of the wild; he is "natural" man because he is by nature a beast. "Nature," "natural," and "unnatural" recur again and again with every shade of meaning and misunderstanding. (1139).*

By the same token Northrop Frye has made his interpretive observations about "the intricate series of puns on 'natural' in *King Lear*," besides the "emphatic repetition of the words 'all' and 'nothing.'" (268). Unlike Harrison, however, Frye emphasizes the connection of "the lower physical nature of the elements" with an "amoral world" to which Edmund as well as the Yahoo or Caliban adheres, in contrast to the "still unspoiled and innocent" world of the fools (Lear, Kent, Gloucester, and the Fool) "in the middle of a fallen nature" (265-9).

John Danby finds that the words "nature," "natural," and "unnatural" occur over forty times in *King Lear*. They cover the "expected range of the Elizabethan meanings of the word," but have "two main meanings, strongly contrasted and mutually exclusive" (19). The "two main meanings" are for Danby two views of nature: first, the benignant nature of Bacon, Hooker, and Lear; second, the malignant nature of Hobbes, Edmund, and the wicked daughters.

According to Robert Fitch, the word "nature" has at least five significations in *King Lear*:

> *So Edmund speaks of "mine own nature" when he simply has reference to the characteristics of his own personality. Edmund may appeal to nature as a goddess who will liberate him from the restraints of custom and of the moral order. Shortly thereafter Lear can appeal to nature as a goddess who will enforce the penalties of the moral order against his daughter. Elsewhere Lear can speak of the natural needs of man in the Hobbesian sense of a natural condition which is short, brutish, and nasty. Then in a religious anachronism someone can speak of Cordelia as a daughter "Who redeems nature from the general curse" where nature is the fallen part of man that stands in need of redemptive grace. (91)*

Wen-chung Hwang has also had a good discussion of the word "nature" in *Lear*. According to his analysis, the word has at least the following six lexical meanings in the text:

a. **the power or force which rules the universe and creates all things in it.**
b. **natural phenomena, like thunder, eclipses, and rain.**
c. **the physical world or universe without spiritual or moral significance.**
d. **the physical strength, body or life of a person.**
e. **the inherent disposition or character of an individual.**
f. **the essential qualities of a human being. (27-28)**

Basically, Hwang's as well as the other critics' interpretations of the word "nature" are all correct. However, I think we can go further to find a thematic pattern woven out of the word and its cognates. This job needs, of course, a thorough investigation of the contexts in which they occur, before the thematic interpretation can be made.

III. The Binary Oppositions

My investigation, based on the Arden Edition (1972) of *Lear*, shows that the word "nature" together with its cognates ("natural," "unnatural," "unnaturalness," and "disnature'd") appears fifty-one times altogether in the play. The words are mostly spoken by Lear (19 times), Gloucester (9 times), Edmund (8 times), and Kent (6 times). But many other characters also use the words in their speech: France (2 times), Cornwall (2 times), Albany (1 time), Regan (1 time), Cordelia (1 time), the Doctor (1 time), and a Gentleman (1 time). The meanings of the words are, to be sure, often ambiguous in their contexts. Consequently, different interpretations have easily resulted. For example, when in the opening scene Lear asks his daughters to tell him the depth of their love for him so that "we our largest bounty may extend / Where nature doth with merit challenge" (51-52), what is meant here by "nature"? The note in the Arden Edition gives two interpretations by Steevens: "Where the claims of merit are superadded to that of nature, i.e., birth. Challenge, to make title to, to claim as one's right"; "nature = natural filial affection; but it means rather 'parental affection,' and *merit*, in the context, means 'filial affection'" (Muir 6). For another example, after Edmund hoodwinks Edgar into fleeting to escape Gloucester's anger and contrives the appearance of a murderous assault on himself by Edgar, the misled father says in private: "... and of my land, / Loyal and natural boy, I'll work the means / To make thee capable" (2.1.82-84). It is noted that here "Gloucester is quibbling on the two meanings of *natural*, 'bastard' and 'feeling natural affection' (opposed to the unnaturalness of his legitimate son)." "But," the note goes on, "since *natural* could mean legitimate as well as illegitimate, he may also imply that Edmund is now his rightful heir" (Muir 61).

Despite the obvious cases of ambiguity as shown above, however, I find it fairly safe to divide the meanings first into two big categories: namely, nature as the Great Nature and nature as our human nature. When the first sense is meant, the word *nature* often has its initial letter capitalized in the printed text and it may take the personified "she" or "her" as its pronoun. For instance, Lear refers to Cordelia as "a wretch whom Nature is asham'd / Almost t'acknowledge here" (1.1.211-2). And later Gloucester refers to Lear as a "ruin'd piece of Nature" (4.6.134). Yet, there are still cases of inconsistency, of course. For example, Lear once reasons thus to himself: "maybe he [Cornwall] is not well: / Infirmity doth still neglect all office / Where to our health is bound; we are not ourselves / When Nature, being oppressed, commands the mind / to suffer with the body" (2.4.102-6). Here the "oppressed Nature" cannot possibly refer to the Great Nature; it may probably refer to the nature of man.

This leads us to a second division. Whereas "Nature" usually refers to the Great Nature and hence it is often personified and apostrophized (e.g. "Hear, Nature, hear" in I, iv, 274; and "Thou, Nature, art my goddess" in I, ii, 1), and whereas "nature" usually refers to human nature and hence it is not personified nor apostrophized, both "Nature" and "nature" can in fact focus on either the physical or the spiritual aspect of them. When Gloucester says, "These late eclipses in the sun and moon portend no good to us: though the wisdom of Nature can reason it thus and thus, yet Nature finds itself scourg'd by the sequent effects" (1.2.100-3), the first "Nature" he mentions in the statement plainly focuses on its intellectual side (it being a "reasoning" subject) while the second "Nature" focuses on its physical facet (it being a "scourged" object). Likewise, when Kent addresses Oswald as a "cowardly rascal" and affirms scornfully that "nature" disclaims in thee: a tailor made thee" (2.2.52-53), the spiritual aspect of our human nature is emphasized. And when, seeing Lear in the heath, he remarks that "the tyranny of the open night's too rough / For nature to endure" (3.4.2-3), his attention is directed mainly to the physical part of our nature, of course.

When "nature" means our physical nature, it refers in effect to our body (in opposition to our soul). This meaning occurs in quite a few contexts in the play. Other examples besides the one just mentioned above are: "Oppressed nature sleeps" (3.6.95), and "Our foster-nurse of nature is repose" (4.4.12). But since our body is where our spirit or soul or any mental quality is supposed to reside, it is often hard to tell in certain contexts which quality (physical or spiritual) is meant particularly. The "nature" in our last example can in fact refer to our mental state as well. As to the "nature" in such contexts as below, the meaning is really ambivalent.

> *Death, traitor! Nothing could have subdued nature to such a*
> *lowness but his unkind daughters. (3.4.69-79)*

> *Nature in you stands on the very verge*
> *Of her confine. (2.4.144-5)*

> *My snuff and loathed part of nature should*
> *Burn itself out. (4.6.39-40)*

> *Cure this great breach in his abused nature! (4.7.15)*

> *Thou hast one daughter,*
> *Who redeems nature from the general curse*
> *Which twain have brought her to. (4.6.202-4)*

In contexts like these, "nature" can indeed mean both physical and mental nature at the same time.

When referring to the spiritual aspect, "nature" in *Lear* mostly means the temper, disposition or instinct one is born with. This is the "nature" when Lear says "I will forget my nature" (1.5.31), when France mentions Cordelia's "tardiness in nature" (1.1.234), when Edmund talks of his father's "lusty stealth of nature" (1.2.11), when Gloucester believes that "the King falls from bias of nature" (1.2.108), when Cornwall judges that Kent marvels at such "smiling rogues" as able to "smooth every passion that in the natures of their lords rebel" (2.2.70-74), and when Albany fears "That nature, which contemns its origin" (4.2.32).

But is one's instinctive nature good or bad? Normally, we suppose everyone is born with instinctive love for his family members; therefore, "nature" is often equivalent, in meaning, to the instinctive affection existing between parents and children, i.e., parental love or filial love. In *King Lear*, such a "nature" is found in such statements as these: "thou better know'st / The offices of nature, bond of childhood" (2.4.175-6), "I may be censured, that nature thus gives way to loyalty" (3.5.2-3), "Edmund, enkindle all the sparks of nature / To quit this horrid act" (3.7.84-85), "Nature of such deep trust we shall much need" (2.1.113), etc.

Since "nature" is supposedly equivalent to "natural affection" between parent and child, it is only natural that in the play the child lacking such affection should be described as "unnatural" or "disnatured." Examples are: Lear's calling his daughters "unnatural hags" (2.4.276) and wishing Goneril's child to be "a thwart disnatur'd torment to her" (1.4.281), Edmund's talking of "unnaturalness between the child and the parent" (1.2.141) and of his brother Edgar's "unnatural purpose" (2.1.49), Gloucester's calling Edgar "Unnatural, detested, brutish villain" (1.2.73-74), etc. Yet, "natural affection" need not be limited to that between parent and child. It can be that between prince and subject as well. Thus, we have such a dialogue between Gloucester and Edmund concerning their being forced to ill-treat Lear:

> ***Glou***. *Alack, alack! Edmund, I like not this unnatural dealing.*
> *When I desired their leave that I might pity him, they*
> *took from me the use of mine own house; charged me,*

> on pain of perpetual displeasure, neither to speak of
> him, entreat for him, or any way sustain him.

Edm. Most savage and unnatural! (3.3.1-7)

Moreover, in the play the terms "natural" and "unnatural" can mean "normal" and "abnormal," respectively, in the consideration of happenings. Thus, France can reply to Lear this way concerning Cordelia's behavior: "Sure, her offence / Must be of such unnatural degree / That monsters it, or your fore-vouched affection / Fall into taint" (1.1.217-9). And Kent can talk, thus, to a gentleman: "...you shall find / Some that will thank you, making just report / Of how unnatural and bemadding sorrow / The King hath cause to plain" (3.1.36-38).

So far I have analyzed the possible meanings of the word "nature" and its cognates in *King Lear*. We have come to understand that the word along with its cognates can refer to either the Great Nature or our human nature, either physical / material nature or spiritual / mental nature, and either natural affection between parent and child or that between prince and subject. Meanwhile, we also understand that human nature is considered basically good (since it is equated to natural affection) but likely to be bad (called "unnatural" or "disnatured"), too. Thus, for Shakespeare in *Lear* at least, "nature" contains a number of binary oppositions such as Great Nature vs human nature, physical / material nature vs. spiritual / mental nature, nature between parent and child vs. nature between prince and subject, good nature vs. bad nature, and normal nature vs. abnormal nature.

IV. The Psychomachia

In the medieval times, Prudentius wrote a Latin allegorical poem entitled *The Psychomachia* (*The Battle of Souls*). The allegory initiates a long tradition of works (as diverse as *Roman de la Rose*, *Everyman*, and *Piers Plowman*) which "defines the earthly life of man as the arena of a Holy War between the contending forces of his own nature" (Spivack 73). In Henry Medwall's *Nature* (1490-1501), for instance, the tradition continues as a pitched battle impending "between the Seven Deadly Sins, led by Man already seduced and depraved, and the forces of virtue whose leader is Reason" (Spivack 86). Medwall's allegorical play is imitated by John Rastell's *The Nature of the Four Elements* (c. 1517), in which the delinquent hero Humanity is seduced by his bad companion Sensual Appetite. It is significant that the medieval, Christian theme of a morality now takes "Nature" as the keyword in the title of a Renaissance allegory. Both Medwall's *Nature* and Rastell's *The Nature of the Four Elements* suggest clearly that nature, containing both good and evil, is the battlefield of the opposing souls.

In the Harvest New Critical Introduction to *King Lear*, Alexander Leggatt points out some relevant passages and concludes that we can recognize from them "the doubleness of nature in its dealings with man: destructive and terrifying on the one hand, beneficent on the other" (23). The "nature" Leggatt refers to here is of course the Great Nature. He thinks that both benevolent and malevolent aspects of the Great Nature "are objectively valid within the play," and he adds, "yet this doubleness of nature, though not simply imagined by the characters, also reflects the doubleness of humanity" (23). "Humanity," as used by Leggatt here, is equal to what we call "human nature." So Leggatt is asserting that in *Lear* the good and evil aspects of the Great Nature reflect the two same aspects of our human nature.

I think Leggatt is all correct in making the assertion. Indeed, I think that the play is a two-level speech act. On the first level, it is the playwright's speech act, by which Shakespeare tells us (through his good and evil characters as well as good and bad things or happenings) that both the Great Nature and our human nature can be either good or bad at times, and that there seems to be a correspondence between them. On the

206

second level, the play is a composite of the characters' speech acts, which may also directly or indirectly tell the same things. Gloucester, for instance, suggests that the "late eclipses in the sun and moon portend no good to us" (1.2.100-101),[1] thus connecting heavenly bodies with human bodies; and the Gentleman says that Lear "Strives in his little world of man to out-storm / The to-and-fro-conflicting wind and rain" (3.1.10-11), thus also linking the external nature with man's inward nature.

It is only natural, of course, that a play, be it a comedy or tragedy, should contain both good and evil dramatis personae. In the light of characterization, however, *King Lear* shows better than other plays Shakespeare's impartial understanding of human nature. The play, as we know, is centered around two families, Lear's and Gloucester's. Lear has three daughters, of whom two are "unnatural" for not showing "a child-like office" (2.1.105). The remaining filial one has two suitors, of whom one does not, while the other does, possess "natural" love for her. The two husbands of Lear's two elder daughters are again opposite to each other by nature: one good, the other evil. The same symmetry is found in Gloucester's family. His "natural" (bastard) son is in reality very "unnatural" (without filial affection) while his legitimate son is "natural" in the sense of showing "a child-like office." Even among the retainers, some characters are good while others are evil (e.g. Kent in contrast to Oswald). Robert Grudin has found this remarkable "pattern of interconnecting parallels and oppositions" (138), and he takes this pattern as a sort of circularity suggesting ethical and temporal roundness. For me, however, this balancing cast of good and evil characters side by side implies, naturally, that like the Great Nature, man's nature can be good or bad.

Furthermore, the characters on the two mutually-contrasting (good vs. bad) sides are all "flat characters,"[2] that is, characters each with but a single dominant trait that remains unchanged throughout the work. According to Enid Welsford, the "good" characters in *King Lear* are those who have the capacity for "fellow-feeling" (138). Such "good" characters as Cordelia, France, Edgar, Albany, Kent, and the Fool do have the capacity for "fellow-feeling," in contrast to such "evil" characters as Goneril, Regan, Burgundy, Cornwall, Edmund, and Oswald, who are selfishly wicked. All such characters are simply "natural" or "unnatural" (if not to use the common label of "good" or "bad") throughout the play. Thus, they are all "flat characters." Essentially, in fact, they are all more or less like allegorical figures. They represent the "natural" (good) souls and the "unnatural" (evil) souls respectively in the psychomachia of humanity.

Besides casting flatly good and flatly evil characters side by side and engaging them in a sort of conflicting war, Shakespeare also utilizes "round characters" (that is, complex, realistic, and changeable characters who are neither downright good nor downright evil) to suggest the theme of psychomachia. Lear and Gloucester, the two family heads, are the "round characters" in the play. They are "round" because they combine opposing (good and bad) character traits in the same person and they grow in personality as "the battle of souls" goes on.

Lear and Gloucester are loving parents, but both favor unfairly a certain child at first: Lear favors Cordelia and Gloucester favors Edmund. Both parents are gullible: Lear is cheated by the sweet words of Goneril and Regan while Gloucester is cheated by Edmund's false words. Both, again, are rash; Lear, therefore, denounces Cordelia unjustly while Gloucester denounces Edgar. Both, then, suffer for the rashness, come to know their stupidity, and repent of their wrongdoing. Meanwhile, both grow wise and show their "fellow-feeling": Lear has "reason in madness" (4.6.173) and takes pity on the Fool, Poor Tom (Edgar) and the blinded Gloucester while Gloucester sees feelingly "how this world goes with no eyes" (4.6.147-9) and sympathizes with the mad Lear. In the end, while Gloucester gropes on patiently for the time of "ripeness" (5.3.11) and finally dies happily reconciled to Edgar, Lear is reunited with Cordelia and finally dies heart-broken after bravely killing "the slave that was a-hanging" her (5.3.273). In both Gloucester's case and Lear's, the end may be tragic in the sense that both involve death. Yet, upon further consideration we know that their deaths are merely physical deaths. Morally they have in fact revived; their final reconciliation to their good children symbolizes that they have returned to their good nature. Therefore, the tragic end is actually like that of a traditional allegory: the Good Soul triumphs over the Evil Soul, as in the psychomachia.

V. The Two Lears

We have mentioned above some critics who see "two natures" in the universe: Harrison sees the contrast between nature as the goddess of natural affection and nature as the goddess of the wild; Frye sees the lower physical nature of the elements vs. the still unspoiled and innocent nature; and Danby sees the benignant nature of Bacon, Hooker, and Lear vs. the malignant nature of Hobbes, Edmund and the wicked daughters. Each dichotomy of nature is justifiable, of course. Yet, it is problematic to refer to "the benignant nature of Lear," as Danby does. Lear does conceive nature as naturally benignant (he thinks nature ought to be good). But does Lear's own nature benignantly good throughout the play? The answer is in the negative, of course. He actually shows two contrasting facets in the play.

There are indeed two Lears in the play. On one hand, we have the Lear that appears in the first two acts of the play. That Lear is seen in his own palace, in the Duke of Albany's palace, and before Gloucester's castle; he is not yet seen roaming on the heath. That Lear is the obstinate, arrogant, and hot-tempered Lear, the Lear that indiscreetly plans to divide his kingdom among his daughters, rashly banishes Cordelia and Kent, and then angrily cries against Goneril's and Regan's ill-treatment of him. That is the foolish Lear, though he is self-assured and overbearing as a parent and a monarch. He is so foolish that he takes words for actions and "has let the ritual appearances replace the internal reality" (Magill116). At that stage, Lear still thinks his power unchallengeable, still wears his regal garments, still tries to keep his train and trappings of royalty, and still demands love from his children and subjects. That is also the selfish Lear, the Lear that has no "fellow feeling" for others.

On the other hand, we have the Lear that appears in the last three acts of the play. This Lear is seen roaming on the heath and exposed to the storm before he is taken to the French Camp near Dover. This Lear is divested of all the accoutrements of kingship and reduced to the condition of a ragged, homeless madman. This Lear has admitted that he is but a "poor, infirm, weak, and despised old man" (3.2.20) or "a very foolish fond old man" (4.7.60), although he still believes he is "a man more sinned against than sinning" (3.2.60). This Lear is no longer the foolish Lear because his wits have begun to turn (3.2.67) and he has certified his evil daughters' "filial ingratitude" (3.4.14). He has in fact become wise enough to tell Gloucester that "A dog's obeyed in office" (4.6.157). In the meantime, he is also no longer selfish. Seeing the Fool still accompanying him in the cold outdoors, he says, "Poor Fool and knave, I have one part in my heart / That's sorry yet for thee" (3.2.72-73). He even takes pity on all those "naked wretches" that have to "bide the pelting of this pitiless storm" with only their "houseless heads and unfed sides" (3.4.28-30).

The foolish, selfish Lear demonstrates Lear's bad nature; the wise, unselfish Lear demonstrates Lear's good nature. In Freudian terms, Lear's bad nature follows mostly the pleasure principle and partly the reality principle. At first, he seeks to "shake all cares and business from our age" (1.1.38) and yet retain the trappings of authority. Later, when his older daughters decide to fail him, he resorts practically to bargaining with them. In contrast, Lear's good nature follows the morality principle. While he swears repeatedly at his evil daughters, he condescends at last to ask forgiveness of his good daughter. More importantly, while he is himself in distress, he has sympathy for the cold Fool, the beggared Edgar, the blinded Gloucester, etc.

It is noted that the play is full of animal images (mentioned animal names include dog, kite, serpent, ant, hog, fox, wolf, lion, sheep, cat, horse, nightingale, herring, boar, fly, tiger, bear, crow, mouse, wren, adder, rat, and many others).[3] Caroline Spurgeon agrees with A. C. Bradley and others that the large number of animal images in the play gives us the feeling that "humanity" is "reeling back into the beast." But she adds that because the images are portrayed chiefly in angry or anguished action, they distinctly augment the sensation of horror and bodily pain that goes with the effect of a tragedy (342). I think both Bradley and Spurgeon are right in their interpretations. However, I tend to agree more with those who hold that the animal imagery in the play "is designed partly to show man's place in the Chain of Being, and to bring out the sub-human nature of the evil characters, partly to show man's weakness compared with the animals, and partly to compare human existence to the life of the jungle" (Muir liv).

Man, as the Renaissance men believed, occupies the middle position in the Great Chain of Being. Thus, human nature is in between beastly nature and divine nature. According to Freudian psychology, man's beastly nature (the libido) normally stays repressed in the id until it emerges in dreams or other unconscious states. Now, in *King Lear*, do we see man's beastly nature revealed only in unconscious states of mind? We see all the evil characters (Goneril, Regan, Cornwall, Edmund, etc.), as well as all the good characters (Cordelia, Albany, Gloucester, Kent, Edgar, etc.), act consciously all the time for their purposes (to gain power, to gain love or to gain other things). But Lear has once gone mad. Is madness a conscious or unconscious state of mind? If it is unconscious, can we say the mad Lear or the unconscious Lear is the "bad-natured" Lear or the beastly Lear?

The mad Lear in the last three acts of the play does speak mad words and act madly. Cordelia says that he is "as mad as the vexed sea"

(4.4.2). Yet, what Edgar observes in the mad Lear is "matter and impertinency mixed; / Reason in madness" (4.6.172-3). And what we observe in him now is a repentant Lear and a righteous Lear that begins to feel sorry for other good suffering fellows. If to be mad is to act wrongly with no sense, then this mad Lear is actually not mad now, just like Edgar, the disguised mad beggar. In actuality, Lear is really mad in the first two acts of the play, that is, when he acts consciously before he goes mad noticeably. Hence, Kent is right in saying bluntly that "be Kent unmannerly, / When Lear is mad" (1.1.144-5) when he tries to defend Cordelia against Lear's fury and unwise dispensation of his kingdom.

If it is hard to say which Lear (the foolish and selfish one or the wise and unselfish one) is really mad, it is also difficult to say which Lear is natural or unnatural. We may think it natural for an old father to be foolish and selfish at times. We may also think it unnatural for an old king to be as foolish and selfish as Lear. Likewise, we may think it unnatural for a mad king to become insightfully wise, and think it natural for an ill-treated father to become sympathetic towards others. If "natural" means "normal," the mad Lear, then, is "unnatural." That is why Gloucester calls Lear "a ruined piece of nature" (4.6.133) and Cordelia asks the kind gods to "cure this great breach in his abused nature," that is, Lear's "untuned and jarring senses" (4.7.14-16). Nevertheless, there is no doubt that the first (foolish and selfish) Lear is regarded as the unnatural Lear and the second (wise and unselfish) Lear is regarded as the natural Lear, for "natural" actually can also mean "original" in the play. Lear is thought to be originally wise and unselfish, but the infirmity of his old age makes him "unnatural" (foolishly rash and selfishly unloving).

Lear himself must be a believer in man's original good nature, for he asks, in the trial scene, "Is there any cause in nature that make these hard hearts?" (3.6.75-76). Gloucester may be a similar believer, for he once blindly asks Edmund to "enkindle all the sparks of nature / To quit this horrid act" (3.7.84). Kent, too, may belong to the group, for he says to Oswald, "You cowardly rascal, nature disclaims in thee: a tailor made thee" (2.2.52-3). It seems that good men believe man is good by nature. How about wicked men, then? Do they believe man is wicked by nature? In the play none among the evil characters have ever pronounced this belief. When Edmund says that "...a brother noble, / Whose nature is so far from doing harms / That he suspects none" (1.2.176-77), the statement may imply that if a man is evil by nature, he can then suspect evil; but it does not imply that man is originally good or evil. Finally, when Edmund is dying, he says: "...some good I mean to do / Despite of mine own nature" (5.3.242-3). This statement implies that he knows he is evil by nature, and that he believes even an evil person like him can become good at last. But it does not imply that he believes man is originally evil. So, we can conclude that in *King Lear* Shakespeare does not suggest that man is all good or all bad by nature. He suggests instead that human nature is subject to change: a good Lear may become a bad Lear and a wicked Edmund may become a good Edmund.

The word "lear" is defined in *O.E.D.* as "instruction, learning; *in early use*, a piece of instruction, a lesson; *also*, a doctrine, religion." And the set expression "lear-father" is said to refer to "a master in learning." King Lear is a father in the play, indeed. But, ironically, he is not a "lear-father." Instead of being a master in learning, he is an old and late learner. He learns too late two lessons: the lesson that human nature is not all alike (some people are good by nature and some are evil), and the lesson that human nature is not as it appears to be (words are not actions; both loyalty and filial piety need evidence). At the end, his learning is still incomplete. Even at the moment of his death, he has not yet learned the lesson that natural justice is not equivalent to human justice (or the lesson that nature's real justice can be other than mankind's ideal justice or "poetic justice"). That is why over Cordelia's death he cries: "Why should a dog, a horse, a rat, have life, / And thou no breath at all?" (5.3.305-6).

According to natural law, every cause has its effect; every fault or folly as well as every guilt or crime has its punishment. Hence,

213

Cordelia's fault (call it pride or stubbornness), no less than Lear's fault or her sisters' and Edmund's crime, may lead to death. Her death is tragic, indeed. But nature is full of tragedies like Cordelia's: an innocent dog, horse, or rat may also come to have no breath at all just because it has committed a fault (in falling into a pit, for instance).

It is sometimes suggested that the death of Cordelia is inevitable because as a patriot or as a prudent playwright Shakespeare simply cannot let France conquer England and save Cordelia and Lear in time. This explanation is too far-fetched. The unhappy ending is in truth only part of Shakespeare's forceful appeal to us to look boldly into the ambivalent face of natural and human reality. C. J. Sisson maintains that "there is in fact poetic justice enough in *King Lear*" because Goneril, Regan, Cornwall and Edmund all perish in their sins and finally Albany proclaims the restoration of the old King to his absolute power, and of Edgar and Kent to their just rights (234). Indeed, if we judge on the basis of the play's entire action (with its double plots finally combined into one), we can only arrive at this "natural justice": every folly as well as every vice must be punished in some way. We may regard Cordelia's death as a "tragic waste," to use a term explicated by Bradley (23). But we must know that Cordelia does not suffer for nothing; she has her own "tragic flaws." To quote Gloucester's cynical remark—"As flies to wanton boys, are we to the Gods; / They kill us for their sport" (4.1.36-37)—as Shakespeare's theme for the play is to totally overlook "natural justice." To ask a happy ending for the play is to ask like a still immature Lear, not yet fully wise about natural justice though already well-experienced in human nature.

VI. Nature vs. Art or Nurture

We have just distinguished the foolish and selfish Lear from the wise and unselfish Lear. We have also recognized the second Lear as not yet fully wise because he still cannot distinguish natural justice from human justice. To be fully wise is in fact to learn a lot of "lears" (lessons). The relationship between nature and art (or between nature and nurture) is another lesson Lear has learned, though.

In Act 4, Scene 6, let us recall, Lear is fantastically dressed with wild flowers. The mad Lear sees Edgar and says to him, "No, they cannot touch me for coining; I am the king himself," and adds, "Nature's above art in that respect" (4.6.83-86). The statement "Nature's above art" in this context may mean, indeed, that "a born King can never lose his natural rights,"[4] since his natural rights include "coining," which is art. Nevertheless, the reference of "nature" need not be restricted to "natural rights" and that of "art" need not be restricted to the art of coining money. The word "nature" may mean anything one is born with, and the word "coining" may mean broadly any act of "making up or devising." Thus, one's naked body is one's nature, too. And to dress oneself up with wild flowers as Lear does is an art of coining, too. In consequence, the statement that "nature is above art" seems to be a general truth pertinent to Lear in various ways.

Lear has in fact learned the importance of returning to nature when he is roaming madly in the wild. Let us recall again that Lear argues at first for the necessity of having superfluities:

> *O! reason not the need; our basest beggars*
> *Are in the poorest thing superfluous:*
> *Allow not nature more than nature needs,*
> *Man's life is cheap as beast's. (2.4.262-5)*

Yet, later when he sees Edgar's "uncovered body" in the storm, he says: "Is man no more than this? ...Thou ow'st the worm no silk, the beast no hide, the sheep no wool, the cat no perfume. ...thou art the thing itself, un-accommodated man is no more but such a poor, bare, forked animal as thou art" (3.4.100-6). After saying so, he tears off his clothes and becomes bare himself. Symbolically, he has rid himself of art (human clothes) and returned to nature (his body). At this mad moment, nature is really above art for him.

Nature vs. art was a topic often discussed in Shakespeare's day. There were people, indeed, who placed art above nature. Sir Philip Sidney, for instance, argues in his *An Apology for Poetry* that "the poet... doth grow in effect another nature, in making things either better than nature bringeth forth, or, quite anew, forms such as never were in nature" and thus nature's world is brazen while the poets' world is golden (Adams 157). Shakespeare, however, does not think that art is above nature. He thinks instead with Lear that nature is above art. But "above" does not mean just "better"; it means "prior" as well. Sidney also agrees that nature is the primary state of existence; all art comes from nature. But he emphasizes the aesthetic superiority of art to nature. Shakespeare's aesthetic idea belongs mainly to mimetic theory, however. For Shakespeare nature is the model for artistic imitation; it is therefore always prior to art. In terms of science and ethics, Shakespeare also places nature before art, "nurture" being the equivalent for "art" in such categories.

In *The Winter's Tale*, Polixenes argues convincingly on this point. He says to Perdita:

> *Yet Nature is made better by no mean*
> *But Nature makes that mean;* so over that art
> Which you say adds to Nature, is an art
> That Nature makes. *You see, sweet maid, we marry*
> *A gentler scion to the wildest stock,*
> *And make conceive a bark of baser kind*
> *By bud of nobler race. This is an art*
> *Which does mend Nature—change it rather; but*
> *The art itself is Nature. (4.4.89-97, emphasis mine)*

In this passage, through the mouth of Polixenes, using a horticultural example, Shakespeare has stated clearly the idea that nature is above art because art is (derived from) nature. This is a scientific truth. And so is the truth told by the King in *All's Well That Ends Well* that "laboring art can never ransom nature / From her inaidible estate (2.1.118-9).

In *The Tempest*, Prospero describes Caliban as "a born devil, on whose nature / nurture can never stick" (4.1.88-89). According to Frank Kermode, learning is a major theme in the romance. While Miranda "is endowed not only with the *melior natura,* but with education," Caliban's education "was not only useless—on *his* nature, which is nature *tout court,* nurture would never stick—but harmful" (1958, xlvi). This Miranda / Caliban contrast implies that Shakespeare does regard nature as the primarily important factor in the development of one's personality, nurture or art being dependent on nature for its successful influence on the person. In fact, Prospero has learned his "Art" at the risk of his dukedom, and finally he decides to forsake his potent "Art" because he knows that whatever is achieved by his "Art" is nothing but "such stuff / As dreams are made on" (4.1.156-7). Ethically, Prospero (or Shakespeare himself) knows that art or nurture can do little to nature. Thus, nature is always above art.

In his book on patterning in Shakespearean drama, William Godshalk enumerates a good number of contrasting loci in Shakespeare's plays: the city of Rome and the forest outside in *Titus Andronicus,* the court of the king and the tent of the princess in *Love's Lobor's Lost,* the court in Athens and the woods outside in *A Midsummer Night's Dream,* the court of Duke Frederick and the forest of Arden in *As You Like It,* the citadel inside the walls of Troy and the Greek camp outside in *Troilus and Cressida,* Rome and Egypt in *Antony and Cleopatra,* Sicily and Bohemia in *The Winter's Tale,* etc. (15-18). As Godshalk further explains, the contrasting loci may stand for the contrasts between order and disorder, illusion and reality, folly and wisdom, artificiality and naturalness, reason and desire, restraint and looseness, time-consciousness and timelessness, harsh militarism and pleasurable love, gloomy winter and hopeful springtime, etc. For me, the two major locales of a Shakespearean play are often representative of the polar contrasts between art and nature, indeed, if art is taken to mean any unnatural human effort made to utilize nature, which is the original substance, material or quality of being. Furthermore, one might argue indeed that in a Shakespearean play "the polarity of place is irrevocably linked with a polarity of character" (Godshalk 19). Thus, for Lear to leave his court and come to the stormy heath is for him to forsake his unnatural self and return to his natural self, just as the natural Duke Senior of Arden returns to replace the unnatural ("artful") Duke Frederick of the court. Behind the polarity of place and of character, there seems to be a Romantic belief that under the greenwood tree of nature, life is better than in a court of art—a theme of *As You Like It*.

When we return to *King Lear*, we find all the characters that die at the end must have learned, if only too late, the vanity and even fatality of their art: the two old sisters' art of speech, Edmund's Machiavellian art, Cornwall's cruel political art, Lear's and Gloucester's parental art, and Cordelia's filial art. But do they repent of their own nature? Shakespeare does not arrange for any of them to reflect upon their inborn nature as the first cause of their behavior. Edmund, the most wicked one, may know that he is himself of evil nature. He may regret that his Machiavellian art has failed. Yet, he only shows that he still has a conscience to do one last good thing. He does not blame his own nature or the "Nature" he apostrophizes as his goddess. Thus, it seems that ethically nature is above art because nature is not blamable while art is.

Why is nature not blamable? It may be logical *and only natural* that good nature should do good and evil nature should do evil. But is one's nature predetermined to be good or evil? Or is one's nature originally neutral (and so it becomes ethically good or evil only after it enters the empirical world)? Let us recall Friar Lawrence's findings stated in *Romeo and Juliet*:

The earth that's nature's mother is her tomb;
What is her burying grave, that is her womb;
And from her womb children of divers kind
We sucking on her natural bosom find:
Many for many virtues excellent,
None but for some, and yet all different.
O, mickle is the powerful grace that lies
In plants, herbs, stones, and their true qualities;
For nought so vile that on the earth doth live
But to the earth some special good doth give;
Nor aught so good but, strained from that fair use,
Revolts from true birth, stumbling on abuse.
Virtue itself turns vice, being misapplied,
And vice sometime by action dignified.
Within the infant rind of this weak flower
Poison hath residence and medicine power;
For this, being smelt, with that part cheers each part,
Being tasted, stays all senses with the heart.
Two such opposed kings encamp them still
In man as well as herbs, grace and rude will;
And where the worser is predominant,
Full soon the canker death eats up that plant.(2.3.9-30)

In this passage, nature refers to anything existing on the earth and it is
conceived as originally all good (all things have "powerful grace" in
their "true qualities"). But later we find this nature can "give some
special good" or "stumble on abuse" from time to time since vice can be
"dignified" and virtue can be "misapplied." Thus, it begins to seem that
two opposed natures (grace and rude will) are inherent in man and things,
and when "the worser" is predominant, death will come. According to
Roland Frye, this passage shows the Friar's theological training and it is
in complete accord with the Christine doctrine that evil springs not from

219

nature but from the corruption of nature.[5] And thus Shakespeare seems to speak through the Friar about two natures: the primary nature, which is all good or neutral, and the secondary nature, which is seen as either good or evil according as grace or rude will prevails. Before man falls, man is in the primary nature without any art; after man falls, man is in the secondary nature with all art. In the fallen world, "Nature hath meal and bran, contempt and grace" (*Cymbeline* 4.227) and man's art or nurture is responsible for any failure in life.

VII. The Humanist Vision

Shakespeare is a Renaissance man. Renaissance is often said to be a period of classical revival, a period felicitous again for secularism and humanism. But we should not forget that the revival is a gradual process going from feudal medievalism, from Christian dogmatism or, in a word, from Hebraism back to Hellenism. Therefore, any Renaissance man simply cannot get clear of medieval thought, Christian doctrine, or Hebraic culture in his classical revival or his return to secularism or humanism, which is characteristic of Hellenism. And, therefore, it is only natural that Shakespeare should combine both Hebraism and Hellenism in his oeuvre.

Robert Fitch claims that in Shakespeare's last plays "there is a bold affirmation of the triumph of innocence over evil." And he adds: "There is a peculiar blending of the Hellenic and of the Hebraic in the resolution of the priorities and the meanings of wisdom and of love. But in the metaphysical concern with *nature*, the moral order, time, and eternity, the Hellenic perspective prevails over the Hebraic" (234, italics mine). I agree that just as Renaissance became more and more secularly Hellenic as time went on, so Shakespeare grew more and more Hellenic and humanistic in writing his plays.

Humanism, as Tony Davies points out, "is a word with a very complex history and an unusually wide range of possible meanings and contexts" (2). For me, Renaissance humanism is a rejection of Calvinistic predestination; it is a belief that recognizes humans "as born not with a burden of inherited sin due to their ancestry but with potential for both good and evil which will develop in this life as their characters are formed."[6] Renaissance humanists do recognize man's middle position in the Great Chain of Being; they recognize the contrast of humans "with other earth-creatures (animals, plants), and with another order of beings, the sky-dwellers or gods" (Davies 125-6). Man is therefore "both mortal flesh, as those below him, and also spirit" and man's struggle between flesh and spirit becomes a moral one.[7] As the Italian Renaissance humanist Giovanni Pico della Mirandola says, man is neither heavenly nor earthly, neither mortal nor immortal; man is the maker and molder of himself; humans can grow downward into the lower natures which are brutes, or grow upward into the higher natures which are divine.[8]

Shakespeare is a poet of nature and a Renaissance humanist. All his plays deal with human nature struggling in the Great Chain of Being, that is, in the Great Nature that includes natural beings (human beings and such non-human beings as beasts, plants, and rocks) and supernatural beings (gods, goddesses, demons, witches, ghosts, spirits, etc.). Human nature is indeed depicted in Shakespeare as capable of growing either downward or upward, either into the lower natures or into the higher natures. In all types of his plays (histories, comedies, tragedies or romances) we see both "good guys" and "bad guys." We see honorable or noble men and women clearly distinguished from despicable or ignoble men and women in histories, comedies and romances. But mostly in his tragic heroes (Hamlet, Macbeth, Othello, Lear, etc.) do we see the characters' own good natures marred by their own bad natures.

We have pointed out two Lears. The two Lears exist not just in *King Lear*. As two opposing natures (the good, wise, unselfish nature vs. the bad, foolish, selfish nature), the two Lears actually appear in all plays and in all societies. The two Lears are forever combating each other like two opposing souls in the psychomachia. They bring about comedies or tragedies now and then as vice and folly affect small figures or great ones. They may make histories, too, by entering "real figures" or make romances by entering "ideal figures."

Drama is an art of representing life or nature. In *King Lear*, Shakespeare's art has tried to turn human ethics and politics into a cosmological debate originated from Greek philosophy. Regarding the state of nature, as we know, there are two lears (doctrines) opposing each other in Greek thought. On one hand, we have Heraclitus and his followers, who believe that "change is ultimate and permanence a mere sensory appearance"; on the other hand, we have Pamenides and his adherents, who believe that "the permanent is fundamental and change a mere appearance" (Thilly 17). At first, Lear is a Pamenidean. He believes "nothing will come of nothing" (1.1.89), that is, "from being only being can come... nothing can become something else... everything remains what it is... there can be only one eternal, underived, unchangeable being" (Thilly 37). We know Lear has at first told Cordelia the truth that ethically no parental love will come of no filial piety, but he has not learned the truth that politically no authority will come of no power. When this drama goes on, it proves to Lear that actually something can come of nothing (Cordelia's lack of sweet words can turn into action of true love) and nothing can come of something (the older sisters' eloquence can turn into no love at all). So, Lear must have become a Heraclitean at last, believing that every person as well as everything can change in time: change is ultimate and permanence a mere sensory appearance.

According to the lear (doctrine) of Heraclitus, "Everything is changed into its opposite and everything, therefore, is a union of opposite qualities"; hence, "the world is ruled by strife: 'War is the father of all and the king of all'" (Thilly 33). In *King Lear*, we do find that Lear is a union of sanity and insanity, love and hate, wisdom and foolishness; Gloucester is a union of insight and blindness; the other characters are the union of virtue and vice; the action of the play is a union of order and chaos, peace and war; everything is a union of nature and art, naturalness and unnaturalness. And the direction of change is from the former element through the latter element back to the former element again. This change is a permanent change, a perpetual alternation of goodness and badness, and hence a natural course seen in nature, implied in all types of drama, and felt in life.

The tempest is a natural phenomenon. It is in fact Shakespeare's recurrent metaphor for one's violent nature or a violent period of life. Thus, a character can speak of a tempest in the heart or a tempest of the soul,[9] and Marina can say, "This world to me is a lasting storm" (*Pericles*, 4.1.20). "The most dramatic blending of the tempest without and the tempest within," as Fitch has suggested, "is in the third act of *King Lear*" (232). But Lear's "tempest in my mind" (3.4.12) must cease like the storm outside. Both a natural storm as experienced by Caliban and Trinculo and an unnatural tempest raised by the Art of Prospero and seen by Miranda must cease, too. There may indeed be a time when foul weather is hardly distinguishable from fine weather as the witches in *Macbeth* have mentioned. Yet, in life as in time it is only natural to alternate foulness with fairness. To stay all fair or all foul is to transcend nature and go into the ideal world beyond nature.

Under the influence of Hebraism, Shakespeare cannot detach himself from the Christian ideal of returning to paradise, the unfallen nature. Hence, there is actually no lack of moral concern in his plays, e.g. in a tragedy like *King Lear* or a romance like *The Tempest*. However, under the influence of Hellenism, Shakespeare is even more immersed in the humanist reality, the everyday nature of human life, which can be uplifted into a higher divine nature or dragged down into a lower beastly nature, depending on whether the superego or the libido prevails. Hence, it seems to Johnson and to us, too, that Shakespeare prefers natural justice to poetic justice since he must hold the mirror of drama to reflect faithfully the changeable fallen nature.

It may not be very sensible to ascribe Shakespeare's art to Neoclassicism or Romanticism as the two terms refer to two post-Renaissance periods. Yet, in the light of nature as a thematic focus, we do find Shakespeare partakes of both Neoclassic and Romantic tendencies. On one hand, Shakespeare's plays do recognize man's middle position in the Great Chain of Being as does Pope's *Essay on Man*, and they do attack "the vanity of human wishes" as does Johnson's satiric poem. Hence, in Shakespeare human nature is always dragged dramatically between conscience and desire; human vices and follies (due to the vain desire for love, power or other things) have constantly brought about comedies or tragedies. In this respect, Shakespeare is a Neoclassical humanist indeed.

On the other hand, however, Shakespeare is also like a visionary Romantic such as Blake, Shelley, and Keats. Like Blake, he envisions man's fall as a fall from "The Universal Man" into "Selfhood," that is, a foolish and selfish fall which perpetuates a cyclical change in life between innocence and experience as the two states of nature. Like Shelley, who places even Jupiter in the process of change, Shakespeare envisions mutability as the sole principle of nature. And, like Keats, he envisions contrariety as the essence of life and nature and tells us the coexistence of binary oppositions.

In a sonnet, Keats compares *King Lear* to a "bitter-sweet fruit" ("On Sitting Down to Read *King Lear* Once again," l. 8). We may not know for sure why Keats should describe the play as both bitter and sweet. Maybe it is because the tragedy is mixed with comic elements—a Shakespearean feature both Dryden and Johnson approve of. Anyway, as Johnson has observed, "Shakespeare's plays are not in the rigorous and critical sense either tragedies or comedies, but compositions of a distinct kind; exhibiting the real state of sublunary nature, which partakes of good and evil, joy and sorrow" (Adams 331). Thus, the entire

Shakespearean oeuvre displays a humanist vision of nature, a vision in which nature contains the primary unfallen nature (which is neutral or all good) and the secondary fallen nature (which is contaminated with art or nurture), and in which human natures romantically group into two Lears, one aspiring with conscience for the innocent, primary nature of the Eden and the other wallowing in the secondary "sublunary nature," letting his good soul forever battle with his bad soul, and allowing binary oppositions to create a mystery of nature in the alternation of life's tragedies and comedies, or histories and romances. This vision allows for the Neoclassic principles of moderation and of morality and yet recognizes the Romantic principles of change and of contrariety.

Notes

1. Gloucester's belief is immediately flouted by Edmund, who says: "...... when we are sick in fortune, often the surfeits of our own behavior, we make guilty of our disasters the sun, the moon, and stars" (1.2.116-8). Yet, Gloucester's belief was common in Shakespeare's time.

2. As first proposed by E. M. Forster in his *Aspects of the Novel*, flat characters are simple, typical and two-dimensional while round characters are unique, fully developed, capable of rotundity and of surprising in a convincing way, and as real to readers as their own acquaintances. See Forster, 72-78.

3. According to Kenneth Muir, "as early as 1879, one industrious critic pointed out the prevalence of animal imagery — 133 separate mentions of sixty-four different animals—and several later critics have commented on the significance of these figures" (liv). A. C. Bradley mentions that a very striking characteristic of *King Lear* is "the incessant references to the lower animals and man's likeness to them," and his list of such animals include "the dog, the horse, the cow, the sheep, the hog, the lion, the bear, the wolf, the fox, the monkey, the pole-cat, the civet-cat, the pelican, the owl, the crow, the chough, the wren, the fly, the butterfly, the rat, the mouse, the frog, the tadpole, the wall-newt, the water-newt, the worm" (214).

4. Quoted from Schmidt in note 86 of Muir's edition of *King Lear*, p. 163.

5. From *Institutes of the Christian Religion* (1.14.3) are quoted these of Calvin's words: "The orthodox faith does not admit that any evil nature exists in the whole universe. For the depravity and malice both of man and of the devil, or the sins that arise therefrom, do not spring from nature, but rather from the corruption of nature." See Roland Frye, p. 217.
6. From "Renaissance humanism" under *Humanism* in Wikipedia [http://en.wikipedia.org/wiki/Humanism].
7. Quoted from "Great chain of being" in Wikipedia. [http://en.wikipedia.org/wiki/Great_chain_of_being]
8. Quoted in Richard Norman, *On Humanism*, p.3.
9. See *3 Henry VI*, 2.5.86, *Richard III*, 1.4.44, *King John*, 5.2.50

Works Consulted

Adams, Hazard, ed. *Critical Theory Since Plato.* New York: Harcourt Brace Jovanovich, 1971.

Bradley, A. C. *Shakespearean Tragedy: Lectures on Hamlet, Othello, King Lear, Macbeth.* 2nd ed. London: Macmillan, 1905.

Danby, John F. *Shakespeare's Doctrine of Nature: A Study of* King Lear. London: Faber and Faber, 1949.

Davies, Tony. *Humanism.* London & New York: Routledge, 1997.

Eastman, Arthur M. *A Short History of Shakespearean Criticism.* Lanham, MD: UP of America, 1985.

Evans, G. Blackmore, ed. *The Riverside Shakespeare.* Boston: Houghton Mifflin Co., 1974.

Fitch, Robert E. *Shakespeare: The Perspective of Value.* Philadelphia: The Westminster P, 1969.

Forster, E. M. *Aspects of the Novel.* New York: Harcourt, Brace & World, 1954.

Frye, Northrop. "*King Lear*: The Tragedy of Isolation." *Shakespeare: King Lear.* Ed. Frank Kermode. London: Macmillan, 1969. 265-269.

Frye, Roland Mushat. *Shakespeare and Christine Doctrine.* Princeton, NJ: Princeton UP, 1963.

Godshalk, William Leigh. *Patterning in Shakespearean Drama.* The Hague & Paris: Mouton, 1973.

Grudin, Robert. *Mighty Opposites: Shakespeare and Renaissance Contrariety.* Berkeley: U of California P, 1979.

Harrison, G. B. *Shakespeare: The Complete Works.* New York: Heinle & Heinle, 1968.

Hwang, Wen-chung. *Language in King Lear.* Taipei: Bookman Books, 1986.

Johnson, Samuel. "Preface to *Shakespeare.*" Rpt. in Adams, 329-336.

Kermode, Frank, ed. *Shakespeare: King Lear.* London: Macmillan, 1969.

——, ed. *The Tempest.* London & New York: Methuen, 1958.

Leggatt, Alexander. *King Lear.* New York & London: Harvester-Wheatsheaf, 1988.

Magill, Frank N., ed. *English Literature: Shakespeare.* Magill Surveys. Pasadena, California: Salem P, 1980.

Muir, Kenneth, ed. *King Lear.* London & New York: Methuen, 1980.

Norman, Richard. *On Humanism.* London & New York: Routledge, 2004.

Orwell, George. "Lear, Tolstoy and the Fool." *Shakespeare: King Lear.* Ed. Frank Kermode. London: Macmillan, 1969. 150-168.

Shakespeare. *All's Well That Ends Well.* In Evans, 499-544.

———. *Cymbeline.* In Evans, 1517-1563.

———. *3 Henry VI.* In Evans, 671-707.

———. *King John.* In Evans, 765-799.

———. *King Lear.* Ed. Kenneth Muir. London & New York: Methuen, 1980.

———. *Pericles.* In Evans, 1479-1516.

———. *Richard III.* In Evans, 708-764.

———. *Romeo and Juliet.* In Evans, 1055-1099.

———. *The Winter's Tale.* In Evans, 1564-1605.

Sidney, Philip. *An Apology for Poetry.* Rpt. in Adams, 154-177.

Sisson, C. J. "Justice in *King Lear.*" *Shakespeare: King Lear.* Ed. Frank Kermode. London: Macmillan, 1969. 228-244.

Spivack, Bernard. *Shakespeare and the Allegory of Evil.* New York & London: Columbia UP, 1958.

Spurgeon, Caroline, F. E. *Shakespeare's Imagery and What It Tells Us.* Boston: Beacon P, 1935.

Thilly, Frank. *A History of Philosophy.* Revised by Ledger Wood. New York: Henry Holt & Co., 1951.

Welsford, Enid. "The Fool in *King Lear.*" *Shakespeare: King Lear.* Ed. Frank Kermode. London: Macmillan, 1969. 137-149.

* This chapter first appeared as a paper in 2010 in National Chung Hsing University's *Journal of Humanities*, Vol. 44, pp. 233-266.

• Chapter 7 •

The Nietzschean and Foucauldean Prospero: Shakespeare's Vision of Power

I. Power as the Origin

In the beginning of Goethe's *Faust, Part I*, there is a scene in which Faust opens a Bible and is "stuck at once" by the line "In the beginning was the Word." In his reasoning, Faust simply cannot grant the Word such merit as creating the world. So he tries to "translate it differently" and comes up with the line "In the beginning was the Mind." It is logical to think that the Word comes from the Mind. But immediately Faust changes the line again to "In the beginning was the Power," for, logically, nothing can be created without the power to do it even if one has the mind and gives the word to create it. Ironically, however, Faust changes the line once more "in a flash" to "In the beginning was the Deed."[1] The rationale now must be: even if you have the power to create the world, there will be no creation at all unless you have the deed of creation. This rationale sounds quite right, but it brings Faust, unawares, to the nonsensical conclusion that the Creation began with the deed of Creation.

Faust does believe in deeds, rather than words. His acts as represented in Goethe's work are his legendary deeds. Yet, he is even more a believer in power. He strives to make himself as powerful as the omnipotent God, by way of black magic in addition to ordinary means. The entire *Faust*, Part I along with Part II, is a story of how the protagonist seeks and uses power. Thus, power is indeed the origin of Faust's Word, Faust's Mind, and Faust's Deed.

Western classical tradition is often said to begin with Homer's epics. The subject of Homer's first epic (*Iliad*) is war: the cause, progress, and consequence of the Trojan War. The Trojan War is said to be caused by love: the love for Helen. But the human cause is itself said to have been caused by a super-human cause: the discord caused by Eris among Hera, Athena, and Aphrodite. Beyond the epic content, however, the historical Trojan War is said to have been caused by an actual struggle for control of the important trade routes through and across the Hellespont, which were dominated by the city of Troy. If this historical interpretation is true, the war was caused not by love for a beauty but by concern for commercial interests. Anyway, war is truly the conduct of using power to gain the power for owning women and / or wealth.

Like epic, drama depicts humans struggling for power. Shakespeare is often supposed to have begun his career as a playwright with the writing of *Henry VI* (three parts), and the last play he wrote (perhaps in collaboration with Fletcher) is often supposed to be *Henry VIII*.[2] Both *Henry VI* and *Henry VIII* are history or chronicle plays. In histories, the subject is usually political and military power. In beginning and ending his playwright's career with history plays, and by writing so many other histories besides *Henry VI* and *Henry VIII* (including *Richard III*, *Richard II, King John, Henry IV* (two parts), and *Henry V*), Shakespeare seems to tell us that power was his lifelong concern.

Besides histories, Shakespeare also wrote comedies and tragedies. Like satires, comedies often aim at human vices and follies. Shakespeare's comedies have attacked various vices and ridiculed various follies. All vices and follies in Shakespearean comedies, however, are linked to high-ranking people's political power and the power of sexual love in some way or other. Behind Bertram's personal blindness of prejudice and unreason lies Helena's unabated love for him. Behind the courtly intrigue of Duke Frederick lies Rosalind's genuine love for Orlando. Behind the villainy of Iachimo lies Imogen's constant love for Posthumus. Behind the king's ridiculous decree for contemplative study lies the insuppressible love of King Ferdinand and the three lords of his court for the princess and the three ladies from France. Besides the flippant fun the merry wives of Windsor have with the roguish Falstaff, there is the love triangle Anne Page is involved in. Besides the laughable rivalry between the reluctant Beatrice and the confirmed bachelor Benedick, there is the serious courtship between Hero and Claudio. Besides the farcical confusion arising from mistaken identity, there is Adriana's increasing suspicion of her husband's infidelity. And besides the pleasurable prudery of the dour Puritan Malvolio, there are the romantic love affairs of Viola / Orsino and Olivia / Sebastian. If we want to see more examples of sexual love related to political power in Shakespearean comedies, we cannot forget the two pairs, of course, in *A Midsummer Night's Dream* (Lysander / Hermia & Demetrius / Helena), nor the two pairs in *Two Gentlemen of Verona* (Valentine / Silvia & Proteus / Julia).

Some of Shakespeare's comedies border on "problem plays."[3] To explore the problem of justice and mercy, however, *Measure for Measure* provides a story of sexual desire that involves Angelo, Isabella and Mariana under the reign of Duke Vincentio. In showing the problem of racism and friendship, *The Merchant of Venice* relates a story of courtship to a story of monetary loan under the juristic judgment of the Duke of Venice. In reflecting the problem of moral and political disintegration, *Troilus and Cressida* tells how politics can corrupt love. None of the problem plays can rid its problem of political and sexual power, indeed.

Some of Shakespeare's comedies also border on "romances."[4] But besides miracles, the romances also display the power of sexual love under the sway of political power: the pure love between Pericles and Thaisa in contrast with the incestuous lust of King Antiochus for his own daughter and the brothel customers' lust for the chaste Marina; the noble love marred by rash jealousy as seen in the case of Leontes / Hermione, in contrast with the true young lovers' love as seen in the case of Florizel / Perdita, which involves the power of two kings; the natural love of Ferdinand, in contrast with the unnatural lust of Caliban, for Miranda, which is controlled by Prospero, the "ruler" of the island.

Many of Shakespeare's tragedies are woven with scenes and themes of sexual love, too. Think of Antony and Cleopatra, Hamlet and Ophelia, Othello and Desdemona, Romeo and Juliet, etc. Even in tragedies where the dominant theme is not erotic, some characters are also tinged with sexuality. In *King Lear*, for instance, there is Edmund's illicit passion for both Goneril and Regan. In *Titus Andronicus*, there is the illicit love between Tamora and Aaron along with the violation of Lavinia by Demetrius and Chiron. But in such tragedies, just as in comedies, sexual love is actually dominated by high-ranking people's political power.

Some Shakespearean tragedies have, indeed, little to do with the power of sexual love. They most conspicuously deal with other themes directly related to political power. Recall, for instance, Coriolanus' pride and military prowess in the power struggle between the Romans and the Volscians, and recall Julius Caesar's pride and self-confidence amidst the power struggle of the Romans. Recall, too, Macbeth's ambition and final downfall for regal power, and recall Timon's hate of ingratitude in connection with the power of his wealth. Like his histories and comedies, Shakespeare's tragedies certainly cannot dispense with political power. That is why it seems that none of his plays can do without a high-ranking authority (an emperor, a king, a prince, a duke, etc.) involved in the political and sexual affairs. And that is why Leonard Tennenhouse can claim that in Jacobean drama, "sexual relations are always political" (124).

Sexual love is itself a strong power, a power occasionally even stronger than political or military power. If it is not, as Freud suggests, the ultimate motivating factor of human psychology and social behavior, it is at least a frequent drive of life, a recurrent element of Shakespearean drama blended with the element of socio-political power. Basically, Shakespeare's characters are all carrying on word wars or sword wars for the sake of power, that is, for the socio-political and / or familial-sexual power in its broadest sense, and their final goal may be just to use the power for wealth and / or for women, or for getting better socio-political and / or familial-sexual positions to keep and / or increase their power. Therefore, power can be regarded as the origin of Shakespeare's dramaturgy, just as it is regarded as the origin of Creation and the origin of the Trojan War.

II. The Will to Power

For Schopenhauer, as we know, the world is driven by a primordial "will to live" (*Wille zum Leben*) and thus the desire of all creatures is to avoid death and to procreate. In challenging this view, however, Nietzsche holds that the "will to live" is but a secondary drive; the primary drive of life is "the will to power" (*der Wille zur Macht*)[5]: except in an extreme condition of poverty and limitation, what all living beings want is not a mere chance to live on but a good chance to gain power, and that is why people are willing to risk their lives in all sorts of "*agon*" (Greek for "contest") just as the Greek heroes did.

Knowledge is an instrument of power. According to Nietzsche, the will to know depends on the will to power: the aim of knowledge is not just to know something, but to master, to have power over something. Science, therefore, is but a way of gaining the power of truth so as to govern Nature. Yet, knowledge or truth is not an "objective" reality; it is a process of "subjective" interpretation serving the will to power. In Nietzsche's mind, therefore, there is no absolute truth: all "truths" are interpretative "fictions." In this world, "fiction" is allowed and it often proves to be useful or practically necessary to life.[6]

Life, in Nietzsche's view, is a plurality of forces, a lasting form of processes, and an intricate complexity of systems which strive after an increase in the feeling of power (Copleston 185). In life's strife, the will to power may seek to overcome obstacles and recognize appropriation and assimilation as proper means for power. Unlike Darwin, who emphasizes the influence of external circumstances, Nietzsche emphasizes one's tremendous power to use and exploit the environment, to shape and create forms from within (Copleston 186). Nietzsche also disagrees with the hedonist view that life's aim is merely pursuit of pleasure and avoidance of pain. For him, pleasure and pain are concomitant phenomena in life's strife for power. Pleasure is the feeling of increased power; pain is the feeling of hindrance to the will to power (Copleston 186).

According to Nietzsche, rank is determined by quanta of power. The mediocre majority may possess greater power than the individuals who are not mediocre. But ascending life should be distinguished from decadent life. Truly great power consists in "the ability to withstand great suffering, to respond creatively to great challenges, and to transform into advantages what seemed harmful" (Thilly 503). For Nietzsche, the will to power cannot be understood apart from "sublimation" (Urmson 281). There is "master morality" in contrast with "slave morality." The Superman (*der Uebermensch*) is one that has "the highest possible development and integration of intellectual power, strength of character and will, independence, passion, taste and physique"—he is "the Roman Caesar with Christ's soul" or "Goethe and Napoleon in one" (Copleston 188). Such a man of great soul is above resentment, delivered from revenge. He has "the free spirit that wills to be responsible" and that spirit "acts as a counter-force to sickly revengefulness" (Mandalios 176). In a word, Superman is the greatest achievement of the will to power.

III. The Exercise of Power

Influenced by Nietzsche and proclaiming himself a Nietzschean, Michel Foucault also knows the universality of the will to power. But Foucault's interest is focused not on power as the target of the will, but on power relations, on how power is exercised in society. For him, power is more limited in sense: it is chiefly political power, seldom referring to such power as going beyond human relationships. Hence, his analyses of power shed light mostly on the means and effects of exercising power in society.

In *Discipline and Punish*, Foucault claims that "power is exercised rather than possessed" (26). It is neither a property nor some substance with its nature and origin directly visible. It is seen only when it is exercised by some agents, such as individuals or institutes. In its entirety, power is constituted by a multitude of "micro-powers." It is seemingly a "strategy" spreading throughout the whole social system, manifested neither globally nor comprehensively but locally. In truth, the exercise of power is like a game of chess: every piece demonstrates a "micro-power" in capturing another piece, but all the moves are directed by the overall strategic arrangement for the pieces. Thus, power is neither located in nor symbolized by the sovereign (as it is traditionally thought to be); it only permeates the society through the state apparatus dynamically and dispersedly (Hoy 134).

For Foucault, freedom is both the condition and the effect of power: to have power is to have freedom, and to have freedom is to have power. No one (no institute) can exercise power without freedom, nor can power be exercised on beings that are not free. Since any exercise of power will inevitably result in some form of resistance as the reaction, to exercise power on a non-resisting slave in chain is not to exercise power at all. Thus, the relation between power and freedom is like that of the opponents in an "agonism"—they are always engaging each other in a contest or combat of reciprocal incitement and struggle.[7] If the exercise of power is like a game of chess, such power is not only the function of the capturing set of pieces but also the result of the possible resistance from the opposed set (Hoy 135-6).

Foucault shares Nietzsche's view that there is no absolute truth. For him, discourse goes with power while knowledge is power transmitted by discourse under the control of power. Powerful individuals or institutes are capable of making truth, morality, and values which come from false consciousness or "regime of falsity" in Foucault's terminology. Thus, real truth can be ascertained only when it is disinterested and in the absence of power relations (Hoy 131).

Foucault finds a great change in the Western history of exercising power in penal institutions such as found in the practice of discipline, surveillance, and constraint. The "Technologies of Punishment" have gone from "Monarchical Punishment," which involves brutal executions and torture, to "Disciplinary Punishment," which involves professionals (psychologists, program facilitators, parole officers, etc.) holding power over the prisoners. The modern disciplinary punishment is so practiced that the human bodies become "docile bodies." Paradoxically, discipline both "increases the forces of the body (in economic terms of utility) and diminishes these same forces (in political terms of obedience)" (Foucault 138). The penal professionals are like masters while the inmates are like obedient slaves useful to the masters.

But it is dangerous for a sovereign to exercise power openly: "the power that does violence to our bodies and our minds must be hidden and dispersed because we are instinctually violent creatures who are prone to the expression of a will to dominate" (Lentricchia 35). Jeremy Bentham's plan of "Panopticon" is for Foucault an example of modern disciplinary technology. A Panopticon is an annular prison-house designed to exercise power based on two principles—visible and unverifiable. It is visible in that the inmate can see himself as constantly under surveillance. And it is unverifiable in that "the inmate must never know whether he is being looked at at any one moment; but he must be sure that he may always be so" (Foucault 201). In such a Panopticon, all the inmates are deprived of freedom, property, and connection between populations. Thus, no internal violence is possible there. Although the Panopticon does not itself possess power, it is an efficient space for the exercise of power.

IV. An Allegory of Power

As we know, *The Tempest* was at first listed as a comedy (differentiated from a history or a tragedy) by the Folio compilers of Shakespeare's works. But, as the last of Shakespeare's complete plays, it is more often than not ascribed to a romance. In fact, its genre has been a puzzle to critics. Gary Schmidgall writes: "The possibilities are admittedly boggling: *The Tempest* as romance, morality play, initiation ritual, refinement of the *commedia dell'art*, topical response to New World voyages, masque, comedy, tragedy, tragicomedy, hymeneal celebration, fairy tale, myth, or autobiographical palinode" (quoted in Daniell 15). Schmidgall has missed mentioning the possibility of "allegory." I think, however, the play is most manifestly an allegory. It may well be "an allegory of Shakespeare's own artistic genius" as many Victorians have thought it to be (Palmer 19). But, interpreted more generally, it is most surely an allegory of power.

Harold Bloom says that Shakespeare should have called *The Tempest* "*Prospero* or even *Prospero and Caliban*" (2). The play is indeed centered on Prospero as the one single protagonist, or on the protagonist and his present antagonist, Caliban. The two central characters, as we can notice, are both allegorical in nature. Prospero and Caliban are clearly incarnations of abstract ideas, just like Fellowship and Death in *Everyman*. They are master and servant, but may stand for general Goodness and Unruliness (Vaughan 278). Hence, R. A. Foakes, among other critics, regards Prospero as "a controller who exercises through his magic a power like that of heaven" and regards the oppositions between Miranda and Caliban as the contrasts between beauty and ugliness or between nurture and nature (145).

August Wilhelm von Schlegel is considered to be the first to adopt an allegorical approach to *The Tempest*. He "related Ariel to the airy elements and Caliban to the earthy, suggesting an allegory which coincides with Elizabethan and Jacobean humor-psychology" (Daniell 50). Later, James Russell Lowell in his allegorical interpretation equated Caliban to brute understanding, Ariel to fancy, and Prospero to imagination (Daniell 51). Interpretations like these certainly can be justified in their own right. However, I certainly wonder why Prospero cannot stand just for prosperity while Caliban and Ariel stand for the earthy and airy elements respectively.

As a male Italian name, "Prospero" does suggest that all he aims to do is to prosper. In the play, we may recall, Caliban occasionally calls Prospero "Prosper": "All the infections that the sun sucks up / From bogs, fens, flats, on Prosper fall" (2.2.1-2); "now Prosper works upon thee" (2.2.83). And Alonso does the same: "and the thunder... pronounced / The name of Prosper" (3.3.99). Even in a stage direction in Act III, Scene 3, "Prospero" is once replaced by "Prosper": *Solemn and strange music; and* Prosper *on the top* (*invisible*). The ending "o" in "Prospero" may be omitted intentionally by the poet for the sake of rhythm (to keep the line's

240

iambic meter). Nevertheless, the poet as well as the characters may really equate "Prospero" to "Prosper" in mind.

To prosper is a mundane idea, as it means "to succeed and do well; to thrive and grow in life." It is often the effect of having power and exercising it well. In *The Tempest*, Prospero tells his daughter on the unnamed island that he was originally Duke of Milan; but he was not content with being "a prince of power" (1.2.55); he became "transported and rapt in secret studies" (1.2.76-77). He never mentions why he became obsessed with "secret studies" and "prized" some volumes of his books "above his dukedom" (1.2.168). But from the fact that he gained magic power over the years on the island, we can infer that Prospero is actually like Faust: his "secret studies" are like Faust's secret contacts with Mephistopheles. Indeed, Prospero is like Faust in coming near to being the Almighty, and in possessing such supernatural power that he may for some time prosper well without limitation. His doings on the island—including his saving Ariel from the cloven pine and making the spirit his servant, his usurping Caliban's island and controlling him as his slave, and, above all, his conjuring up the eponymous tempest and bringing about the revelation of Antonio's evil nature, the redemption of Alonso, the suppression of Caliban and his accomplices' revolt, the possible marriage of Ferdinand and Miranda, etc.—all bespeak his prosperity in exercising his hard-won supernatural power before he comes to know the limitation of such power and prosperity. Thus, the play is indeed an allegory of power, of how a mundane and yet Faustian hero wills to have infinite power for prosperity, gains it, exercises it, and finally reflects upon it.

Many other characters in the play also show that they, likewise, willed to have supreme power. Prospero's brother, Antonio, usurped his dukedom in order to become the "absolute Milan" (1.2.109). Alonso, the King of Naples, helped to supplant Prospero and married his daughter to Tunis in order to have more power. Sebastian was once tempted to murder Alonso for power. Stephano, supported by Caliban and Trinculo, was about to murder Prospero and become king of the island. Gonzalo once stated what he would do if he were king on the isle. Miranda said: "Had I been any god of power, I would / Have sunk the sea within the earth... " 1.2.10-11). Ferdinand said, "I am the best of them" and "myself am Naples" (1.2.432 & 437), supposing his father was already dead. Saying that he was "first my own King" (1.2.344), Caliban, naturally, wished to have power to take back his isle and win Miranda to people "This isle with Calibans" (1.2.353). Through all these characters' deeds and thoughts, Shakespeare suggests undoubtedly that all people, regardless of their ranks, races, and genders, have the Will to Power. Thus, the play is indeed an allegory of power.

V. The Types of Power

As an allegory of power, *The Tempest* is fraught with power of various types. Firstly, it has both *natural power* and *supernatural power*. Natural power is seen in the storm that sinks the ship, the sea that drowns the men, and the land that provides "all the qualities of the isle" (1.2.339). Supernatural power is felt when the men's drenched garments hold "their freshness and glosses" (2.1.60-61) and when music is heard "played by the picture of Nobody" (3.2.124-5). Supernatural power goes with Ariel, of course, who performs Prospero's behest, and with Prospero himself, who controls everything on the isle, including Caliban's "dam's god, Setebos" (1.2.375).

As a human being, Prospero ought to be confined to his *human power*, which is to see, to hear, to feel, to think, and to do things like other human beings. Yet, he wishes to have *superhuman power* into the bargain. His "secret studies" have finally made him a god-like being, as he has acquired the superhuman power to foresee things, to charm people from moving, to command spirits, to change fates, and to create the future at his will.

Other characters in the play behave like most human beings. Alonso used *military power* to help Antonio extirpate Prospero out of his dukedom and to win more *political power* for himself as well as for Antonio. All that Sebastian, Stephano, Gonzalo, Ferdinand, and Caliban once dreamed of was the highest political / military power, too, that a king might have.

All individuals have *physical power* and *intellectual power* for life. In the first scene of *The Tempest*, the mariners are exerting their strength (physical power) to handle the ship against the storm and surges while the boatswain is exerting his skill and knowledge (intellectual power) to fight in the same tempestuous situation. The boatswain is wise enough to tell Gonzalo the practical truths: "What care these roarers for the name of King?" (1.1.16-17); "if you can command these elements to silence, and work the peace of the presence, we will not hand a rope more" (1.1.21-23). In certain situations, authority is really of no avail while laborers' physical power and professionals' intellectual power are of great importance. This idea is reinforced in Prospero's understanding that his authority cannot dispense with Caliban as his slave and Ariel as his minister.

All intellectuals know that there is *legal power* in social laws and there is *lingual power* in human languages. Legally, power goes with rank: a king has his supreme authority in his kingdom, a duke, in his dukedom, just as a ship-master has his top command in a ship. That is why so many characters in *The Tempest* are shown to try to keep their high ranks if they have them, or try to usurp others' high ranks, or dream of having the highest rank. Legally, marriage is entitled to both name and property, which yield social and financial power. That is why Alonso married his "fair daughter Claribel to the King of Tunis" (2.1.68), and that is why Prospero is arranging his daughter Miranda's marriage to King Alonso's son and heir Ferdinand. Legally, alliance can augment power. That is why Antonio allied with Alonso first and sought to ally with Sebastian next, and that is why Caliban would ally with Stephano and Trinculo. And legally, ownership also has power to keep what one owns. That is why Caliban claims to Prospero that "This island's mine, by Sycorax my mother, / Which thou tak'st from me" (1.2.333-4).

Terry Eagleton suggests that "the name of Prospero's language is Ariel, who symbolizes his word in action" (94). In truth, lingual power is seen in all sorts of speech act. It is seen in Prospero's revelation and consolation to Miranda, his promise and praise to Ariel, his threat and command to Caliban, his accusation and explanation to Ferdinand, his reproach and admonition to Alonso, Sebastian, and Antonio, etc. Language has power mostly because it tells truths, but it may have power, too, when it tells lies. What Prospero has told Miranda about his past may all be true, but it is surely a lie to say Ferdinand is "a traitor" coming to the island to work "as a spy" (1.2.463 & 458). The lie, however, has the power to justify Prospero's testing toil imposed on Ferdinand. Very often lies may not be easily differentiated from truths. In Caliban's mind, Prospero is truly "a tyrant, a sorcerer that by his cunning hath cheated me of the island" (3.2.40-41). But for Ariel it is a lie to say Prospero is such a person. Prospero himself may refuse the appellation, but we know he is truly tyrannical to Caliban, has magic power like a sorcerer, and has truly "cheated" him of the island somewhat like what a colonist did to the natives of a colony.[8] Anyway, despite Ariel's ascribing it to a lie, Caliban's description of Prospero does have the power to justify Stephano and Trinculo's joining Caliban in the scheme to murder the tyrannical sorcerer-usurper.

To lie is immoral. In human society, the importance of *moral power* cannot be overestimated. In *The Tempest*, Prospero plainly acts as a moralist facing and trying to redeem "three men of sin" (3.3.53). He stands for the moral power that can cease to be revengeful, get reconciled with enemies, rectify their misdeeds, and bring the entire society to a blissful ending.

Love is the core of morality. One may be moved by *the power of beauty*, but one is even more moved by *the power of love*. Sexual power often comes from beauty. Ferdinand and Miranda "are both in either's powers"(1.2.453), as soon as they see each other's divine appearances. As Robert Grudin has observed, there is a vein of anti-lechery in the play, since Caliban is stopped from raping Miranda, Ferdinand is enjoined to refrain from premarital sexual intercourse, and Venus is left out in the Masque that calls upon goddesses to bless the young couple (200 ff.). Beyond sexual love, it seems, the parental love that Prospero bears to Miranda is more important: the entire play is a father's effort and arrangement to ensure his daughter's future prosperity. It is the power of such parental love that moves us and sets in motion all the acts of the play.

Beyond the parental love, then, there is also the compassionate love, the love that goes with the sense of community and fellowship. When Ariel says that his affections would become tender towards all the charmed prisoners if he were human, Prospero replies:

> *Hast thou, which art but air, a touch, a feeling*
> *Of their afflictions, and shall not myself,*
> *One of their kind, that relish all as sharply*
> *Passion as they, be kindlier moved than thou art? (5.1.21-24)*

In the end, Prospero does show his merciful and compassionate love towards everybody, including the ugly, monstrous Caliban. In Prospero's mind, *ethical power* is really placed above *aesthetic power*.

In actuality, Shakespeare has his Christian conscience, and that makes him naturally place ethical power or moral power above all worldly powers. It is only that Shakespeare is, after all, a poet of nature rather than a moralist. He tends to show us not the ideal way of living

245

but the true picture of life, in which man keeps using all types of power to win better socio-political and familial-sexual positions, to have wealth and women, and to gain security and prosperity in life.

VI. The Nietzschean Prospero

Prospero is indeed a Nietzschean hero. He manifests Nietzsche's idea of "will to power" and he can be considered as a near example of Nietzsche's "Superman." Originally as the rightful Duke, Prospero did not have to struggle for existence when he was in Milan. Yet, he was obviously not content with the political / military power that his rank allowed him. He made himself obsessed with "secret studies," and that led him to neglect his ducal duty. Thus, he seemed to forsake political power in pursuit of supernatural power. And thus his "will to power" is of the highest kind.

In seeking for infinite, supernatural power, Prospero is quite like Faust. Unlike Faust, however, Prospero does not make any deal with the Devil, nor does he surrender moral integrity in order to achieve power and success. Although he is said to have done "secret studies" and to own a magic staff and some magic books, there is no mention that he has ever made any pact with Mephistopheles. Moreover, what he does on the island after he has divine power is not for such worldly pleasures as Faust has indulged. His greatest pleasure, it seems, is to show the power of his "Art," while his goal is to ensure the prosperity of his family.

Frank Kermode regards *The Tempest* as a pastoral drama concerned with the opposition of Nature and Art. In his interpretation, the main opposition is "between the worlds of Prospero's Art, and Caliban's Nature" (xxiv). Prospero's Art, "being the Art of supernatural virtue which belongs to the redeemed world of civility and learning, is the antithesis of the black magic of Sycorax" (xli). Such Art has two functions: to exercise "the supernatural powers of the holy adept" (xlvii) and to control Nature (xlviii). In this interpretation, Prospero is regarded as a good mage.

As a good mage, Prospero is almost a Superman, an ideal man of power in Nietzsche's terminology. He knows he has the tremendous power to master, to govern Nature. He has appropriated the island, assimilated Ariel, mastered Caliban, exploited the environment, and caused the tempest to shape and create the future of his family and the other members of his world. But the increase in power does not spoil him. Instead, he is sublimated in a way. He has the "master morality" to set himself above resentment and deliver himself from revengefulness. He is indeed like a holy adept, exercising his supernatural power to counter the evil powers and to tame the wild.

But Prospero is not yet a complete Superman. As his mind is still restricted by his mundane idea of personal prosperity, not yet extended to the ideal of wishing to withstand great suffering for the whole world and make the entire human race prosperous (as Goethe's Faust finally wishes to), he is at most just on the way to the highest status of Nietzsche's Superman.

VII. The Foucauldean Prospero

As a Nietzschean hero with the highest Will to Power and almost achieving the status of a Superman, Prospero is, nevertheless, a Foucauldean expert as well in his exercise of power. Prospero knows well the Foucauldean truth that "power is exercised rather than possessed." That is why he perpetually tries to show his magic power by exercising it. His raising the tempest, controlling Ariel and Caliban, teasing Alonso and his followers with a magic banquet, calling spirits (of Ceres, Iris, Juno, and nymphs) to perform a nuptial dance for Miranda and Ferdinand, and driving the plotters with magic hunting dogs, etc., as well as his saving Ariel from the cloven pine, are all acts of showing magic power by exercising it. And all these acts stand for some of the "micro-powers" that constitute the entirety of his almighty power, which is independent of his dukeship.

Prospero also knows well the Foucauldean truth that freedom is both the condition and the effect of power. As he has the power to control even Setebos, Caliban's dam's god, and "make a vassal of him" (1.2.376), he knows he can enjoy freedom on the island at will. In contrast, all those in his power (Ariel, Caliban, and the shipwrecked Italians) are no better than slaves under his control and at his mercy. Many of them want to resist or even revolt, but they are all overpowered and therefore without freedom to do things at will.

Readers may wonder why Prospero decides to forsake his "potent Art" by breaking his staff, burying it "certain fadoms in the earth" and drowning his book (5.5.50-57). Barbara Traister thinks that "Prospero knows the limits of his power" (120). Why, then, does he know the limits of his power? It may be because he knows his potent Art is actually nothing but "rough magic" (5.1.50). It may also be because he knows that "We are such stuff / As dreams are made on" (4.1.156-7): power and man are both inconstant. But it is more probably because he knows the Foucauldean truth that to exercise power on a non-resisting slave is not to exercise power at all. In the end of *The Tempest*, all the other characters are so overpowered by him that it becomes meaningless to exercise power again on them. It is as if an "agonism" has lost its opponents. Furthermore, it is even more probable that Prospero has come to realize that he himself is enslaved by both his Will to Power and his Way of Exercising Power: since he has achieved his goal of ensuring prosperity for his family, to keep showing power to his non-resisting slaves is no other than to make himself a slave of power.

Prospero knows, too, the Foucauldean truth that there is no absolute truth; power can control discourse and make truth. In telling Miranda what had happened to him and her in Milan, Prospero was constructing (or reconstructing) a truth in his informative discourse so that his doings to the shipwrecked Italians may be justified. In accusing Ferdinand of coming to act as a spy on the island, he was making a lie (a false truth) to further his plan on him. In refuting Caliban's remarks that he usurped his island and ill-treated him, Prospero was replacing Caliban's truth with his own truth so that his government on the island might be justified. In admonishing the shipwrecked Italians, he was uttering a moral truth to justify his treatment of them. Indeed, Prospero always claims (in speech and in mind) that he has the truth. But his truth is never disinterested and in the absence of power relations. In actuality, his truth is often no better than expedient discourse made to justify his exercise of power.

What Prospero practices on the island is what Foucault calls "Disciplinary Punishment." The island is in essence a Foucauldean "Panopticon," in which the prisoners (Caliban at first, and later the shipwrecked Italians) have become "docile bodies" held under strict discipline, surveillance, and constraint. In this Panopticon, Ariel represents the agent that makes the modern power of imprisonment both visible and unverifiable. He really keeps an eye on every "inmate," allots places for them, manages matters separately with them, and stops them from dangerous schemes—and all these things he does invisibly (as an airy spirit), with his unverifiable power. This Panopticon is indeed a great success. It is so successful that all guilty and mischievous malefactors are chastised there in time, and everything just goes smoothly there in complete accord with Prospero's ideas. Prospero is indeed the governor, and the play is "patterned around ideas of governing, of the master-servant situation in its multiple aspects" (Godshalk 166).

VIII. The Vision of Power

All great writers are visionary poets. A great work often envisions something significant. Dante's *Divine Comedy*, for instance, is a Christian vision of the afterlife told in an allegorical manner. And Goethe's *Faust* is a romantic vision of man's quest for the infinite. Now, I say *The Tempest* stands for Shakespeare's vision of power: it is told partly in an allegorical manner and partly in a realistic / fantastic manner to depict a partly Faustian and partly Nietzschean hero exercising his power in a Foucauldean method. Furthermore, this play is like our famous novel, Tsao's *Dreams of the Red Mansions*,[9] in that it envisions man's perpetual, and yet vain, strife for power and prosperity.

I have said above that *The Tempest* is an allegory of power as it shows its protagonist (Prospero) and many other characters all striving or dreaming to have supreme power. Now, we must say that the play's title and the play's setting are also allegorical in nature. Northrop Frye suspects that "tempest" suggests "the Latin *tempestas*, meaning time as well as tempest, like its French descendant *temps*, which means both time and weather" (Sandler 178). I think the tempest is both a storm of the world and a storm of the mind, that is, both an elemental storm and a mental storm. As an elemental storm, it may wreck ships and ruin bodies. As a mental storm, it may stir minds and change mentalities. In the play, as we see, the tempest raised by Prospero has truly done no harm to the shipwrecked Italians: the tempest is just a means to redeem them morally. Thus, allegorically, the tempest really stands for any critical time created by Heaven or by man as a "brainstorm" to confuse and / or clear up one's mind.[10]

I have also said above that the anonymous island in *The Tempest* is Prospero's Panopticon used to hold Caliban and the shipwrecked Italians under strict discipline, surveillance, and constraint. Upon further consideration in the light of allegory, however, the island is, even more justifiably, an epitome of the mundane World of Power. In this World of Power, everyone keeps struggling for power—for supernatural power or for various types of human power (political, intellectual, legal, lingual, moral, sexual, etc.). In this World of Power, when one has become the Lord of Power (as Prospero has), one will exercise one's power to further prosper oneself and one's family (as Prospero does to prosper himself and Miranda) in one's interactions with others, including one's ministers (the Ariels), slaves (the Calibans), friends (people like Gonzalo), foes (people like Alonso, Sebastian, and Antonio), and other related persons (people like Ferdinand, Stephano, Trinculo, Adrian, Francisco, the ship Master, Boatswain, Mariners, etc.). In this mundane world, as each one struggles with a Will to Power and exercises one's checked or unchecked power for prosperity, usurpation (of a position, a land, resources, rights, etc.) is frequent, mental tempests are even more frequent than elemental tempests, and very few, if ever, can understand the vanity of seeking and showing power. Thus, all are enslaved by power in trying to increase power, show power, or overpower others. "Liberty!" may become the most common outcry when conscience sees through power.

Interestingly, towards the end of *The Tempest*, Prospero discovers Ferdinand and Miranda playing at chess, and we hear this dialogue:

> *Mir. Sweet lord, you play me false.*
> *Fer. No, my dearest love, I would not for the world.*
> *Mir. Yes, for a score of kingdoms you should wrangle, And I*
> *would call it fair play. (5,1.172-5)*

Here is Miranda's teasing talk about chess-playing, of course. She is teasingly showing her strong love for Ferdinand since she says she would call it fair play if Ferdinand should wrangle for a score of kingdoms by playing her false. Here, however, we also see a truth bearing on the World of Power. Just as the kingdoms of chess are the targets of moves with chess-pieces, the kingdoms of the world are the targets of tactics with human powers. One may wrangle for a score of kingdoms at chess or in the world by playing false, but one may be pardoned or even praised for doing so by one's lover or partner, who likes power no less than this one. This dialogue actually suggests that the innocent Miranda and Ferdinand will get ready to enter the World of Power, and thus there ensues another generation of power struggle.

Upon seeing Ferdinand and Miranda obsessed in playing chess, Alonso remarks: "If this prove / A vision of the island, one dear son / Shall I twice lose" (5.1.175-7). For Alonso in the story, the scene is not a vision, of course. But for an allegorist who sees life as a game of chess, this scene is certainly "a vision of the island" as a "brave new world, / That has such people in it" (5.1.183-4). It is a world where "goodly creatures" (5.1.182) are true opponents forever maneuvering with power for power.

The world of *The Tempest* is in fact the dramatic world of Shakespeare in miniature. It is the condensed Shakespearean world in which all characters in tragedies or comedies and in histories or romances exercise power to increase or keep power, be it superhuman power or human power, physical power or intellectual power, political power or sexual power, legal power or lingual power, aesthetic power or ethic power. In this world of power struggle, glimpses of vanity may occur to the "goodly creatures" occasionally and elevate them to a Superman's level temporarily. But as Everyman is after all only a worldly Prospero—a person aiming at prosperity in this world, not at perpetuality in the other world—the tempests of power, inward and outward, are forever there, challenging all temporal figures.

This vision of power is in fact a universal vision. It has often been reflected in Western literature since Homer's epics. It is most impressively reflected in Goethe's *Faust* as well as repeatedly reflected in Shakespeare's plays. In the East, I find, it is most significantly reflected in Tsao's *Dreams of the Red Mansions*. In that great novel, as we see, the red mansions refer to the Mansion of Prosperity and the Mansion of Security, in which powerful people, while still struggling for women and wealth, for weal and for woe, dream to have security and prosperity all the time, hardly knowing that *la vida es sueño.*[11]

It is significant that *The Tempest* begins with a mage's tempest which seems to threaten safety, and ends with the same mage's promise of safety with "calm seas, auspicious gales" (5.1.314), while the in-between is a series of temporal words and deeds expressing the ways of the world in struggling with power for power. Towards the end of the play we do hear Prospero swear to abjure his "coarse magic" by breaking and burying his staff and drowning his book (5.1.50-57). But we do not see him carry out the oath in the play. Will he carry it out, now that he has resumed his dukedom and secured his daughter's prosperity? I say, "Nobody knows." Yet, unless Prospero has truly become a Nietzschean Superman caring for sublimity more than prosperity, he might just go back to Milan, still bringing with him his staff and book so that he might still keep his magic power to ensure his own (and his family's) security and prosperity forever. After all, in Shakespeare's vision of power, a prosperity-minding man must consider security first and a secured man will go on with his Will to Power to seek prosperity by exercising power like a Foucauldean. To prosper is to have women and wealth, and to lose power is to lose prosperity. This is all Prospero knows, and all he needs to know.

Notes

1. See lines 47-60 of the scene "Faust's Study" in *Goethe's Faust*, translated by Louis MacNeice (1951), Oxford UP, 1808.

2. Scholars have not been able to decide as to when Shakespeare started to write plays. In his *Shakespeare: The Complete Works*, G. B. Harrison says that "Shakespeare probably first began to write plays in 1591 or 1592; but some scholars dispute this and claim that he had been actor and playwright since 1587" (9). It is for this uncertainty that Harrison places *Henry VI* along with six other plays as the first plays that had been written by 1594 (see his *Introducing Shakespeare*, p.164). But many books simply place *Henry VI* and *Henry VIII* as Shakespeare's first plays and last one respectively though they may be dated differently. In Frank Magill's *English Literature: Shakespeare*, for instance, the three parts of *Henry VI* are listed as the first plays and dated from 1589-1591 while *Henry VIII* is listed as the last play and dated from 1612-1613. In Louis Wright and Virginia LaMar's *The Folger Guide to Shakespeare*, we see *Henry VI* and *Henry VIII* also placed first and last in the chronology of Shakespeare's plays but they are respectively dated from 1590-1592 and 1612-1613.

3. The term "problem plays," as coined by F. S. Boas in *Shakespeare and His Predecessors* (1896), refers to such plays as *All's Well That Ends Well, Measure for Measure,* and *Troilus and Cressida.* For me, they refer to any plays that raise problems in the plays' subject matter or generic classification.

4. Many scholars take for romances such later plays as *Pericles, Cymbeline, The Winter's Tale,* and *The Tempest.* Several common features have been suggested for such plays. For me, the most important feature is: they contain magic and other fantastical elements.

5. In his *The Will to Power,* Nietzsche says: "This world is the Will to Power—and nothing else!" (917). In *Thus Spoke Zarathustra,* Nietzsche makes Zarathustra say: "Only where life is, is there also will; but not will to life, instead –thus I teach you—will to power!" (90).

6. These and the following Nietzschean ideas are clearly stated in Copleston, pp.182-188.

7. It is noted that as Foucault's neologism, "agonism" is "based on the Greek *agōnisma* meaning 'a combat,' which implies 'a physical contest in which the opponents develop a strategy of reaction and of mutual taunting, as in a wrestling match.'" See Faubion, p. 348.

8. It is noted that since World War II, Caliban as a colonial victim has dominated the interpretive paradigm throughout the Third World and even within the Anglo-American orbit. See Vaughan, p. 280.

9. Referring to 曹雪芹《紅樓夢》。The novel's title is variously translated into English. David Hawkes & John Minford's translation is: *The Story of the Stone.* C. C. Wang's is: *Dream of the Red Chamber.* Hsien-ye Yang & Gladys Yang's is: *A Dream of Red Mansions.* I prefer to translate it into *Dreams of the Red Mansions* or *Dreams of the Red Houses.* For explanation, see [翻 19] in 「大家一起翻」 in DGD English-Learning Website (http://dgdel.nchu.edu.tw).

10. It is interesting to note that in British English "to have a brainstorm" is to suddenly become forgetful or unable to think clearly, while in American English "to have a brainstorm" is to suddenly have a clever idea.

11. The Mansion of Prosperity is 榮國府 and the Mansion of Security is 寧國府. On the surface, the two mansions claim to bring prosperity and security to the nation (國). They actually seek prosperity and security only for their dwellers. In the novel it seems that only Jia Bao Yu (賈寶玉) came to know Pedro Calderon de la Barca's theme: *la vida es sueño* (life is a dream).

Works Consulted

Bloom, Harold, ed. *William Shakespeare's The Tempest*. New York: Chelsea House Publishers, 1988.

Copleston, Frederick. *A History of Philosophy*. Vol. 7, Part II. New York: Image, 1994.

Daniell, David. *The Critics Debate: The Tempest*. London: Macmillan, 1989.

Eagleton, Terry. *William Shakespeare*. Oxford: Basil Blackwell, 1986.

Faubion, James D., ed. *Essential Works of Foucault 1954-1984*. vol. 3. Trans. Robert Hurley et al. New York: The New Press, 2000.

Foakes, R. A. *Shakespeare—The Dark Comedies to the Last Plays: From Satire to Celebration*. London: Routledge & Kegan Paul, 1971.

Foucault, Michel. *Discipline and Punish: The Birth of the Prison*. New York: Vintage Books, 1979.

Godshalk, William Leigh. *Patterning in Shakespeare's Drama*. The Hague & Paris: Mouton, 1973.

Grudin, Robert. *Mighty Opposites: Shakespeare and Renaissance Contrariety*. Berkerley & Los Angeles: U of California P, 1979.

Harrison, G. B. *Introducing Shakespeare*. London: Penguin, 1966.

———, ed. *Shakespeare: The Complete Works*. Boston: Heinle & Heinle, 1952.

Hoy, David Couzens, ed. *Foucault: A Critical Reader*. Oxford: Basil Blackwell, 1986.

Kermode, Frank, ed. *The Arden Shakespeare: The Tempest*. London & New York: Methuen, 1980.

Lentricchia, Frank. *Ariel and the Police*. Brighton, Sussex: The Harvester Press, 1988.

Magill, Frank N., ed. *English Literature: Shakespeare*. Pasadena, CF: Salem Press, 1980.

Mandalios, John. *Nietzsche and the Necessity of Freedom*. New York: Lexington Books, 2008.

Nietzsche, Friedrich. *The Will to Power*. Trans. Walter Arnold Kaufmann, Walter Kaufmann, & R. J. Hollingdale. New York: Vintage Books, 1968.

——. *Thus Spoke Zarathustra*. Trans. Adrian Del Caro & Robert B. Pippin. Cambridge: Cambridge UP, 2006.

Palmer D. J., ed. *Shakespeare: The Tempest*. London: Macmillan, 1991.

Sandler, Robert, ed. *Northrop Frye on Shakespeare*. New Haven & London: Yale UP, 1986.

Shakespeare, William. *The Tempest*. Ed. Frank Kermode. London & New York: Methuen, 1980.

Tennenhouse, Leonard. *Power on Display: The Politics of Shakespeare's Genres*. London & New York: Routledge, 2005.

Thilly, Frank. *A History of Philosophy*. New York: Henry Holt & Co., 1951.

Traister, Barbara Howard. "Prospero: Master of Self-knowledge." In Bloom, 113-130.

Urmson, J. O & Jonathan Ree. *Concise Encyclopedia of Western Philosophy and Philosophers*. New York: Routledge, 1990.

Vaughan, Alden T. & Virginia Mason Vaughan. *Shakespeare's Caliban: A Cultural History*. Cambridge: Cambridge UP, 1993.

Wright, Louise B. & Virginia A. LaMar, eds. *The Folger Guide to Shakespeare*. New York: Washington Square Press, 1969.

* This chapter first appeared as a paper in 2010 in *Intergrams*, which is an e-journal of the Department of Foreign Languages and Literatures, National Chung Hsing University.

語言文學類　PG0610

The Visionary Shakespeare

作　　者 / 董崇選（Alexander C. H. Tung）
責任編輯 / 林泰宏
圖文排版 / 陳宛鈴
封面設計 / 王嵩賀

發 行 人 / 宋政坤
法律顧問 / 毛國樑　律師
印製出版 / 秀威資訊科技股份有限公司
　　　　　114 台北市內湖區瑞光路 76 巷 65 號 1 樓
　　　　　電話：+886-2-2796-3638　傳真：+886-2-2796-1377
　　　　　http://www.showwe.com.tw
劃撥帳號 / 19563868　戶名：秀威資訊科技股份有限公司
　　　　　讀者服務信箱：service@showwe.com.tw
展售門市 / 國家書店（松江門市）
　　　　　104 台北市中山區松江路 209 號 1 樓
　　　　　電話：+886-2-2518-0207　傳真：+886-2-2518-0778
網路訂購 / 秀威網路書店：http://www.bodbooks.com.tw
　　　　　國家網路書店：http://www.govbooks.com.tw
圖書經銷 / 紅螞蟻圖書有限公司
　　　　　114 台北市內湖區舊宗路二段 121 巷 28、32 號 4 樓
　　　　　電話：+886-2-2795-3656　傳真：+886-2-2795-4100

2011 年 9 月 BOD 一版
定價：300 元

讀 者 回 函 卡

感謝您購買本書，為提升服務品質，請填妥以下資料，將讀者回函卡直接寄回或傳真本公司，收到您的寶貴意見後，我們會收藏記錄及檢討，謝謝！如您需要了解本公司最新出版書目、購書優惠或企劃活動，歡迎您上網查詢或下載相關資料：http:// www.showwe.com.tw

您購買的書名：＿＿＿＿＿＿＿＿＿＿＿＿＿＿＿＿＿＿＿＿＿＿＿＿＿

出生日期：＿＿＿＿＿年＿＿＿＿＿月＿＿＿＿＿日

學歷：□高中 (含) 以下　　□大專　　□研究所 (含) 以上

職業：□製造業　□金融業　□資訊業　□軍警　□傳播業　□自由業
　　　□服務業　□公務員　□教職　　□學生　□家管　　□其它＿＿＿＿

購書地點：□網路書店　□實體書店　□書展　□郵購　□贈閱　□其他

您從何得知本書的消息？

　　□網路書店　□實體書店　□網路搜尋　□電子報　□書訊　□雜誌

　　□傳播媒體　□親友推薦　□網站推薦　□部落格　□其他＿＿＿＿＿＿

您對本書的評價：(請填代號　1.非常滿意　2.滿意　3.尚可　4.再改進)

　　封面設計＿＿＿　版面編排＿＿＿　內容＿＿＿　文／譯筆＿＿＿　價格＿＿＿

讀完書後您覺得：

□很有收穫　□有收穫　□收穫不多　□沒收穫

對我們的建議：＿＿＿＿＿＿＿＿＿＿＿＿＿＿＿＿＿＿＿＿＿＿＿＿＿

＿＿＿＿＿＿＿＿＿＿＿＿＿＿＿＿＿＿＿＿＿＿＿＿＿＿＿＿＿＿＿＿＿

＿＿＿＿＿＿＿＿＿＿＿＿＿＿＿＿＿＿＿＿＿＿＿＿＿＿＿＿＿＿＿＿＿

＿＿＿＿＿＿＿＿＿＿＿＿＿＿＿＿＿＿＿＿＿＿＿＿＿＿＿＿＿＿＿＿＿

11466
台北市內湖區瑞光路 76 巷 65 號 1 樓
秀威資訊科技股份有限公司　　　收
BOD 數位出版事業部

··

（請沿線對折寄回，謝謝！）

姓　　名：＿＿＿＿＿＿＿＿　年齡：＿＿＿＿　性別：□女　□男

郵遞區號：□□□□□

地　　址：＿＿＿＿＿＿＿＿＿＿＿＿＿＿＿＿＿＿＿＿＿

聯絡電話：(日) ＿＿＿＿＿＿＿＿＿　(夜) ＿＿＿＿＿＿＿＿＿

E-mail：＿＿＿＿＿＿＿＿＿＿＿＿＿＿＿＿＿＿＿＿＿